MW00617184

The Stars May Rise and Fall

The Stars May Rise and Fall

Estella Mirai

The Stars May Rise and Fall by Estella Mirai

© 2018 Estella Mirai

ISBN: 978-1-68454-753-1

Cover by MiblArt
Page break graphic by Freepik
Excerpt from "Hurry Go Round" ©1998 hide with Spread Beaver

To the dreamers

The Stars May Rise and Fall

Chapter 1

Teru wasn't going to call the number on the card.

It was a joke. That was all it could be—a prank, left by someone who had heard him singing to himself before the show, had seen the way his fingers trembled as he lined his eyes in black and smeared pink glitter above his eyes.

I can help you. Call me.

Someone had been watching him. Watching the way he scanned the dressing room, searching the decades' worth of graffiti and backstage passes that papered the walls. Someone had heard him singing—to the marker-scrawled names of his idols, hidden among them. To the ghosts of the live house, even though most of them were still alive.

Yasu would have been his first bet. Teru could almost see his friend writing the message, holding the pen in his fist to disguise his handwriting, to form the wavery, deliberate words.

"Minori finally convince you to sing backup?" he had joked before the show, wedging himself between Teru and a guy from one of the other bands at the mirror. Or maybe he had been serious; with Yasu, it was hard to tell.

Teru had snapped his mouth shut, killing the song mid-verse. "You know I can't sing while I play."

"Well, it's not like your drumming could get any worse." That was definitely supposed to be a joke, but it didn't help that Teru suspected it was true.

He sat down on his futon, turning the card over and over again in his hand. It was a plain white business card, the kind you could make for a thousand yen on a machine in Shinjuku Station. One side was blank; the only things printed on the other were a phone number and an email address.

I can help you. Call me.

That was scrawled above the number, in handwriting that could have belonged to a kid.

He could practically hear Yasu's voice, half teasing, half concerned. "I've known you what, six years now?" he'd said. "You've been doing this since high school—singing, or humming, or drumming on the table when you think no one's listening. It means something's up."

Teru guessed it probably did.

"I'm just worried about the band," he had said. It was mostly true. The longer they struggled, the fewer fans they seemed to have—and while he knew twenty-one wasn't exactly old, Teru had been around for long enough now to see eighteen- and nineteen-years olds come out of nowhere and get record deals in a month. He was starting to feel some kind of expiration date creeping up on him, some kind of deadline for getting out of this rut before he ended up like the guy he'd replaced—working three jobs, as far as anyone knew, and off the stage for the past two years.

Yasu had laughed. "La Rose is a decent band," he'd said. "And besides, this is just a first step."

That was Yasu in a nutshell. He never let anything

bother him—not his weight, not his rural Niigata accent, and definitely not the fact that they'd only sold nine tickets that night. He really believed, with all his heart, that he would be a star someday. Teru wasn't so sure.

He put the card aside and pulled his sweaty costume out of his bag. Pleather shorts and a vest, a long-sleeved fishnet bodysuit and sparkly purple tights with a few unintentional holes in the knees. Maybe the card was from a millionaire fan, wanting to invest in some new costumes. Teru rose from the futon and tossed the tights and bodysuit into the sink with a sigh.

He didn't have any better ideas. It couldn't have been Seika, La Rose's bassist, even though he had caught the tail end of Teru and Yasu's conversation as he waltzed into the dressing room with his blue curls trailing down his back and a blue-black boa wrapped around his shoulders.

Sure, he'd probably seen the way Teru flinched when he had draped the boa across his neck, when he'd announced, "Set lists, boys!" and deposited them on the table with a flourish. Maybe Teru's ivory foundation hadn't been enough to hide the flush on his cheeks, or maybe Seika had caught the way his body reacted—only sometimes, he reminded himself—without the permission of his brain.

I can help you. Call me.

But it wasn't Seika's style. He wasn't shy about his sexuality, and his teasing was frequent, loud, and clear. If he thought Teru needed that kind of help, he wouldn't have written an anonymous card.

I can help you. Call me.

Teru hardly dared to hope that it was real.

15

It was possible. Maybe someone—some talent scout—had actually seen him play. Maybe they'd admired the effort behind his glam-goth makeup and his fountain of hot pink, spray-stiff hair. Maybe someone had seen the way he came alive onstage, the way the sticks and the drums became an extension of his body, how the music beat like blood through his veins. And maybe that someone had felt bad for him, because after six years he was still playing the same old rhythms, the same simple riffs under guitar and bass lines that made his nerves stand electric on end.

I can help you, because you obviously love what you're doing. *I can help you*, because you suck at it, all the same.

Or maybe it wasn't about the music at all.

Maybe it had been someone backstage—someone who had heard Minori and Bara arguing after the show.

"...after the key change," Teru had heard Minori say from behind the too-thin dressing room door. "I know you can hit it, but you need to hit it every time."

"Fine." Bara had sounded bored. "Is that all?"

It wasn't, of course. He had sung the second verse twice and left out the third. He'd come in late after the bridge. He was screaming his way through "Boutoku no namida," and—

"And this is visual kei," Bara had retorted, "not the fucking opera. You know as well as I do I'm the only reason half our fans show up."

Minori did know that, and that was probably why the fight had ended as soon as it had. Bara's fans, like a lot of the girls who haunted these little venues, didn't care that he couldn't sing. They would show up as long as he was there, screaming into the mic with silver roses in his blood-red hair and his muscular, fishnet-clad legs on display. The only problem was, there weren't that many of them, and at pay-to-play venues like Rock Eden, La Rose was losing money—and status—with every show.

I can help you. Call me.

Maybe it was wishful thinking, but the message seemed intended, if not for Teru, at least for the band.

"Hey, Minori." Teru had smiled, trying to pretend he hadn't overheard. He'd sat down at the mirror, grabbed a pack of makeup remover sheets from his bag—and the card had fluttered out, landing cocked against his drum pedal on the floor.

"What's that?" Yasu had read it over his shoulder. "Someone trying to scout you?"

"Yeah, right."

Yasu had just shrugged, pulled his orangey-blonde hair out of his face, and gone back to scrubbing off his eyeliner. He was a hell of a guitarist, but not much of an actor. If it had been him, Teru wasn't sure he would have been able to keep a straight face.

I can help you. Call me.

Teru ran his finger around the edge of the card. Maybe it *had* been a mistake. Should he call, and let whoever had left it know?

He opened the window and lit a cigarette. The smoke floated out into the muggy Tokyo night.

"This is stupid," he said aloud. "It's one in the morning. Whoever it is, they're asleep."

But Teru wasn't asleep. His bandmates probably weren't asleep either. If it was a musician who had left the card, one in the morning was better than one in the afternoon.

I can help you. Call me.

He picked up his phone and dialed.

It rang once, twice—and Teru cut the connection. *This is stupid.* But he didn't feel stupid. He felt guilty, like he'd been doing something he shouldn't.

He stubbed out the cigarette and walked across the room to the refrigerator. Nothing but a pack of noodles and a flat Diet Coke. Even though he'd already had a couple with the guys after the show, what Teru really needed was a beer.

On the other side of the room, the phone rang.

The floor was littered with clothes and magazines and Playstation controllers. Teru almost tripped as he lunged for the phone, and then only crouched there, watching it, with his nerves wrapped around his voice box like a snake. There was no name with the number, but Teru knew it by heart. He'd only been staring at it for the past hour.

The ringing stopped. An engine rumbled outside Teru's window, and a train clattered over distant tracks. Upstairs, slippered feet padded across a tatami floor. The air was thick with an anticipation far from silence—but just as easily shattered by the trill of a different ring.

Teru's fingers fumbled to open the text.

I heard you sing.

He stared, waiting for the words to sink in. They didn't, though. They made no sense.

It had only been a mistake after all.

You've got the wrong number, he replied. *This is Teru, the drummer for La Rose Verboten. I don't sing.*

18

And then: *You should.*

The phone rang again.

"Hello?"

"You have a beautiful voice."

It wasn't Yasu. It wasn't anyone he knew.

"Hello?" Teru repeated. "Who is this?"

"A friend." The voice was male, deep and effortlessly sensual in a way that Seika would have envied. It made Teru distinctly uncomfortable.

"Look," Teru said. "I think you want Bara. I'm not the singer. I'm the drummer. The one with pink hair?"

"I heard you," the man pressed. "In the dressing room. I can help you."

In the dressing room?

"Is this some kind of joke?"

"Not at all."

"What do you want?" Teru whispered.

"To teach you. To help you. Will you meet with me?"

Teru's palms were sweaty, his face flushed. It was partly exhaustion, partly a lingering buzz... but it was more than that. He felt dirty. This was worse than what he felt with Seika—and it was just a voice on the goddamn phone.

"There's a studio in Koenji," he heard himself say.

"No!" the man snapped, and he took a sharp, hissing breath. "No studios. You may come to my apartment."

"Your apartment?"

"Please. It is... difficult, for me to go out."

"Um... okay." What the hell did that mean?

"I live in Meguro," the man said. "Near the live house. I can send you the address. If you'll come." There was a plea in his voice, a quiet desperation. Teru swallowed, hard.

"You want to give me singing lessons?"

"Yes."

This was insane. "When?"

"Whenever you are free."

Teru glanced at his calendar. June, 2000. Three years, almost to the day, since he had stepped off the night bus from Niigata. After all that time, he didn't even have anything to lose.

"Okay," he said. "I work the morning shift on Thursday. I guess I'm free that afternoon."

"Very well. Call this number when you arrive at Meguro Station. I will give you directions from there."

"Okay."

"Goodnight, Teru."

The connection went dead. Teru lay on his futon, staring at his phone for a long time before he dropped into uneasy sleep.

Chapter 2

He almost called back. In the space between Sunday and Thursday, between work and rehearsal and snatches of sleep, Teru caught himself a dozen times with his finger over the redial button.

He knew what he would say. It had been a mistake. He'd been tired and drunk and upset because his bandmates had been arguing. He didn't really want to sing. He definitely didn't want to do it at a stranger's apartment. Minori and Bara had seemed okay at Tuesday's rehearsal—well, Bara was still off-key and Minori was still unhappy about it, but at least he'd managed to restrict himself to glares and barely audible sighs. Yasu was right—La Rose was a decent band. There was no reason to risk that for some unknown voice on the phone.

But they were decent. They weren't good.

And when Teru clocked in to work on Thursday morning, he still hadn't made the call.

The sky overhead was dark and gray; by eleven the rain began to fall. It turned the streets of Koenji into shallow, fast-moving canals and the windows of the convenience store into watercolor paintings.

Teru lingered in the back room after his shift, folding and refolding his uniform and messing with his hair in the mirror until he finally had to admit to himself that the rain wasn't going to let up. If he was going to back out, this was his chance. He could blame the weather, blame work. It would be easy—and he could conveniently forget to reschedule.

He created a blank text, and for a minute his finger hovered over the key that would have begun an apology. But curiosity won out. Teru shook his head, threw the phone into his bag, and stepped out into the rain.

The station was only five minutes away, but by the time Teru passed through the ticket gates and onto the covered platform, his pants were soaked from the knees down and his socks had absorbed enough water to fill a bucket. The train was crowded—people who typically rode bikes or motorcycles were being forced out of the rain and onto public transportation—and Teru stood against the door with someone's elbow in his side, his breath fogging the glass as he watched the wooden Koenji storefronts give way to Nakano's cookie-cutter condos, and finally to the maze of lights and corporate logos that was Shinjuku.

At Shinjuku he transferred to the Yamanote loop line, and the skyscrapers vanished into the foliage of Yoyogi Park, the pop culture mecca of Harajuku and Shibuya, and then to the upscale elegance of Ebisu and Meguro. Teru didn't come to this area often, and when he did it was usually for a concert. It was easy to forget that Meguro was a wealthy neighborhood, full of ritzy apartment buildings and five-star restaurants. He'd never met anyone rich or famous outside of record signings, and he wasn't sure how he would—or should—react if his mystery contact turned out to be a bona-fide celebrity.

That's ridiculous, Teru told himself, but he

double-checked his reflection in one of the mirrors on the platform.

The train closed its doors and continued on its southbound course. Teru pulled out his phone. His fingers hovered over the keys for a second. A minute. He dialed.

The answer was immediate. "Yes?"

"I'm at the station."

"Go out the West Exit."

"Okay." He went down the stairs, fed his ticket to the automatic gate and fumbled to open his umbrella with one hand while holding onto the phone with the other.

"Go up the hill," the man said, "past the live house. Take the second right. The building is called Green Heights Meguro. Apartment 108."

The connection fell silent.

Green Heights Meguro was easy to find. It was a long, low apartment building, four stories tall with a brick façade and wrought-iron balconies facing the street. The main entrance was unlocked; Teru stepped through the double doors into a lobby. The walls were lined with postboxes, each one bearing a tiny lock and a black and gold nameplate with the room number and family name of the resident. Teru thought of his own postbox, which would not close all the way, much less lock, and on which he had written his name with a black magic marker.

He glanced at 108, but the box in the lower right-hand corner, next to 107 and below 208, was conspicuously blank.

The corridor was cheery, with white and yellow tile floors and fluorescent lights that never so much as flickered. Most of the residents had custom nameplates or welcome signs for their doors, and Teru's stomach growled at the aroma of garlic and butter from 105.

When he reached 108, however, the doubt in his gut bled into cold, quiet panic. There was nothing outside—no flowers, no knick-knacks, no welcome mat. The window onto the corridor was dark, and the door was nearly as blank as the postbox, bearing only an inspection sticker from the Meguro water department and another from NHK, indicating that the TV tax had last been paid six years ago, in 1994.

It was a prank. A joke. Or something worse.

But what if it was? The band, as it was, was going nowhere. He knew it, and his bandmates had to know it too. He'd be back at his parents' house in a couple of years with no job, no education, nothing but a repertoire of overdone drum riffs and a stockpile of overdue bills.

Teru rang the doorbell. There was no response. His phone, however, began to ring.

"Hello?"

"The door is unlocked."

Teru opened it onto an interior that was darker and only slightly less desolate than the outside. "Hello?" he called again. "Is anyone here?"

"The door at the end of the hall. Come in."

Teru kicked off his shoes, turning them around to face the door, and leaned his dripping umbrella against the shoe cabinet in the position that seemed least likely to leave a spot.

There were four doors leading off the short hallway. The two on the left were dark and closed. The door on his immediate right was also closed, and narrower than the others; it probably led to the bathroom. The door at the far end, however, stood slightly ajar, and a faint light danced out from beneath it.

The handle was cold in Teru's grip, and a breath of cool air escaped from around the edges of the door. This was it. His last chance to turn back. But he remembered the voice on the phone.

Please.

Teru pushed the door open. The room was dark, lit only by the glow of a computer monitor. His host, seated before it, was a shadow, shrouded in black and veiled with blue hair too bright and too perfect to be anything other than a wig.

"Stop." The man raised a pale hand in warning. "Come no closer."

Teru stopped. The room wasn't especially small, but it was crowded. There was a leather sofa, so buried under piles of sheet music and CDs that it would be impossible to actually sit. A coffee table was similarly decorated, and some of the mess had spilled onto the floor. The far wall consisted of floor-to-ceiling windows, cloaked with black curtains and blocked with a second wall of mixing equipment, cabinet speakers, and amps. The man had a full-size keyboard plugged into the computer, but the only guitar in the room was a wreck of shattered wood and twisted strings that definitely didn't look playable.

"Close the door."

Teru did.

"Now, sing."

"Now?" Teru asked. "But I just –"

"Do you want my help or not?"

"Yes," Teru said. "But—"

"Then do as I ask."

"Okay," Teru said, but there were more questions than songs running through his head. "What do you want me to sing?"

"Anything you like." The man pressed a key, and a note sounded in the dark. "'Unfinished'?"

It was the song Teru had been singing in the dressing room, an old X Japan ballad that, under any other circumstances, he could have performed in his sleep. But when he opened his mouth, the voice that came out was weak and thin, and after a few bars he wasn't sure if he was still on key.

"Stop."

"I'm sorry. I'm not a singer. I—"

"You are holding back." The reply was cold. "You are wasting my time. This apartment is soundproof. No one can hear you. Now, sing for me the way you would sing for the world. 'Kurenai'!"

It was another X Japan song, from the same '89 album. But louder, faster, heavier. More difficult, even if he'd had a proper accompaniment. Still, Teru tried, his confidence buoyed a little by the knowledge that the people next door would be unable to hear.

He was less than halfway through the first chorus when the man raised his hand. "Very well." He turned, his face still in shadow. "Your English pronunciation leaves much to be desired. Do you speak any other languages?"

Teru shook his head. "No. I—I barely finished high school... sir. And English wasn't my best subject."

His host considered this. "Well," he said at last, "it is never too late to learn."

He turned back to the computer.

"Teru," he said. "I wish to propose a deal. You will sing my songs, and in exchange... I will make you a star."

"But I'm not a singer."

"You will be."

"But Bara—"

"Bara," the man said, "could never sing this." He raised his hand and pressed a single key, and this time a full accompaniment swelled into being in the dark and cluttered room.

"La Rose Verboten's new single," he proclaimed. "'Yami no hanabira'."

And he sang. His voice was soft, but it filled the room, echoing and reverberating even though there shouldn't have been any acoustics to speak of. The song began in a minor key, a lament that crescendoed into a chorus that, musically speaking, should have been triumphant—but which, when coupled with the lyrics, managed to be even sadder than the verse. He sang of loss, but also of hope, and it was the very hopelessness of the delivery that drove the song, with all of its implications, home.

> "*Kouya wo oikakusu*
> *Yami no hanabira*
> *Furitsuzuku shikkoku no yuki*
> *Ai ga sakikaeru made*"

"It's beautiful," Teru whispered, as the final chorus

faded into the night. It was a hit, a number one single—the sort of ballad that would bring in fans who cared nothing for the makeup or the fishnets or the hair. He wanted it. He wanted to sing it, even if he wasn't really sure that he could.

"It's yours," whispered the man, as if he had read Teru's thoughts. He raised his head to look Teru in the eye.

Teru started. Beneath the cloud of blue hair, the man behind the voice was absolutely beautiful—at least, so was the part of his face Teru could see. His skin was pale, his cheekbone high, his eyebrow sculpted to perfection. He might have been anywhere from twenty-five to forty; the makeup he wore made it impossible to tell. Teru thought his eyelashes would be nearly as long without mascara, though, his lips nearly as dark and well-defined without lipstick.

That was only the left side of his face, however. The right side, as well as his nose and most of his forehead, was hidden behind a mask.

It was a beautiful prop, mimicking the contours of his face in a liquid silver that looked like polished steel. It would have looked brilliant on stage—but Teru couldn't understand the need for it in the comfort of his own home. He didn't ask, though. He couldn't. His tongue seemed incapable of forming any words at all.

"It's yours," the masked man repeated. "The song—take it. I ask only that you perform it as it deserves to be performed."

"But what about Bara?"

"Leave Bara to me."

"What does that mean?"

"You play next week?"

Teru nodded. "A week from Sunday."

"Here." The man took a folder from his desk. "You can read music, I assume?"

Teru blushed as their hands brushed against one another. "Um... a little," he answered. It had been a long time since his mother had finally let him stop taking piano lessons.

"Very well, then," his host said. "Share this with the others. Tell them you wrote it, if you like. Or tell them the truth. It doesn't matter to me."

Finished with the conversation, he turned back to the computer and, manipulating the mouse with his left hand, began to rearrange some part of the accompaniment.

"The door is unlocked," he said. "You may let yourself out."

"Wait," Teru ventured. "Who are you?"

"Someone who can help you. Does anything else matter?"

"I—no. No, I guess not," Teru said. "Can't you at least tell me your name?"

"My name?" the man repeated. His shoulders stiffened, and he sat up a little straighter. His voice grew soft. "They used to call me Rei."

Chapter 3

Teru couldn't get the song out of his head. He tried to remember it, picking out the melody on his undersized keyboard and humming it to himself at work, in the men's room, in the shower. He tried to forget it, renting the catchiest pop singles he could find and turning up the volume on his Discman so high that businessmen and old ladies gave him even dirtier looks than usual. At night, when he lay in his futon in the moments before sleep, he swore he could still hear Rei—singing it and then, in the same breath, asking Teru to take it, to sing it, to leave Bara to him.

He had taken it. But he wasn't sure what he was supposed to do with it now. He couldn't show it to the band; they would never believe that Teru, who had never written a note in his life, had suddenly turned out a showstopper. And the truth would be no better. *A masked stranger wrote the hit of the decade and just gave it to me, for no reason at all.*

He didn't hear from Rei again until Monday evening. He was standing in the entranceway, one shoe off and one shoe on, on the way to rehearsal when his phone rang. Shoving his foot into the remaining boot, he answered the phone with one hand and grabbed his keys with the other.

"Hello?"

"Teru."

"Yeah?"

"Are you busy?"

No, he almost said, but that would have been a lie. "Kind of. I'm about to be late to rehearsal."

"Rehearsal," Rei repeated. "I look forward to hearing what the others think of the song."

Teru's mouth went dry, and his bag—with Rei's sheet music inside—seemed to double in weight on his shoulder. He hadn't had the heart to take it out, but he wasn't sure he'd be able to screw up the courage to show the band.

"Yeah," Teru said. "I mean, me too."

"I wanted to ask you something," Rei went on. "On Sunday night, after the concert... do you have any plans?"

Teru hesitated. "No," he said, turning his key in the lock. "I don't think so."

"Good. I would like to see you again."

Teru's hand shook; he almost dropped his keys down the gutter instead of into his bag. He wanted to say yes, although he wasn't sure why. And he was also afraid to, even though there wasn't a good reason for that either.

"Sure," he said, struggling to keep his tone light. "I'll get you a pass. If you want to come to the show."

"That won't be necessary," Rei said. "I will be watching from the balcony. But I would like to see you after the show, as well."

"Um... okay." Teru took a deep breath. Once more, he felt as though he had done something forbidden. It was the fifteen-year-old thrill of his first smoke, the seventeen-year-old thrill of his first fuck... but why? He shook his head in disbelief. Had he really developed some stupid fanboy infatuation after one song?

"I'm looking forward to it," Rei said, and hung up without saying goodbye.

Teru looked up; he was waiting at a crosswalk where the signal was already green. The clock on his phone read 7:56, and he was still a good ten minutes from the studio. He tossed the phone into his bag and broke into a run.

Eight minutes later, out of breath and exhausted, Teru burst into the studio and, for a moment, was relieved to find that rehearsal hadn't started without him. "Sorry... I'm late..." he gasped. "Where's Bara?"

Minori shrugged, but his lips were set in a thin, angry line.

Yasu shook his head. "Give him a few minutes. He had to work. Maybe they kept him late?"

"Fashionably late." Seika laughed, but the atmosphere in the room was tense.

Teru nodded, trying not to think about Rei and what he had said: *Leave Bara to me.* There wasn't much he could do. Whatever else Rei was, he was Teru's secret, at least for now.

He opened his bag and took out his sticks. At least he could practice while they waited.

"Hey, what's this?"

A page of the score, a page of "Yami no hanabira" had fluttered out of his bag, and Yasu was holding it, looking at it... reading it.

"Where'd you get this?" he asked.

Leave Bara to me.

Teru bit his lip, shutting out the voice in his head. "I...

I don't know."

"Let me see it." Minori put his guitar on a stand and peered over Yasu's shoulder. He mouthed the lyrics, hummed a scrap of the melody. "Do you have the rest?"

"Yes?" It came out sounding like a question.

As Minori flipped through the score, his eyes grew wide. He handed it to Yasu, who picked up his guitar and began to play a bit of the intro. He made a mistake, stopped, and repeated the phrase again.

"Damn. This is tough." Yasu gave the remaining pages to Seika, but kept repeating the bit of introduction, stopping every few bars to try a new fingering or a different position.

Seika nodded. "The bassline is crazy." He smiled. "Who is this, Teru?"

"I don't know," he lied again.

Minori's eyes widened further. "Did *you* write this?" The studio grew quiet; all eyes were on Teru.

"No," he whispered. "No, I didn't. It's... A friend of mine wrote it, and said we could use it. If you guys want to, I mean."

Seika nodded. Yasu scowled, and Teru knew that he was running through a mental list of their common friends, trying to think of someone with the ability to write such a piece and the insanity to give it away. Minori, however, simply picked up his guitar and began to play.

"Let's do it," he said. "Let's give it a try while we're waiting for Bara. Yasu, you want Guitar 1 or 2?"

Yasu shook his head. "Doesn't matter, does it? Both parts are killers. Take whichever you want."

Teru turned his attention to the drum kit and began, as

slowly as he could, to adjust his settings. There was no way he could play the drumline as written, at least not without a lot of practice. He pretended to tune the snare, which already sounded just fine, wondering if the other guys would mind if he improvised something simpler, at least for today.

He never had a chance to find out, though, because the door flew open—and Bara stormed in.

His face was nearly as red as his hair, and in his fist he held a stack of papers, which he waved angrily in Minori's face. "What the hell is this? Who the *fuck* do you think you are?"

Minori looked up in surprise. "What are you talking about? Calm down. What is that?" He reached for the papers, but Bara snatched them away.

"You don't even have the balls to complain to my face now? Twice a day for the past goddamn week! Emails at three in the morning. Attacking me on a public forum! This is... this is...."

But he didn't seem to know what, exactly, it was.

"Bara, calm down!" Minori repeated. "I don't know what you're holding. I haven't sent you anything that I didn't send to everyone else in this room. You know we'd tell you if there was a problem. Now, calm down. Let's sit down and talk."

"No!" the singer declared, his face growing redder and redder. "No more talking, no more meetings! I'm sick of this shit. Have fun trying to sell tickets without me." He threw the papers at Minori and stormed out.

"Bara, wait!" Minori picked up two or three of the offending pieces of paper and followed him.

Teru bent to pick up one of the pages. It was an email message, sent from Minori to Bara a week ago. "We really need to talk about this," he read. "Your lack of ability and dedication is holding back the rest of the band."

"Sounds like Minori," Yasu said. But Teru didn't think it really did.

"These songs should have a melody," Seika read. "Those screams and moans you pull out whenever you can't hit the notes aren't going to cut it."

"This one's worse." Yasu quoted, "Your rock star attitude isn't doing us any good. You're taking attention from the rest of the band, who actually practice and work hard to sound the way they do."

Teru cleared his throat and read the rest of his. "This band has been around for two years. We should be thinking about touring or recording, but instead I'm just worried about selling twenty tickets for Sunday."

"This looks like a flyer." Yasu held up one of the others. "Or a page from a magazine." It was the photo from their latest flyer, skillfully edited to remove Bara from the center. There were only the four of them, above an abbreviated version of their upcoming schedule. It was a grainy, pixilated copy, but it looked like a copy of something real.

"That wasn't printed anywhere," Teru said.

Seika frowned. "It looks like it was."

"Bullshit," Yasu muttered. "Even Bara wouldn't believe that was real."

That was true; he probably didn't. The messages had been designed to do two things: call attention to Bara's deficiencies as a singer, and make him believe that Minori was behind them. It was a petty, cheap attack—but it had hit him where it hurt. Except for Teru, Bara was the only member of the band who didn't sound one hundred percent professional. He knew it, and it bothered him. Rei, apparently, had known it too.

Minori re-entered the studio—alone. His shoulders were slumped, and his voice, when he spoke, was quiet and raw. "You guys know I didn't do this, right?"

"Of course," Teru said, a little too quickly. Yasu and Seika only nodded.

"Look," Minori said. "I don't want to have to ask, but if any of you know anything...?"

"I don't even have a computer," Seika said.

"Me neither." Teru shook his head. "Bara should know that." The band had a BBS, a simple online message board, but Minori and Bara, as well as a handful of fans, were the only ones who regularly posted. Sure, it was possible to type and hit "Reply" on a cell phone, but between the time and the data charges, Teru hardly bothered to read it, much less comment.

"Same here," Yasu turned the Photoshopped flyer around so Minori could see it. "I don't think any of us know how to do this."

"It wasn't even my email address." Minori frowned. "Look at this." He held out one of the pages he had taken with him. It was a printout of the BBS, with two posts from Minori and three from Bara. "This is me." He pointed to an announcement about the next show. "See? I've got an underscore, but this one's a hyphen."

"Did you show that to Bara?" Yasu asked.

"Of course. But... I don't know. I didn't write these, but to be honest, I agree with a lot of what they say. Bara's been looking for a reason to quit, and maybe I've been looking for a reason to let him. I hate to say this, but... maybe this is for the best. We'll cancel Sunday, take a break—"

"Wait." Seika interrupted. "Cancel Sunday? That's an Urgent Venus event. We were lucky to get invited." He looked pointedly at Minori and Yasu. "Can't either of you sing while you play?"

Minori shook his head. "I didn't write those songs for myself. I know it's a big event, but with substandard vocals.... No offense," he said, with an apologetic smile.

"None taken." Yasu smiled back. "I can't sing. But..." He shot Teru a sidelong glance. "The karaoke king of Sanjo Minami High School could."

Teru cringed at the years-old memory. "No," he protested. "I can't."

It was, apparently, what Rei wanted. But not here. Not like this. Not so soon.

Minori raised an eyebrow. "You don't even sing backup. Think you can hit the notes?"

"Yeah." That, at least, was true. "But...."

"You know the lyrics?"

"Of course."

"Can you scream?"

Teru hesitated, then shook his head. "I can try... but not like Bara, no."

Minori picked up his guitar. "We'll do better with a drum machine than with no singer. We can change the set list if we have to. Let's at least see what you sound like."

The room was silent. No one played a note; they only watched as Teru put his drumsticks in his bag and walked to the microphone. He took it in his hand, testing its weight—and then Minori launched into one of La Rose's signature songs.

Teru closed his eyes, felt the absent beat as the guitars and bass swelled into being around him. He nailed his cue.

And he sounded good. The song had been written for Bara's range, much narrower than his own. It was... effortless, freeing. Like a fish in water, except that fish couldn't fly. A flying fish, then, soaring over the guitars and bass as the crowd that wasn't there roared its eternal devotion.

The last note seemed to last forever, trembling in the air until Teru was sure he'd held it way too long—but it died at the same moment the guitars did, and the band burst into applause.

For the first time that day, Minori's smile seemed genuine. "All right, Teru. Get to work programming that drum machine. For now, at least, we need you more behind the mic."

Chapter 4

"Let's hear from the lead guitar. Whenever you're ready."

Teru heard Minori strike a chord, then launch into an ad-libbed solo behind him, but his attention wasn't on the sound check. The stage hadn't changed—it was the same old Rock Eden. But the place had never looked as vast or as intimidating as it did now, with his bandmates invisible behind him and nothing but the mic stand to use as a shield.

It was nothing like it would be during the show, of course. The hall lights were on, and the bassist from Urgent Venus was restringing his instrument in the front row while a couple of staff girls collated the flyers and questionnaires. The balcony was empty except for the sound technician. But even this was a little bit terrifying.

"Thanks." The sound tech's voice interrupted his thoughts. "Rhythm guitar, are you ready?"

Yasu started to play, and Teru took the microphone, shifting it from one hand to the other as he tapped his foot to a restless beat that existed only in his head. He took a few steps to the right, rested a foot on one of his monitors, leaned out over the imagined crowd. He wasn't used to having to move around onstage; it hadn't really occurred to him until now that he would have to.

"Great. Let's hear the bass, then?"

"Sorry," Seika said. "I'm not quite ready. Why don't you work on the vocals first?"

"All right." The voice from the sound booth didn't change, but to Teru it suddenly seemed stern and ominous. "The lead singer, then?"

Teru's palms were sweating; he replaced the microphone on its stand and wiped his hands on his jeans.

"Ah! Ah, ah!" He half-spoke, half-sang a few notes into the mic, and was almost shocked to hear them echo out into the hall. "Ma, mi, mu, me, mo...."

And it was over. "Sounds great. Thanks. Bassist, are you ready?"

"Okay," Minori said, when Seika was done. "Let's run the first song from beginning to end, and then if we have time I want to go through the guitar solo in the third. Teru, take it from your introduction?"

Teru took the mic, sending a rustle through the speakers as his hand brushed the grill. "Good evening, Meguro!" He forced a smile for the empty chairs. "We're La Rose Verboten!"

The drum machine kicked in, and the guitarists stepped to the front of the stage. Teru turned his back to the hall in a bit of last-minute choreography. Turn the crowd's attention to Yasu and Minori, and then....

He closed his eyes, took a deep breath, and belted out the first line. It sounded okay. He lunged over the speakers, pulling the mic in close to his face. *Just like karaoke,* he told himself, but of course that wasn't true. He hated going to karaoke with strangers, and now the staff girls were looking up at him—smiling. Laughing? Watching, anyway, and that was bad enough. Teru looked away, into the darkened spotlights and up to the balcony.

"All right," Minori said into his mic. "That sounded good." From the balcony, the sound engineer nodded his agreement. Teru wondered if he would be able to see that far when the lights went down, and his heart tightened at the thought. It was bad enough to know that Rei would be watching. Teru wasn't sure if he'd be able to sing a note with that mask staring down at him.

—※—

Two hours later, he stood on the stage again. The hall was dark; the curtain was close enough to touch, and Teru found himself holding his breath, half afraid that the mic would pick it up and somehow expose his nerves to the crowd.

"Ready?" Minori whispered.

No, Teru thought, but he looked over his shoulder and nodded.

The curtain opened, and the hall rustled with a whisper that might as well have been a roar.

"That's not—"

"Where the hell is—"

"What happened to—"

Bara.

"Good evening, Meguro!" Teru said—a split second too late, out of sync with Minori's triumphant chord. "We're... La Rose Verboten."

He was dimly aware that he had started to sing, pulled into the song more by instinct than by will. When Bara had sung this song, the five or six girls who always staked out a place in the front row had screamed, lunging at the stage and thrusting their arms in the air. Now they only stared in disbelief. Teru didn't think they would actually walk out—wouldn't make it look like they'd come up to the front by mistake. But it didn't seem like they would give anyone but Bara a chance, either.

He stumbled through two verses and a chorus, wincing as he went flat on the last note. When Yasu stepped forward for his solo, Teru turned his back and escaped upstage. He didn't want to risk looking out to the crowd, didn't want to see the disinterest on their faces. And he didn't want to look at the balcony either.

Without the drum set, he was naked. The microphone was his lifeline, and he clung to it, closing his eyes and gripping it with both hands. He didn't move; he couldn't. It was all he could do to finish the song—and when it ended, it was to nothing but the polite applause he'd heard at so many mediocre shows.

"Next song," Teru whispered in what was supposed to be an ominous tone. "'Boutoku no namida.'"

He closed his eyes, shut out the sounds of the crowd, and sang into the mic as though it was the only thing in the world. The song was about doubt, about guilt, about giving up your dreams to fit society's norms. The message was ambiguous, and Teru wasn't sure that he liked what it had to say, but in the dark, in that moment, he almost believed it. It wasn't his job to make it personal—he was just a character, playing a role.

"Hello, Meguro!" There was no response. "I hope you're enjoying the show. I, uh... guess a lot of you are seeing us for the first time. So, let me introduce everyone. On bass, Seika." This was greeted with polite applause. "On guitar, Yasu." Applause again. "On guitar, our leader, Minori." A few halfhearted cries. "And I'm Teru. The lead singer."

Another whisper ran through the crowd.

"Um... for some of you, I guess this is a surprise. Our vocalist has... left the band. I was the drummer, but... for now, at least, I'm singing. So, um... here's the next song?" He turned around to plead with his bandmates. This wasn't going well.

The next song was an easy one, a bright, upbeat number with a catchy refrain. Bara had usually tried to scream it, but Teru focused on the melody, drawing it out one note at a time. By the time it was over, a couple of Bara's fans had managed to escape to the back of the hall—but to Teru's surprise, a group of girls he'd never seen before had taken their place. They were smiling, laughing, nodding their heads to the beat—and Teru was fairly sure he heard someone whisper, "He's cute!"

They could have been talking about one of the other guys. In fact, they probably were. But the positive comment from this largely tepid crowd gave him courage, and his second speech went much better than the first.

"Thanks for coming tonight." The newcomers greeted this with a cheer. "If you like what you see, come see us again—July second, at Cynic in Ikebukuro. It's a little far from Meguro, but—"

"It's not far!" cried a voice from the back.

Teru grinned. "Or for some of you, not so far. Anyway, we'd love to see you there. We've got a demo tape for sale—800 yen for three songs, you can buy it outside. And photo sets. Okay, so... we have two songs left. Next, I want to sing a ballad for you, kind of a love song."

Seika began to play the intro, slow notes dropping from his bass like water into a pool. The lights dimmed and faded to blue... and from that moment, the crowd was theirs. Teru still clung to the mic like a life preserver, but either it worked with this song or the girls had just decided to forgive him his nerves, because those in the front row began waving their arms to the beat.

The last song was a heavier rock number, and it brought a few others to the front of the crowd to jump, headbang, and scream. Teru put the mic back on the stand, let his eyes meet those of the girls in the front. It wasn't too bad. They weren't going to tear him apart. They just wanted the music, and right now that meant they wanted him. It wasn't bad at all.

Minori and Yasu ran to the front of the stage, dragging out their improvised solos as the song rode into its climax. Yasu raised his hand, tossing his pick out into the crowd and strumming the last phrase with his thumb. On sheer impulse, Teru followed suit. He pulled the studded bracelet from his left wrist and hurled it over the heads of the girls in the front row. A hand shot into the air to catch it, and the curtains closed to what was, by the standards of an event this size, positively thunderous applause.

—⋇—

"Oh, there's the singer!" A voice called from across the lobby.

"Shhh, Kana! I'm sure he heard you!" And two voices giggled together.

The girls who'd come up to the front during the third song were standing by La Rose's unmanned merch table, holding copies of the year-old demo tape. "We wanted to buy your tape," the first girl—Kana—said, "but we couldn't find your staff!" She pouted, but her eyes were still smiling.

Teru smiled back. "I'm sorry. It's just the four of us right now," he explained. "But I'd be happy to sell you a tape. They're 800 yen."

Kana and her friend each bought a tape, and by the time Teru had counted out their change, they were the first two customers in an actual line. He fell quickly into the rhythm he always found behind the register at work, only looking up when the door to the hall, and through it to the balcony, opened.

Even when the other guys arrived to help him, Teru stayed busy, and they were relieved only when a staff girl for one of the other bands ducked out to the convenience store and bought them a couple of beers. They toasted the band over a stack of tapes that lasted only a little longer than the 350-milliliter cans.

Soon the demo tapes were replaced by a handwritten sign reading "Sorry. Sold Out," but the girls kept delivering their questionnaires. Teru barely had time to wonder where Rei was, if he had come to see him sing at all. The fans all wanted to make small talk; a couple of them asked Teru if he was single. His head was already spinning when he noticed the girl across the room.

At first, he thought she must be lost—that she had gone through the wrong door on her way to the restaurant upstairs. On the street, Teru never would have given her a second glance, but here she looked decidedly out of place in a linen skirt and sweater set in a sea of fishnets and safety pins. It was only when she approached La Rose's table that he noticed the black leather bracelet—the one that, until about two hours ago, had belonged to him—and realized that she actually had attended the concert.

"Excuse me?"

Her voice was soft and familiar, though Teru had no idea where he would have heard it before. She was young, no older than he was, with shoulder-length hair just a little too light to have been her natural color. Her wallet, which she held in one manicured hand, was Louis Vuitton, and everything else about her looked expensive as well.

"Excuse me?" she repeated. "Is it too late to buy a CD?"

Teru smiled. "Demo tape. And I'm sorry, but we just sold out."

"Oh. Well, then, how about photo sets? Do you have any of those left?"

Teru pulled a photo set out of the box. "Five photos for five hundred yen. They're a little old, but—"

"Okay," she cut him off. "I'll take three."

Teru shook his head. "It's just the one set. I can sell you three, but they'll all be the same photos. We'll be taking some more as soon as—"

The girl laughed. "Masato Ijima!" she whispered. "You haven't changed a bit."

"E—excuse me?" Teru's heart seemed to stop, and he glanced around, hoping that none of La Rose's fans had heard his given name. "Do I know you?"

"Of course you do. I'm Kiyomi, silly! Kiyomi Nakamori? From high school?"

"Oh! Uh... long time no see?" Teru remembered Kiyomi Nakamori from high school, but he never would have guessed that this was her. Kiyomi had been shy, her long hair curtaining her face, and her body buried under bulky sweaters and jackets that had earned her more than a few uniform violations. This girl, however, held her head high and proud, her smile framed now by stylish layers, and let her sweater hug her curves rather than hide them.

She smiled again and took a carefully-folded questionnaire from her bag. "I know, I look totally different. But it's me! I can't believe you're playing here. You were really good, um..." She laughed again. "What was your stage name again?"

"Teru."

"Like the guy from GLAY?"

Teru flushed, and looked down at his shoes. No one ever believed him when he tried to explain that his stage name had nothing to do with the frontman of one of the biggest visual—well, ex-visual—bands in Japan, and the actual story behind it wasn't anything especially impressive.

"Sorry." Kiyomi's smile faded. "I shouldn't have laughed. I was just expecting something a little closer to your real name, like Yasu."

"No, it's okay." Teru shook his head. "I get that a lot. But it's not really the same. He writes his name T-E-R-U, all caps, and mine's kanji, like 'kagayaki'?" He traced the kanji character for "shine" on his palm.

Kiyomi laughed again, and bowed deeply, as though she had been introduced to a celebrity. "It's a pleasure to meet you, Teru-like-kagayaki."

"How long have you been here?" Teru asked. "In Tokyo, I mean?"

"Only a few months." She reached into her bag again and pulled out a planner. "Let's see. Two months and thirteen days, according to this. I'm working at a hotel in Yokohama. It's good money, but I haven't had a lot of time to make friends." She looked almost sad for a moment, but then smiled brightly again. "How about you? That hair... wow. I guess you haven't given up and put on a suit yet, then?"

"Uh, no..." Teru ran his fingers through his hair. It had been long-ish at the end of high school, but pink definitely hadn't been allowed. "Actually...."

"Excuse me!" They were interrupted by a harried-looking woman in a Rock Eden T-shirt. "We're closing for the evening," she reminded Teru and Kiyomi. "You're welcome to continue your conversation outside."

Kiyomi looked at her watch. "It is late," she said. "Look, it was really nice to talk to you again. Do you think... I mean, I know it's kind of inappropriate for a fan to do the asking, but do you think I could have your phone number?"

"Um..." Teru looked around, making sure all of his actual fans were out of the building. "Sure. Just a second."

He reached into his bag for a pen, but when he couldn't find one, took out his cell phone instead. "I guess I can just put you in my address—fuck!"

Kiyomi frowned. "Is everything all right?"

"Yeah. Yeah, I just..." *I'm supposed to be at Rei's apartment in five minutes.* "I forgot. I've got an appointment, and—"

"At ten o'clock at night?"

"I'm sorry." Teru grabbed the box of photo sets. "Look, I'll email you later. Did you write your address on the questionnaire?" he asked over his shoulder as he started up the stairs.

"Yes, but—"

"I'll send you my number, then. I'm really sorry, Kiyomi." He loaded the box into the back of Minori's van. "I'll be in touch, I promise. I just... this is really important."

"Sure," she sighed. "I guess I'll see you around then, Masa—Teru."

Teru slid the questionnaire into his bag and looked again at his phone, cursing under his breath when he saw the time. He didn't know Rei very well—didn't know him at all, really—but he wasn't too anxious to find out whether or not he was a stickler for punctuality. Teru pulled up the call history, silently rehearsing excuses and apologies as he made his way up the hill.

Chapter 5

The apartment building was silent, though lights shone in more than a few of the windows. Teru nearly tiptoed down the corridor, as conscious of the fall of his footsteps as of the accelerating beat of his heart. It was hard to believe that, less than a ten-minute walk away, his bandmates were opening the night's first bottle of beer in the noisy fluorescent cheer of some chain izakaya.

"Hello?" he called. "I'm sorry I'm late."

The only answer was the light from Rei's computer screen, spilling into the hallway through the half-open door. Teru kicked off his shoes and stepped up into the hall.

He slipped through the door to the music room, closing it behind him this time without being told. Rei was seated at the computer, his back to the door. Teru could see nothing of him but the cascade of royal blue hair that seemed, if anything, brighter and more unnatural than it had been the week before.

"Have a seat." Rei gestured toward the sofa. The papers and CDs that had previously littered it were gone, and Teru was able to sit, though his nerves kept him from really relaxing. The coffee table had also been cleared of its clutter, and was now occupied by a bottle of cognac, an ice bucket, and a glass.

"You may pour yourself a drink," Rei continued, though his eyes never left the screen. The edges of the mask shone in the electronic light like some clichéd silver lining.

"Thank you," Teru whispered, and poured himself a bit of cognac over a generous amount of ice.

Rei lifted a matching glass from his desk and raised it to his lips without a toast. "Do you understand, now," he asked, "why I wanted you to sing?"

"It was great," Teru admitted. "But you lied to Bara, and Minori."

Rei raised an eyebrow. "Was my criticism untrue?"

"That's not what I mean. You could have broken up the band."

"It was for your own good."

That was also probably true. No one seemed to believe that Minori had really written the messages, and they all seemed happier now that Bara wasn't around to argue. Teru took a deep breath. "You hurt Bara."

"Yes," Rei agreed. "Are you angry with me?"

Teru thought about this. "I should be," he said. It hadn't been fair. But he could still hear the ghosts of the crowd. "But not really."

"Then enough about Bara. We are here to discuss *your* performance. Your voice is stronger than you think, Teru. The ballad was especially lovely."

Teru wet his lips from his own glass, and was relieved to find the cognac smooth and far easier to drink than the cheap whisky he kept at his own apartment. Whether it was the effect of the liquor or of Rei's words of praise, Teru felt the tension in his body begin to subside.

"You have promise." Rei took another sip. "But it was all too obvious that you had never sung on stage before. They liked your voice, yes... but they took pity on you too."

Teru nodded. He couldn't argue with that.

"You hid your face with the microphone as though you were terrified. Your speech was stiff and awkward... though the second time was better than the first. You hardly moved, and you failed almost entirely to make eye contact with the crowd."

"I'm sorry."

Rei shook his head and turned away from the computer, his drink still in his left hand. "Don't be. Everyone has a first show, and most go much worse than tonight did. Have you been practicing the song?"

"Yes." Teru hesitated. "But I don't know how long it'll be before we can play it. It's a lot harder than anything else we've got, and—"

"You will play it on the second. At Cynic." Rei's voice was soft, but it left no room for argument. "We must record your new single as soon as possible. 'Yami no hanabira' must be your first priority."

Teru nodded. "Okay, but—"

"Excellent. Then let us work on your staging." Rei turned back to the computer and replaced his glass on the desk. "Use the microphone in the corner. Do you need the sheet music?"

"No."

"Good. Now, I want you to think about the lyrics. Feel them. Let me see them in your posture, in your face."

Teru took the mic stand from the corner and placed it in the middle of the room. Even the tiny stages he played on were much larger than Rei's music room, but he could see that this kind of practice might help. Teru wasn't very good at ad-libbing; even as a drummer he seldom strayed from the piece as written. Mapping out his staging beforehand—getting into character, as it were—would be better than jumping into it blindly as he had tonight.

"Start with the mic on the stand," Rei suggested, "and take it into your hand during the bridge. Lower the stand a little." Teru fumbled with it, and Rei nodded. "That's fine. Not so close to your mouth. Let the crowd see your face. Let's run through it once. Do whatever feels natural."

Teru was relieved to find that he did, in fact, remember the entire song, and was able to sing it without any major mistakes. More than once, however, he caught himself clutching the microphone as he had on stage, so focused on the notes, the breathing, the dynamics, that he forgot to pretend he was in front of a crowd.

"Not bad," Rei said. "Your voice is perfect."

"Thank you."

"Now, when you take the microphone, put the stand behind you, so it doesn't get in your way. Ideally, of course, you would have a roadie to do that, but for now...." He smiled a half-smile beneath the mask.

They ran the chorus a few more times, until Rei was satisfied with both Teru's facial expressions and his handling of the mic. "Now, the third verse, after the key change." He turned back to the computer and clicked on something. "This is where you almost give up, but decide to go on. Look up!

Into the spotlight!" Teru did. "Now, hold the mic in your left hand, and raise your right to the heavens. Plead with God. Plead with the angels! No, no! Stiffen your wrist!" Teru tried, but it looked awkward, unnatural. "Palm up, toward the sky!" He tried again. "No, not like that!"

"Can't you show me, then?" Teru cried, exasperated. "I don't understand what you want me to do."

"That's—" Rei almost shouted, then lowered his voice and went on. "That's good enough for now. Once more, from the second key change."

They ran it once more, from beginning to end. Teru wasn't completely confident about the staging, but it was a hell of a lot better than what he had come up with on his own.

"Thank you... Rei." It was the first time he had spoken the name aloud. "Is... is this what you do before a show?"

Rei drew in a deep, sharp breath, and let it out slowly. "Yes," he said. "It often helped me to work out the staging... before I went on."

So he is a musician then. Teru wanted to ask what band Rei was in, how long he had been in the business, why his name and face weren't all over every live house in the city. He wasn't sure, exactly, what stopped him.

"Teru?"

"What is it?"

"About the song," Rei continued in a quiet, controlled voice. "I need you to talk to the others. Set a date. Tell your friends that I have taken care of everything—it won't cost them a thing. There is only one condition." He lowered his eyes. "I would like to produce the CD myself."

"You're going to pay for us to record a CD? We can't accept that."

Rei's response was smooth and immediate. "I insist."

"But I barely know you. It wouldn't be right. And besides..." Teru's curiosity got the better of him. "Why don't *you* sing it?"

Rei closed his eyes and lowered his head, allowing a curtain of blue hair to fall over his face. He didn't speak, and neither did Teru. Rei had heard him, and it was his prerogative to respond, or not, as he chose.

"I can't."

"Th—that's ridiculous," Teru protested. "Your voice... it's..."

"I can't." Rei bit off the words, spitting at the screen. "I can't!"

He brought his fist down, rattling the keyboard and sending a stack of papers fluttering into the air like a downed bird's feathers. His shoulders shook; the black cloak sloughed away, pooling around his waist and sliding, trailing, dripping to the floor.

Rei fumbled to catch it, but Teru was there first. His fingers closed around the soft, well-worn fabric and he lifted it up, extending his hand in the same gesture of drilled-in politeness with which he would have returned a dropped pencil or a train pass or a key.

And then he froze.

In the wan, artificial light of the monitor, Teru got his first good look at Rei's face, and any words he might have had dried up in his mouth. The skin on Rei's chin and neck was twisted, puckered into a single endless scar. The silver mask glowed blue in the light, and his eyes—one wide and furious, the other nearly hidden behind a wall of plastic hair—seethed.

He drew a sharp breath and tried to swivel the chair, to turn away before Teru could see any more. But it was too late. He already had.

Rei's right arm was held against his chest by a complicated brace, a sling of metal and plastic that cradled his elbow, supporting his emaciated wrist. His fingers were pale and curled towards his palm—limp and completely useless.

Something twisted cold and sharp in Teru's gut. "What happened?"

Rei closed his eyes. "Does it matter?"

"No. Of—of course not. I just...."

"Please," he whispered. "You must sing my music. It's... it's all I have left."

Teru took a step back. "So... you're giving it to me?" He shook his head. This didn't make sense. "But you don't even know me."

He couldn't help but think of that phone call from Yasu, over two years ago now, couldn't help but remember turning on the TV to see that Hideto Matsumoto—hide, X Japan's lead guitarist—had been found dead, asphyxiated with a towel on his bedroom door. Teru had felt sick then, like someone in his own family had died. And he felt sick now, even though whatever had happened to Rei had happened before they had ever met. It was like watching a friend, or an idol, rendered helpless by some silly, stupid accident.

"I am giving it to you," Rei echoed. "I need your voice. I need your band."

Teru nodded, again and again until the gesture lost all

meaning. "We'll record your song. I promise," he said, though he had no right to do so.

Chapter 6

Teru slumped into a chair in the studio lobby and shook two cigarettes from the pack, offering one wordlessly to Yasu.

"You all right?" Yasu asked. "You kind of look like shit."

"Thanks," Teru muttered, but he didn't argue. Shit was pretty much what he felt like. His back was sore from restocking the shelves at work and he hadn't really been able to sleep since the show.

"Where'd you disappear to the other night, anyway?"

Teru shrugged. "Nowhere special. I just... had plans with a friend."

"A friend, huh?" Yasu smiled and leaned in closer, lowering his voice. "Is there something you're not telling me?"

"Not a girl." Teru took a long drag on his cigarette and let it out as a sigh. "Just a friend," he said. "The guy who wrote the song."

"Yeah?" Yasu raised his voice to include the whole room. "Hey, have you guys been practicing Teru's song?"

"It's not mine," Teru protested, but if the others heard him, they didn't reply.

"Is that a challenge?" Seika smiled.

"Maybe."

Minori grimaced. "No thanks. I'd embarrass myself if I tried."

"Awww." Yasu stubbed out his cigarette and stood, gesturing for the others to follow. "Come on."

"I've been busy."

"Then we practice now. Right, Teru?"

Teru looked at Seika, half hoping he'd refuse, but he shrugged. "I'm game. Minori can sight-read."

"It won't be sight-reading."

"Then what are we waiting for?" Seika tossed his empty can into the recycle bin and followed Yasu into the studio.

They played it through twice. The first time was rough; Yasu and Minori stumbled a little during the complicated twin solo, and Seika swore his timing had been off. Teru struggled with some of the higher parts, too, but he didn't think it sounded too bad. It was a song about desperate hope, after all; if he sounded a little desperate to reach the notes, he could probably make that work in his favor. The second time went even better; despite the tragic tone of the piece, Teru found himself soaring out of the last chorus with a smile.

"That was pretty good," Minori admitted. "Maybe, with a little more work—"

"I think we should play it." The words were out of Teru's mouth before he had time to consider them.

"You mean live?"

"At Cynic," Teru said. "Why not? We sounded great, and..." But he couldn't think of another argument, at least not one that he wanted to make public.

"I'm not sure." Minori shook his head. "We've always

written our own music. It's one thing to mess around in the studio, but—"

"Teru's right." Seika smiled. "We sounded fabulous. Does it matter who wrote it, if it's good?"

"Thanks," Teru said. "I... I know this is strange. But it would mean a lot to my friend if we did."

Yasu shook his head. "I don't get it. It's a great song. But why give it to us? Why the hell would he just give it away?"

"He's not, though," Teru objected, though his hands were shaking and he was sure his face had gone a hundred shades of red. "He—he wants us to record it. He said he'll produce. He'll take care of everything. We just have to—"

Minori frowned. "We can't afford that."

"My friend can."

"Even so, I—"

"We do need to think about recording again," Yasu interrupted. "Either that or make more copies of that demo tape, and—"

"I know. We need something with Teru's voice on it, but—"

"It sounds great to me." Seika shrugged. "Face it, love. You're outnumbered."

"Fine." Minori sighed. "But that doesn't change the fact that we've only rehearsed it a few times. We don't even have a drummer."

"Teru can play." Seika smiled, but Teru looked away. The drumline was completely beyond his ability. It would be a challenge even to program it into a synthesizer, and Minori—and Rei—would probably insist on live drums for the recording. "Or," Seika continued, "I could call in a favor. I've got a friend at work who's an excellent drummer—and he owes me one."

"All right." Minori sighed, putting his guitar back into its case and holding up his hands in surrender. "You guys win. We play it on Sunday. Beyond that, I'll think about it, okay?"

Rehearsals always went in reverse order: the first band to play was the last to warm up, and La Rose was slated to go on second. With less than an hour between their rehearsal and the opening of the doors to the public, they went into the sound check in full makeup and then, with time to kill and plenty of nerves to be ironed out, gathered around one of the bar tables at the back of the long, narrow hall to watch the final band warm up.

"Thorne," Yasu read from the schedule. "Anyone heard of these guys?"

"I don't think so." Seika took their flyer from the top of the stack and squinted at it, but if he knew any of the faces in the grainy, Xeroxed black-and-white group photo, the recognition didn't show. He pointed to the dates at the bottom. "You think this is really their first show?"

"Nice timing." Yasu snorted. "La Rose and Thorne?"

"Ibara," Minori translated under his breath.

The band onstage looked young, with black makeup smeared around their eyes and down their cheeks in painted expressions of sorrow. Their hair was short and spiky and—as had become a fad in the scene lately—their costumes were little more than black suits overladen with silver mesh and studded jewelry. They were bent over their instruments, the drummer and the guitarist running through their tuning while the singer consulted with the bassist over a stack of paper held between them.

There was nothing special about them, but as Minori watched, his frown grew thinner, harder. Angrier.

And when the singer looked up, Teru knew why.

His hair was shorter, his nose was pierced, and the silver roses that had once flowed down his back had been reduced to a single blossom, peeking jauntily—if a concoction of silk and glitter could be jaunty, anyway—from his lapel. One eye was milky white, the other jet black—contacts, without a doubt, but still unsettling—but Teru would have known that cocky, self-sure wink anywhere.

His mouth fell open, but Yasu beat him to the punch.

"Bara," he muttered, and swore.

Minori tapped a cigarette from his pack. "Where the hell did he find a new band in a month?"

"They're not new," Seika offered. "The name is, but the other three have been together for awhile."

"We gonna stick around and watch?" Yasu asked, but no one bothered to answer, and no one attempted to leave.

Thorne played over an electronic backing track full of throbbing echoes and cries like breaking glass, a steady stream of eighth notes from the bassist and a drumline that Teru could have hammered out in his sleep. The guitarist's output was warped so far that it was hard to tell it apart from the sound effects, and—to the band's surprising benefit—so were Bara's vocals.

If there were lyrics under all of the distortion, Bara himself probably wouldn't have heard them. But Teru didn't think anyone would care. They would come for what they always had: Bara, with his weight on his left hip and the mic held casually between the second and third fingers of his right hand, dangling there like an oversized cigarette. His mismatched eyes were rolled up to the ceiling, his mouth half-open in a mockery of feeble-mindedness or insanity. He growled what passed for the melody into the mic and then, at the end of every line, turned straight to the audience and screamed.

"They're not bad," Seika admitted. And they weren't. This style of visual kei wasn't Teru's thing, but he had to admit that the music actually did suit Bara's voice. He could practically see the girls, bracing themselves against the tables while they headbanged until it was time to throw themselves at the stage in time with Bara's screams.

"Come on." Minori grabbed the flyer, crinkling the corner, and stomped out of the hall and into the stairwell.

The entrance to Cynic's dressing room was practically outside, halfway up the flight of stairs to the street. With less than an hour before Thorne would take the stage, fans were starting to trickle in beneath the aluminum-foil sign, leaning against the flyer-covered walls with their tickets and their cell phones and calling out to La Rose as they ascended the stairs.

Minori waved, and the others followed, but they didn't stop to talk. They slid through the door next to the box office and, ignoring the sighs of disappointment from the girls, found a spot in the corner to talk.

"Hey," Yasu said, "it's no big deal. No one was expecting him to drop off the face of the earth, right?"

"His music's completely different," Teru chimed in, but Minori only tightened his grip on the flyer.

63

"Look at this," he said through gritted teeth. "Look at the schedule."

Teru did. Like the rest of the flyer, it was an obvious rush job—handwritten beneath the blurry photos and run off on a convenience store copy machine.

Seika saw it first. "Here," he said. "In August. They're playing with us again."

"Could be a coincidence," Yasu said.

"If it was only one." Minori shuffled through his bag until he'd come up with one of La Rose's flyers. "It's not, though. Look at this." He held them up, side by side.

"Fuck," Yasu said. "Will you look at that? Every single date." It was true. Thorne hadn't booked all of the same venues—but they had managed to get a gig *somewhere* in Tokyo on every night La Rose was playing, at least for the next three months.

"Why would he do that?" Teru asked, but the answer came from behind him.

"La Rose Verboten. Imagine meeting you here." Bara shook his head, but without his long hair to punctuate the gesture, it lacked the flair he had probably intended. "Amazing coincidence, isn't it, Minori?"

Minori gritted his teeth. "Astonishing."

"I suppose it works out for the best, though, since my fans already had those nights off."

That did make sense. Teru nodded in spite of himself.

"I have to admit," Bara continued. "I was surprised to see your new lineup. Are singers really in such short supply?"

That should have hurt, but from Bara it was almost expected.

Yasu rolled his eyes. "Give it a rest. Teru's good."

"I'm sure he is. And who do you have on drums these days?"

"Bara?" The Thorne drummer bowed his way into the conversation. "We're on in ten."

"Thanks." Bara nodded to his former bandmates. "Now, if you'll excuse me, I have a show to do. Listen in if you like." He directed this last to Minori. "Who knows? You might actually learn something."

"Learn something?" Yasu snorted, when the door had closed behind him. "Who the hell does he think he is?"

"He's right, though," Minori said. "That's the new trend. Their look, that electronic sound."

"It's a cross between Malice Mizer and Dir en Grey. Who cares? We've got our own sound."

Rei's sound.

Seika smiled. "And it's going to take everything we've got just to get through 'Yami no hanabira.' Right, Teru?"

Teru tried to smile. "We'll be fine."

Minori nodded. "Okay. Let's do this. We'll blow them away. And Teru?"

"Yeah?"

"Call your friend as soon as this is over. Tell him we're free to record whenever he is."

Chapter 7

They cancelled rehearsal that Wednesday, and booked a recording studio instead.

Teru had worked an eight-hour shift the night before, and though he was exhausted, he couldn't sleep. He lay in bed for four hours, tossing through bouts of intermittent dreams. At five o'clock, he gave up and retreated to the shower.

By eight, when he left for the studio, his hair was closer to fuchsia than to the baby pink it had been the night before, and his black roots were as close to gone as his unprofessional hands and a bottle of drugstore bleach were going to get them. He'd shaved every visible inch of his body, plucked his eyebrows—and then he had finally emailed Kiyomi.

He'd put it off for over a week, but once he got started, the words came easily. It had been a long time since he'd had a personal conversation—if that's what you could call this—with anyone but Yasu, and longer still since a girl had shown any non-band-related interest in him. He'd started out writing to give Kiyomi his phone number, but ended up telling her about recording and about the next couple of gigs as well. If she wanted to interpret that as flirting... well, maybe he would let her.

Even after all of that, Teru was early. Rei had booked a studio near Yurakucho Station in Tokyo's Ginza district. It was a more upscale part of town than even Meguro, asserting its pride in the hundred-year old brick storefronts as surely as in the towering glass skyscrapers. The display windows boasted shoes and handbags that cost as much as a mid-range car, and even the music stores made Teru feel too shabby to touch the merchandise. No matter what the guidebooks said, he'd always found the area more intimidating than charming.

The studio was no exception. Teru didn't really have anything to compare it to; the demos he'd recorded before had been done in rehearsal studios, then pieced together on Minori's computer at home. Even the most affordable recording studios really weren't when you were living on convenience store wages—but he didn't need experience to know that this place wasn't exactly the bottom of the barrel.

The automatic doors swept away, admitting him to a stark white lobby that had more in common with a sci-fi movie set than with any studio Teru had seen. Almost at the same moment, another door opened in what had previously appeared to be a seamless, almost luminous wall, and a receptionist in a jet-black uniform greeted him from behind an equally achromatic desk. "Good morning, sir. You are with La Rose Verboten, is that correct?"

"Yeah—yes. That's right. Is, uh... anyone else here?"

"Not yet. Feel free to relax, and someone will call you when the studio is ready." She bowed again and disappeared through the same door.

Minori was the next to arrive, with his guitar case over his shoulder and a look of awe on his face. "Wow..." he whispered. "This is nicer than I was expecting. Is your friend here yet? There are a couple of things I want to talk to him about before we get started."

"I don't think so." Teru checked his phone, but there was nothing from Rei or anyone else. "The receptionist said I was the first one."

"And we thought we were going to be early!" Seika burst through the doors and into the conversation, followed by a shorter, quieter man lugging what seemed to be half a drum set. "Tetsuya, this is Minori. Teru. And this is Tetsuya, as fabulous on the drums as he is in bed."

"You wish," Tetsuya said. "It's nice to meet you guys. Can I get a little help with my stuff?"

"Sure," Teru said. He followed them out to the street, where a large purple van with "Club Passion" airbrushed on its side was parked in a no-parking zone with its hazards blinking.

"Boss's car," Tetsuya explained.

"You work with Seika?" Teru asked as he took one side of the bass drum and helped Tetsuya carry it into the lobby.

"Yeah, unfortunately." Tetsuya laughed. "Why, don't I seem like the type?"

"No. I mean, yes. I mean…." Teru blushed, not quite sure what he meant. Tetsuya didn't seem gay, that was it. He was just a guy—short, tan, muscular. Masculine. Seika's polar opposite.

"Yes," Seika said. "Well, there's no accounting for taste, and our boss attempts to cater to a variety." He smiled and deposited Tetsuya's cymbals and his own bass next to the rest of the instruments on the floor.

Yasu was the last of the band to arrive, cursing the subway station and its multiple exits as he dragged his guitar and amp through the door on a trolley. "Should have seen the look on some of those suits' faces when I got on the train with this." He glanced at the clock on the wall.

Minori looked at Teru. "Do you think we should call your friend? Is he usually late?"

"No," Teru said. "I mean, I don't think so." He didn't think it would help to explain that he'd never seen Rei outside his own apartment before. "Let's give him a few more minutes? We can set up our equipment, maybe warm up."

Tetsuya enlisted Teru to help him set up the drums. "Nice kit," Teru commented, desperate to change the subject. "I play too, you know."

"Yeah." Tetsuya laughed. "I heard the whole crazy story. What do you use?"

"I've got a couple of snares—Tama and Gretch." Teru shrugged. "My apartment's not big enough for much else."

"I get that." Tetsuya smiled. "Well, if you ever need a better paying job, I can introduce you down at the club."

"No thanks," Teru said. "I'm not—" But Tetsuya wasn't listening. He, like the rest of the band, was staring at the door.

Rei stood in the doorway, tall and silent, his hair spilling carefully across his face. He was dressed, as always, in black—layers of skirts and flowing sleeves. He surveyed the room, taking in the equipment, the instruments, the musicians. His eyes met Teru's, making him feel naked, exposed.

"It is... a pleasure." He inclined his head, not quite

bowing, the image of grace and perfection. Then he stepped into the room, and the illusion was shattered.

His steps were awkward and uneven, taken at half the pace of the sound engineer who slunk into the room behind him and bowed fitfully to the band. His right arm was concealed within the folds of his robes, and his left, aided by a cane, seemed to be bearing nearly half his weight. Rei did not speak; he seemed entirely focused on the task of walking.

His manner, his attitude, his *aura* refused assistance, and the look on his face as he lowered himself into a chair behind the mixing board dared the band to make any comment at all. No one but Teru, who had seen him in the comfort of his own home, seemed to recognize the nervous twitch at the visible corner of his mouth, or the look of utter terror in his eyes.

"Well, then." His voice was quiet, firm. "Shall we begin?"

To Teru's relief, none of his bandmates were anything but polite. They ran through the song, speaking very little, taking Rei's advice with murmured consent and quiet nods. Seika hadn't lied about Tetsuya—he was an excellent drummer, and the others had obviously been practicing; Teru, at least, had been singing "Yami no hanabira" in his head for weeks.

"That was fine," Rei announced. "We will begin with the drums. Guitars, bass, you may do as you like, as long as you are not in the way. Teru?"

Teru jumped. "What?"

"We will record the vocals last, when we have a backing track to work with. Until then"—he indicated the seat beside him—"will you join me?"

Teru glanced at Minori, but the band leader only shrugged. "Go ahead."

The mixing booth was raised above the floor of the studio; Teru had to step up in order to reach it. It was strange, looking down on his bandmates, though the height difference couldn't have been more than thirty or forty centimeters. Stranger still was the idea of sitting here, in front of a panel of instruments that meant next to nothing to him, with Rei close enough to touch, close enough to send shivers up his bare arm.

The engineer was seated on Rei's left, which put Teru next to the door on his right. He could see almost nothing of Rei's face. It was hidden by the mask, and that by the wig. Teru stared in spite of himself—at the wig, the long cloak, the cane that now lay propped against the mixing board, at once the most innocent and the most sinister thing in the world.

Tetsuya was brilliant, even on such short notice, and Teru was glad of that. It gave him something else to focus on, something to think about when Rei's arm or shoulder or cloak—Teru didn't dare look over to see which—brushed against his elbow, or when he reached across the mixing board, trailing his blue hair over Teru's forearm and causing him to jerk away. The slightest touch was like a shock—Teru would draw back and then, feeling the eyes of his bandmates upon him, force himself back to a stiff, straight-backed position, ignoring the contact points that might as well have been fire on his skin.

"That was nearly perfect," Rei said after the first complete take, in a flat voice that didn't make it a compliment. "Once more, from the top."

"But he was great," Teru said.

Rei nodded. "Yes. Almost perfect. What good is almost?"

One almost perfect take became seven, and then six more for the bass. "That will do," Rei said at last, dismissing Seika with an inclination of his head. "You may take a fifteen minute break. Teru?"

"Yes?" Teru jumped. His mind had started to wander.

"You may take fifteen minutes as well. Mr. Tashiro?"

The engineer looked up. "Hm?"

"A glass of water." Rei looked pointedly at the clock. "Fourteen minutes, now. I want the guitarists and Teru back here at twelve-thirty."

Teru stood on shaky legs. Lunch, it seemed, was out, and he'd probably be sitting in that booth for another three hours before he had a chance to even start on his own part. He grabbed his phone, lighter, and a pack of cigarettes and shoved them into his pocket on the way to the lobby.

"So..." Minori shook a cigarette out of his own pack and lit it. "What's with the costume?"

"I don't know," Teru lied, glancing over his shoulder to make sure the studio door was closed. It wasn't. "I've never asked."

"Is he in a band?" Yasu frowned. "I haven't seen him around, but he sure as hell knows what he's doing."

Seika only laughed. "If he wants to be mysterious, let him. I'll never get this cheapskate to give me that many takes." He shot a look of mock disgust at Minori. "Besides, I learned a long time ago that what other people do—and wear—is none of my business."

"So how long have you been collaborating?" Minori asked.

Teru was trying to come up with an answer when his phone rang. "Just a second, guys." He excused himself to the other side of the lobby. "Hello?"

"Teru?"

"Kiyomi?"

"Oh, you did recognize my voice!" She laughed over the staticky connection. "How are you?"

"I'm okay. We're recording today. I told you that, didn't I?"

Kiyomi laughed again. "That's why I'm calling. I figured you'd be having lunch, and I just wanted to say good luck, and maybe ask if you were free this weekend?"

"This weekend?"

"Go for it!" Yasu mouthed from across the room, and Teru turned away.

"I'm off all day Saturday," Kiyomi said. "I know you're busy. We can decide the details later. But let's say dinner? Saturday night?"

"Saturday night?" Teru sounded like a broken record, but the part of his mind that was aware of this didn't seem to be communicating with his mouth. "Yeah, sure. I can do that. Send me an email, okay?"

"Okay. I'll see you on Saturday."

As soon as Teru hung up the phone, the rest of the band converged on him with questions. They were about Kiyomi now, and not about Rei, but that didn't make them any less uncomfortable.

"Is this the girl from the show the other night?" Minori

asked.

"Yeah. I... I guess she was there. That's okay, right?"

"Sure it is," Yasu answered. "She's a friend from high school, not a fan. A date with Kiyomi Nakamori!"

"It's not a date," Teru said, but the smile on Yasu's face grew wider.

"Excuse me?" the engineer interrupted, opening the door a little wider to let his voice carry into the lobby. "Mr... ah, Rei wants to see the guitarists as soon as you're done here."

"Okay." Minori pulled a portable ashtray from his pocket and passed it around. "We'll be right in."

They recorded the guitars together, then separately, putting down at least ten different tracks for each part. Teru sat in the sound booth, achingly aware of Rei's presence beside him and even more aware that, since the break, he had said almost nothing at all. He muttered commands to the engineer in an angry tone, and asked Teru for help only once, when he needed to adjust a knob that was too far away to be comfortably reached with his left hand. Teru was beginning to wonder if he had offended his mentor when Rei finally announced that he was satisfied with the guitars, and that recording of the vocals could begin.

Teru entered the booth, adjusted the heavy studio headphones over his ears and pulled the microphone closer to his face. He looked up at Rei for confirmation, to make sure he was doing this right, and when Rei nodded he said, "I guess I'm ready."

"Good," Rei said. "You may begin." He cued the recorded accompaniment, and music flooded into Teru's ears.

When he had sung this song on Sunday, he had tried to think of losses in his own life—tragedies from which to "bloom again," as the lyrics said. Teru didn't have much to draw on. There was the silent feud with his mother, who hadn't really spoken to him since he'd announced he was moving to Tokyo to become a rock star. The death of his grandfather, a bitter old World War II vet who hadn't had the sense to shut up about his outdated political views. The breakup of his first band—that one had almost worked. But today, when he sang, he could only think about Rei.

> *"Hanabira no kakera*
> *Sajin no you ni, kaze ni..."*

> *Fragments of petals,*
> *Like sand dust, in the wind....*

What had his life been like, before? He had been a musician—had he played in a band? Had he played at Rock Eden? At Cynic? At Vicinity? Had he ever recorded? How well had it sold? Who were his bandmates? His fans? His girlfriend? Teru imagined Rei as he must have been, the life that he should have had... and then he looked up at that beautiful, terrible mask and saw it all falling apart.

His voice trembled on the final note, and he grimaced. The half-fabricated tragedy had worked too well. "Sorry," he said, as soon as the red light went off.

"No." Rei shook his head. "There is nothing to be sorry about. You have finally learned to sing with a bit of emotion."

It was a compliment, but there was an edge to it that

stung. *Why are you so angry, Rei? What did I do?*

The music started again, but this time Teru, too, was angry, and the pity and sympathy he had felt minutes before were gone. By the third attempt, he was back to thinking of the night his first band had broken up and the silly, childish tears he had tried so hard not to shed.

"Fine. Enough." Rei flipped a switch, and the music came to a stop. "We are obviously done here. The first take will be fine."

Teru nodded, but he didn't think it was fine. Something had happened. Rei was upset. Teru's failure to repeat his original performance may have had something to do with it, but he didn't think it was all. Rei had been cold since the break, and Teru could think of absolutely nothing he had done that would have angered him.

"Nice job, guys." Minori smiled. "What do you say we go celebrate? Have a beer?"

"Or three?" Yasu added.

"Sure," Teru said. "That sounds great."

Seika looked up at the mixing booth. "How about you?" he asked. "Rei, was it? Come join us for a drink?"

Rei answered without missing a beat. "No, thank you," he said. "I am afraid I have... other business to attend to. Teru?"

"Yes?"

"May I have a word with you alone?"

His tone made Teru stand up straighter. "Yeah, go on, guys. I'll catch up with you outside."

"Three things," Rei began, when the others were gone. "First, thank you for being discreet about... my appearance. I assume you will continue that discretion in the future?"

"Sure. I mean, yes. Yes, sir."

"Second, if you are serious about a career as a singer, I strongly advise you to stop smoking."

Most of Teru's favorite singers smoked, and he kind of liked the way it roughened their voices, but he nodded. "Yeah. Okay."

"Finally, regarding your relationship with Ms. Kiyomi Nakamori." Rei took a deep breath. "Perhaps things have changed since... the end of my career, but as far as I am concerned there are two types of musicians: those who are in it for the music and those who are in it for the girls. Which are you, Teru?" He raised his hand. "No. Don't answer that. Just think about it. If you want to succeed in this business, your fans must remain fans."

She's not a fan, Teru almost protested, but he forced himself to swallow the words. "Okay," he said. "I understand." He glanced at the door. "Is that all?"

Rei's voice was soft, but firm. "That is all. Now go. I have work to do."

Chapter 8

Teru stood outside the Alta department store, between a group of girls with bleached hair and tanned skin and an outdoor display of folding fans and yukata, and scanned the crowd for Kiyomi. Shinjuku on a Saturday night was a veritable fashion show. From trendy to trashy, from campy to couture, every imaginable style and subculture was represented. Teru was, however, the only man on the sidewalk with bright pink hair. It would be easier to relax and let her find him.

The boots he had chosen were a little too tight, and he shifted uncomfortably on his feet. He wanted a cigarette, no matter what Rei said, but he had just eaten half a pack of breath mints. The thirty thousand yen that was the last of his "emergency fund" was burning a hole in his wallet, and he wasn't quite sure if he was dreading or looking forward to the prospect of going to a love hotel if dinner went well. It had been too long. He wasn't any good at dating. Maybe he ought to call Kiyomi and cancel the whole thing.

"Teru!"

He heard her before he saw her—a tiny, elegant figure standing on her toes and waving to be seen over the crowd. "Sorry I'm late!" she cried. "I took the wrong train from

Shibuya. Still not used to the big city, I guess."

Teru hesitated before taking her hand. "I've only been here a few minutes," he said. "Are you hungry?"

"Starving." Kiyomi grinned. "I hope you know somewhere good." She clutched her bag as though it might fly away, and looked up at the department store with its oversized TV screen and the neon skyline beyond with an expression that could have been wonder or fear.

"I know a few places." Teru smiled. "Is sashimi okay?"

"It's perfect!" She squeezed his hand tighter. "I'm so glad you were playing that night," she said. "I'm just so glad we ran into each other."

Teru wasn't sure what to say to that, so he said nothing as he led her down the crowded streets of Kabukicho to the izakaya that Seika had recommended. It didn't look like much from a distance—a wood-paneled storefront on the first floor of a five-story building, hung with paper lanterns and centered with a curtain fluttering in the wind from the tires on the main street beyond. It wasn't until they got closer that Teru—and Kiyomi—could see the chalkboard specials, propped beside the sliding door, and the large, built-in tank in which several of said specials still swam.

Kiyomi drew a breath, and beside her, Teru smiled. He'd have to remember to thank Seika later.

The hostess was good—she hardly gave the pink hair and pleather pants a second glance. She led them to a booth in the rear, big enough for four and surrounded by a bamboo curtain for privacy. "Will this table be all right?"

"It's beautiful." Kiyomi slid onto the worn bench. Teru sat across from her, and the hostess bowed before leaving them with a menu painted in dancing calligraphy on thick, unevenly edged paper.

Teru ordered a beer, and Kiyomi a pomegranate sour. "I haven't had one of those in ages," she said. "Maybe not since the night we graduated."

"The night we graduated?" Teru raised an eyebrow. "I don't even remember what I did." He glanced at the menu. "Is there anything you don't like?"

Kiyomi shook her head, and her silver earrings sparkled in the light. "You choose," she said. "I like everything. It takes me forever."

When the waiter returned with their drinks, they gave him an order so long that he had to reconfirm it twice. Once that was done, though, and the bamboo curtain drawn, Teru raised his glass and looked Kiyomi in the eye. "Well..." he began. "Here's to fate, I guess. And old friends."

"To old, dear friends," she echoed. "Kampai!"

"So," Kiyomi said, when they had taken the obligatory first sips, "what have you been doing? Besides the band, I mean?"

"Besides the band?" Teru laughed. "I don't have time for anything else. I live in Nakano, work at a convenience store. How about you?"

"Just work," she said. "I work and go to shows on my days off. And I think..." she continued, running a manicured finger around the rim of her glass. "I think I'm going to let myself get very drunk tonight."

"Not yet!" Teru laughed. "The food isn't here yet, and it's"—he checked his phone—"not even eight o'clock."

"Well, then, I'll drink slowly. For now. Do you

remember sports day our third year?"

"Sports day? Umm... not really. Should I?"

"I don't know." Kiyomi laughed. "Do you remember Kenji Watanabe?"

Before she could finish her story, though, the waiter reappeared with an entire flounder, delicate slices of sashimi arranged around the rest of the fish—which, despite being flayed and mounted on skewers, continued the charade of breathing.

"This looks absolutely delicious!" exclaimed Kiyomi.

It was, and so was everything else that followed. Mackerel and sea bream and flying fish, octopus and sea urchin and abalone—fare that would have been unusual enough when they'd lived with their parents. It was a once-a-year—hell, at this rate, maybe a once-a-decade kind of splurge. But Kiyomi's wide eyes and obvious delight made it worth it. "I feel like such a pig!" She giggled. "Really, I don't usually eat this much."

"It's fine," Teru said. "I'm glad you like it."

"It's perfect! Much better than our graduation trip. Do you remember that?"

Teru leaned back and listened to her reminiscing, smiling and nodding in the right places, but finding that he didn't have much to contribute. He remembered most of the things she was talking about, but it felt like they had happened not only long ago, but to someone else entirely.

Beer and cocktails came and went, and Kiyomi's stories grew more and more animated as she finished off each glass. After awhile, Teru stopped talking entirely, and listening took a backseat to watching as he tried to focus on the curve of her wrists and the way her eyes shone softly in the dim light. Maybe going to a hotel wouldn't be so bad. Maybe, this time, he could make things work.

"One more drink?" he suggested. "If you're up to it, that is?"

Kiyomi cocked her head, and Teru wondered what it would be like to kiss that secretive little smile, to run his fingers through that long blue hair....

He blinked, and shook his head hard. How had *that* thought worked its way in there?

"Teru? Are you okay?"

"What? No. I mean, yes, I'm okay. Just tired. Did you want to have another drink?"

"I just said I'd love to." She laughed again, but the sound lacked most of its previous charm.

Maybe I am just tired.

"If you're up to it, that is?" She echoed his earlier words with a smile.

"You know, Teru..." Kiyomi blushed. "It still feels strange, calling you that. I wouldn't say this, if I hadn't been drinking, but... I still remember the first time I saw you, at our school entrance ceremony. I liked you even then. Even in a uniform, with black hair and bushy eyebrows, you looked pretty good. And you still do."

Teru drained the last of his current beer and pushed the glass aside to make room for the next. He wasn't sure how to answer that. "Um... that's..."

"Here you are, sir. One beer, and one Kahlua Milk. Will that be all?" the waiter asked.

"Y—yes. Thank you."

Kiyomi raised the glass to her lips, and when she returned it to the table, a drop of milk lingered there, on her upper lip, as innocent and provocative as the curve of her neck, the line of her jaw. She was so pale. Just like Rei. Pale and fragile and needy and proud.

"Teru?"

"Wh—what is it, Kiyomi?" *That's right, Kiyomi. I'm with* Kiyomi.

"Are you sure you're okay? Your face is bright red."

Teru shifted uncomfortably in the booth. His pants had shrunk significantly, his body alive with feelings that might have been pleasant were they not tainted with the same guilt, the same horror that had come with his mother's discovery of a girly magazine stuffed under his bed—and Teru's unreasonable surety that she could see, somehow, the unwanted images that had crept into his head when he'd tried to use it, flat chests and tight asses obscuring the curves on the page.

"I'm fine," he stammered. "But—but maybe you're right. I'm sorry. I had a really good time, but maybe we ought to think about heading home?"

"Of course," Kiyomi said. "I'm sorry. I shouldn't have had so much to drink either—Oh, don't worry about me!" she protested. "I'm fine. There's always next time. Do you need to go to the restroom or anything?"

Teru shook his head. "No. I'm fine. Thanks, Kiyomi. Let's do this again?"

Kiyomi grabbed his hand and pulled him to his feet, though she had had just as much to drink as he had. "It's not goodbye yet," she said. "At least walk with me to the station."

They walked to the station in silence, though it was more of a peaceful silence than an uncomfortable one. Kiyomi believed Teru when he said he'd just had too much to drink, and since that *was* a part of it, it wasn't hard to fake. If she noticed the bulge in his pants, she was either kind enough or embarrassed enough not to mention it, and Teru was happy to keep it that way.

"Are you sure you're okay from here?" Kiyomi paused at the bottom of the stairs to the Chuo Line platform. "I've got to take the Yamanote to Shibuya. Call me when you get home, okay?"

"Okay." Teru nodded. "I'm fine, but thanks for worrying."

When he reached the platform, the train was just pulling away. Teru sighed, but it wasn't really a problem. Another one would be along in five or ten minutes; new lines were already starting to form around the "Car 4" markers on the ground. He pulled out his phone and checked the time. It was almost eleven. He had no mail, and no missed calls.

There had been nothing at all from Rei since that day at the studio, not since... *not since I made this date.*

Teru shook his head. That was a stupid thought. As far as Rei was concerned, he was a voice, a performer, just one more instrument on the CD. But his fingers were already scrolling down the list of names in his address book until he found the one he was looking for.

"Yes?" Rei answered.

"It's Teru."

"Yes. I know that." He sounded tired. Or maybe just annoyed.

"I know this is strange, but... are you busy? Tonight? Now?"

There was a long pause, and Teru was afraid he had lost the connection—or that Rei, perhaps, had terminated it.

"No."

"Can I..." Teru took a deep breath, and let the words come out in a single insane rush. "I'm in Shinjuku. Can I come over?"

Another long pause. The lights on the platform began to flash, and a voice on the PA system announced the arrival of the next train, but Teru was already on his way back down the stairs.

"I don't suppose that telling you no would do any good."

The words were harsh, but Rei's tone had softened, and Teru breathed a silent sigh of relief. "I guess not," he said. "I'll be there in thirty minutes."

Chapter 9

Rei answered the door with his wig askew and a cloak thrown haphazardly over his shoulders. It didn't quite hide his arm, out of its sling and hanging at his side, and it didn't quite hide the fact that he was dressed—for bed?—in a turtleneck and once-black sweatpants that had faded to something closer to navy. Only the mask was neat, perfect, as much a part of his face as his lips or his overly-plucked eyebrow. Teru wondered if he'd been wearing it, even alone.

He led Teru to the music room, taking a seat on the sofa and resting his right leg on one of a pair of ottomans. Teru was left to sit on the other, at the far side of the coffee table. "I apologize," Rei said, "for taking the best seat." He forced a bitter laugh. "It hasn't been a very good day."

He shrugged the cloak from his shoulders and draped it over the far end of the sofa, exposing the outline of his body in the tight turtleneck. For all his height, Rei was no bigger around than Teru was. His thin, flat stomach rose and fell with each breath, his pelvis and collarbone pronounced even under his clothes. Where his left shoulder and bicep were firm and rounded, his right shoulder fell away at an unnatural angle, like it had been dislocated and never repaired.

Teru stared. He knew he was staring, fascination and pity and morbid curiosity warring in his gut, as Rei lifted his right arm with his left and arranged it on his lap in a position that would have looked more or less natural, if the hand at the end of the sleeve hadn't been so discolored and clawed.

"Does it hurt?" Teru asked.

"Immensely."

There was nothing to say to that. Teru nodded and looked away.

"I've been talking to record shops about the single." Rei went on as though this had been the topic of conversation from the beginning. "Badge 10, Tesla Coil, Rock Amour, Fifth Phase. There's a shop in Shizuoka that has expressed interest, and one in Niigata—"

"You mean Toxic?"

A smile spread across Rei's face. "So you are from Niigata. I thought I recognized your accent."

"Yeah, Sanjo," Teru said. "I didn't think anyone could tell."

"Only when you're tired. Or drunk." Rei gave him a stern look. "Stick to the Tokyo dialect on stage. Now, if you'll take a look at that folder"—he nodded to the coffee table, where a single clear folder lay between a stack of minidiscs and a half-empty bottle of Suntory whisky—"you'll find two designs for the CD jacket. I prefer the one on top, but it is your decision."

"Okay." Teru glanced at the designs, but they looked almost identical. "I need to ask the guys."

"As you like. I would appreciate your answer by Sunday." Teru didn't answer immediately, and Rei sat up a little straighter. "Teru?"

"Yeah? Sunday, right? That's fine."

"Your date... did not go well?"

Teru laughed. "No." He could only hope that the reason wasn't quite as obvious. "No, I guess it didn't."

"That makes two bad days, then. Shall we have a drink?" Rei eased his leg from the ottoman and took the whisky from the table. He poured two glasses and, without waiting for Teru's reply, gave him one. "A toast. To La Rose Verboten. To the single. To you, Teru."

Teru raised his glass, knowing that more alcohol in his system couldn't be a good thing. "Not to me. Just the music, okay? Kampai."

"Speaking of music," Rei said, "I have a surprise for you." He returned his glass to the table and took an MD from the top of the stack.

Teru took it, turned it over, pulled it out of its case, but there was nothing written anywhere on it. "'Yami no hanabira'? Is this the final mix?"

Rei shook his head, and his smile spread to his eyes. "Listen to it."

Teru crossed the room to the computer and inserted the disc.

Music flooded the room. It was not "Yami no hanabira." Where the twin guitars had made passionate love to one another in that song, they warred in violent harmony in this one. The drums were thunder, rather than heartbeats, and the bass beat like a heart that was about to explode. Where "Yami no hanabira" grieved and hoped, this song wailed in fruitless despair. It was violent. It was angry. It was bitter—and yet it managed to be the saddest thing Teru had ever heard.

The vocals were, to Teru's surprise, smooth and melodic, completely at odds with the raw anguish of the backing band. The voice was Rei's, of course—Teru could see him onstage, the rays of the spotlights burning crystal lines in his hair. It was easy to imagine him, perfect and whole, leaning over the crowd as he gripped the microphone, caressing it, making love to it with both hands.

"It's beautiful," Teru said. "But there's no way I can sing it. Not like that."

"You must," Rei insisted. "You are the only one who can." He closed his eyes and fell back against the sofa, as oblivious to Teru's discomfort as he was to anything that was not his own music, his own pain. "You will sing it, or it will die."

"I—I didn't mean that." Teru felt his face grow red, and his tongue stumbled drunkenly over the words. "I just can't sing it like *that*. Like you. Your voice is... it's beautiful. I could never sing it like you."

"And I could never sing it like you. Does that make either of us better, or worse?"

Teru shook his head. "I guess not. I—I just meant..." But he didn't know what he meant, not really. He didn't know what anything meant, anymore. "I'm sorry. I should get going. The last train—"

"Has come and gone."

Rei pushed a strand of hair out of his face. Teru retrieved his bag from the floor and glanced at his phone. It was after 12:30. The Yamanote Line might be running, but there wouldn't be any connecting trains out of Shinjuku. "I'm fine," he said. "I can take a taxi home."

"Don't be ridiculous." Rei looked Teru in the eyes. "You will take the song, and you will sing it. Modesty is one thing, but you must be grateful when given a gift. And that means," he explained, gathering the cast-off cloak into his lap and carefully situating his bad arm on top of it, "that you will thank me when I offer to let you spend the night."

"I—I can't," Teru stammered.

"You will." Rei gestured to the now-empty space beside him. "I insist. Tonight, you are my guest—not my student. Come, sit with me. Tell me about yourself."

Teru's glass was nearly empty; he took the bottle of whisky from the table and, without asking permission, poured himself a second. Before taking a seat on the sofa, he downed half of it in a single gulp. "There's nothing to tell."

"Everyone has a story." Rei sipped from his own glass. "Where did you come from? Why are you here?"

Teru shrugged. "I'm from Sanjo, Niigata, like I said. I came to Tokyo be a star, like every other guy in the business. Why talk about me?" Teru took a deep breath. "I'd rather hear about you."

"That," Rei said, "is a very long story."

"Like you said, the last train has come and gone."

"I don't know what you want me to tell you," Rei whispered.

"I want to know you."

Rei shook his head. "This isn't who I am."

That was it, Teru thought. The conversation was over. Rei would ask him to leave now, to take a taxi after all. Teru wouldn't even blame him if he did.

But Rei said nothing. He simply sat, staring down at his hand, at his leg, at his broken body as though assessing the damage for the first time.

"We were on tour," he began. "Our first. It was our big chance—or so the record label said. They had a contract for us, if the tour went well. If the tour went well, they would see what they could do. Our first album, on shelves within the year. It was all we could think about." He shook his head, refusing to look Teru in the eyes. "And the tour was going well."

He drained the last of his whisky, and his hand trembled as he replaced the glass on the table. "We were on our way to Sendai. Five of us, in a van on the Tohoku Expressway. A band with a future. Stupid boys with stupid dreams. And when I woke... I was alone."

Rei lowered his head, allowing the wig to conceal his face completely. "They told me I was lucky. I was only crushed *half* to death, you see." He laughed bitterly. "Lucky!" he cried. "An interesting definition of luck."

"So, all of this..."

Rei laughed again. "Shall I spell it out? My left leg was broken, my right shattered. There's more metal in there than bone. Broken ribs, a collapsed lung. My arm..." His voice fell to a whisper again, and he raised his head to look Teru in the eyes.

"I couldn't feel a thing. Not even the pain, not then. I called the nurse. I had to know. Years, I told myself. Years, before I could play the piano again, or the guitar. I had prepared myself for the worst, and then...."

"She told you never."

Rei nodded, tears pooling in the corner of his eye. "Nerves, apparently, cannot knit themselves back together as neatly as bone. Not that the bones have done a wonderful job of it either." He took a ragged breath. "And then..."

Teru took Rei's hand and held it, stroking the back of it gently with his thumb. It wasn't enough, but it was the only thing he could think of to do.

"And then?"

A tear slipped down Rei's cheek.

"You can tell me. What happened?"

"I asked for a mirror."

Teru nodded. "So, the mask..."

Rei jerked his hand away. "You don't understand."

"How can I understand if you won't tell me?"

"How *could* you understand?" From beneath the mask, beneath the waterfall of hair, nearly-black eyes accused and pleaded. "You've never been anything but beautiful. How could you—"

"Let me see you." Teru, surprised by the strength in his own voice, raised a hand to stroke Rei's cheek. "Please. Let me understand."

Rei pulled away. "I can't."

"I don't care what you look like."

"You would, if you knew." Rei shook his head. "What are you imagining, Teru? A few scratches, a few burns?"

"I don't care!" Teru insisted. "You're—you're beautiful too."

He reached up and touched the mask, meaning to pull it away. He would show Rei that there was more to him than pink hair and power ballads, that he could deal with whatever it was. He touched Rei's face, and Rei flinched. Teru pulled him back, but instead of removing the mask, he leaned in until he could smell Rei, feel his breath on his cheek.

The kiss was simple, chaste, lasting only a moment. Teru drew back and opened his eyes.

Rei looked away, then pulled away, rising to his feet as quickly as he could. He pulled the cloak around his shoulders, hugging his arm to his side.

"Rei, I—" Teru didn't know whether to apologize or explain.

"You should sleep," Rei said. "I have work to do." He hesitated in the doorway, looking back. "The first train is at 4:33. Goodnight, Teru."

Teru wasn't tired, not anymore, but he curled into a ball on the sofa. It smelled like leather and whisky... and Rei. "Goodnight," he whispered, more drunk than sleepy. The lights went out, and darkness swallowed him whole.

Chapter 10

A narrow beam of sunlight cut a path across the room, teasing Teru's eyes open and then forcing them shut. He opened them again and blinked, unsure for a moment of where he was. He was lying on his back, an unfamiliar blanket across his chest and an unfamiliar ceiling above. His mouth was dry and his eyes were filled with an unpleasant grit. Hangovers, at least, were familiar territory. What *had* he been doing last night, anyway?

He closed his eyes, preferring darkness at the moment to even the sliver of light, and forced himself to replay the previous evening in his head. He had been with Kiyomi; he remembered that. They'd had a lot to drink, but he hadn't taken her to a hotel. They had said goodbye at the station, taken their separate trains....

But we didn't. They had gone to the station, and said goodbye. *But I took the Yamanote Line too.*

His head was made of iron, and it throbbed like a drum under a disjointed piano line repeating itself in his mind. It felt like a missing part of something, though Teru couldn't remember what the rest of the piece had been. Over and over again, the same series of notes, an insubstantial countermelody that seemed a strange thing to be stuck on mental repeat. It was impossible to think like this—what *was* this damn song?

The phone call. The song. The story. The kiss.

Teru's eyes flew open.

The unfamiliar ceiling gave way to walls that were familiar enough, to the flicker of a computer screen and to the dark figure who sat at the keyboard, picking out another bit of melody with his left hand, over and over and over again until he was finally satisfied.

Rei clicked and dragged something and pressed another key, setting the music into motion and bringing the nausea in Teru's stomach up to his throat with a violent jolt. What had seemed to be two meaningless lines of notes came together to form a beautiful, organic melody. It had not been a bit of something forgotten, but a half of something whole—a piano piece written for ten fingers, played instead on two sets of five.

Teru rolled onto his side. His head still hurt, and he would have killed for a drink of anything but whisky, but for the moment it was enough to lie here, silent, watching the music trickle from those fingers in broken pieces. He couldn't imagine what it must be like, to have a complete song trapped in his head, being forced to break it into parts and reassemble it in the outside world.

Rei glanced at the screen once more, adjusting something before returning his attention to the keyboard, and Teru felt an uncomfortable twinge. He had gone too far last night, and alcohol hadn't been the only contributing factor. He wasn't even sure whether or not he regretted what he had done.

Rei's lips had been soft, hesitant, but welcoming and warm. His eyes had burned with pain, with longing... and maybe with relief. His body, too, was almost alluring in its imperfection, though it made Teru's stomach turn to admit it. Was this some kind of weird fetish? Was it even possible to have something like that and not know it? Or, maybe, was it just because it was Rei?

"You can stop staring now."

Teru jumped. "Wh—what?"

"I said, you can stop staring." Rei reached for the mouse. His eyes never moved from the screen. "The trains should be running. It's after ten o'clock."

Considering the amount he'd had to drink, Teru was surprised he'd managed to wake up before noon. "Look. About last night..." His tongue was a dirty sock in his mouth.

"It was a mistake."

Teru's heart sank. "Yeah. So, I'm sorry, okay? It won't... It won't happen again."

He sat, and the world began to spin. His head felt twice its normal size. *A mistake.* That was all it had been. Rei had been vulnerable, Teru had felt sorry for him, and that had led to a situation neither of them had intended. It would be stupid to interpret it any other way.

Teru's bag had fallen to the floor during the night; he picked it up and checked its contents: wallet, phone, keys, a handful of receipts, cigarettes and a lighter, a condom, and the things that Rei had given him, the cover art and the minidisc. He had everything. The trains were running again. There was no reason to stay, and yet his feet did not want to carry him to the door.

"Rei?"

He lifted his hand from the keyboard. "Yes?"

Teru slung his bag over his shoulder. "Look. I know I can't understand what you've been through. But if there's anything I can do...?"

"Forget it," Rei said. "I am fine."

"I really don't care, you know..."

Rei's shoulder stiffened and he sat up a little straighter in his chair. "I told you," he began, "it was a mistake. As we seem to be in agreement on this issue, there is no need for further discussion. I am a busy man, Teru. You are not my only concern, and at the moment you are keeping me from my work. Is that clear?"

Teru nodded.

"I am waiting for your decision about the cover. That will be all."

Rei began to tap out the next piece of melody, as if Teru had already left. There were no goodbyes, no plans to meet again. Rei would remain in the darkness, in the world of solitude he had created for himself. And Teru would step into the sunlight, cursing his long hair and pleather pants on a hot summer morning as he was forced to face the world.

The sky was a bright, clear blue, sprinkled only with the innocent sort of clouds that couldn't have shed a drop of rain if they'd tried. Wealthy mothers and their pampered children were out in force on the streets of Meguro, shining in their brand-name clothes and their brand-name strollers, the epitome of happiness and naïveté. No one but Teru could see the dark cloud that hung over the day. No one but Teru was grieving for something that had happened on the Tohoku

Expressway years ago, and for something else that had died before it had had a chance to happen at all.

He had wanted it, or at least a part of him had, and he wasn't sure if it was the desire itself that was bothering him or the fact that it had gone unfulfilled. Teru wasn't gay. He couldn't be. He had slept with girls, and he'd liked it, well enough. Sure, he looked at men, but it wasn't because he wanted them. He just wanted to be *like* them. Of course he thought Yoshiki and Gackt and Sugizo were sexy... but that was natural, wasn't it? They were his idols and besides, they looked like girls anyway, most of the time.

"Fuck." Teru leaned against one of the advertisements lining the walls of the station, closing his eyes against the sunshine as he dug through his bag for his cigarettes. This was too much to deal with right now. He had rehearsal to think about, that damn CD cover... and then there was Kiyomi.

That, at least, was a safer line of thought. She was sweet, pretty, successful—and it would be a hell of a lot easier to start that phone call to his parents with "Remember Kiyomi from high school?" than with "Look, I met this man...."

The battery on his phone was low, but there was enough left to make a quick call. Teru took a deep breath. This was the right thing to do. The *only* thing to do. His date hadn't been a smashing success, but it hadn't been a total failure either. There was still time to do things the way they ought to be done.

"Hello?" Kiyomi answered, her voice groggy with sleep. "Masa—Teru? Can I at least call you Masato on the phone?"

"Um, Kiyomi?" Teru didn't feel like addressing that particular issue at the moment. "How are you? I mean, we both had a lot to drink."

Kiyomi laughed. "That's an understatement. But I'm off today. I'll live. Are you okay? You seemed kind of distracted."

"Yeah, well... the band and all," he lied. "I've just been busy. I had a great time, and I meant what I said. I really do want to see you again."

"Me too." Teru could almost see her smile. "Call me sometime?"

"Yeah, sure. And you can call me too."

"Anytime," she agreed, and they said goodbye.

Teru tossed the phone back into his bag with a smile. Even after their not-quite-disastrous date, talking to Kiyomi made him feel good. With her, there was no danger, no guilt, no pity. It would be so easy to fall in love with her...

Then why the hell can't I stop thinking about him?

Chapter 11

Teru went home. He flipped through an old magazine, looked through his rack of CDs. There was nothing he wanted to listen to, so he sat on the floor in front of the TV and flipped through the channels. News. More news. A sumo tournament. A soap opera that looked like it might be watchable until he realized the afternoon's melodrama revolved around a mother estranged from her gay son. He tossed the remote to the floor, and took a hot shower instead.

Rehearsal was scheduled for seven, but Teru left a little after five, tossing a pair of drumsticks into his bag along with his wallet and phone and the little white MD. Maybe all he needed was to pound the hell out of something; if no one had the studio before them, some private time with the drums might be just the thing to get all this shit out of his system.

La Rose was booked into Studio C from seven to nine and, as luck would have it, the previous band finished at six. Teru was welcome to use the studio for that hour, the receptionist explained as she penciled him in, promising to let his bandmates know when they arrived.

He didn't bother to tune the drums, didn't give a damn about how he sounded. A few minutes were all he needed to adjust the height of the snare and the cymbals, and then there was all the time in the world just to play.

Teru closed his eyes and let his body go where it wanted. It found a rhythm easily enough, the same pattern over and over again—nothing showy, nothing difficult, just all of his guilt expressing itself in varying degrees of loud.

Crash. The kiss had never happened. *Bang.* He didn't give a damn about that mask. *Boom.* And he hadn't been walking around in a fucking *cloud* all day feeling *sorry* for some stuck-up *bastard* who was getting all the *pity* that he *needed* from him*self!* He punctuated each burst of anger with a beat, ignoring the protests of his muscles as he drove toward a frustrated climax. He did care. That was the problem, and no matter how long he spent in this studio, pounding out his problems on these drums, concern didn't turn to hatred quite so easily.

"Damn!" He threw the drumsticks to the floor and buried his face in a ragged towel.

"Teru?"

Teru flushed at the sound of Minori's voice, not daring to look up. He had no idea what his face would look like when he did. "Did you see that?" he asked, into the towel.

"Some of it," Minori said. "I, uh... guess this wouldn't be the time to tell you we've got a lead on a new drummer?"

"Really?" Teru looked up, curiosity overriding shame. "Who?" He glanced at the clock; Minori was ten minutes early. It wasn't really worth it to complain about the loss of his private studio time, though. He was done, and the sooner he could hand that MD off to someone else, the better.

Minori propped his guitar case against the far wall and unzipped the outside pocket,. "Ever heard of Dear My

Roman?"

"Dearmie what?" Teru's tongue tripped over the English words, and he flushed. "I guess that's a no."

Minori smiled. "They were a visual band. Broke up about six months ago. Drummer was a guy called Nao." He handed Teru a CD. "Sound quality is shit, but he sounds all right, and seems like a decent guy."

"Sounds good."

"You're okay with that, then? If you'd rather we look for a new singer, I—"

"No, he wouldn't." Yasu threw the door open and barged into the conversation without so much as a hello.

"I guess... whatever you guys think," Teru said. "Whatever's best for the band, right?"

"All right," Minori said. "I'll run it by Seika too, and—"

"Hey, Minori?" Teru took the MD out of his bag. "Before I forget, I..."

"What's that?" Yasu asked. "Another number one single?"

"It's just a song." Teru looked at his feet, still resting on the pedals. "From my friend."

"Rei?"

"Yeah." Teru's face burned; he had forgotten for a moment that the rest of the band had actually met Rei. "That's right. From Rei."

"Good evening, boys. Hope I'm not interrupting." Seika swept into the room with a wink and a smile—just a part of his act, Teru told himself, but he looked away.

"Not really," Yasu said. "You're in a good mood."

"I spent the night in the arms of the most wonderful

boy," Seika gushed. "Not that any of you would be interested."

Minori winced, even though he had to know it was mostly for show. Yasu laughed, but Teru remained silent. Maybe he hadn't exactly spent the night in Rei's arms, but Seika's love life didn't seem like much of a joke anymore.

"Save it for later, okay?" Minori warned. "Teru, we'll listen to this after we practice."

"Okay, sure. Let's do it," Teru said. "Let's play."

They ran through "Yami no hanabira" first, at Teru's insistence. He wasn't going to be able to focus on anything if he spent the evening worrying about having to sing Rei's song. Better to get it over with, get it out of his system. Once it was gone and the only thing left to dread was that MD, staring at him from its vantage point atop the amp, he really did start to feel better.

Minori stopped rehearsal at a quarter to nine. "All right, guys. That was good," he said. "Let's listen to this song while we're cleaning up, and then I've got a few more things I want to discuss over dinner."

He slipped the MD into the stereo system, and the not-quite-cacophony of Rei's newest song filled the air. The first time Teru had heard it, he'd been focused on the melody and on the contrast of the operatic vocals and death-metal guitars. The second time, he knew what to expect, and could take the time to appreciate the details.

The guitars were real. That was the first thing he noticed, though it took him a verse and a half to convince himself that it was true. The guitars, the bass, the drums: none of them were synthesized. Someone had actually played this, and it couldn't have been Rei. He'd hired someone, then. It wasn't inconceivable. But it also seemed like a lot of trouble for a demo, when a synthesizer would have worked just as well.

"Your friend's not a bad guitarist, is he?" Yasu raised an eyebrow, and there was more than one question there.

Teru shrugged. "I don't think he played it all himself."

"I don't care who played it," Seika said. "It's incredible. Do you have the tab?"

Teru shook his head. "Not yet. I can ask him for it. I, uh, need to talk to him anyway."

When the instruments had been returned to their cases and the studio fees paid, the four of them relocated to a Royal Host and ordered a table full of greasy delicacies. "Ahh, the joys of gourmet dining," Seika remarked with a good-natured smirk as they dug in.

Minori ran the potential drummer's name by Yasu and Seika. They hadn't heard of him either, but they agreed to invite him to their next rehearsal. "Make sure he knows about the crazy shit Teru's friend writes," Yasu joked. "Drummer wanted. Must be willing to dislocate own neck on demand."

"Tell him yourself, if he agrees. Now, I have news, good news, and great news." Minori smiled. "First, this." He took a magazine from the pocket of his guitar case and opened it to an advertisement in the back.

"Crisis Cross Omnibus, Volume 3," Teru read. "A CD?"

"They're accepting demos now. It'll be eight tracks, two of them by existing Crisis Cross bands. That leaves six slots open for newcomers. They're an indie label, but some of their acts have done pretty well. We only need a rough cut. We could redo something we recorded with Bara, or there's Yasu's new song."

Yasu laughed. "Or Rei's."

Minori nodded. "Think about it. Now, the good news: our next show, two weeks from today. We already have nineteen names on our list, and about half of those have never booked through us before."

Teru's eyes grew wide. *Nineteen?* Even with Bara's fans, they had never had nineteen reservations two weeks before a show. "That's... that's..." *That's intimidating*, he admitted to himself. "That's great."

"It is," Minori said, "but it's nothing compared to this." He took a piece of paper from his pocket and unfolded it on the table. "It came yesterday. From one of the editors of *Shokker*. They want to do an interview."

"No way," Yasu said, and Teru shook his head. *Shokker* was a major visual kei magazine. Sure, they covered indie bands as well as major, and they'd give a blurb in the back to anyone who would pay for it—but an interview?

"When?" Teru asked. "How?"

"I still need to talk to her about the specifics," Minori admitted. "But she must have been at Cynic."

Seika raised his Coke in a one-man toast. "Well done, Teru. I believe you've saved this band."

"It wasn't me," Teru mumbled. "I just... oh, shit! Sorry," he said, when the rest of the band looked up at him in alarm. "It's nothing. I just forgot. I promised Rei I'd ask you guys about the CD cover." He took the designs from his bag and laid them in the middle of the table. The color schemes were a little bit different; one was darker and one was brighter, but they were more or less the same.

"I like this one." Minori pointed to the darker cover.

"Really?" Seika picked them up and compared them under the light. "I like this one. The song's not that dark. It's hopeful, isn't it?"

Teru shrugged. "Rei liked the darker one better, too."

"I'd go with the brighter one," Yasu said. "But if the composer likes this one..."

"The darker one it is, then," Seika conceded. He flipped a blue curl over his shoulder and turned his attention to his salad.

"Okay." Teru slid the designs back into his bag. "I'll, uh... call him tonight, then."

"All right, Teru." Yasu clapped him on the shoulder. "Now that the business is taken care of, we can get to the important stuff—your date!"

"My date?"

"Last night? Kiyomi? How'd it go?"

Minori and Seika exchanged a look, but neither of them attempted to change the subject. Teru couldn't believe that it had really been last night—that it had been twenty-four hours, and not twenty-four days, since he had met Kiyomi in front of Alta. "I don't know." He shrugged. "It was okay. We were both tired."

"Are you going out again?"

"I don't know, Yasu. Get off my back."

"Teru, that's your *problem!*" Yasu frowned. "You never know what you fucking want. You come to Tokyo to be a drummer, but the first time you hit a plateau you decide you suck and just stop trying. You're a decent singer because you've got natural talent, but you don't seem to care about that either. There's a hot chick who probably spent most of high school writing your name in the margins of her notebooks, and you don't fucking *know* if you want to go out again? I'm saying this as your friend, man. Decide what you want and fucking go for it."

Minori cleared his throat. "Well, then, on that note... Teru's not the only one who had a rough Saturday night. Let's call it a day. Go home, rest. I'll see you Thursday night in Koenji?"

The others nodded their agreement and, when the table was clear, they left the restaurant together. "Anyone need a ride?" Minori asked, and Yasu accepted.

"Just the two of us on the train, then," Seika said. "You live in Nakano?"

"Nakano's the closest, but I'll probably walk from Koenji," Teru explained. Koenji was one station closer and twenty yen cheaper, and the extra five minutes' walk would be good exercise. "You?"

Seika smiled. "Okubo."

"Koreatown?"

"The rent's cheap, and I can walk to work. Beyond that, I wasn't picky."

"Yeah..." Teru nodded. "Hey, um... Seika?"

"Yes?"

"Do you have to work tonight?"

Seika shook his head. "No, I'm off."

"Ah," Teru said, cursing himself for his shyness. It was one thing to be nervous around Rei, but Seika? They'd been playing together for almost two years. If he couldn't ask a stupid question.... "Look, I was actually, uh... wondering if I could ask you something?"

"Of course," Seika said, in an uncharacteristically serious tone. "Is something wrong?"

Teru took a deep breath. "Can we go to a coffee shop or something?" They had a little more than an hour before the last train. "It won't take long. I promise."

"Okay." Seika nodded. "Coffee sounds good."

They found a Starbucks by the station, and were able to snag a corner table with low armchairs and enough privacy that Teru wouldn't have to be too embarrassed about what he was about to ask. "Look... I know we don't know each other very well. And this is, uh... kind of personal. So if you don't want to answer—"

"Just ask me, Teru. You know I'm not shy."

"How did you..." Teru cleared his throat. "How did you know you were gay?"

Seika's eyes grew wide. "Is there a reason you're asking?"

"Never mind." Teru shook his head. "You don't have to answer. I'm sorry, I—"

"I'm not upset." Seika took a slow sip of his coffee. "I just wasn't expecting that particular question. I guess I've always liked men. It wasn't a matter of realizing it so much as it was admitting it to myself."

"So you never dated girls?"

"No. I dated girls. I tried to do what my family, what society wanted me to do. But one day... it wasn't that anything changed. I just realized that what I felt for those girls wasn't

108

the same as what I felt for... for him."

"Okay." Teru nodded. "Thanks." He wasn't sure that any of that was very helpful. It hit a little too close to home to be much of a comfort.

"Teru?"

"Hmm?"

"Is there a reason you're asking me this?"

Teru could only stare at the table.

"Whatever you tell me stays here. I just don't think you're that interested in *my* personal life."

Teru took another sip of his coffee. "Maybe," he said at last. "I don't know."

"Okay." Seika nodded. "It's okay not to know. You know that, right?"

"I kissed a man."

"Good for you."

"What?"

"I may not be the best person to learn life lessons from," Seika acknowledged. "But I don't think you'll ever know, unless you try."

"Okay." Teru said. "That... that helps, actually. Thanks."

"Go home. Take a hot bath. Relax. If it's meant to be, it'll be. And if not..." Seika shrugged. "I could always introduce you to someone from the club?"

That bath didn't actually sound like a bad idea. As soon as Teru got home, he set the hot water running and pulled his futon out of the closet, collapsing onto it and opening the mail folder on his phone. He was going to have to talk to Rei, sooner or later. He would just have to keep it professional, that was all.

He hit the send button before he had time to regret it and retreated to the bath, half-hoping the reply would be waiting for him when he was done.

Chapter 12

Three and a half days later, Teru woke to the ringing of his phone. He rolled onto his stomach and groped for it in the mess of CDs, beer cans, and magazines cluttering his floor. It wasn't Rei. It hadn't been Rei for three and a half days, and there was no reason to think it was now. Teru told himself that, and he believed it. But that didn't stop him from being disappointed every time it turned out to be true.

Under all the junk, Teru was half surprised to find the phone on its charger. He pulled it off, pressing a button to illuminate the screen. *One new message,* it said, but when Teru opened it, his heart sank. It was from Minori, marked priority, and the subject was "Tonight's Rehearsal."

"Damn." Teru rolled onto his back and closed his eyes. *Rehearsal.* It was the last thing he wanted to do. How was he supposed to tell the guys that he still didn't have the score when he was supposed to be friends with its source? Minori was already suspicious of Rei, and it wouldn't take much for Seika to make the connection between the half-regretted kiss and the suddenly strained relationship with the masked composer.

Teru opened his eyes. It might help to read the message, at least. Maybe rehearsal had been cancelled.

"Just a reminder," he read. "Rehearsal tonight. New drummer'll be there. Let's cut that demo if we can. Teru—did you get that score?"

Teru hit the reply button, but his mind was a blank. He could promise to have the score by tonight, but there was a pretty good chance he'd only prove himself a liar. "Hey, Minori," he typed, but deleted it, unsure of what should come next. "About tonight...." That wasn't right either.

Fuck you, Rei. He ran an angry hand through his hair and winced when it caught in a tangle. So they'd gotten drunk, made a mistake. *But any half-decent human being would have forgotten about it by now.* Teru was letting his mind rot, dwelling on this. He'd barely eaten, hadn't touched his music in days. He kept hearing Yasu, telling him that he didn't care about anything, didn't know what he wanted in the first place.

I want to know. *I want to know whether he felt anything. Whether any of this means anything at all.*

At the very least, he had to get that music.

Teru hit the delete button again. "Rei," he began. "We have rehearsal tonight. I get off at 4, and I could come by and get that music if it's okay with you. Let me know. Thanks."

He reread it five or six times, trying to convince himself that it was okay, that it didn't sound too forward, or angry, or impatient. Rei hadn't known about rehearsal, and there was always a chance the original mail hadn't gone through. *Not much of a chance,* he reminded himself firmly—but a chance, all the same.

—⋆—

Teru didn't look at his phone all day. He set it to vibrate and buried it in his bag, then refused to set foot in the back room during his shift. A smoking break would only turn into a watching-the-phone break, and so he didn't take one, letting his body's cries for nicotine go unanswered. It was only four hours, after all—and if he couldn't wait four hours, he hadn't really earned the smoke or the email.

But when his shift finally ended, the little light next to the antenna, which should have been blinking yellow-green if anyone had called, emailed, or texted him, was dark. He opened the mail folder anyway, but Minori's message was still on top. There was nothing from Rei at all.

The cigarette came next, but the pack was a cheap substitute for his favorite brand; it left a strange, stale taste in his mouth that wasn't much of an improvement over nothing at all. He stubbed it out before he really had to, and threw the half-empty pack back into his bag. *Well*, he told himself, *at least you've got some time before—*

The phone began to vibrate on the table.

Teru snatched it up, and jabbed the call button. "Hello?"

There was a long silence, and then Rei took a deep, trembling breath on the other end of the line.

"Hello?" Teru repeated. "Did you—"

Rei didn't let him finish the question. "Come."

Teru shrugged out of his uniform, watching each piece as it crumpled to the floor. His own clothes were flashy: a tight pair of pants with one black leg and one red, adorned on either side with meaningless buckles and straps, and a black tank top with silver studs around the arms. His hair was

113

pulled back, and would have to stay that way since he didn't keep styling product in the back room at work, but he had dressed for Rei as much as he could.

"I'm heading out," he called to his shift manager. "See you tomorrow!"

"Have fun on your date!" She smiled at him, and Teru blushed. Did it really look like he had dressed for a date?

"Uh... yeah. Thanks," he stammered, not bothering to correct her.

The train was quiet. It was still too early for summer vacation, but Teru thanked whatever force had kept the usual crowd of students out of this particular carriage. He needed the quiet to rehearse what he was going to say. Of course, there was a good chance that Rei would give him the music and tell him to get lost. And if that was the case, Teru couldn't really blame him.

"Next stop, Shinjuku. The doors on the left side will open. Please change here for the Yamanote Line, the Saikyo Line, the Shonan Shinjuku Line...." The announcement droned on, listing all of the train lines that connected at the massive hub. Teru stood up and waited by the door. He had never commuted to Shinjuku for work or rehearsal, but this transfer was beginning to feel routine—like he'd done it so often he could manage it in his sleep.

The Yamanote Line was just pulling away from the platform as he reached the top of the stairs, and he took the three-minute interval between trains to send a text to Rei. He wasn't expecting a reply, and he didn't get one. But if Rei didn't want to be seen without the mask and wig, it would be polite to give him some idea of when to expect company.

The walk from Meguro Station, too, was beginning to feel routine, though it was a little strange to feel that way about going to someone else's home. Teru had always preferred to take girls out instead of bringing them to his tiny, messy apartment, and he'd never been close enough with a girl to be invited to her apartment either.

Why was Rei different? He wasn't a girl, for one—but Teru didn't hang out much at his friends' apartments either. Was it because Rei *couldn't* leave? But he'd seen Teru play. He'd been at the studio. Just because he acted like an invalid most of the time didn't mean he really was one.

Teru shook his head; he was here to get the sheet music. If that went well, maybe he would be able to apologize—and that was it. Life would be a lot easier if he started the process of backing away.

He rang the doorbell, and waited.

Rei came to the door a minute or two later, fully clothed in his long skirt and a kimono-like robe. He wore no makeup, but the mask was in place, and the long blue wig was tangled, as though he had slept with it on. He looked Teru over, starting with his feet and sliding his gaze up until their eyes met. Teru looked away.

"You came."

"Yeah." Teru cleared his throat. "I came. Can I come in?"

"I suppose." Rei stepped back, allowing Teru to enter the apartment. "We did not part on good terms. I am sorry."

"No. I mean, *I'm* sorry. It was... inappropriate."

"It was," Rei agreed. "Forget about it."

Teru nodded. He didn't want to forget about it, and he

couldn't even if he'd tried. But he could shut up about it, and that would have to be just as good. "Do you have the music?" That was a much safer subject.

"Yes." Rei showed him to the music room. "It's on the table. Have a seat. Make sure everything you need is there."

"Okay." Teru did as he was told. The music seemed to be in order: four copies in a plastic folder, regular musical notation as well as guitar and bass tab. "This is great," he said. "I mean it. We could never repay you for this, but if there's anything at all—"

"Stay."

"What?" Teru blinked, sure he hadn't heard correctly.

"Don't go." Rei took a deep breath. "Please."

Teru shook his head. "I can't. Not now. I have rehearsal, and—"

"Tell them you're sick. Tell them the trains have stopped. I'll call and tell them you've lost your voice, if you like. There are things I need to tell you, Teru, and if I don't do it tonight, I may never find the courage again."

Teru sunk back into the couch. "I... I guess I could call them." The words came out as whispers.

"Thank you." Rei smiled a nervous smile. "Now, where would you like to go for dinner?"

"Dinner?" Teru was halfway through the list of names in his phone, on his way to the M's. "We don't have to—"

Rei straightened his shoulders and back, standing as tall as he could. "I am not much of a cook," he said. "But our conversation will go better with good food and drink. Let me take you out, just this once. Anywhere you like."

"I—I don't know." For all the lines Teru had rehearsed,

he had never imagined the conversation taking this turn. "I don't know this area. I don't know what you like, and..."

Rei nodded. "Call your friends, and think about it. It may take me awhile to get ready."

"Okay." Teru returned his attention to the phone and brought up Minori's number.

"I was starting to worry about you," Minori said. "Did you get the score?"

"Yeah. Yeah, I did, but..." Teru took a deep breath, grateful that Minori couldn't see him over the phone. He was sweating, though the apartment was cool, and his face must have been painted a hundred shades of crimson. "Look, I know it's bad timing, but I don't think I'm going to be able to make it. I'm burning up." That, at least, wasn't a lie. "Fever, headache... I should be fine for Sunday," he explained quickly, "but I need to get some rest right now."

There was a long pause. "...Okay," Minori said, but his voice was gruff. Unhappy. "We'll cut that demo next time. Get some rest, call me tomorrow, okay?"

"Okay."

"Take care."

"Yeah." Teru tried to make his voice a little scratchy. "I will."

When Rei returned nearly half an hour later, his face was made up, and he had replaced the rumpled blue wig with a shorter one that was somewhere between lavender and steel. "I like your hair," Teru admitted, unsure whether the compliment would be appreciated. He had no idea if the wigs were a fashion choice, or just one more part of the disguise.

Rei stiffened, and something like anger passed over his eyes. When he spoke, though, it was with a light tone, and he thanked Teru for the compliment. "I prefer the blue, myself," he said with a forced smile. "But it would have taken too long to style."

Teru had never worn a wig, but Yasu had had one in high school, when they hadn't been allowed to have extreme hairstyles of their own. The thing had been a mess, perpetually tangled and fake-looking. Rei's were obviously of better quality, but even so, Teru imagined they required a bit of upkeep. He smiled with what he hoped would be interpreted as sympathy.

"Shall we go?" Rei nodded toward the door. "Have you decided what you'd like to eat?"

"I don't know Meguro very well," Teru said. "If we went to Shibuya or something..."

"Fine. Shibuya it is." Rei turned, leaning heavily on his cane.

Teru cleared his throat. "Um... Rei?" He was fairly sure that what he had to say next wouldn't be taken well. "Don't you think... I mean... shouldn't we call a taxi, or something?"

Rei laughed, but there was no humor in the sound. "Why would we want to do that?" he asked. "No one takes a taxi from Meguro to Shibuya. The trains are much cheaper."

—⟩⟨—

It took a good thirty minutes to make a walk that should have taken ten, and though Rei didn't complain, he was out of breath by the time they reached the station. When a middle-aged lady offered him her seat, he took it without thanks or apology.

At Shibuya, they were swallowed by a crowd of high school girls in uniform skirts and blazers. Teru nearly had to shout to be heard. "I don't think we want to deal with Hachiko tonight." The square on the west side of the station tended to be at least as crowded as Alta in Shinjuku, and the crowd was usually younger. "Let's head out by the Tokyu Line? There are a few izakayas over there, too."

Rei nodded his agreement, and they took an escalator to the ground floor. The east side of the station was busy too, but compared to Hachiko it was a ghost town. "I don't really know this side of the station," Teru apologized. "But most places have the menu posted outside. If you know what kind of food you want..."

But Rei had already stopped in front of a tall building marked by a strip of restaurant and karaoke logos trailing up its side. "Here," he said, his voice powerful and decisive. "The ninth floor."

"The ninth floor?" Teru wondered if Rei's stubborn pride was going to assert itself on those stairs as well. "Are you sure—"

"Don't be silly, Teru." Deep brown eyes sparkled with what may have been genuine mirth. "No one takes the stairs to the ninth floor. The elevator is much faster."

Chapter 13

The izakaya was bright and lively; laughter rang out from the surrounding tables, and the atmospheric music was upbeat and modern. The young host did a double take when he saw the two men with pink and purple hair, but he recovered quickly enough and escorted them to a central booth. It was separated from the other tables on three sides with curtains, but the fourth side faced a busy aisle where waiters and customers passed by on their way to the kitchen and restrooms.

"Is this table all right?"

"Of course," Rei said. "It will be fine."

"You don't mind being in the middle of all these people?"

"Being stared at, you mean?" Rei shook his head. "I don't mind if people stare at my hair or makeup any more than you do."

Teru nodded, though he didn't fully understand.

"I choose to look like this," Rei explained. "I don't mind being stared at for something I can control."

"Oh. Okay." That made more sense, but it also hit dangerously close to the list of subjects Teru had promised himself not to bring up. He turned his attention to the menu.

"So, uh… what's good?"

The waiter took their drink orders and returned with two glasses of shochu and tiny dishes of some sort of vegetarian appetizer.

Rei lifted his glass. "Why don't we try our toast again?" he suggested. "To music. And to you."

Teru blushed, but he lifted his glass and let it clink against Rei's before taking a small sip. There was a fine line between drinking and getting drunk, and tonight he was determined not to cross it.

The waiter had brought wooden chopsticks in paper sleeves; Teru pulled his out and broke them neatly in half, straight down the middle. A sign of good luck. He smiled and looked up at Rei. "Do you think…" he began, but when he saw the expression on Rei's face, his smile faded and his mouth snapped shut.

Rei was fighting a silent war with his chopsticks, attempting to force them apart with one finger while using the other four for leverage. Teru forced his attention back to his food. He had caught Rei in a moment of weakness, and he wasn't sure whether to help or to pretend he hadn't noticed. It didn't help that the weakness itself was oddly compelling; Teru's eyes seemed to wander of their own accord.

"Rei?"

Rei said nothing, though Teru couldn't be sure if he was being ignored, or if the effort of separating the chopsticks had honestly consumed Rei's attention. He was beginning to suspect the former when the chopsticks popped apart, one of them flying across the table to rest against a tiny bottle of soy sauce. "Yes?" Rei said through gritted teeth.

"Were you left-handed? I mean, before…"

Rei retrieved the missing chopstick and clumsily raised a bit of spinach to his lips. "Does it look that way to you?" he growled.

More food arrived, and they ate in silence, watching each other. Rei picked at his food, taking tiny bites and chewing carefully. His upper lip didn't always seem to move the way it was supposed to, and Teru wondered if that was the product of some kind of reconstructive surgery. It was strange, but not unattractive; Teru had to force his attention back to his food.

"The guys liked your song," he said, more to his plate than to Rei.

"I'm glad." Rei took a long sip of his drink. "Teru?"

"Hm?"

"I hope I haven't made things awkward, with your friends."

"Awkward?" Teru shrugged. "I don't know. Everything's just happened so fast, I guess. Minori's a good guy. But it's always been his band. His music, his costumes, his decisions. Yasu's just shocked I have a life he doesn't know about, and Seika…" *Seika's probably got me all figured out by now.* "They probably know you had something to do with Bara leaving, and they're probably not going to thank you for it. But I don't think they hate you for it either."

Rei nodded. "Has Nao contacted you yet?"

"Nao?" Teru frowned.

"The drummer?"

"Oh, right. You had something to do with that, too?"

"It is not difficult to contact people who post their

email addresses on public forums," Rei said. "But yes, I suggested that he answer your ad."

"He's coming for an audition... tonight, I guess," Teru said with a guilty shrug.

Rei nodded and took a deep breath, as if steeling himself for something unpleasant. "Teru, there was a reason I brought you out tonight, and it wasn't to talk about your band. I wanted to apologize, and I wanted to... explain.

"I have been alone," he said, "for a long time. When I heard you singing in the dressing room, I..." He lowered his eyes to the table. "I knew that you were the one. I knew that you could sing my songs, and when I heard you talking to your friend, I... I can't remember the last time I have *wanted* something as badly as I wanted to talk to you that night. For years, I had been waiting for the right voice, the right band. I thought that I could risk getting close... but I was wrong."

"Wrong?" Teru echoed. "I—don't understand. You don't want to work with me anymore?"

"No. Listen." Rei drained his glass and set it aside. "I was wrong," he said, "because you were... too good. I am not trying to fire you, Teru. I am trying to tell you that... that kiss was not an accident."

"Wh—what do you mean?"

Rei's eyes grew distant; he shrunk back into the folds of his cloak. "I am sorry, Teru. I shouldn't have..."

"No." Teru shook his head. He couldn't let this stop here.

"It is early," Rei continued. "You can still make it home. I—I'll walk you to the station."

Teru heard his own voice as though it came from

somewhere outside his body. "No," he repeated. "Please. Not yet." His mouth moved without permission, taking orders only from the burning sensation that had spread from his heart to the pit of his stomach and continued to make its way down. "I mean, what I'm trying to say is... I guess I meant it too." A weight fell from his shoulders, and cold panic rushed in to take its place. "Don't leave. I don't want you to go."

"So," Rei breathed after a long moment, his eyes softening and his smile growing shy. "What happens now?"

"I don't know." Teru picked up his glass and touched his lips to the rim. His hands needed something to do, and the cool, wet glass was refreshingly *real*... "I've never said anything like that to... to a man, before."

"And I haven't said anything like that for years."

"Rei." The name spilled from Teru's lips. "I'm so sorry. You don't deserve this. Any of this."

"I don't deserve you."

"That's not what I mean. I—"

Rei raised his hand, and Teru's mouth snapped shut. "I know. You didn't mean it, but it's true. You don't know me, Teru."

"I want to."

"I am not a good person."

"That's not true."

Rei looked up, into Teru's eyes. "You really want to be with me?"

Teru nodded. "I want to know what this means."

It wasn't a very good answer, but it was apparently good enough. Rei rose from the table with the aid of his cane and, taking the bill between his ring and little fingers, turned toward the front of the restaurant—toward the register and the door.

Teru followed, reaching for his wallet. "I only have big bills," he said. "Can we—?"

"No." There was a smug satisfaction in Rei's voice as he passed the bill across the counter. "We cannot. What is the use of a generous insurance settlement if you cannot use it to take someone special to dinner?"

"I—I don't... I mean...."

Rei looked over his shoulder and smiled. "The correct answer," he lectured gently, "is 'Thank you.'"

Teru had never been treated to dinner before. He'd never even gotten to the point where he felt comfortable going Dutch. But he knew from years on the other side of the bargain that it wouldn't be polite to look at the bill or the register to see exactly how much he was being treated to. Instead, he stood by the elevator, trying not to stare as Rei fumbled with his wallet.

I like him. Teru tested out the words. To his surprise, they didn't sound bad. *I'm attracted to him.* That was weird, but not as wrong as it would have seemed a few days ago. *I love him.* No. It was too soon for that. *How can I love someone I barely know?*

"Teru?"

"Yes?"

"Let's go."

It wasn't so much an invitation as a fatalistic plea. And there was only one path to take now, out of the elevator and toward the other side of the station, where a string of love hotels—rentable by the hour or, at this time of night, until morning—waited. "Let's go," Teru echoed. "Can I call us a taxi? Please? I know we don't need it, but...."

Rei pressed his lips into a hard line. "You spent a year of your life learning to walk," he said. "A year of your life. And I spent two. Do you understand?"

"No." Teru's heart sank. "I don't understand... but I'll walk with you. Is that enough?"

"For tonight," Rei said, "I think it is."

Chapter 14

They made their way up the hill in silence, oblivious to
the strains of music pouring from the windows of passing cars
and the tired, drunken chatter of the students and office
workers trudging in the opposite direction, towards home.
Teru said nothing, and Rei said nothing, and the silence was
infinitely more comfortable than their conversation had been.

"This one." Rei's breathing had grown steadily heavier
since they'd left the restaurant. Teru couldn't be sure whether
it was the result of nerves or of physical exertion, but when
they stopped at last beneath a white-and-blue blaze of neon
kanji that would have been elegant in any other medium, his
voice was little more than a throaty gasp.

"Rakuen," Teru read aloud. *Paradise.* The building was
dark, covered in a mock stone façade that, had it not been for
the neon sign and the table of room rates beneath it, might
have made the place look like a castle.

Two sets of automatic doors, tinted nearly black for
privacy, opened with a breathy purr. The lobby, as well, was
decorated in shades of black, except for a lighted panel with
photographs of the available rooms.

Rei showed no sign of emotion; he wore two masks
now, the second of mock indifference, and he held himself

with the same elegance he had struggled with in the studio. "Good," he whispered, resting his cane against the lighted wall as he traced the numbers at the top of the board. "The deluxe suite."

Teru longed to offer to help him with his wallet, but he bit his tongue and let Rei pay the exorbitant fee on his own. The reception here was unmanned—no fully staffed love hotel would have allowed two men to enter together—and a few bills and the push of a button were all he needed. A small key fell into a dark cubbyhole, not unlike that on a typical vending machine, and Teru bent down to take it before Rei could try.

"Upstairs." Rei's voice was distant, but not angry. *He's nervous too.* The thought was strangely comforting.

The room was on the fifth floor, at the end of a hallway paneled in the same black and blue. The plaque beside the door shone with a turquoise light that went out the second Teru's trembling hands turned the key in the lock. When the light came back on, it was red. *Occupied.*

Rei sat on the lip of the entranceway to remove his boots, needlessly complicated things that stretched nearly up to his knees, fastening with enormous buckles and straps. There were plenty of similar styles that would have been easier to get on and off, and no one would have noticed the difference. They were ridiculous. But Teru had to admit that the process was admirable, as well. Rei and those buckles had a mutual understanding, an established routine that eventually led to the removal of both boots and their careful placement against the wall.

Teru's boots were of a simpler, cheaper make: mock leather with elastic bits on the side that allowed them to be slipped off in less than a minute. By the time he had arranged them in the cupboard, Rei was still in the process of struggling to his feet. Teru said nothing—there was nothing to be said—but offered his hand, and was only a little shocked when Rei took it and allowed himself to be helped into the room.

The suite was four times as large as Teru's apartment, papered in iridescent pink and draped with filmy silver curtains with no windows behind them. A television equipped with a Playstation, a karaoke set, and a collection of pornographic videos stood watch at the far end of the room, flanked by a mini-bar and a small counter. Soft, soothing music, carefully synthesized with only the slightest hint of a melody, floated in the air. There was a panel of controls that could be used to raise or lower the music and lights. And there was a bed.

"Shall we sit?"

Teru hesitated. Sure, he had come here to... do what? To face his feelings, to see how real they were. But the bed seemed so... final.

"Okay."

He sat on the edge, near the headboard, and Rei took a quiet pose on the opposite end. His cane fell against the mattress, dividing it neatly in two, and his cloak slid from his shoulders to darken the foot of the bed.

Their eyes met for a single panicked heartbeat. Teru looked down, and when his nerves had calmed enough for him to raise his eyes again, Rei had moved the cane to his other side, leaving only a wall of air and nerves between them.

Slowly, deliberately, giving Teru every chance to stop

him, Rei raised his hand to the collar of his shirt and slipped the top button from its hole.

"Help me," he whispered, and Teru nodded—a promise that had little to do with clothes.

He inched his way across the bed, his chest too tight for the want and fear that throbbed there. Rei tensed as Teru reached for him, for the second button first and then, when he realized that wouldn't work, for the orthotic brace he wore over his shirt.

It was metal and plastic and neoprene, and Rei's sleeves beneath it so long that no skin above his hands was exposed. Still, as the heat of their bodies met in the vanishing space between them, Teru had to force himself not to tremble. "Let me know if I hurt you," he said as, one by one, he peeled the straps and cuffs away.

"You could never hurt me," Rei said. "You should know that, before we... begin. I am in constant pain." He closed his eyes. "Every second, every minute, every day. It hurts when you touch me, Teru."

Teru shied away, but Rei took his wrist and forcibly pulled him back. "It hurts when you touch me," he repeated, looking Teru evenly in the eyes. "But it hurts even more when you don't."

Teru nodded, but when he turned his attention to Rei's high-necked shirt, he made an effort to move slowly. More buttons fell away, exposing a prominent collarbone. Teru traced the line of it with his fingers, barely touching the skin, and Rei stiffened, inhaling sharply.

Teru raised his hand to Rei's neck, running his fingers over the scar tissue there. His other hand continued to unbutton the shirt, widening the collar until it fell away. The right side of Rei's neck was contorted into an endless, seamless scar, a mass of twisted flesh that snaked around his shoulder to his back, pulling the skin around it into puckered swirls. Teru brushed the side of the neck with his fingers. "Is this okay?"

"It's fine," Rei said, but he was jumpy, on edge.

Teru's hands moved slowly downward, seeking permission for every fraction of a centimeter and finding it in Rei's terrified, eager eyes. The shirt sleeves, modified at the cuffs to close with Velcro instead of buttons, slid easily down his arms. A cascade of scar tissue gave way to smooth forearms and the warm expanse of Rei's back. He was soft, delicate... but also taut and seething with strength in a way none of the women Teru had been with could rival.

Teru exhaled his admiration, as his fingers continued to explore. "Oh, Rei..." he gasped, as he ran his hands up to his shoulders—and then, just as quickly, pulled them away.

"Please... don't stop. It's been so long." Rei's voice was laced with desperation. "Teru. Please?"

"Can—can you feel this?" Teru brushed his fingers hesitantly against the bicep. The muscles there were withered, pale skin clinging to the bone, and Rei shuddered as Teru's touch found other, less offensive scars—marks not of destruction but of attempted healing.

Rei closed his eyes and let out a measured breath. "Would it repulse you if I said no?"

"Of course not," Teru said, and, pushing his grief down as deeply as he could, let his hesitant fingers make their way to Rei's chest and stomach. He was slim in the way that many visual kei musicians were—not soft, exactly, but trimmed by efforts that depended more on starvation diets than on exercise. Another scar stretched down the length of his chest, but his abdomen was flat and unblemished, a stretch of creamy skin interrupted only by a trail of curly black hair leading down...

Teru paused, his fingers light on the waistband of Rei's pants. They were the kind of thing you could get in any inexpensive shop in Harajuku—long and flared to look almost like a skirt, rendered one-size-fits all by an elastic waistband.

"Just a second." He wrapped his hands around Rei's waist and pushed the elastic down as far as he could. "Lie down."

Teru slid his hands up to the small of Rei's back and guided him to the bed, watching with satisfaction as the tension in his features dissolved. "I can't hurt you, remember?" he said, and slid the elastic over Rei's slender hips with a smile.

There was a long scar on his right hip, and he wore Velcro supporters on his knees and ankle. "Can I take these off?" Teru asked. Rei nodded, and Teru nearly cringed at the sound they made when he did. Rei's legs were streaked with scars—on the knees, shins, ankles—but they were mostly hidden by soft, curly hair that teased at Teru's fingers as he worked his way back up to the sloping pelvic bones and to the prominent peak beneath the black boxer briefs that were now the only clothing Rei wore.

Teru reached up, his fingers again on the waistband—and then a warm hand pulled his away.

"No," Rei whispered, dropping Teru's hand as he

fought the mattress to return himself to a sitting position. "Not yet. It's my turn."

His fingers caressed Teru's temple, tracing a loose strand of hair, bringing back a half-remembered childhood, a pillow and a bed and someone sitting beside Teru as he drifted into sleep. Teru closed his eyes as a now-familiar heat spread through his groin.

What the hell is he doing to me?

Rei was, in fact, doing very little. He grazed Teru's cheek and neck with his fingers, leaving trails of goosebumps in their wake. His touch was light, hesitant. *Afraid.* Rei slid his hand under Teru's shirt, grazing his nipples, and Teru's body shuddered in response. His mouth flew open in a soundless moan.

He let Rei undress him, working one side of the shirt and then the other in turns, until at last he pulled it over his head and to the floor. His pants put up less of a fight; from behind him, Rei unfastened the button and zipper deftly with one hand, and let Teru complete the task, pulling them over his legs and letting them fall. Only a pair of faded plaid boxers remained, relics of his high school days that wouldn't have made it into today's wardrobe if he'd had any idea....

Rei slipped his arm around Teru's waist, and Teru shivered. Soon the boxers would be gone too, and he would be Rei's completely.

"Come here," Rei whispered and pulled Teru close. "You're so beautiful, Teru. So beautiful."

"So are you. I wish you would believe that."

"Shhh," Rei urged, and his fingers began to work their way down.

Teru tensed.

"What's wrong?"

"Nothing." *Something. Everything.* "I don't know."

Rei broke their embrace. "It is too soon," he said. "You're not ready."

"I am," Teru protested, but he knew it wasn't true. He wanted Rei, ached with wanting him—but until a few hours ago that thought had disturbed and terrified him. "I want to be," he amended.

Rei's eyes grew distant—like he was not seeing Teru at all, but someone else. Another place, another time.

"Rei?"

"Don't say things like that."

"Like what?"

Rei shivered, and shook his head. "Forget it," he whispered. "I... am not ready either."

And then Teru had Rei in his arms, his breath hot against his chest and the skin of his back warm beneath his fingers. "Rei?" he said. "Listen to me. I—I really do want this."

"I know that. I—"

Teru lifted Rei's chin and kissed him with a force that he hadn't consciously intended, pushing his tongue past those soft, yielding lips and daring Rei to answer him in kind. They drank from one another with a raw need, unrelated to pleasure or play. It was more like eating, or breathing—simple and blunt, and necessary above all.

"Lie down with me," Rei breathed in his ear, and Teru did.

Rei lay on his back, his hair splayed across the pillow. Teru touched it, forgetting for a moment that it was only a wig, that Rei couldn't possibly be receiving the same pleasure he had given earlier. He cradled his bad arm against his chest, and his breathing was shallow and rough.

"Are you okay?"

"No."

"Does it have anything to do with me?"

"Teru?" Rei asked, ignoring the question.

"What's wrong?"

"Are you... are you happy?"

Teru frowned. "What do you mean? Of course I am. Aren't you?"

"I... don't know what that means."

Teru rolled onto his side. "Do you trust me?" he asked, and Rei nodded.

"Let me see you." The words came out of nowhere. He hadn't been planning to ask the impossible.

"No." Rei shook his head. His voice faltered, and his eyes grew wide. "I—I can't."

"I want to know you, Rei. I want to know all of you." Teru touched the edge of the mask. Rei flinched, but he didn't pull away. "Let me see your face. Please."

Rei nodded, but the look in his eyes was that of a child, waiting for the results of a test he knew he had failed. "Okay," he whispered dryly. "Okay."

Chapter 15

Rei closed his eyes; he gripped the edge of the comforter, steeling himself for some unimaginable pain. "Please," he gasped. "Do it quickly."

The wig was lighter than Teru had expected; it came away in a lavender cloud.

"Oh, Rei."

The scars on his neck snaked upwards, cupping the side of his head like a many-fingered hand. The hair that remained was patchy and short—shaved, probably, to accommodate the wigs—and studded in places with silver. Teru stroked it, let it scour his palm before tracing the paths of melted skin, down to an ear that was little more than a hole set in a mound of molten flesh. Teru jerked away as he grazed the lump, unsure whether it was his hand or his heart that had been burned.

Rei clenched his teeth. "Just end it. Please."

Teru nodded. His arms were sluggish, mechanical. The nerves in his fingers sparked. He touched the mask, right below Rei's cheekbone, and the muscle there hardened.

Teru swallowed. He closed his fingers around the edge of the mask. And then he ripped it away.

His mouth fell open; his hand went limp. The mask

tumbled, forgotten, to the floor.

"Teru?"

Teru took a step back. "I—I think I need some time."

He fled. The bathroom door slammed behind him and he crumpled to the floor, his head in his hand and his hand on his knee and his chest heaving with dry, uncontrollable sobs. He thought he would cry; he thought he would be sick. Bile rose in his throat, and he sobbed as he choked it back down.

Pink and black, pink and black. The tiles on the floor marched on in perfect synchrony, but the glitter embedded within them was as random as the stars. Teru closed his eyes and, when that wasn't enough, pressed the heels of his hands into the sockets until they burned.

It was all he could see. That face... that *monster* who couldn't be Rei, because Rei was beautiful, and human, and alive. The slash of an eye, with no brow and no lashes, narrowing to a crooked slit when he blinked. The skin, pulled tight around the socket and over the hollow of his cheek, stretched like a pale balloon. The mouth, lipless at the corner, contorted into a permanent sneer. And that nose... the nose that was not a nose at all but a gaping, lopsided hole where once there had been cartilage and skin.

Teru clenched his hands into fists, digging trenches with his fingernails in his palms. He wanted to hurt. He *needed* to hurt, to punish himself for what he had done.

He crawled to the shower and twisted the knob. Icy water assaulted him, soaking his boxers and plastering his hair to his neck. Teru arched his back, recoiling from the cold, but he forced himself to stay, letting the water freeze and then burn him as he turned the knob as far into the red as he dared.

The mirror on the wall had clouded over; Teru wiped at it with the back of his hand. Pulling the elastic from his hair, he leaned back and let the water hit him, full and hard and scalding, in the face. His eyes, when he opened them, were bloodshot, his cheeks seared pink. He tore at his face in the mirror, whitening the skin as he stretched it as thin as he could. But when he let it go, it sprung back into place: young and healthy and whole.

"Monster," he whispered, not to Rei but to himself. "Who's the fucking monster now?"

He stopped the shower, let the mirror re-fog. Water dripped from his hair, turning lukewarm as it streamed over his shoulders and pecs, then cold as it dribbled to his thighs. He held up his hands, his thick drummer's forearms and wrists. There was a dot of a chicken pox scar on the inside of his right elbow, and a reddish spot on the back of his left hand where he'd been burned by a sparkler as a kid.

His boxers were soaked; he peeled them off and threw them into the garbage can with a thunk. Then he wrapped a fuschia towel around his waist and, swallowing a lump, opened the bathroom door.

Rei was asleep on top of the comforter, half-dressed with the mask askew on his face. The wig lay on the floor in a tangled heap; Teru picked it up, smoothing it out as well as he could, and laid it on the bed next to Rei.

"I'm sorry." He reached out, stroked Rei's temple. "I..." But the words wouldn't come.

"No..." Rei moaned, and Teru's heart seized. But he

slept on, kicking at the comforter as his chest rose and fell in ragged gasps.

Slowly, gently, afraid that he would wake, Teru lifted the mask from his face.

His eye was half-open, a blank white stare; his breath wheezed through the corner of his mouth. The skin, too thick in places and too thin in others, looked more like plastic or clay.

Teru leaned over and, closing his eyes, placed a single kiss on that cheek. He crawled into bed with his back to Rei, with his warmth and the sound of his breath to remind him of what he had done, what he had lost—and what he hadn't been good enough to give.

Chapter 16

Teru woke to find Rei fully dressed, his clothes creased in all the wrong places and his wig badly in need of a comb. The far side of the bed was tidy and cold; he had not slept there for long.

"Get up."

He spoke to Teru, but stared only at the windowless curtains. "Get out of bed and go home."

—→⁑←—

Teru had every intention of doing just that, but by the time the train swept into Shinjuku Station, overshooting its mark and forcing the passengers on the platform to rearrange themselves round doors that were suddenly in all the wrong places, he was beginning to change his mind. He didn't want to be alone right now. He couldn't remember if he was supposed to work today or not, but if the manager called him, he could always pretend to be sick. *I do feel like shit. Isn't even a lie.*

He stood on the platform, balancing a lit cigarette in one shaking hand and his cell phone in the other, searching his speed-dial list for someone he could talk to in pseudonyms and what-ifs. Someone who would understand enough of what he didn't want to say.

"Hey." Yasu answered. "Feeling better?"

Right. I skipped rehearsal last night. "I'm okay."

"You don't sound okay. What's up? Where are you?"

"Shinjuku."

"See you there in thirty minutes?" Yasu's voice was full of concern, and Teru felt sick to his stomach again.

"Yeah. Sure. I'll be outside the East Exit, okay?"

His cigarette had burnt, forgotten, down to a stub. Teru stamped it out with his foot, turning a blind eye to the No Smoking sign perched cheerfully above a timetable not three meters away. The lights on either side of the platform began to blink, a warning chime proclaimed the arrival of the next train, and Teru fled to the stairwell and down into the less carefully controlled chaos of the pedestrian walkway below. He stumbled past a group of middle-aged ladies, earned a stern look from an older businessman and a mildly interested one from a homeless man around the same age. A couple of girls stopped what they were doing to whisper to each other at the sight of him. On any other day, he might have cared. But at the moment, Teru was concerned with nothing but getting outside, lighting up that next cigarette and trying to replace the rot in his heart with nicotine, with sunshine—with anything at all.

By the time Yasu arrived, Teru had smoked seven cigarettes down to the filter, scattering the butts in the apathetic beginnings of a mountain at his feet.

"What happened to the Clean Shinjuku Campaign?" It was a lame joke, and Yasu knew it; the smile on his face apologized more than encouraged, but it made Teru feel

141

better than anything else that had happened that day.

He didn't bother to answer the question. "Hey."

"What's up?"

"Don't really want to talk about it here." Teru shook his head and stamped out cigarette number eight. "Can we go somewhere? Sit down?"

"Sure." Yasu nodded. "Coffee?"

"Yeah. That's good. Just... somewhere close, okay?"

There were a hundred coffee shops within a three-minute walk of the station, and they found one with cheap coffee, sandwiches, and an empty corner booth that was the closest they were going to get to privacy in the middle of the biggest city in the world. Teru poured a tube of sugar into his coffee and stirred it too fast, sloshing more than a few drops onto the table. He wanted to tell Yasu everything; he wanted to tell him to forget it and go home.

"How'd rehearsal go?" Teru hoped he sounded more relaxed than he felt.

Yasu gave him a funny look. "It was okay. Minori wanted you there, to tell the rest of us if the new guy's worth his shit." Teru couldn't tell if that was a joke or not, but he feigned a smile. "He seems all right, though. Minori's got us some new gigs, and he wanted to talk about that Crisis Cross thing."

Teru nodded, but his already heavy head was starting to throb.

"Yeah, I remember. Weren't we going to record something..."

"Yesterday?" Yasu smirked. "We've got a couple of weeks. Minori'll live. But you didn't call me here to talk about

142

band shit." He leaned across the table. "What happened last night?"

Teru stared into his coffee. "I wasn't sick," he admitted. "I was with someone."

"And...?"

"Have you ever felt like... like you'd met someone really special? Only, you didn't realize how special they were until they were gone?"

"Who hasn't?" Yasu grimaced. "Fucking sucks."

"Yeah." Teru took a sip of coffee. "Yeah, it does."

"Hey, look. You don't have to tell me anything you don't want to, okay? But, you know... Hell, I'm no good with girls either. But I'm sorry, man. I really am."

"It's okay," Teru said. Yasu was probably right—he definitely wasn't the best one to ask when it came to advice about girls. But Rei wasn't a girl, was he? Maybe he could at least ask for advice about guys.

"Hey, Yasu?"

"Yeah?"

"What would you do if... if you had a secret? Something like, I don't know, an ugly birthmark or an extra toe?" Those were bad examples, but Teru couldn't think of anything better—at least, he couldn't think of anything that wouldn't give away the fact that he was talking about someone Yasu had already met, spoken to, and probably wondered about as well. "And what if you decided to show this girl," he went on, "because you thought she would be different? That she'd be able to look past whatever it was."

Yasu raised an eyebrow.

"And what if..." Teru continued, unable to stop the

143

words once they had started, unable to stop the self-loathing that had crept into his voice, or the tears that were caught in his throat and threatening to work their way up to his eyes. "What if, when you showed this girl, who should have been different... what if she hated you, and she ran? Could you ever forgive her? Could you ever take her back?"

"Damn." Yasu whistled. "So, you saw this chick's extra toe and freaked? Do you even *want* her back?"

Teru shook his head. "I didn't *freak*. I was just... shocked. But I do want... you know."

"Okay, okay. I get it. I don't know if she'll take you back or not, but if it was me, I guess I'd apologize. Then take her out to dinner. Or somewhere fun. Bowling, skating, I dunno... someplace where she doesn't have to think about it, she can just have fun and remember what a great guy you are when you aren't acting like an ass, right? And then, you just ignore it. Don't mention it again, and she gets it—you don't care."

"I don't care," Teru repeated. It seemed too simple, but it made a kind of sense. Never mind that the thought of dragging Rei to a bowling alley was either too funny or too tragic for words. *He's already feeling sorry for himself. If I want to be with him, I have to help him forget. Apologize, ignore it, have fun.* It would be easier said than done, but... "Thanks. That actually sounds okay."

"No problem." Yasu shrugged, but then his eyes grew wide. "Oh, shit," he said. "No fucking way." He smiled, then laughed, then had to put his coffee down before he spilled it all over the table. "'I was with someone last night?' It was Kiyomi, wasn't it?"

144

"N -no. I..."

"Come on, give me your phone." Yasu reached across the table, plucking Teru's phone out of his open bag. "Lemme see. Na, Na... Nakamori. Here she is!"

"Yasu, wait!"

"Here." Yasu thrust the phone into Teru's hand and leaned back, evidently sure he had done his friend a favor.

"Hello?" Teru heard Kiyomi's voice before he could get the phone to his ear. "Hello?"

"Um... hi." He shot Yasu a look that should have been poisonous, but Yasu only laughed and smiled.

"You caught me on my lunch break," she said. "Let me guess. No show this week, and I haven't talked to you in ages. Yes!"

"Yes?"

"To your invitation, silly. How does Sunday sound?"

"Sunday?"

"Unless you have to work?"

"No. No work. I mean, yeah, Sunday's fine," Teru stammered.

Kiyomi laughed. "Why don't we meet in front of Alta again and decide from there? Everyone else in the world will be meeting for lunch at noon, so I'll see you at eleven forty-five."

"Sure. Okay. I'll, uh, see you on Sunday, then."

Teru hung up the phone in a daze. *Rei. Kiyomi.* Now there were two clouds hanging over his heart. He'd have to hurt one of them. Or both. *Fuck. Fuck fuck fuck.*

The mental curse became a spoken one as his phone began to buzz. It was the CombiMart. He must have been scheduled to work today after all.

Chapter 17

Teru almost didn't recognize Kiyomi when he saw her. She was dressed in black from head to toe, her makeup too heavy and her heels too high. Only her hair and her elegant wristwatch betrayed her as the successful young businesswoman that she was; everything else could have come from the closet of one of his fans.

"Don't laugh!" She spread her arms as wide as she could in the crowd and spun around, modeling the costume like a little girl. "I look ridiculous, don't I?"

"You look fine." Teru shook his head, gesturing to his own T-shirt and jeans. "But I'm a little underdressed."

Kiyomi laughed again, and this time Teru joined her. It was a little funny, after all.

Take her someplace where she doesn't have to think about it... just have fun... ignore it... you don't care.

Teru shook his head, trying to forget Yasu's words. Kiyomi wasn't the one who needed to forget. She wasn't the one who needed to have fun. *Ignore it,* he told himself again. *You don't care.*

"Teru?" Kiyomi asked. "Are you all right?"

"No," he said. "I mean, yes. I'm fine. Just tired. I missed work on Friday and got hell for it last night." It wasn't much of an excuse, but it was true: he had been given all of the least desirable jobs as not-so-subtle punishment for his absence. Kiyomi gave him a sympathetic smile.

"Lunch first?" she suggested as soon as they had pulled away from the Alta crowd. "Let me guess. Single guy, living alone... no breakfast, right?"

Teru laughed. "Right. But I don't mind waiting, if you're not hungry yet."

"Are you kidding?" Kiyomi took his hand. "Single girl, living alone? I haven't eaten since last night's instant ramen."

They chose a chain Italian restaurant, where they were shown to their table by a young waitress with an "In Training" badge pinned to her blouse. "Here you are." She handed them their menus upside-down and continued into a sales pitch for a lunch special that was apparently valid only on weekdays.

"Poor girl." Kiyomi smiled at the waitress's back as she scurried off at the summons of her manager.

They ordered, and when the same girl returned with their salads, she seemed to have composed herself a bit. "I'm sorry," she apologized. "I think I must have given you the wrong specials."

"It's fine," Kiyomi reassured her. "Thank you."

"So, um..." Teru wanted to say something, to compliment her on the way she had spoken to the waitress. He wanted to tell her how kind and how wonderful she was, how she deserved so much better than him. "What do you want to do after lunch?" he asked instead. "I hadn't really made any plans."

"After lunch?" Kiyomi frowned. "I don't know. Take

me shopping?"

Teru shrugged. "That sounds okay. What do you want to buy?"

Her eyes met his across the table, and she smiled that shy, conspiratorial smile. "Well, I've been thinking. Your band has a CD coming out, right?"

"Right." Teru nodded.

"And no staff?"

"Not right now, no."

"So, perfect!" Kiyomi's smile widened into a grin. "I have Sundays off; you usually play on Sundays. I'm not busy, and I'd be going to your shows anyway. So... all I need is a new wardrobe, and you've got yourself a staff girl. Take me to Marui One?"

Marui One was the visual kei department store: seven floors of almost nothing but visual, punk, and gothic fashion. It was the perfect place for Kiyomi to get what she wanted, but there was nowhere in Tokyo—nowhere in the country—where Teru was more likely to be recognized, and no better time for it than a Sunday afternoon.

"I don't know..." He picked at his salad. He hadn't been to Marui One in ages, and while he couldn't really afford anything, it was never a bad idea to see what was in style. But La Rose Verboten was more popular than they had ever been, and for Teru to take a girl shopping in the middle of the afternoon.... "I might be recognized," he said. "If anyone asks, I can't tell them you're my date. But if they see you at the staff table at the next show...." Minori might not like it. As far as the fans were concerned, they were all single and straight, and therefore available. Too much of the business depended on that image to risk it.

But I am single. She isn't my girlfriend; she'll be staff. And Rei...

Teru shook his head. Kiyomi was right. They were going to need someone to sell their CDs, to hand out flyers and collect questionnaires. "Okay." Teru forced a smile. "Let's go."

———※———

The first floor was consumed by the chaos of an early summer sale, huge bins of "Spring and Summer Bargains" that differed from the fall collections only in the ratio of gauze to satin and mesh to canvas. It was all black, it was all expensive, and in the wide eyes of Kiyomi, it was all wonderful. Tokyo had given her a more mainstream sense of fashion, taught her to dress the way society expected, and to do so well. But the girl that she had been—that shy, awkward girl who longed on some level for darkness, for a dangerous and exotic beauty on the stages of Niigata and Tokyo—that girl wasn't gone, and here she was finally in her element.

"What do you think of this?" She pulled a dress from the nearest rack and held it to her chest, letting the skirt brush against the tops of her shoes. It was sleeveless, with buckles and faux leather straps that would, when fastened, highlight the curve of her arms. Though the front of the dress was modest, the back was low and open. It was sexy, it was daring... and the thought of Kiyomi wearing it, in front of his bandmates and his fans and whoever else happened to be there....

"I don't know," Teru said. "It's a little... I mean, there

are lots of shops upstairs too. Why don't we look around a little more?"

Kiyomi returned the dress with a giggle. "In other words, it's too sexy and probably way too small anyway." She let out a little sigh. "Not me, is it? Okay, let's keep looking, then. The jewelry's in the back, right?"

The corner of the first floor that had not been overrun by sale items was, indeed, home to a small jewelry shop. Kiyomi ran a finger down the edge of the display case as she walked, taking in each piece with a glance, but the shop sold mostly men's jewelry, and she was apparently uninterested in wearing handfuls of clunky rings and piles of men's necklaces like some of the girls did. "Not me," she proclaimed again with a smile. "But this would look wonderful on you!"

She plucked a necklace from the display. "What do you think?"

"What is it?" He took the pendant and held it up to the light. It had wings, maybe. Bat wings or demon wings, spidery and membranous, but everything else was... obscured. Whatever it was, the artist had portrayed it in a state of agony, some mythical creature struggling against invisible bonds. It was tragic. It was hideous. Teru loved it.

"How much is it?"

"That one is twenty thousand, sir," the salesgirl answered. "It's one of a kind. The artist has designed all sorts of jewelry and costumes for the stage...." She rattled off a list of bands, some of them better known than others. But Teru heard only one thing. *Twenty thousand.* There was no way.

"I'll think about it." He handed the necklace back to the clerk.

"Wasn't it perfect?" Kiyomi whispered in his ear as they stepped onto the escalator. "It would look so good with your costume!"

Teru shook his head. "Not for twenty thousand yen."

He accompanied her into shop after shop, watching as she tried on everything from leather pants to lace-trimmed Victorian gowns. She paid with a credit card, signing away in an instant an amount of money that Teru hadn't spent on anything but rent and taxes in years. He was a little jealous, but tried not to let it show. Kiyomi had worked hard for what she had, and he had chosen his lifestyle as well. There wasn't any reason to begrudge her a little shopping spree.

"Ready?" Teru picked up her bags; if he couldn't pay for her shopping like some guys would, at least he could be a gentleman when it came to this.

"Excuse me?" The clerk called to them as they turned to leave. "Are you the singer from La Rose Verboten? I saw you last week. You were great."

Teru felt his face color, a mixture of embarrassment and pride. "Y—yeah," he managed to mumble. "Um, thanks."

"I can't wait for the new single," the girl said and then, remembering where she was, she bowed. "Thank you very much for your business!"

"Thank you," Teru and Kiyomi echoed in unison, and all three of them started to laugh.

"That was nice of you, to carry my bags." Kiyomi leaned in to thank him when the clerk was out of earshot. "And being recognized wasn't too bad, was it?"

"Not really."

"Do you have to go?" She looked at her wristwatch. "I

don't want to keep you if you're busy, but…"

Teru shook his head. "I'm not busy. What is it?"

"Well…" Kiyomi bit her lip. "How do you feel about CD shopping? I'm dying to see the posters for your single."

"Are they up already?"

"I think so. Wait here just a second, okay? I'm going to run to the restroom."

When she returned, Kiyomi was beaming. "Sorry to keep you waiting," she said, but it didn't really sound like an apology, and when she took Teru's hand again and forcibly closed it around her own, he understood why. He opened his fist, already knowing what he would find. It was a bat, or a demon, or maybe an angel trying to escape from its own personal hell, frozen forever in an artist's steel rendition.

"I thought you were going to the restroom," Teru said. "I can't take this."

"You have to," she said. "No returns. Consider it repayment for the bracelet."

"From the show? That was cheap, Kiyomi. This is…."

She shook her head and, taking his hand, began to lead him toward Tesla Coil, the closest music shop specializing in visual kei.

"Kiyomi, I…" Teru didn't know what to say. He was having a good time, but he knew that she was having a better one. And enough of him still wanted to help Rei, if he could. *I can't be with you, Kiyomi. God, I want to. Or I want to want to. But it's different with him.*

It was what he should have said, but he didn't. "I'm glad we did this," he said at last. "I had fun."

She squeezed his hand in reply. "Me too."

Tesla Coil was a small shop, but prestigious in its way—those who knew visual kei shopped here, and those who didn't, didn't need to. The store sometimes played host to CD signings and handshake events, but if anything had been scheduled today, it was long over by the time Teru and Kiyomi arrived. Two or three girls were browsing the shelves, one with a bored-looking boyfriend in tow, but they hadn't picked a terrible time to come.

La Rose weren't big enough to merit poster space in the front window, but as soon as he entered the shop, Teru was greeted by an image of himself: an old photo that had been blown up and worked into the middle of a large, dark poster taped to the counter beneath the register. The name of the single—it sent a shiver up his spine to see it in print—and the release date were printed in the lower right corner, and information about making a reservation had been hand-written next to it by the shop's staff.

"Wow," Kiyomi whispered. If it weren't for the stares of the employees behind the counter, Teru might have said the same. This was real. He was here, in one of the best-known visual kei shops in Tokyo, looking at his own photo under the register. It was like a dream. And it was all thanks to...

"Rei."

"What?" Kiyomi asked. "Did you say something?"

Teru shook his head. "This just reminded me of someone, that's all."

"Rei?" Kiyomi's voice was half-teasing as she asked, "A girl? A girlfriend?"

Teru shook his head. "Just a fellow musician. Someone

154

I used to know."

Chapter 18

The following Sunday was a new beginning, in more ways than one. The formerly empty merch table was manned by Kiyomi, beaming in her new clothes as she arranged and rearranged stacks of the CD single. "Hi, Teru!" she called as he trudged down the stairs. "Looks good, doesn't it?" She held up one of the CDs for his approval.

Rei had kept his end of the bargain. The CDs had arrived four days ago, sent to the band's PO Box with a typed, impersonal label. They did look good. They sounded good. But that didn't stop Teru from feeling like shit about the whole situation.

Rehearsal should have been amazing. The new drummer, Nao, was something of a genius. At nineteen, he was twice the player Teru was; after two rehearsals—one of which had been mostly spent on Minori's demo—and a week's worth of long nights with a tape player, he had managed to learn enough of La Rose's songs to put together a passable set.

The drums were the heart of the band. Teru had always believed that, and the others were proof, feeding off of Nao's sound in a way they never had with the too-perfect drum machine. The band around him was on fire, but Teru was cold and numb.

"Sorry," he muttered as they returned to the dressing room, stealing one last look at the balcony before the door closed behind him.

"No need to apologize," Minori said with a smile. "We sounded pretty damn good, and we'll be better with a real crowd. Well done." He said it more to Nao than to the others, but they all nodded. "I'm going to check out some of the other bands. Anyone want to come?"

Teru shook his head. He wasn't sure that he wanted to be here either, in the dressing room where Rei had first heard him sing—but at least he was fairly sure that Rei couldn't *see* him in here. *Stupid,* he told himself. *He's not here anyway.* But he still didn't want to spend any more time than he had to in the hall.

He dragged Yasu and Nao to the convenience store, where they loaded up on coffee and rice balls and snacks. They sat on the sagging sofas in the smoking area to eat, watching the other bands come through with their costumes and instruments.

"So," Nao said between bites. "You guys play here a lot?"

"Yeah," Yasu said. "Here, Cynic, Sound Junction. Vicinity sometimes. Where'd you guys used to play... what was it, Dear My Lemon?"

"Roman. As in romance?" Nao laughed. "Not my idea. This was our home base too. I guess we must have a fan or two in common."

"You still don't know who sent that email?" Yasu asked, shaking his head. "Some of these fans can be really weird. Minori tell you what happened with our last singer?"

157

Teru's hand holding his coffee froze. "That's... I'm sure there's no connection," he said, and forced himself to take another sip.

Nao frowned. "He did, but what I got wasn't anything like that. Just 'Check out this band, they're kind of your style.'"

"Well, if you ever find out who it was, remind me to thank them." Yasu pulled out a pack of cigarettes and offered one to Teru, who took it with trembling fingers.

"You okay?" Nao asked him. "You don't look so good."

Yasu laughed. "Don't mind him. Teru gets starstruck every time we play here, that's all. Doesn't seem to realize the rest of the world doesn't get all worked up just because X spent twenty minutes on that stage twenty years ago."

"Give me a break." Teru groaned. "I need a smoke, that's all."

"Well," Nao said, "take it easy. I hear those things can really mess up your voice."

"Yeah." Teru stood, crumpling his empty coffee can in one hand and lifting the cigarette to his mouth with the other. "I'll keep that in mind," he said, and stomped up the stairs to the lobby.

He would have to apologize to Nao later. It was a stupid thing to say to a singer who smoked, but Teru knew he'd either been joking or honestly concerned. He had no way of knowing that Rei had said the same thing to Teru three weeks ago, when they'd sat together in the sound booth, recording the CD that was now laid out in front of Kiyomi on the merch table.

"Hey, Teru." She smiled up at him. "Are you here for

the set lists?"

"The set lists? Uh, sure. Let me take them down to the guys."

She handed over a stack of paper—five sheets with the song titles hand-written in a rounded, feminine script. "Thanks," Teru said. "I'll pass these around."

"Wait," Kiyomi said. "Do you have to get dressed already?"

"I guess not. Do you need some help?"

"No, it's nothing like that. There's something I want to show you." She stepped around the table and took Teru's hand, leading him into the hall, right under the balcony, and through a heavy door on the far side.

It was only the stairwell leading down to the restrooms, but Teru didn't need to ask why they were here. Just as the dressing room had been decorated by musicians, the stairwell had been decorated—with twenty years of graffiti—by their fans.

The legends of Rock Eden were all here, inscribed on its walls in permanent marker and ballpoint pen. X was here, in a dozen expressions of love for the music, the memories, the cult following they had had in the beginning and the nationwide phenomenon they had been in the end. Luna Sea was here too. Someone loved Shinya, someone else loved Sugizo, and here was a large block of text proclaiming obsession with the band as a whole. There were more recent acts too: Sex Machineguns and Dir en Grey, indies bands—popular ones like Due'le Quartz and smaller ones, many of whom Teru had played with or spoken to or drunk with at three in the morning.

"Here it is!" Kiyomi pointed to a smaller inscription, near the bottom of the stairs. Teru squinted to make out the message, written in tiny letters between odes to GLAY and L'Arc~en~Ciel. "La Rose Verboten," he read, and laughed aloud.

Kiyomi smiled. "It's official. You're a part of visual kei history."

Teru laughed again. It was true, there were a lot of famous names on these walls. But there were also a lot of bands he had never heard of. Still, it was nice to know they had a fan.

"Oooh, Teru, did you see this one?" Kiyomi pointed to another inscription. It was large and multicolored, incorporating drawings as well as text. Teru knew immediately who it was for. The drawing in the middle was a pink spider with butterfly wings, and there was only one musician who would be associated with an image like that.

"hide..." he whispered. The sudden death of X Japan's lead guitarist had shaken the world of visual kei, claimed the lives of several of his fans in suicide, and had deeply affected Teru. It must have affected Kiyomi, too; her breath hissed through her teeth as she bent to read the inscription—a name, a date of birth and a date of death, the picture, and a quote: "Mata haru ni aimashou."

Let's meet again in the spring.

But hide had died in the spring, hadn't he? Over two years ago now...

It wasn't the only memorial message; Teru was surprised, in fact, to see how many there were. Not only for hide, either—there was Kami of Malice Mizer, dead last year of

160

a brain aneurism; Hizumi of Madeth Gray'll, killed in a car
crash on the way to hide's funeral. There were others as well,
names that he had heard before and names that he hadn't.
Teru caught himself holding his breath. He'd never realized....

"It's terrible, isn't it?" Kiyomi whispered.

Teru didn't answer. He let his half-smoked cigarette fall
to the floor. The epitaph beneath his fingers wasn't the
biggest, or the boldest, or the most well-done. It was older
even than hide's, though that wasn't what made it stand out.
To anyone but Teru, it might have meant nothing at all. It
was an epitaph to a name lost to history, lost in the memory
of the past five years—an epitaph not for an individual, but for
an entire band.

AETERNUM
January 5, 1995
Rei
Saki
Iroha
Taka
Mako

Teru read the names, first to himself, then aloud.
"Rei."

"Oh, wow... Is this who you were talking about? Rei?
Your friend? He's *dead?*"

Teru shook his head. "I'm not sure."

January 5, 1995. Teru had been not quite sixteen, a kid
who'd never been to Tokyo, who hadn't even played his first
show. *Five years.* It seemed like a very long time.

Teru took Kiyomi's hand, but his own hands had gone cold, and the voice that came from his mouth didn't sound like his own. "Hey, they're, uh... they're probably letting people in by now. Let's go."

He stamped out the still-smoldering cigarette and took her back up to the merch table in a daze. He had known what had happened to Rei, but seeing it on the wall, like that... *A part of history. Just like Kiyomi said.* How could he sing those songs, now that he had seen where they came from? An entire band... their music, their lyrics, the world they had created on stage, wiped from the world in a single night. Not five minutes had passed, and Teru had already forgotten their names. It wasn't fair.

"Hey."

Teru jumped. "Yasu. Sorry, I.... What is it?"

"Are you sure you're okay? You know Nao didn't mean anything by that, right?"

"What? Oh, that.... Yeah. No. It's fine. Where is he? I ought to apologize."

"Downstairs, getting ready. I came up to ask you about the uchiage. You in?"

"There's an uchiage? But we have that interview tomorrow."

"Yeah. But we can't put out a CD without a party. The fans would skin us alive." Yasu laughed. "We'll all be in the same boat. And it's just an interview, no pictures. What do you think?"

"Okay." Teru sighed. He wouldn't be going to Rei's tonight—maybe going *somewhere* would be better than sitting at home and dwelling on that fact. "Yeah, why not? I'm in."

"Good." Yasu glanced at the clock. "Minori already put your name on the list. And you better start getting ready, unless you plan on going onstage like that."

"Thanks," Teru said, and followed him into the dressing room.

———※———

Teru stood in front of the mirror, holding up the necklace Kiyomi had given him. He fastened it around his neck, but it weighed a hundred times what it had outside the department store. *What if Rei's here?* He wasn't, of course, but if he was... *He'll see it. He'll know.* Teru fumbled with the clasp. He'd wear it the next time he took Kiyomi out, but he didn't want to wear it right now.

"Teru? What are you doing?"

Minori stood behind him, holding his guitar in one hand and a case of effect pedals in the other. Like Teru, his face was made up, his white-blonde hair sprayed into stiff perfection. "You look fine. Come on. Ten minutes to set up—you know the drill."

The fans had been kept waiting; they rushed to the edge of the stage as soon as the curtain opened, shouting for Teru and the band. When Nao took the stage, whispers mixed with cheers ran through the crowd. In the looks department, at least, they approved.

The first song was one of Minori's, a heavier, fast-tempo number. Teru had worked with Rei on the staging for this, too, and he felt a twinge as his body remembered the way Rei's hand had felt on his, showing him how to hold the mic, how to gesture to the crowd, how to cry from the pit of his soul.

"Good evening, Meguro!" he called. "We're La Rose Verboten!" The crowd had their part down; they answered with a cheer. "You may have noticed a new face up here tonight. Let me introduce our new drummer, Nao." Nao answered with an improvised riff that made the audience go wild.

"He may look a little scary," Teru continued with a wink, "but he's really a nice guy, so be sure to say hi after the show. Now, for our next song—our new single, available in the lobby"—another cheer—"'Yami no hanabira'!"

He sang. He sang well, and if there were tears in his eyes when it was over, he could have ascribed them to happiness. "Thank you so much. All of you." Teru turned his back, took a drink of water, and when he looked back out at the hall he spoke directly to the balcony. "You're my inspiration."

The rest of the set went well—not flawlessly, but well, and Teru had spent enough time on the other side of the curtain to know that no one was going to care that his breathing had been off during the second chorus, or that Yasu had leapt into the twin guitar solo a beat behind Minori. Those were small mistakes; the energy in the room would have all but erased them.

"That was great!" Minori beamed. "Let's get this stuff cleaned up and get out to the lobby as soon as we can. They're going to be waiting for us."

And they were. Although the curtains had closed and the elevator music that filled the hall between sets had started up again, the crowd wasn't quite ready to let go of La Rose.

"Encore!" someone called, and someone else echoed her. "Encore! Encore!" A handful of voices took up the chant, and soon it sounded like the entire hall. "Encore!" they cried, and Teru frowned.

"We don't have an encore, do we?"

Minori shook his head. "We can play something from the set again." He glanced at Nao. "Or if you're okay with the new one?"

"The new one?" Rei's new one, "Phoenix." Teru had looked it up: fushicho. A bird that would die and be born again in flames. "Don't you think it's a little soon?"

"Nah." Nao smiled. "I can handle it if you guys can."

Minori nodded to the girl working the curtains, and she pulled them open again. The spotlight streamed into Teru's eyes, blinding him, making it impossible to tell if Rei was up there in the balcony or not. *He's not,* he told himself firmly.

The screams from the crowd were incredible. A new single, a new drummer, and now a new song, all in the same night. It was too much to be believed, and Teru took the overreaction for a blessing. Maybe no one would really hear the way he stumbled over the lyrics, the way his voice trembled where it should have soared. He held the microphone like a shield, like he had that first night when Rei had scolded him for it. He could think of nothing else to do. The song was too desperate, too pitiful... and the crowd absolutely loved it.

This is visual kei, after all. Who doesn't love a good tragedy?

He finished the song with his head held high, still looking straight into the spotlight, still grasping the mic with his sweaty, trembling hands. The curtain closed; the world went dark. The screams of the crowd died out, and someone clapped Teru on the back, herding him off the stage, through the dressing room and up to the lobby. The other guys had their equipment to pack up. It was just Teru and Kiyomi, alone with a mob.

"It was brilliant!"

"When's your next show?"

"Can I touch your hair?"

"Sign my CD!"

A silver paint pen and a copy of the single were thrust under Teru's nose.

"Thank you," he heard himself say, and there were questionnaires being pressed into his hand. He was smiling—he *must* have been smiling, because they smiled back, a hundred faces that might have been one. "Yes," he said. "Of course." Of course we'll be at the uchiage. Of course we have more flyers. Of course you can take my picture and touch my costume and tell your friends I really meant it with *you*.

The Rock Eden staff were his salvation—at ten o'clock they came through the lobby with brooms and dustpans and stern looks on their faces, telling the girls to take their conversations outside. They would wait, of course—there was even a word for it: demachi, to wait outside the venue until the musicians emerged. For the moment, though, Teru was grateful for the reprieve. He leaned against the wall with a sigh. "Well, I guess we did it."

"We did." Yasu, who had come up from the dressing room sometime during the madness, grinned. "Nice job on that encore, by the way. It's a killer."

"More for you than for me." Teru shrugged. "Thanks, though. I guess it went pretty well."

"How did we do, Kiyomi?" Minori picked up the remaining stack of CDs.

Kiyomi glanced under the table. "Most of the first box is gone. Over fifty, I'd say."

"Wow," Teru said. "Nice work, guys. Thanks, Kiyomi."

He caught her trying to stifle a yawn; she'd had a long day, too. "It was a great show. Now..." She turned the yawn into a smile. "We drink until dawn!"

"Makeup off," Minori said, "and equipment in the van."

"I'll, uh, be right back. Okay?" Without waiting for an answer, Teru turned and slipped back into the hall.

The stairs to the balcony were blocked by a rope, and a sign warned anyone without a backstage pass to keep out. Teru had a pass; he pushed the sign aside. The stairs were unlit, but with the show over and the fans sent out to demachi in the street, the balcony was as bright as the rest of the place. Bright, and cramped, and deserted.

"Rei." Teru sunk onto one of the low benches and buried his head in his hands.

There were footsteps on the stairs, and Teru looked up. A girl—a woman, really, maybe around thirty—wearing a Rock Eden T-shirt and carrying a broom stepped onto the balcony and gave him a tired smile.

"Sorry," he said. "I was just leaving."

The woman leaned the broom against the sound board and wiped her hands on her jeans. "He was here," she said. "He saw you play."

Teru's heart leapt, but he kept a straight face. "I don't know who you're talking about."

She sat next to him on the bench. "You don't have to lie to me. I've known him for a lot longer than you have. He gave me a message for you. I'm not sure if you want to hear it, but...." She shrugged.

"A message?"

"Don't look so hopeful. He's pissed off, and not just about whatever fight you had. 'Leave the merchandise and the fraternizing to your staff. If you fail to act like a star now, how do you expect to become one? To them you are a performer, not a friend. Fans can be delusional. But they are not idiots. If you continue to parade your girlfriend in front of them—with or without a pass—they will figure it out.' Don't shoot the messenger," she added. "His opinion, not necessarily mine."

"Yeah," Teru said. "Okay. I get the point. I'll—"

"Wait." She stopped him as he stood to leave. "I wanted to talk to you too."

"About what?"

"Like I said, I've known him for a long time. Rei is a self-centered bastard, most of the time. But he's also a human being, and he lost... everything. Since he met you, he's been different. Maybe 'happy' is too strong a word, but hopeful. You've helped him more than you know."

"I haven't done anything. What could I—"

"You gave him a reason besides guilt to get out of bed in the morning. That's something, isn't it?"

"...I guess."

"Look." She sighed. "He's mad at himself, not you. I don't know what the fight was about, but—"

168

"It wasn't a fight," Teru said. "It was... me. He showed me his face and I freaked, okay? He's not mad at himself, he's—" His voice caught in his throat, and she gave him a sympathetic smile.

"I think you're wrong." She shook her head. "He knows what he looks like. But he also thinks he deserves what happened. How much has he told you?"

"I don't know. Everything?" *Nothing? How the hell am I supposed to know?*

"I doubt that. Personally, I wouldn't blame you if you walked out that door tonight and never came back, but... he doesn't really want to lose you."

"He told you that?" Hope swelled in Teru's chest, and for a moment he was afraid that his eyes really would fill with tears.

"No. But I know him, remember?" She took a tiny square of paper from the pocket of her jeans and pressed it into his hand. "I'm Chizuru," she said, "and as much as I hate him, I'd rather see him with something to live for. Let me know if there's anything I can do."

Chapter 19

In the dressing room, Teru sifted through a pile of makeup, picking out the things that belonged to him and returning them to his case. Brown next to black, red next to brown. There had never been any order to his cosmetics before, but it seemed important that they be sorted, placed into the little compartments in an arrangement that made as much sense as anything could at the moment.

He had to stop thinking about Rei, about Chizuru—about the piece of paper in his pocket, unread and unopened and destined to stay that way until he could get a minute alone. His fans were waiting, and the night wasn't over yet.

The makeup case closed with a satisfying click, and Teru tossed it into his duffel bag with his costume. He replaced his sweaty top with a clean, skintight T-shirt and attempted to run a brush though his hair.

"Done," he said, as much to the voices in his head as to his bandmates. "Let's go."

"Like that?" Seika asked. "You're not going to take your makeup off?"

Teru glanced at his reflection. He didn't really want to be Masato Ijima right now. "Do I have to?"

"Not if you don't care about your pores." Seika had traded his own makeup for a pair of black sunglasses, but his boa was still around his shoulders, and he waved it admonishingly at Teru. "I can wait for you," he said, in a kinder voice, "if you want."

"Nah." Teru shook his head. "I'm fine like this. Give the fans what they want, right?"

Seika shrugged. "Suit yourself. Are we ready to go?"

The others nodded and, groaning half in jest as they toted the final load of costumes and instruments up two flights of stairs, made their way into the muggy summer night. Minori's van was waiting for them at the curb, its back doors thrown open and its hazards blinking furiously.

"All right, guys. Everything in the van!" Minori placed his bag on top of the CDs and called to a group of girls lingering outside. "Are any of you waiting for the uchiage?"

They nodded, and one of them called back, "We're not the only ones, are we?"

Seika took over, draping his boa around the girl's shoulders and making a show of dragging her away from her friends. "No," he said, "but you're the only ones with a special escort." The girl squealed and ran back to her friends, who laughed and pulled her back across the sidewalk toward the van.

When the equipment had been loaded, Minori closed the doors and grabbed his keys. "You guys know the place?" Teru and the rest of his bandmates nodded. "Good. I'm going to take the car around to that flat-rate lot. Take these ladies with you, okay?"

"Not a problem." Seika wrapped his boa around a

second girl's shoulders, and Teru laughed in spite of himself. This was their job, right now. It didn't matter what Rei said. It didn't even matter if he was gay, or whatever he was. It was his job to flirt, to flatter, and to let himself be flattered in return.

By the time they reached the izakaya, all seven of them were laughing, and Teru was almost sad to see the three girls led to the far side of the room. The bands were seated closer to the door, and Kiyomi was sitting with the other bands' staff at one end of the fans' table, so immersed in conversation that she barely looked up when Teru and the others arrived.

Beer was waiting for them, too. The singer from one of the other bands poured, and when Minori ran through the door a few minutes later, the party began in earnest. He grabbed a bottle with one hand and his mug with the other, and headed to the front of the room. "Here's to a great night!" he began, and was greeted with a cheer. "Kampai!"

"Kampai!" Teru raised his glass, clinking as many of the others as possible before the guys holding them headed to the other side of the room to toast the fans and staff. Yasu dragged Teru to his feet and they joined the crowd, tiptoeing through a minefield of bags and cushions to the fans' table, where they were given a warm reception and a refill.

He didn't know what Rei's problem was. Drinking with the fans was good for business—everyone knew that. Teru didn't understand why Rei didn't want him to do this, and he *really* didn't understand why he had to send his... whoever she was with the message. He downed his third beer and watched the world go fuzzier, trying to tell himself that he didn't care.

Empty beer glasses and overflowing ashtrays began to

crowd the tables and the night gave way, nominally at least, to the following morning. Every time the waitress came around, Teru asked her for another beer, until he had lost count of how many he'd had. *Fuck you, Rei.* If only he could get drunk enough, maybe he could forget. But the more he drank, the clearer the memories grew. The voice in his head grew louder and colder, but the words didn't change, and the faces across the room—those beautiful faces of youth and freedom and femininity—didn't grow any more attractive, or more attainable.

"Hey, Yasu?" He sounded drunk, even to himself; his words were slurred, but his mind was clear enough to be embarrassed by it. "I'm, uh, gonna go to the restroom. Okay?"

"Sure, man. Whatever you want." Yasu laughed, and when Teru stumbled to his feet he only laughed harder. "Try not to fall on your face, yeah?"

Teru shuffled to the bathroom and leaned against the wall, closing his eyes and bending his knees until he was almost sitting on the floor. *I can't stop thinking about him. I can't stop loving him, and I can't stop hating him, and I... I just can't.* "Dammit, Rei," he whispered. "What the fuck am I supposed to do?"

He took the piece of paper from his pocket. It was a business card, folded into a tiny work of origami; he worked his finger into the fold and slid it open. What was this, anyway, more criticism? A more personal attack, that Rei didn't want his flunky to hear?

But the message, when he saw it, filled Teru with a different type of rage.

Stupid.

His knees gave way, and he crumpled to the floor, clutching the piece of paper in his fist.

Stupid!

He punched the floor; pain flared across his knuckles, bringing tears to his eyes.

So fucking stupid.

He opened it, read it again. It was nothing. The girl's name, Chizuru Sakata, and a phone number. That was all.

Teru pinched the card between his fingers and ripped it, watching it turn from one scrap of nothing into two, four, eight, a million, until no one could have pieced the thing back together. There was nothing left. No reminder, no evidence that he had ever spoken to her. No evidence that he had ever given a damn.

The pieces spiraled down the toilet, gone with a single flush. Teru opened the door and stepped back into the hallway, full of voices and laughter and smiling faces that should have been the perfect backdrop to the role he was expected to play.

"When are you coming to see us?"

"We're sitting in the corner, okay?" A smile, a laugh. "Promise?"

"There's something I want to show you!"

"I still haven't gotten my autograph!"

And another voice, more familiar but no less clouded by drink and fatigue. "Where were you?" Kiyomi stumbled out of line for the ladies' room. "I thought you left!"

"I've been right here, Kiyomi. Are you okay?"

"I'm drunk!" she admitted gleefully, falling backwards to rest her head against Teru's shoulder. A few of the other girls snickered, but Teru didn't see what was so funny.

"Come on," she whispered in his ear. "Come on, Masato..."

Teru flinched at the use of his given name. "Ki—Kiyomi!" He gripped her wrist with more force that he intended, and she cried out. "Dammit. I'm sorry. Let's... let's sit down. Have some water, or juice."

"I don't want to sit down." Kiyomi pouted. "I want to have fun. This is a party, isn't it?"

"Y—yes. Yes, it is. And we need to get back to the party."

Kiyomi took a few steps in the direction of their room, letting Teru lead her as far as the sliding doors. "Come on," he pleaded. "Take off your slippers."

"Masato..." She whispered his name in his ear.

Teru shook his head. He shouldn't be doing this. He had to get Kiyomi back to her table, back to the other girls. He had to get her to sober up, somehow, before she said something they'd both regret.

"Oh, Masato!" She raised her voice, and Teru put a finger to her lips. *Dammit. Maybe Rei was right.*

"Kiyomi, you need to calm down."

"Come here!" She giggled and, with a surprising burst of strength, pulled Teru away from the party room and into a side hallway.

"What is it?" he asked. The beginnings of a headache throbbed at the base of his skull.

She giggled again. "Do one little thing for me, and then I promise to go back and be good."

Teru sighed. "Fine. What is it?"

She leaned close, her eyes sparkling with mischief. "Are you sure?"

"Yes," he said. "I'm sure."

The hairs on his ear prickled as her lips nearly brushed against the lobe. "Kiss me."

Teru took a step back. "Kiyomi..."

She pursed her lips. "You promised."

"Not here."

And then those lips met his, and forced him to swallow his words.

Her kiss was sweet and firm and teasing, dancing from one corner of his mouth to the other with hints of better things to come. Teru kissed her back, in spite of himself. She was good, and he responded to her reflexively.

But then she plunged into his mouth, and his heart went cold.

"Stop." He drew back, wiping at his mouth with the back of his hand. "Please. Just... just stop."

Kiyomi frowned. "What did I do?"

"I'm sorry." He shook his head. "I can't do this. Not with you. Not here." He put an arm around her waist; tears spilled from the corners of her eyes. "Come on, Kiyomi. Let's go back to the party."

He led her to the end of the table where, until about thirty minutes ago, he had been sitting with the rest of the band. Minori and Seika had moved over to the fans' table, but Yasu and Nao were still there.

He called to a waiter. "Excuse me! Can we get a glass of orange juice, please?"

"Yes, sir." The waiter nodded and ran off to get the

drink.

"Teru?"

Well, at least she got my name right this time. "What is it, Kiyomi?"

"I'm... sleepy." She rested her head on his shoulder.

Teru wanted more than anything to push her away. He could touch her pulse, smell her perfume... but he felt nothing. Nothing but the terrible, twisting guilt, and an unbearable desire that had nothing to do with Kiyomi at all.

I have to see him.

The waiter came back with the juice, and Teru lifted it to Kiyomi's lips. To his relief, she was awake enough to take it with her own hands, and calm enough to take a sip. "Is that better?"

"A little," she said. "I had too much."

"It's all right." He tried, without much success, to keep the urgency out of his voice. He couldn't let Kiyomi know how desperate he was to be somewhere else. "Why don't you lie down?" he suggested. "Here, take this." He offered her the cushion he had been sitting on. There wasn't a lot of room on the floor, but with two cushions, in a fetal positon, she would probably be able to rest for a few hours.

"Teru...?"

"I'm here." He brushed a strand of hair out of her face. "Just go to sleep, okay?"

"Feels... good..." she whispered, and was silent.

When Teru was sure she was asleep, he pulled Yasu and Nao aside. "Look," he said. "I've got to go. It's kind of an emergency. Make sure Kiyomi gets to the station in the morning, okay?"

"You're not coming back?" Yasu frowned.

"I'll be at the interview tomorrow. Please," Teru begged. "A friend needs my help." *At two-thirty in the morning. Again.*

"What are we supposed to tell Minori?" Nao asked. Minori would be furious if he knew that Teru was blowing off the uchiage for... not even a date. A desperate fucking plea.

"Just tell him the truth," Teru said. "Tell him something more important came up."

Chapter 20

The night was thick with humidity. Teru's shirt clung to him as he walked, and his hair fell flat against the back of his neck as hairspray fought a losing battle with the combined forces of heat and nerves. He must have looked like shit.

He forced himself to not to run, to put one foot in front of the other at a pace as steady and even as the pounding of a bass drum. There was no need to rush; there was every reason to fly. This was the right decision, and this was possibly the only chance he would have to make it—while he was just sober enough to know that what he was doing was insane, and just drunk enough to do it anyway.

Gold footlights illuminated the building, making it look like a movie set, a false façade against the backdrop of the night. Teru walked up to the door, past the postboxes and into the corridor, past room 101, 102... 107. To the nameless, trinketless door of 108.

The door was locked. Rei was asleep, or else he had locked himself in his music room with that computer and a hundred angry chords. Teru didn't care. He crushed his hand into a fist and began to pound. He didn't stop when no one answered; Rei was here. He had to be.

"Rei!" he called. "It's me! Dammit, it's Teru! Please.

Open the door!"

He repeated the words until they were meaningless and his voice, exhausted already from the show, threatened to fail. His shouts became pleas, but he kept knocking with one hand and ringing the doorbell with the other. The neighbors would hear—how could they not? It was only a matter of time before someone woke up and told him to leave. He'd be forced to go back to the uchiage with raw knuckles and vocal chords and nothing to show for it at all.

"Rei!" His final cry was raspy and hoarse, and when it, too, met with no reply, Teru forced himself to step away. His hand was numb, his fingers barely willing to uncurl. This was useless. He could stand here until the sun came up, but if Rei didn't want to talk to him...

There's not a damn thing I can do.

A siren wailed and then fell silent. There was nothing but the ringing in Teru's ears, the pounding of his heart, and the sleeping, dead, movie-lot apartment building.

And then the silence was gone, replaced by the turning of a deadbolt and a rush of stale, air-conditioned wind.

"What do *you* want?" Rei's voice was crisp and livid.

"I wanted to see you."

Rei stood in the entranceway in his bare feet, covered from head to ankle with a hooded cloak. What Teru could see of his face was set in a thin-lipped frown—the expression of a man who had been woken up at three in the morning by someone he hadn't particularly wanted to see in the first place.

"You wanted to see me?" Rei repeated the words as if they belonged to a foreign language. "Here I am. I do sleep, on occasion, you know."

"I'm sorry." Teru stepped into the entranceway, holding the door with his foot in case Rei tried to slam it in his face. "This wasn't the way things were supposed to happen. I need to see you. Now."

He touched the hood, and Rei flinched. "You had your chance." He shook his head, but there was more fear than anger in his tone.

"I'll close the door," Teru said, and he did. "No one will see you. Only me. Give me another chance, Rei. I know I don't deserve it, but—"

"No." Rei took a step backward and almost tripped on the step up into the apartment. "Not... not here."

Teru took off his shoes. His socks were damp; he took them off too and shoved them into the toes before following Rei into the music room.

Rei lowered himself onto the sofa and then, to Teru's surprise, nodded to the seat beside him. "You wanted to see me?"

"Y—yes." Teru sat. He reached for the hood again, and this time Rei didn't object. He held his breath, impossibly still as Teru pushed the hood away. "I want to look at you," Teru said. "I want to see *you*, not just..."

Rei closed his eyes and exhaled. "There's nothing to see."

The mask was held in place with some kind of theatrical adhesive. The first time Teru had removed it had been at the end of a long day; it hadn't taken much effort to pull off. But now the tape was fresh, and it came away with a ripping sound like a bandage being torn from a wound.

181

His stomach turned, and for a moment he thought he might really be sick. It was bad. It was as bad as he remembered, or worse. But it was also Rei: the Rei who had given him his music, who had given him a way out of a cycle of homemade demo tapes and single-digit turnouts. *He gave me everything. And this is the only thing I have to give him in return.*

The hand holding the mask fell to his lap, and with the other Teru reached up, tracing the line of Rei's forehead, his temple, down to his cheek and chin. He said the only thing he could think of that was neither negative nor untrue.

"It's not as bad as you think it is."

Rei shook his head. "We have to stop this, Teru."

"No we don't. You're so beautiful, Rei, in so many ways." It was the alcohol talking, but he let it. It wasn't saying anything that wasn't true.

"You don't even know me."

"I know enough! Dammit, Rei, look at me!" He did. "I love you," Teru said. "I barely even know you, but I can't stop thinking about you. Let me help you, like you helped me."

"You are singing my music. It's enough."

"Not for me!"

"Teru." Rei's voice was cold, and Teru's heart went colder. "Don't say those things. You don't know what they mean."

"Yes, I do."

"You say you love me." Rei looked down at his right hand, clawed and useless in his lap. "You don't know what I did."

Teru took Rei's hands in his own—the strong and the broken, he held them as though they were the same. "I don't understand," he said. "What don't I know? What did you do?"

Rei lowered his head. It was an action born of years of habit; if he'd been wearing a wig, Teru wouldn't have been able to see the single, silent tear that trickled down his cheek as he spoke.

"I killed him."

A chill ran up the back of Teru's neck. "That isn't..." he stammered. "You killed who?"

"Saki. And the others. I killed them all."

Teru let Rei's hands fall back to his lap. "I don't understand," he said again, but a heavy weight had settled into his gut. "Who's Saki? What do you mean?"

And then something clicked.

Saki. Aeternum. January 5, 1995.

"In the accident..." Teru whispered, and another tear fell from Rei's eye. "He was your bandmate." But something about the way Rei said the name told him that couldn't be all.

"He was the only man I've ever loved."

"No." It was barely more than a breath, and it was all Teru had left inside him. It was too much. Too much to take in. Too much for one person to lose. "Rei," he said, "I..."

"How old are you, Teru?" Rei looked up, and then turned away just as quickly. "Never mind. If I am not twice your age, I am rapidly approaching it. I am... too old to love again."

Teru said nothing. He could think of nothing to say. He heard the words, could have repeated them verbatim—but they fell on him like dull, meaningless blows. *Saki. I killed him. The only man I've ever loved.* That wasn't a story; it was a nightmare.

"I'm sorry." Rei's shoulders shook, and he struggled to cover his face with his good hand.

Teru didn't dare to touch him, didn't dare to draw closer. He had too many questions, and didn't want the answers, and somehow needed them, anyway. "Why?" he asked. "Why are you sorry?"

"I loved him." Rei lowered his hand. His ruined face was distorted even further with grief and pain. "I loved him, and I killed him. If I dare to love you..."

"What?" Teru snapped, a raw, newfound anger now warring with sadness and confusion. "You're going to kill me too?"

"...I'll hurt you. You don't want to be with me."

Teru's head was throbbing. "That's bullshit," he said. "You don't know what I want. You've never even bothered to try."

Rei shook his head. "I'll hurt you," he repeated.

"Maybe. It happens."

"But I *killed* him!"

"Listen to me." Teru forced himself to lower his voice, to breathe the shock and the frustration out with his words. "It wasn't your fault. It was an accident." He wrapped an arm around Rei's shoulders. "Am I hurting you?"

Rei shook his head; his eyes were miserable, but he didn't seem to be in any physical pain.

"Then talk to me. Rei? Please."

"I don't know if I can."

"Try." Teru ran his fingers over Rei's patchy hair. How long had it been since someone had touched him? Listened to him? Let him cry? "Tell me about him... about Saki."

"I shouldn't have been driving." Rei's voice was paper-thin. "We had a fight. I was upset. I..."

"Okay." Teru ran his fingers down Rei's neck, and he shuddered. "I'm sorry. Did I—?"

"No."

"Okay. Tell me about him," Teru said again. "Not about the accident. Tell me something good."

Rei considered this. "Saki *was* good."

"He was your bandmate?"

"Our lead guitarist. I should have told you..."

"It's okay." Teru let his hand fall to Rei's lap, let their fingers intertwine. He squeezed, and Rei squeezed back, and it didn't matter that he had run out of questions, of comments, of words.

"He might have liked you," Rei admitted. "You remind me of him. Sometimes."

"I do?"

"Only sometimes. Saki wasn't quite as... aggressive as you."

Teru wasn't sure if he was being given a compliment or not. He'd never thought of himself as aggressive. Hell, he wouldn't have gone out for the La Rose audition if Yasu hadn't dragged him. But he was here, wasn't he, at three in the morning, being compared—favorably or not—to the ghost that had haunted his relationship since the beginning.

"I wonder, sometimes, what he would think of me now."

"I don't know." Teru wished he had something more encouraging to say. Everything was different now: every lyric

Rei had written, every glimmer of pain in his eyes. Every moment of the past few weeks—had it really been weeks and not years?—was repainted in a new light, and Teru wasn't sure what he was seeing anymore.

"How can you love me now?" Rei's voice was very small, and very tired. "How...?" His head fell to Teru's shoulder. Where Kiyomi's weight had been a burden, Rei's was a cross that Teru was willing to bear.

He couldn't answer. His head was swimming with drink and confusion and fatigue. It had been a long day—for both of them, Teru guessed—and if he was going to love Rei, if he was going to take care of him, it seemed like he ought to start by putting an end to this terrible conversation and seeing him to bed.

He lowered his arm to Rei's too-thin waist. "We should get some sleep. I have that interview tomorrow, and—"

"Interview?"

"With *Shokker*?"

"You didn't tell me."

"I guess we weren't speaking to each other."

"*Shokker*. That's... wonderful."

"And it's tomorrow." Teru shook his head. "You look tired. I know I am. Can we get some sleep? We'll have time to talk later. About everything."

"You'll stay?" Rei asked, as if he still couldn't quite believe it.

"If you want me to."

"Until morning?"

"Yeah. Sure." It was already morning, but Teru decided not to mention that. "Should I... should I sleep on the couch

186

again?"

Rei hesitated. "No," he said. "That will not be necessary." He rose, leaning on his cane. "Come with me."

He led the way out of the music room, to the nearest of the doors off the main hallway. "This is where I sleep." Rei opened the door. His fingers hovered over the light switch, as tense as the rest of his body and trembling in the remnants of light. "Please, don't say anything."

He turned on the lights, and a lump rose in Teru's throat as he stepped inside. This room hadn't been designed for sleeping; it was larger than the music room and shaped oddly, with a kitchenette by the door and a large open space at the far end. If this apartment had been inhabited by anyone else, this would have been the living room. Instead, it looked more like a hospital suite.

The kitchen counter was cluttered with pills and ointments. If there was any food in the place, it must have been locked away in the refrigerator, a silver monstrosity that might have been state-of-the-art ten years ago. The table, under a low-hanging light, was strewn with makeup and piles of clothes, and in the corner, a folded-up wheelchair lurked in the shadows.

In what should have been the living area, the shattered guitar Teru had seen on his first visit crowded a sagging, dilapidated loveseat. Next to it, a row of shelves held a selection of wigs that a costume shop owner might have envied. The blue and lavender, in different lengths and cuts, as well as colors Teru hadn't seen before: red, black, silver, and an orange he privately thought would look terrible against Rei's pale skin. The masks were there too: five of them, plus the one they'd left in the music room, all crafted from the same liquid silver. Propped against the bedside table was a crutch—one of those that wrapped around the arm instead of going under the armpit—and on the table itself, a tangle of metal and plastic that Teru recognized as the brace for Rei's arm.

The bed itself was a steel monster. It was large, at least a double, but robbed of any luxuriousness by the starkness of its frame and by the mechanical parts that, Teru supposed, would allow the back to be raised. It was different from a hospital bed only in the absence of rails—but it would still feel like a prison, to sleep in this room. To wake up every morning confronted by the reality you were trying so hard to avoid.

Rei had lost his band, his looks, his freedom. It had never occurred to Teru that there were worse things to lose. He'd come here to fix what he had broken... but Rei's heart had been broken long ago. Teru had only ground the pieces into dust.

"Can I stay?"

"If you want."

Teru sat on the bed. It was soft enough, despite its appearance, and his neck and back and shoulders ached with the fatigue of one of the longest days he had ever known. "Thank you." He lay back, and all of the energy flooded from his body at once.

Rei sat on the far side of the bed, watching Teru as he pulled the terrycloth blanket up to his chin.

"Aren't you going to sleep?"

"Maybe," Rei said. "If I can. Right now, I just want to watch you. To make myself believe you're really here."

"I'm here." Teru rolled onto his side, closing his eyes at first as Rei touched the side of his face, tried to run his fingers through his sticky, matted hair. Then he forced himself to open them, to look at Rei's face, marred at this angle only by the lack of a nose.

"Rei?" he whispered. "I'm so sorry."

Rei closed his eyes. "So am I."

—⋇—

"Teru?"

Teru grunted and rolled over, burying his face in the pillow and pulling the blanket over his head.

"Teru, wake up."

"It's too early," he said, but he opened his eyes. Rei was awake, sitting on the bed as though he hadn't moved since the night before.

"What time is your interview?"

Teru kicked the covers off and jumped, nearly falling out of bed. "Fuck. Oh, shit. Oh, fuck, fuck, fuck."

"Teru?"

"What time it is now?"

"Ten thirty."

"Fuck." His mind was already racing down the street to the station, back to his apartment, and to the *Shokker* offices in Ginza. The interview was supposed to start at twelve. There was no way in hell he was going to make it.

"Is there anything I can do?"

"Hell, I don't know, I..." Teru tried to take a deep breath, but it came out just as rushed as everything else. "Can I use your shower?"

"My shower?"

"Please. I don't have time to go home. I smell like shit, and—"

"You smell like a live house," Rei said, and gave him something that was almost a smile.

"Yeah. I smell like I didn't go home last night, and... you know. That's not going to look good."

"It wouldn't," Rei agreed. "Go ahead."

Teru crossed the room with large, hurried strides, trying to focus on the interview and not on the relics of pain. It might have helped if he had ever been interviewed before. For better or worse, he had no idea what to expect, and it didn't help that his eyes and his mind kept wandering to the evidence of Rei's life and near-death. At least that was better than the only other thing he seemed able to think about.

Saki. It wasn't much in the way of an upside, but at least oversleeping on the day of his interview gave him an excuse not to talk about *that.*

He slammed the bathroom door, and the walls shook with the blow. Teru swore. Was falling in love supposed to feel so *bad?*

He peeled his clothes off, wrinkling his nose. They really did smell bad, but there wasn't a lot he could do about it. Showing up in last night's clothes would tell the guys he hadn't been home, but showing up in something of Rei's would tell them why. He was just going to have to hope that the shower put him somewhere on the other side of completely revolting.

The bathroom mirror was cracked, fine lines radiating from a central impact point. The sink was full of soapy water, and what looked like at least one dark blue wig was soaking in it. Brushing his teeth would be out, then.

The bath itself was no cleaner than Teru's own, but it was deep and long enough to hold the family the builders had been planning for. Teru was half-tempted to fill it and give it a try. He felt a twinge as he noticed the handrails and the plastic chair with suction-cup feet that looked like something his great-grandmother would have owned.

He squeezed some liquid soap into the palm of his hand and worked it into a lather. Hot water streamed down his scalp, plastering bits of hair to his cheeks and neck as it washed away the remnants of last night's hairspray and mousse. He left the water running, letting it pour over his body as he reached for the shampoo.

He pressed down on the pump, but the only thing that spurted out was a gasp of transparent bubbles. "Shit." Teru cursed aloud. There were three more bottles, but they were no better, and when Teru read the labels he cursed again. They were just soap, all of them, used-up soap bottles that no one had bothered to throw away.

There'd been a wig in the sink, though, hadn't there? Teru didn't know what was typically used to wash wigs, but there was at least a chance that whatever it was would at least be better than soap for getting last night's gunk out of his hair. He stopped the water and opened the door.

The best thing he could find was a discount-store bottle of shampoo and conditioner in one. When he emerged from the shower a few minutes later, his hair was no longer standing in a thousand different directions, but it didn't feel any less like straw, and was unwilling to do anything but trail lifelessly down his back. It had been a long time since Teru had worn his hair down—it was usually either tied back for work or teased up for a show.

"I'm trying a new look," he explained to his fragmented, unshaven reflection. There was no way the guys were going to buy that. He looked like he hadn't been home the night before, and that was all there was to it.

Rei was sitting upright in the bed when he returned, the mask and wig hiding his face. "I'm sorry," he said. "The bathroom is dirty."

"No worse than mine." Teru smiled. "Thanks."

"Teru?"

"Yeah? What's wrong?"

"Don't go."

Teru shook his head. "I have to."

"I know."

"Rei." Teru took a step forward, but stopped. There wasn't enough time. He had to be at that interview, and if he sat on the bed, if he put his arm around Rei, he didn't know if he'd be able to tear himself away. "Look," he said, "what you told me last night? That doesn't affect how I feel, okay?"

"It should."

"I wish you wouldn't say that." He sighed. "I have to go to this interview. But I promise—Rei, I *promise*—that I will be back."

"Tonight."

"I can't." Silently, Teru cursed himself and his boss at the CombiMart. "I've got the night shift. How about Thursday?"

"Thursday?" That was three days away, but it was the

best Teru could do.

"Yeah. I've got the whole day off. We can go out. Do something fun."

"Something fun."

"We don't have to. It was just an idea."

Rei looked up. He was smiling—a sad smile, but it was a smile all the same. "I would like that," he said at last. "I would like that very much."

"Okay. Thursday, then." Teru pulled his shirt over his head and ran his fingers one last time through his hair. "Thanks for letting me stay."

Rei followed his gaze to the clock. "Don't let me keep you from your interview."

It wasn't "good luck," but it was going to have to do.

Chapter 21

The date—if that's what it was—had been Teru's idea, but he had no idea what they were going to do. He wasn't sure what guys did when they went out together, or if, for that matter, they went out at all. There were men like Seika, and clubs like the one where he worked, where it was okay for two guys to go and act like—well, like they were a couple. Teru didn't want to go to a gay bar, though, with or without Rei, and none of the typical date spots he could think of seemed like very good ideas either.

He didn't want to sit in a dark movie theater, forced to be silent and still while there were so many things they needed to talk about. Getting drunk hadn't worked in their favor last time; bars and izakayas were out. Bowling alleys and video arcades would only make Rei uncomfortable, and while he supposed they could go to karaoke, they did enough singing as it was.

Still, the only thing they really had in common was music, and in the end that was what Teru went with. He arrived at Meguro Station early and bought two tickets to Ochanomizu. It was a part of town primarily known for instrument shops, which seemed like a good idea, but also made him a little nervous. The goal was to get Rei to enjoy himself—and musical instruments and sound equipment were obviously things he enjoyed. But Teru couldn't help thinking of the shattered guitar, of the bathroom mirror that had shared a similar fate... and of Saki. Dead Saki. Perfect Saki. Lead guitarist Saki.

Teru shook his head. He'd had three days. Seventy-two fucking hours, and this was the best he'd been able to come up with. It was too late to think of something new.

He saw Rei coming from across the rotary—long blue hair, head-to-toe black robes that, even in a neighborhood with two visual kei live houses, stuck out in the summer heat. His limp was more noticeable at a distance, but the people around him didn't seem to care. They pushed past him, around him on their way to the station, leaving him straggling at the back of the crowd as the green pedestrian light started to blink.

"Hey." Teru smiled, trying to keep his tone light. "You, uh, ready?"

Rei nodded. He didn't ask where they were going, didn't say anything at all as Teru led him through the ticket gate and up the escalator to the platform.

"So, the interview went pretty well," Teru said. "It was pretty basic stuff. They didn't even really ask about our music. Favorite brands, favorite colors. Silly stuff like that."

Rei nodded, and muttered something that might have been "Typical."

"We sent in 'Blood on the Moon' for that ominibus. It's one of Minori's songs. I, uh, don't know if you've heard it...."

Teru glanced at Rei, hoping for some kind of reaction,

but he stared straight ahead, not hearing the conversation at all.

"I, uh, guess we'll hear back about it soon."

They took the train to Tokyo Station. There were three routes they could have taken. Shinjuku was the most familiar, but it was also supposed to take the longest. The subway usually involved a lot of stairs—sometimes three or four flights of them, depending on the line. So Tokyo it was.

"You know," Teru said. "I've lived here for three years, and I could probably count on my fingers the number of times I've actually used Tokyo Station. Hey..." He stopped. "You seem preoccupied. Is everything okay?

"I'm fine," Rei said, but his hand shook, and his eyes were focused on something that wasn't there.

"I'm sorry." Teru rested his hand in the crook of Rei's arm. The crowd shifted around them as they stopped, suits brushing against suits as critical eyes looked and judged and quickly looked away. "I wish I had a car or something." *Hell, I wish I had a license.*

It took them longer to get to the Chuo Line platform than it did for the train to get to Ochanomizu. Like Tokyo, it was a station that Teru didn't use often. There were plenty of music shops in Shinjuku and Shibuya, but this was a quieter part of town—frequented by musicians, but not so much by fans. "I hope this is all right," Teru said as the train doors closed behind them. "I don't really know what else you like."

"It's fine," Rei said, and tried to smile.

The station was situated on the bank of the Kanda River; between the breeze from the water and the greenery surrounding it, the area was... not quite cool, but not as stifling as the rest of the city. Across the street, a row of music shops stretched off into the distance, their signs competing with one another for space against the sky.

"You want to go in here?" Teru stopped in front of the first store. It was primarily a guitar shop—no drums, but there were "Keyboards and PA Equipment" on the fourth floor.

Rei hesitated.

"We don't have to, if you don't want to. We can—"

"No." Rei gritted his teeth and tightened his grip on the cane. "We should. It has been too long."

The automatic doors opened and closed behind them, and a tense-looking man in a STAFF polo shirt stepped out from behind the counter. "Good afternoon," he greeted them, and continued to shadow them as they walked around the floor. "Is there anything in particular you're looking for?"

"Just browsing, thanks." Teru gave him a smile that was supposed to add "...so leave us alone," but the guy either didn't get the message or chose to ignore it. Teru turned to Rei. "Want to go upstairs?"

The second floor was bass guitars, and the third was acoustics. Rei paused in front of a lovely instrument made of light wood and inlaid with mother-of-pearl. He reached out to touch it, leaning his cane against the wall. "Can you play?" he asked softly. "I would love to hear what this sounds like."

Teru shook his head. "Sorry. Yasu tried to teach me once, but..." Playing the guitar, like driving, was one skill he had never thought he would need. "You really don't want to hear me try."

The fourth floor, as Teru had suspected, was the most interesting. He didn't really know what made one speaker or mixing board better than another, but Rei was in his element, scanning the cards attached to each piece and nodding at the information they contained.

The walls were covered with equipment—there was no good place to lean the cane, and so Teru took it whenever Rei wanted to look more closely at something. After awhile, he stopped handing it back and just carried it, watching as Rei ran his fingers over knobs and dials, muttering to himself.

"What's that?" Teru asked, when Rei pulled a smaller box from a shelf. It was too big to be held comfortably in one hand, but Rei turned it over somehow with his long fingers, scanning the fine print on the back.

"For you," he said, and handed it to Teru.

"A mic?" Teru glanced at the box. "Is it different from the ones you've already got? It's, uh, kind of expensive, and...."

Rei stiffened, holding out his hand for the cane. "You don't need to worry about money."

"But today's supposed to be my treat."

Rei hooked the cane over his wrist and dug in the folds of his cloak for his wallet. "Then treat me."

Teru took the wallet and the mic to the register. While he was waiting for the clerk to fill out the warranty card, he turned on one of the display keyboards and started to plunk out a one-handed rendition of "Twinkle, Twinkle Little Star."

"You play?"

Teru blushed. "Not really. My mom made me take lessons when I was a kid, but..."

"Play for me."

He added the left hand, simple chords to go with the

simple melody. "I quit when I was in the third grade. This is the only thing I really remember."

The clerk called Teru back up to the register to get his warranty card and the microphone, packaged in a paper bag with the store's logo in gold. "Thank you very much, sir," the clerk said. "Please come again."

Teru took the bag, but before he could reply, the room filled from behind him with the melancholy strains of a familiar melody.

He turned to find Rei, seated at a digital piano, playing a version of "Für Elise" that may or may not have been perfect—but it was sure as hell better than Teru's "Twinkle, Twinkle Little Star." Teru didn't know if he was hitting every note or not, but he was coming close, using the pedals to draw out notes that needed to be held and moving his hand up and down the keyboard in a blur.

The clerk followed Teru's gaze, as did the customer behind him, but they only nodded—impressed but not amazed—and returned to their transaction. At this distance, from this angle, Rei was just a guy in a music shop, playing "Für Elise" on the piano. As far as Teru could tell, no one even noticed he was doing it with one hand.

Rei threw his head back, exposing the mask and the scars on his neck for the world to see. The piece—or at least the first part of it—came to an end; he didn't attempt the more difficult second section.

"That was amazing," Teru said.

Rei took his cane, rose to his feet, and led the way in silence to the stairs.

Outside, Teru tried again. "You play classical piano?"

"Are you surprised?"

"Not... not really. It was gorgeous."

"It is not a difficult piece."

"Did you just do that off the top of your head?"

"I expect even you have heard of Beethoven."

That wasn't what he'd meant, and they both knew it. "Of course I have," Teru said. "I meant... never mind. Do you want to look around some more?"

They walked side by side, never really touching. Teru was hyperaware of Rei—of his breathing, of his footsteps, of the shadow he cast at the edge of his peripheral vision. His body heat, his nerves... or were those Teru's own, projected into the space between them?

They passed a violin shop, and one specializing in wind instruments. The next shop down the road, though, was definitely more their style. The first couple of floors were guitars, but the sixth and seventh were blocked out together on the floor guide, with "Drum Center" written in the middle in a large, bold font. "Do you mind if we check this out?" Teru asked, and Rei shook his head.

The place actually had an elevator, and the drum section was at least as large as the floor guide had led them to believe. Rei sat and watched while Teru had fun, messing around on equipment that he probably wouldn't have chosen and definitely wouldn't have been able to afford on his own—but he felt a little guilty, too. He'd done his best to come up with a date that wouldn't be too hard on Rei. He'd avoided the subway, with its endless stairs and squat toilets, and made a point of steering away from zoos and amusement parks and anything else that required a lot of walking. It hadn't occurred to him that window shopping could be just as tiring when you weren't twenty-one, with nothing worse than the flu in your medical history.

An hour passed, maybe an hour and a half. Teru took more time than he needed, feigning more interest—and a higher budget—than he actually had when the floor manager offered him some catalogues. When he finally said goodbye and nodded his thanks, he was pretty sure the guy thought he'd made a future sale.

"I wasn't aware you were looking for a new kit." Rei gave him a half smile, and Teru shrugged.

"I can dream."

"Is there anything you want?"

It was an offer; Teru knew it, but he couldn't accept. "Not today." He shook his head. "Maybe not ever, unless I can afford a bigger place."

"Ah." Rei nodded his understanding. "I remember those days." He smiled again, a little sadly.

"So, what do you want to do now?" Teru asked. "We could have an early dinner. Or—"

"Let's go upstairs."

"Upstairs?"

There was only one floor above the drums, marked "Used and Vintage" on the guide. It was, Teru thought as he stepped off the elevator, the kind of place that Yasu would have loved. The walls were lined with old instruments—more "Vintage" than plain old "Used," and even to Teru, who could only tell one guitar from another if it was a model one of his friends used, the selection was impressive. A 1974 Gibson Les Paul, a 1971 Marshall Tremolo amp. Yeah, Yasu would be in heaven here, if only he could afford a fraction of the price tags.

He said as much to Rei, and Rei gave him another sad smile in reply. He was thinking about Saki, Teru knew. Saki, whom he knew absolutely nothing about... he probably would have loved this place too.

"Are we looking for anything special?" Teru asked. Just being here made him nervous. Some of these instruments looked like they might break if he looked at them the wrong way—and there was no way he could pay for the damage if they did.

"Not—" Rei began, but then he stopped in front of the counter, ignoring the clerk and his open-mouthed stare in favor of a guitar—an extremely expensive guitar, it seemed, in a glass case with the word "ASK" where the price should have been.

"Not particularly," he lied.

It was a Fender Stratocaster, according to the head, painted orange in the middle and fading to red and then to black around the edges. It was old—that much was obvious, even without the handwritten tag reading *1964*—and well-used. The neck was dull, worn between the frets, and in more than a few places the paint had been scratched and flecked away by what at least looked like use, rather than abuse. "A guitar?" Teru asked.

"A '64 Stratocaster."

"It's in good shape," the clerk said, finally forcing his mouth shut and a professional expression onto his face. "A little worn, but all original parts. Sounds like a dream. You want to play it?"

He looked at Teru, and Teru shook his head. "Not me."

"How about it?" He turned his attention to Rei, and for a moment—Teru was sure—Rei considered it. The piano had worked. Rei had made it work, but Teru couldn't think of any way, other than childishly strumming the open strings, to play the guitar without at least some use of both hands.

Apparently Rei couldn't either. "Not today."

"You sure?" The clerk didn't look especially disappointed. He probably saw guys dressed just like this—well, just like Teru—every day, and they probably had about as much money to spend on vintage guitars as Teru did.

"How much is it?"

"Two million, four hundred thousand. Still has the original case."

"I see." Rei nodded. "I'll think about it. Thank you."

"Sure," the guy said. "Don't forget, we do have installment plans."

Money wasn't the issue, though. Two million, four hundred thousand yen was as much as Teru made at the CombiMart in a year... but he had a pretty good feeling that Rei, if he wanted to, could handle it.

"It was nice," Teru said, when the elevator doors had closed behind them.

"Nice?" Rei echoed, as though the word was an insult to the guitar. "Do you have any idea...?" He raised his hand, still holding his cane, and punched the wall. "What's the use, Teru? What's the use of money, when..."

"You should have bought it," Teru said. "Or played it. Touched it. You wanted to."

Rei clenched his teeth. "What would have been the point?"

———✦———

They took the train to Shinbashi, and then to Odaiba. The man-made island was swarming with kids—high school and college students just out for the summer, holding hands and sharing sodas under webs of colored lights and standing in line for the Ferris wheel overlooking Tokyo Bay. The bay itself was dark and murky—muddy or polluted, Teru wasn't sure which—but the first hints of a sunset colored the sky in swirls of orange and pink, and the skyline was crowned with the red-gold point of Tokyo Tower.

Teru bought two bottles of green tea from a vending machine and hesitated before twisting the top from Rei's. They sat on a bench, watching the waves lap the concrete shore, just close enough that Teru's arm—and large parts of the rest of him—prickled with the thrill of the almost-contact.

A young couple ran down the path in front of them, laughing and tugging at one another's hands and arms and clothes until the girl stumbled and almost fell, and the boy pulled her up into a hug. Rei shivered, or shuddered, and Teru inched closer, wanting to hold his hand, to put an arm around his waist, but not sure if he had the courage to do such a thing here, where the entire world would see.

"What am I supposed to say?" Rei whispered, breaking the silence. He stood; Teru followed, to the rail that separated the concrete bridge from the sea. "Should I pretend that I am not reminded of him with every step I take, with every note I hear and with everything I see? Should I lie? Should I tell you that we never stood here"—he tossed his cane aside; it fell to the pavement with a clatter—"on this spot, or close to it, speaking of a future that would never be? Should I pretend that I am who I was? That I can walk with you, as I did with him? That I can be with you, unafraid to be seen?"

He lowered his eyes, looking not at the waves but at the ground, at the cracks in the concrete, at his own hand on the rail. "Should I be honest?" he asked. "Should I tell you how badly I hurt? How much worse I know tomorrow will be? Should I—"

"Stop." Teru's eyes were full of tears. "Just... just stop. Today was supposed to be fun. I'm sorry if I picked a bad place. I'm sorry if I did something wrong. But, Rei, every day can't be like this. If you need to talk to me, then do. If you need to rest, if you need any help, I'll do whatever you need. But you have to let me know. I can't read your mind, Rei, and... and I think you expect me to try."

"That isn't true."

"It feels that way to me."

"I'm sorry."

"Don't be," Teru said. "I didn't mean to hurt you."

"You didn't." Rei turned, lifting Teru's chin with the tips of his fingers until their eyes met. "You didn't," he repeated.

"Okay," Teru said. "Do you want to go home?"

"No."

"Do you want to have dinner?"

"Yes," Rei said. "But not yet. We should ride the Ferris wheel."

"Are you sure?" That had been the plan, but after

everything that had happened, it seemed childish. Stupid.

"Isn't that why we're here?"

"Well, yeah," Teru admitted. "You can see the whole city from the top."

"Then we should do that," Rei said. "The Ferris wheel is... new. We should have something that is ours, and ours alone."

They stood in line, waiting as friends and couples and a few families bought tickets before them. Everyone was laughing, smiling, happy to be here on a summer evening that was just starting to turn not-hot-but-warm. Teru listened to the conversations around him, unable to think of anything to say, any conversation of his own that would be safe to start. It all came back to Saki, to that night, to whoever Rei had been before.

He paid for two tickets, though it felt like a party of three, and they took the elevator to the ride entrance. At the top, a kid with scraggly hair and acne eyed Rei's cane as he ripped the tickets in half. "You have to step up," he said, "while the wheel's still moving. Are you capable of boarding in that manner?" It was a memorized speech, not a personal attack, but Rei bristled.

"We're fine," Teru said, holding out his hand. It took Rei a second to realize what he was trying to do, but when he got the message he nodded, looping the cane over Teru's wrist and taking his hand instead. The kid held the door for the previous couple to get out, and when they had, Teru and Rei stepped up to the platform together.

It wasn't the most graceful climb up to a Ferris wheel car in the history of the world. Teru stepped up first, and let

Rei use his arm as leverage to pull himself into the car. It wasn't pretty, but he didn't fall or even come close, and Teru had to resist the urge to tell the kid off as he locked the door behind them.

"Thank you," Rei said. "I didn't think about that."

"Yeah. Me neither. I'm sorry."

Rei smiled. "Don't be. This is very... normal."

"Yeah." Teru said, and he laughed. "I guess it is."

"Do you come here often?"

Teru looked at Rei's face, searching for a hint as to whether or not that was supposed to be a joke, but he seemed to be as serious as always. "No," Teru said. "I don't really date much. You?"

"Only once," Rei said, and looked away.

Teru followed his gaze out the window, to the darkening sky and the glittering skyline, streaked with expressways and spangled with lights, and colored with the pillars of Rainbow Bridge. "So," he ventured, "why a '64?"

"That is the year I was born."

Rei looked at Teru, gauging his reaction, but Teru only nodded. He'd known that Rei was older. If he'd been on the verge of a major debut five years ago... maybe he'd been a little old for the indies scene, but Teru had met guys trying to make it into their thirties and even forties before. Fifteen years between them, then. It wasn't a small difference, and Teru might have cared, if he'd known earlier. But now?

"That's a good reason," he said.

The car approached the apex, and what conversation there had been between them fell dry. They looked out the window, taking in the sky, the bay, and the city—their city—beyond. *We should kiss at the top*, Teru thought. There was no time like now, no place like here—with the door locked and the rest of the world a hundred meters below. No one would know. No one would care.

They reached the highest point, and the car rocked as its center of gravity shifted, as the iron rod holding it went completely vertical for a moment and then began to shift in the opposite direction.

It was now or never. Teru let his hand fall, accidentally-on-purpose, from the edge of the window to Rei's knee, and when, after a fraction of a second, he thought the silence was his answer and tried to pull away, Rei stopped him, kept him there with a quiet, deliberate strength.

The ride wasn't over, but Teru's eyes were no longer on the skyline. He closed them as, at last, their lips came together in a kiss that was more a promise of intimacy than an intimate act itself.

"Thank you," Rei whispered. "Thank you for today."

"It doesn't have to be over. We could have dinner or something?"

"Teru..."

Things were going so well, at least at the moment. He didn't want to give Rei a chance to say no. "We still have time. We could—"

"Shhhh." Rei pressed his index finger to Teru's lips. "Dinner is on me. I can only hope the place I am thinking of is still there."

—⟶⁝⟵—

Teru was half expecting to be taken to some overpriced

restaurant with a foreign menu and more forks than there were things to eat with them. He was both shocked and pleasantly surprised when, instead, Rei led him under the train tracks by Yurakucho station to a salaryman's haven of greasy, run-down, counter-service-only kinds of dives.

The place was still there—a tiny, smoky hole-in-the-wall serving little more than grilled chicken skewers and beer. The tables were made of particle board and plastic crates, and the chairs were stools with holes in the vinyl upholstery.

"This doesn't seem like your kind of place," Teru commented as he scanned the walls for the specials. There would be no menu in a restaurant like this—most of the prices were posted on boards nailed vertically to the walls, and seasonal specials were tacked next to them, written in permanent marker on printer paper just like the set lists at La Rose's shows.

"It doesn't?" Rei gave him another sad—or maybe just nostalgic—smile, and they toasted with frosty mugs. "I wasn't always so well-off, you know."

Teru nodded. "The insurance money."

"Among other things."

The food arrived—thigh meat and skin and various innards, with leeks and garlic for flavor. It was simple, but it tasted good, and it was all on skewers—no chopsticks required.

"Where are you from?" Teru asked between bites. He was captivated by this Rei—not the reclusive composer or the star who had almost been, but the boy who, like himself, must have come to the city once with a pocket of change and a dream.

"Aomori," he replied. "I came to Tokyo when I was

sixteen. It took me a very long time to have any success with my music."

Teru nodded, hoping there would be more to the story. "Did you know him, then? Saki?" A lump rose in his throat.

"No. He was younger." Rei sipped at his beer. "Too young."

"I'm sorry."

"It's not your fault."

"It's not yours either." Teru reached across the table and took Rei's hand. "It's not, okay?"

Rei nodded. Overhead, a train clattered out of the station, rattling the walls and causing the businessmen at the next table to raise their raucous laughter over the din.

The second they were home, Rei disappeared into the kitchen and returned with a wheeled cart on which he had placed a bottle of whisky, two glasses, and a pail of ice.

"Thanks." Teru took a glass and raised it. "To a great night?"

"To a wonderful day."

Rei sat on the sofa, just close enough for Teru to run his fingers through his hair. "Do you mind?" he asked, slipping them beneath the edges of the wig, and Rei shook his head.

The mask was next; Rei flinched, but Teru felt only an echo of the discomfort that he had before. He nodded, exhaled, and moved on to the cloak that hid Rei's too-thin frame.

"Wait." Rei reached into one of the inner pockets and

withdrew a handful of pills. "Painkillers," he explained, and downed them with a mouthful of whisky.

"Did I—"

"I don't sleep well," Rei said. "Without those, I don't sleep at all. It was a good day. And now I am tired." He smiled what would have been a gentle smile, had the twist of his lips not made it ghastly. "I don't want to hide from you anymore, Teru. I am... very tired."

"Rei, I—"

"Stop." His voice was firm, and Teru said no more. He reached up and, waiting for the quiet nod of permission, began the act of freeing Rei's bad arm from its sling.

Rei sighed. "Do you pity me, Teru?"

"I... I don't know." Teru hesitated. "Maybe. I can't imagine..."

I can't imagine what it would be like. To have so much talent and be unable to use it, unable to stand onstage and earn the crowd's applause. That had seemed like the worst of it, but today he had seen so much more. Teru couldn't imagine being unable to carry a couple of glasses, to open a stupid plastic bottle, to get on a Ferris wheel without a hand up. It was everything. Every minute of every day, a reminder of that night and what Rei had lost.

"I feel sorry for you," he admitted. "I guess. Sometimes. But that's not why I'm here. You know that, right? You—you changed my life, Rei. You've touched so many people with your music."

"Have I?"

"Of course you have. There's me. And the guys. Our fans." Teru grasped Rei's hand. "And that girl—Chizuru—she cares about you."

Rei raised his eyebrow. "That is news to me."

"She was worried about you the other night. About us, I guess."

"My personal life is not her business."

"Who—who is she anyway?"

Rei withdrew his hand and stood, limping across the room to the wall that held his CD collection. "Here." He selected an 8-centimeter single in a paper case and carried it back to Teru.

The cover was a familiar one. The song, a catchy pop ballad by some busty idol singer, had topped the charts a few summers ago, and though that kind of thing wasn't usually Teru's style, he had to admit that it had been a guilty pleasure. But there was no way the capped teeth and flawless skin on the cover belonged to the girl he had met at the live house—it would take more than a couple of summers to make that kind of change. Teru turned the case over, looking for an answer—but what he found raised a whole new set of questions.

Music and lyrics by Chizuru Sakata. "She's a composer?"

"No," Rei smiled. "I am a composer. She is a face."

"You sell your music under her name." That explained how one insurance settlement had managed to provide not only for medical bills and a basic standard of living, but for an apartment in one of the most expensive parts of Tokyo and recording equipment that rivaled a mid-range studio.

"Yes." Rei sank back onto the sofa. "Teru?"

"What's wrong?"

"I am going away. For a few days. I need to see him."

"For Obon?" Teru frowned, returning the CD to the table and taking another sip of whisky. The festival of the dead was only two weeks away, but Teru hadn't really thought much about it. There was no chance of him going back to Sanjo, to sit at his uncle's table and listen to cousins he'd never heard of ask him when he was going to get a real job, and then fork out money he didn't have as an offering to dead relatives he had never even met. But it made sense that Rei would want to see Saki, wherever he was.

"Tomorrow," Rei said, and Teru nearly dropped his glass.

"But it's still two weeks away."

"I always go early. His family would not want to meet me there."

"When are you coming back?"

"I don't know."

"But we have a show on Sunday."

"I know. I'm sorry. We never talked about this." Rei closed his eyes. "We never talked about what would happen, if one of us went first. I have to ask him. I have to..."

"Okay," Teru said. He didn't know what else to say. He had never been there, never experienced what Rei and Saki had had or what they had lost. "Take your time."

"Thank you."

"We should go to bed."

Rei was obviously exhausted, and between the drugs and the whisky, far enough from the pain that a few hours of sleep might be possible. Teru pulled him close, until Rei's head was in his lap. He closed his eyes, letting his own head fall to the arm of the couch, and they lay there in a tangle of arms and legs and frustrated longing until sleep, at last, claimed them both.

Chapter 22

The first three days passed in a blur. Teru's schedule was so full that he hardly had time to miss Rei—unless, of course, you counted the empty time between dark and sleep, or the lull before the curtain went up on Sunday's show.

The tension in the live house was palpable, an electricity that bounced between Teru and his bandmates, pulling them together and pushing them apart and magnifying the ache—not quite nerves and not quite longing—that had been sleeping in his gut since Rei had left. Minori was on edge because Bara was there; Teru was restless because Rei wasn't. The rest of the band tiptoed around them like they were walking on glass.

Teru floated through the set, the emotion in his voice as carefully scripted as the lines Minori and Rei had given him to work the crowd between songs. He was there and he wasn't, a character posing beneath the spotlight, unsure how in control of his actions he was.

"Last song," he whispered into the mic, and the fans sighed their disappointment, right on cue. "Yami no hanabira."

It was the showpiece, the song that was supposed to bring the crowd—and Bara—to their knees. As petty as that was,

Teru couldn't help but smile at the thought. The song Minori had chosen to show off with wasn't one of his own, but Rei's.

I'll have to tell him later, he thought, as he raised the mic over his head, letting the applause wash over him, keeping him in character for a moment longer. He tried not to look at the balcony, dark and empty overhead, and he tried not to think about when, exactly, "later" would be.

Bara was waiting for them in the dressing room, squinting at himself in the mirror as he worked a glob of mousse into his hair. "Not bad," he admitted with a short, begrudging nod.

"Thanks," Teru said, but Minori only frowned.

"You're in a good mood."

"You could say that." Bara smirked. "Haven't you heard the news?" He slid a flyer across the table.

Minori didn't say anything, but his face, in the glow of the dressing room lights, went pale. "Congratulations," he muttered, in a voice that squeaked like it was being forced out. "Hey, guys, I'm going to go help Kiyomi. Come on up when you're ready, okay?"

"Yeah." Teru nodded. "Sure."

"Sure," echoed Seika, but Yasu said nothing. He was still staring at the flyer.

"Crisis Cross? Isn't that that CD—?"

Nao picked up the flyer and read it slowly, his eyes visibly traveling the paper from top to bottom and back again. Yasu leaned over his shoulder, and Teru, unable to resist his curiosity, followed suit. "Crisis Cross Omnibus Volume Three," Nao read under his breath. "Coming in December to a record shop near you."

216

Beneath the announcement were pictures of the participating bands. Two of them were no surprise: they were signed to the Crisis Cross label and had been included from the beginning. But the other six were news to Teru. He had seen the names around, of course, but he only really knew two of them. There was Urgent Venus, who had organized the event that had become Teru's vocal debut—and there, in the bottom right corner, was Thorne.

Seika plucked the flyer from Nao's hands and returned it to Bara. "Congratulations."

"Thank you." Bara stood, adjusting the rose—red today—in his lapel. "You came close, by the way. 'Musically competent, but sadly dated.' Give Minori my condolences."

"Yeah, whatever," Yasu muttered, in a voice that was just loud enough for Teru—and Bara—to hear.

Teru nodded, and mumbled his agreement. But looking at Yasu, Seika, and Bara standing next to each other, he could kind of understand what Bara meant. Yasu's long hair and pleather were straight from the 80s, Seika's gothic skirt and feathers the 90s to a tee. Were bands like Bara's really the future? Horror-shock visuals and screams passed off as songs? Teru didn't want to believe that—but there was the flyer. And La Rose was nowhere in sight.

—⋇—

"Forget it," Minori said. "It was a good show." He raised his beer mug. "Kampai."

They were in what must have been the most out-of-the way drinking establishment in Meguro. Unsure of where Thorne was having their after-show drinks and without a reservation on a Sunday night, they'd ended up in a tiny izakaya on the first floor of the elderly Okinawan owner's home. The walls were covered with tapestries in large, bright floral patterns, and a pair of shisa lion-dogs bared their wooden teeth from the top of a clunky analog karaoke set that was the most modern thing in the room.

"Go ahead and sing if you like," the owner had said with a silver-and-tobacco-stained smile, but none of them were exactly in a festive mood.

"So, you already know the bad news," Minori began. "The lineup for Crisis Cross is out, and we're not on it."

Teru nodded and sipped at his beer. Beside him, Nao picked at the goya campur they'd ordered to be polite, even though none of them had really wanted it.

"I'm sorry. I was going to tell you guys after the show. But, look. We had a good night. We sounded great, and we sold another"—he consulted his notebook—"ten CDs."

Yasu nodded. "Not bad."

"Especially since most of our regulars have already got it. We're doing better now than ever, and we need to keep moving forward." Minori glanced around the table. "I think we should put it out anyway."

Seika raised an eyebrow. "'Blood on the Moon'?"

"Why not?" Nao shrugged. "It's as good a time as any."

Yasu nodded; Teru followed. There was no reason not to, not really.

"Great. Then we'll start working on it at our next rehearsal. There are a couple of things I don't love about the arrangement, but we can polish that up. And if everyone's okay with it, I want to start thinking about a new look."

Yasu winced. "Some of us are broke, you know."

"I know. But we need to do this. Nao's still wearing his stuff from his old band, and the rest of our costumes were designed to work with Bara's."

"Minori." Seika frowned. "I know you and Bara were friends, but—"

Minori set his beer down with a thunk. "This isn't personal. Bara was right. We're good at what we do. But what we're doing was big last century. If we're going to change our image, now's the time."

"Change our image?"

"Why not? New single, new costumes. I'm not talking about copying Bara—just something more mainstream, more masculine."

Seika glanced at Yasu; Yasu glanced at Teru. Teru cleared his throat.

"I'm not asking you to cut your hair or pierce your faces," Minori went on, "and I don't want to distort our music beyond all recognition. But we could play with this electronic stuff, tone down the theatrics and take it in a poppier direction. Think less X, more hide solo?"

"Teru does do a mean 'Pink Spider,'" Yasu joked, and Teru shook his head.

"I—I think we should..." *I think we should ask Rei.* But that wasn't an option. Rei was... somewhere. With Saki. "I think we should wait."

The smile that spread across Minori's face was, Teru thought, more of a growl. Like the shisa, he was baring his teeth. Ready to protect his turf against his competition. "If we keep waiting, we're going to lose our chance. These fans are fickle. They'll move on to someone else, and—"

"Let's think about it," Seika said. "We just got off stage. I'm with Teru. This isn't something to rush into. An image change is a big deal, and we're doing pretty well the way we are."

Minori tapped a cigarette from his pack and fumbled with his lighter, flicking it two or three times before he finally got a flame. "Fine," he said. "Take a few days to think about it. But that omnibus comes out in December. I want to have something by then."

Under the table, Teru glanced at his phone. No texts. No calls. And it had been three days.

—⋇—

He was dragged out of bed on the sixth morning by a phone call from Minori. "I wanted to talk to you first," he said. "Are you really interested in recording?"

"Of course." Teru yawned. "Why wouldn't I be?"

"I'm just checking. You're the only one we can't replace in the studio. And, ah... how about Rei?"

So that's what this was about.

"Do you think he'd be willing to help us out? I'm not talking about the money or anything, but—"

"I don't think he'd want us to do it without him." Teru's voice was strained, his throat constricted, and his heart was playing speed metal in his chest. Six days ago, he would have been sure of that—Rei wouldn't have wanted Teru in the studio without him. But he'd been gone for longer than just a few days, and now that Teru was forced to think about it, he had no idea what that meant.

220

"Great," Minori said. "Do you think you could make it to Kichijoji on Saturday? I want to talk about recording, and a few other things. If Rei's available...?"

"Okay," Teru said. "I'll ask him."

He said goodbye, and pulled up Rei's number. And then he just sat there, staring at it for a very long time.

Even with all of Rei's health problems, there was no reason to think he wouldn't be able to get home. Teru strongly suspected he didn't drive, and if there'd been a train or bus accident it would have made the news. Those thoughts crossed his mind, but they didn't stay there for long. What stayed, and what really bothered him, was the thought that Rei might already be back—and that something else was preventing him from calling.

Minori called him again on his way home from work, but Teru didn't answer. He had nothing to say that he hadn't said that morning, and he didn't feel like having to explain why he hadn't been able to get in touch with someone who, as far as the rest of the band was concerned, was his friend.

The sun was on its way down when Teru reached his apartment, and still, Rei hadn't called. Again, Teru brought his number up. Again, he shook his head and put the phone aside. He did a load of laundry, boiled some spaghetti and, finding nothing remotely resembling sauce in the cupboard, seasoned it with soy sauce and stale sesame seeds. He charged his phone—still silent—and hung the laundry in the bathroom while pretending to listen to the TV. When that was done, he dug out a stack of CDs and picked one at random. Working on his own music would remind him of Rei; listening to someone else, he hoped, would distract him.

Teru stripped down to his boxers—it was too hot and humid for pajamas—and lay on top of his futon, staring at the ceiling while the CD played on. He pulled on the chain for the overhead light: once, twice, and then the room was completely dark. Teru closed his eyes and listened to the music, trying to pick out each instrument one at a time, tuning the others out, and then letting them flow together again.

The phone began to vibrate beside him.

"Hello?"

"Teru."

"Rei." Teru sat up, fumbling for the chain. "You're back."

"I am back. How was your show?"

"My show? It was okay."

"That's good."

"I—I wanted to talk to you. About the band. Minori wanted me to ask if—"

"May I see you?"

"Now?"

"The trains are still running."

"Okay." Finding the cord at last, Teru pulled it, and the lights flickered on. "I'll be there as soon as I can."

He dressed quickly, in the same clothes he had worn earlier that day, stuffed a change of clothes into an Isetan shopping bag and ran a comb through the most tangled bits of his hair. Then he threw on a pair of shoes and rushed out into the night.

The trains running in the opposite direction, from Shinjuku out into the suburbs, were overflowing with sweaty, suited workers, their bodies pressed against the windows and each other like sardines in a can. The train Teru took, on the other hand, was nearly empty; there weren't many people rushing to get *into* the city on a weekday night.

He almost ran from the station to Rei's apartment, and when there was no response to his knock on the door, he turned the knob and let himself in. The entranceway was dark, the doors on his left closed. The only light in the apartment came from the music room.

A wave of déjà vu swept over him. Rei, bathed in a pale bluish light, sat at the computer with his back to the world. And he played. Only the music was different. It wasn't visual kei, but something older, heavier, dark in a completely different way. It sounded outdated, like the Scandinavian metal Yasu liked, but it was also incomplete. Two guitar lines and a keyboard part seemed to be more or less there, but the bassline died out after the chorus, and there were no drums or vocals at all.

"You came." Rei said, never taking his eyes from the screen.

"How was your, um... trip?"

"Do you like this song?"

"Sure," Teru said, but Rei's non-answer resonated like a sour note in the middle of a show. "It's not finished."

"It was," Rei said. "I am trying to remember. I want you to sing this. For me."

"Okay." He tried not to make it sound like a question. The song wasn't really La Rose's style. But they could deal with the rest of the band later; here, tonight, he would sing what Rei asked.

Rei pressed a key and restarted the music. "The ending needs work," he admitted. "What do you think?"

"I like it," Teru said. "But..."

"It's not your style."

"It's just... different." Teru frowned. "Did you write it?"

"I co-wrote it," Rei answered softly. "I told you that I came to Tokyo a long time ago."

Teru nodded.

"Visual kei didn't exist then, at least not as we know it. I experimented with glam rock, heavy metal. Saki found this amusing." Rei looked at Teru, smiling sadly. "He wrote this for me, as a joke. A relic of a song for a relic of a singer. But we worked on it together. I wrote the lyrics. I need to do something, Teru. I need to keep his memory alive."

"Okay." Teru was surprised by his reaction. A week or two ago, this would have bothered him, but now... "Look, the guys are meeting on Saturday, and they want you to come. I think we should get this ready."

"Saturday..." Rei repeated. "Two days. I don't know if I can remember it all."

"I'll help you."

"That is kind of you. But—"

"Got any drumsticks?" It was meant as a joke, but as soon as the words were out of his mouth, Teru's face began to burn. "I'm sorry. That was a stupid question."

"No." Rei shook his head. "No, it wasn't. In the front room. To your right, next to the front door. There is a bookshelf on the far side." He closed his eyes, remembering. "Next to it you will find a box. Number fourteen. There should be drumsticks inside."

Teru nodded. He had known, of course, that there was another room in the apartment. The door had always been closed, though, and the window blacked out. Teru turned the doorknob slowly, and groped in the dark for the lights. There were three bulbs in the fixture, but only two of them worked, and all of them were coated with dust. Someone had swept the floor fairly recently, although the bookshelf hadn't been touched. It was dusty and cluttered, crammed full of records and cassette tapes, magazines and books of sheet music.

The box was where Rei had said it would be, marked with permanent marker in a neat, flourishless hand. Next to it was another box, and on top of that, another. Some of them looked like they had been opened at some point and closed again, but number fourteen was nearly new.

The top had been folded shut, and Teru opened it, feeling a little like he was treading on sacred ground. It was full of clothes. They looked like costumes, and he felt a little dirty touching them, moving them out of the way—had they belonged to Rei? To Saki? Or to one of the others, about whom he knew nothing at all?

The drumsticks were at the bottom of the box. Teru took the pair that seemed the newest and left the room in a hurry.

Rei was still at the computer, immersed in his work. "Thank you." He clicked and dragged something on the screen. "That will do, for now. Now play."

The music started again. Teru tapped one stick on the edge of the table. His other hand joined in, following intuition more than anything else, and he let his foot take over the beat as something akin to a real drumline materialized around him. It wasn't fancy, and it sure as hell wasn't brilliant, but Rei watched and nodded his approval.

"Try this," he said, when the music had stopped. With his drum pad, he began to play a simplified version of what Teru had done. Then he added another layer—this one more detailed, with cymbals and accents. Finally, he played the rhythm of the bass drum. One bit at a time, tapped out with his fingers—but when he put it all together, it sounded good.

Teru picked up the rhythm, hitting the air where the cymbals and toms should have been and using the table as the snare. It worked. They had thrown it together in the space of a few minutes, but somehow, it actually worked.

"That will do, for the chorus." Rei said, though he didn't take his eyes from the screen. "Do you have to work tomorrow?"

"Yeah."

"Then I will work on the rest alone. Tonight, I want to hear you sing."

The music began again, and this time Rei sang along:

"Kusarikitta kono tokai"
This rotten metropolis
"Tamashii suitsukusu."
Sucking up my soul
"Ore no aijin. Ore no hametsu."
My lover, my destruction
"Nigeru basho nado nai."
I got nowhere to run

They sang together, one line at a time until Teru had

memorized the lyrics, and then he tried it alone. It rubbed his throat raw, the almost-screaming he had to do to get into the upper registers without resorting to a falsetto. He wondered if he was damaging his voice, but Rei didn't say anything, and that was usually a good sign.

He slept on the sofa while Rei played on, and in the morning he borrowed the shower again, changing into the clothes he had brought before heading to work. Rei asked what time he would be back—"tomorrow" clearly was not an option—and Teru gave him a late estimate, deciding to stop by his apartment for another change of clothes, just in case.

"Tonight, then." Rei was visibly exhausted, but he smiled as they said goodbye.

When he returned after work, with not one but two changes of clothes, Teru found the music room carpeted with sheet music, CDs and MDs, and dozens of pages of notes and lyrics and scribbled ideas. "What's this?" Teru picked up one of the loose sheets, but whatever it was, it was practically illegible.

"The rest of your album."

"Album?" Teru surveyed the room again. "Where did this come from?"

"Listen."

They listened to one song after another, some full demos with live instruments and vocals, others rough a capella or keyboard performances. Sometimes Teru sang. Other songs were listened to and rejected, and a set of newer compositions were included without discussion. They put what they had on a stack of MDs, printed out the lyrics that were saved on the computer, and made a list of songs that had

227

yet to be transcribed.

Teru slept when he was tired; Rei seemed not to sleep at all. Thursday turned into Friday; they ate, at Teru's insistence, but whether it was breakfast, lunch, or dinner, neither of them could say for sure. When Teru looked at his phone, it was Saturday morning, a quarter to three. They had narrowed down the library of songs, but it was still enough to fill four or five albums. They packed it all into a faded black duffel bag and, with only nine hours until the meeting, crawled into bed—too exhausted to do anything but sleep.

The meeting had been set for noon, in a family restaurant in Kichijioji, a thirty or forty minute train ride from Meguro. Teru's alarm went off at ten, and after a prolonged battle with the snooze button, he crawled out of bed and into the shower at ten-thirty. Rei was quiet as he, too, showered and dressed, double- and triple-checking every aspect of his appearance in the cracked bathroom mirror.

The train was crowded with Tokyo natives and tourists alike, enjoying the first day of most big companies' summer vacations. Teru and Rei earned more than a few interested stares, and when a crowd of Europeans speaking a language Teru couldn't place tried to take their picture, he stepped between the lens and his companion, ruining the shot with a cloud of pink hair.

The restaurant was only five minutes from the station, even for Rei with his cane and Teru with the overstuffed duffel, and they managed to arrive before noon. The hostess seemed to be expecting them; she led them to a long table in the back, where the rest of the band was already seated. Teru suppressed a groan. He hadn't dared to hope they would be first, but he hadn't expected *everyone* else to be there, to see them arrive together.

He forced a smile. "Hey. I, um, guess most of you remember Rei." Yasu and Minori nodded; Seika only smiled. "This is Nao, our new drummer." Nao gave a nervous nod that was almost a bow. "And... Kiyomi."

Teru's mouth fell open. No one had told him she had been invited. "What are you doing here?" he asked, realizing too late that he'd been rude.

Kiyomi looked as shocked as Teru was, and more than a little embarrassed. She'd barely spoken to him at the last show, other than to apologize. Teru had smiled, told her it was nothing. But it still bothered him that she was here.

She nodded and murmured a greeting before looking away. Teru knew that look. He'd seen it on the faces of hundreds, thousands of people all over the city, whenever he'd been out with Rei. She was trying so hard not to stare that she *was* staring—at everything else. Her napkin, still folded on the table, had grabbed her attention at the moment, and she spoke to it quietly. "Minori asked me to come," she said. "I don't know anything about music, but you're all so busy. I just thought I might be able to help with... with something."

"Kiyomi's our target audience," Minori explained. "I want to know what she thinks. And there are things that need to be done that don't require any musical ability. Costumes, flyers, postcards..."

"Very well." Rei's reply was cold and final. Kiyomi

could stay.

Teru deposited the bag on an empty chair and pulled out another for Rei, aware of his friends' eyes on him as he did. They knew. They had to know, and Teru was sure that they were judging him, blaming him, for letting his personal life interfere with the band—even if that interference had been mostly positive.

"Well, then," Minori said. "If everyone's ready...?"

"Wait," Rei said, in a tone that left no room for argument. "Minori."

"Yes?" Teru had to give Minori credit. He flinched, for a fraction of a second, but then he looked back, straight into Rei's eyes.

The rest of the band was watching them, the leader and the composer squaring off. There was no reason for Rei to be angry with Minori. But Teru knew him—and that tone of voice—well enough by now to be ninety-nine percent certain he was. "This band," Rei went on, "is not a competition. Bara's success—if you can call it that—does not detract from yours."

"I know."

"Am I wrong, then? Are we not here today because... because Thorne"—he overenunciated the name—"was selected for that omnibus, while La Rose Verboten was not?"

"It's important to—"

"What is important is the music."

Now the customers at the adjacent tables were staring as well.

"Of course." Minori shook his head. "Of course it's about the music. "

"Good. Then you will agree with me that Crisis Cross is a mediocre label that has yet to propel a band to mainstream fame."

Minori nodded.

"And you will agree with me that while 'Blood on the Moon' is a good song—"

"Thank you."

"...that while it is a good song, it is not a great one. It is not enough. Teru?"

Teru zipped open the duffel bag, extracting one of the folders of sheet music he and Rei had prepared.

"What's this?" Minori asked.

"Your album."

"Our album?" Yasu echoed.

"It's not all recorded." Teru half-bowed in apology. "But it's all—"

"It's yours," Rei said, relaxing at last into his chair. "Use anything you want. I ask only that I am allowed to produce."

Minori shook his head. "We can't accept this."

"I insist."

Seika raised an eyebrow. "That's generous of you." There was a question there, but neither Teru nor Rei chose to answer it.

"An album." Minori tested out the words. "It seems soon." But Teru could tell he was considering it.

"I think we should," he said. "The songs are brilliant. At least listen to them."

Nao was already flipping through the first of the folders, tapping out a drumline on the arm of his chair.

Minori glanced around the table. "Kiyomi?"

"Yes?"

"Can you start thinking about album titles, jacket designs? Just in case," he clarified, with a sharp glance at Teru. "*If* we're going to do this I want to do it as professionally as we can. We'd need to look into studios—"

Rei smiled. "I have already spoken to Mr. Tashiro."

"All right," Minori said, when his notes had sprawled onto their fifth page and Rei's untouched coffee had long since gone cold. "This seems like a risk, without a label behind us. But we need to do something, and"—he nodded to Rei—"it does actually sound like you've thought this through. We'll think about it," he said, emphasizing every word—but the half-smile that played at the corner of his mouth told Teru that he already had.

Kiyomi took the check and began to calculate the amount each of them owed. "Well, until we do have a label to finance these meetings," she said, "you owe me nine hundred apiece. Or if everyone pays for their own..." She began punching numbers into her phone, but Seika, who had also ordered only coffee, stopped her.

"Nine hundred's fine with me." He glanced at Rei—everyone else would have owed more than that anyway—but Rei's attention was commanded by his wallet, hidden in the folds of his cloak.

"It's fine." Teru spoke up before Rei had a chance. Ignoring the looks from his bandmates, he pulled out his own wallet and handed Kiyomi two thousand-yen notes. "I've got his."

"Teru—" Rei whispered.

"It's okay." Teru shook his head, took his change, and put his wallet away, painfully aware that the bills Kiyomi was holding were his last. "You've done a lot for us—for me. It's the least I can do." It sounded phony, like the line that it was, but it would save Rei the embarrassment of having to fumble with his wallet in front of Teru's bandmates—people who maybe, just maybe, had a chance of respecting him for his music alone.

"Well, I hate to break things up, boys, but I need to get home and change." Seika paid his share of the bill and shouldered his bag.

"Yeah." Teru grabbed his things. "I guess I should get going too."

"You have to work tonight?" Yasu passed his money to Kiyomi and pulled a pack of cigarettes from his pocket. The restaurant was non-smoking, but the lobby area wasn't. If Rei hadn't been there, Teru would have joined him—as it was, he was seriously considering it.

"No, I'm off. Just tired."

"Wanna grab a beer?"

Teru's eyes unconsciously sought Rei's.

"Will you walk me to the station first?"

"Sure. Is that okay with you guys?" Teru wasn't sure if Minori and Nao were included in the invitation or not, but he addressed the question to all of them.

Rei was tired; the meeting had gone well, and there was no reason to think that his silence on the way to the station was due to anything other than fatigue. Their goodbye was quiet, understated for the benefit of the crowd around them. Teru put what he could into words: "Thanks. For everything."

Rei shook his head. "I should thank you."

"Are you sure you can get home okay?"

"I am fine."

Teru nodded. "I'll see you later then."

"Teru?"

"Hm?"

"Here." Rei held out his wallet. "Take what you need."

Teru shook his head. "I can't do that. I'll go to the ATM. I—"

"Teru, I have something to ask you." Rei took the wallet back, but didn't put it away. Teru's heart was in his throat, making it hard to breathe or talk or do anything other than nod. He also had things to ask. He wanted to ask about their relationship, about those six days, about where Rei had gone and what he had done and what, if any, decisions he had reached in that time. But he couldn't, not here. Not in the middle of the station with half the world swarming around them.

"We will be very busy, from now on. You will need to devote yourself to your music."

"Of course."

"You know that you don't need to work anymore."

"What do you mean?"

"I want you to quit your job." Once more, Rei extended the wallet. "You don't have to worry about money. You don't have to worry about anything but the music. Let me take care of you."

"I..." Teru began, but he didn't know how to finish. *I can't. I shouldn't. I'd love to.* More than anything else, he wanted a cigarette. His hand strayed to his pocket.

Rei's eyes followed, and he frowned. "Of course, my time and money will be ill-spent if you continue to destroy your voice. Think about it." He took the wallet back, holding it against his chest with his forearm as he pulled out a 10,000 yen bill. "The offer does not expire."

Chapter 23

Recording began two months later, on a cool Tuesday in October. Teru woke early, sliding out of bed so as not to wake Rei, who was still asleep, half-buried in his pillow.

He took his shower first, with shampoo he had bought himself and placed on the shelf where the empty soap bottles had been. He shaved, dried his hair, brushed his teeth. There were wigs in the sink waiting to be washed, a tangle of lavender and blue that didn't look dirty, but turned the water a murky shade of grayish brown after only a few seconds of scrubbing. Teru wrung them out and rinsed again—a strangely intimate act, washing Rei's hair while he slept in the other room.

When the water rinsed clear he hung the wigs to dry, then headed to the music room where one of the long blue ones, set aside for today's use, was waiting. He sat on the sofa and laid it over his knee, combing it and wiping away the static.

At nine, he returned to the kitchen. Teru wasn't much of a cook, but he did what he could to make sure Rei was eating—if not well, at least something. If the omelette he came up with was a little raw in the middle and a little burnt around the edges, it would still be edible. He cut it in two with the edge of the spatula and scooped the halves onto chipped brown plates.

"Rei? You awake?"

"No."

"Come on, get up. I made breakfast."

Rei groaned, but he sat up, reaching for the eyedrops he kept on the bedside table. Teru looked away—he had seen it before, but it seemed inappropriate to watch as Rei moistened the eye that never completely closed.

"Is Chizuru coming today?" Teru asked over his shoulder as he searched the refrigerator for something to drink.

"Yes," Rei said. "She is."

"Okay." Teru nodded. "I'll get my laundry ready." His clothes were heaped in a pile in the corner. Like the rest of their relationship, the laundry arrangements seemed to have gone from entirely separate to old married couple—with a maid, no less—without any of the milestones that should have come between.

Rei ate his eggs, drank his juice, and left for his own shower. Teru washed the dishes, took out the trash, and brought in the mail. Letters addressed to Rei—to his real name, anyway, which neither of them ever used—went on the table. Junk mail went into the trash. And the postcard from a music store addressed to Sakito Koyanagi... Teru folded that in half and crammed it into his pocket. He would call the store later, let them know that the recipient was no longer at this address, and that, he hoped, would be the end of that.

When Rei had finished his shower, he let Teru help him dress. Today was going to be a long day, and that meant he'd need all the support that Teru could convince him to take: knee supporters, an ankle brace, a wrist brace to keep his paralyzed hand from curling into a claw. Sometimes Rei refused these things, but today he accepted them without complaint. Teru could only hope this meant that he knew how important it was to be focused on the music, and not the pain, today, and not that the day was shaping up to be a bad one before it had started.

"Is that all right?" Teru asked as he pulled the sling over Rei's good shoulder.

"Fine," Rei muttered, but he reached up with his left hand and tightened the strap. It was too hot for the cloak just yet, although Rei never left the apartment without it. Teru helped him with the mask and wig instead; that would be enough for Chizuru, and they could deal with the rest when the time came.

Teru grabbed a strip of prescription painkillers and shoved them into his pocket. "Do we need anything else?"

"No," Rei said, and then, "Wait. Yes. I need that pedal from the front room."

Teru was on his hands and knees, digging through a box of guitar equipment when the doorbell rang. He heard the door open and close a second later; Chizuru never waited for an answer.

"Last month's royalties," he heard her say. "I took out my share. And this is the contract for the TV commercial."

"Yes," Rei replied. "This is fine."

"Here." There was a rustle of paper; Chizuru had handed him something. "You're taking them, right?" Medicine, then. Rei didn't take his pain meds, not every day,

238

and when he did they didn't always seem to work. But Teru didn't think Chizuru needed to know that.

Another door closed, and their voices were dulled to wordless cadences of frustration. Teru was more or less used to Chizuru and her presence in Rei's life; she lent her name and face to the songs he sold to more mainstream artists and took care of the chores and errands that Rei was unable or unwilling to do on his own. But she'd seemed so worried about him, that night Teru had met her at Rock Eden—and lately, it seemed all they did was argue.

Teru knocked at the bedroom door, giving both of them the time to put on whatever faces they wanted to show. Chizuru looked up, but quickly went back to making the bed. Rei was sitting at the table, putting on his makeup.

"Did you find it?"

Teru held up the pedal. "Yeah. Is there anything else?"

"No." Rei's voice was muffled; he held a tube of mascara between his teeth as he unscrewed the top and applied it, with a steady hand, to the single set of lashes on his left eye. "We are almost ready. Ms. Sakata?"

"Yes?" She raised an eyebrow at the formality.

"You will accompany us to the studio, please."

She glanced at Teru. "What about the housework?"

"You will only be needed until we arrive. Since you are so concerned about my well-being, I thought you might like to carry our bags."

"Of course," Chizuru said through clenched teeth, her mouth frozen in a phony smile.

Teru could have carried everything himself, but he held his tongue. It was a power play, some reaction to what had passed between Rei and Chizuru in the hall, and he knew that speaking up would only make things worse—and that that might make the rest of the day unbearable. So he walked with Rei as Chizuru stormed ahead with the equipment, blazing a trail of palpable tension.

—>⋅<—

Seika and Minori were waiting at the studio, their heads bent over a magazine. They looked up, in unison, at the opening of the door, and Teru, feeling Seika's eyes on him, took a stumbling step backward, away from Rei.

He didn't know how much his bandmates had figured out, and he wasn't sure how much he wanted them to know. But judging by the scowl on Minori's face, today wasn't going to be the time.

"Hey," Teru said. "Is that the interview? It's out?"

"Advance copy," Minori said, but he didn't really sound excited.

Rei sat at the mixing board and silently extended his hand.

They scanned the article together, Teru glancing over Rei's shoulder as he read. It was a two-page spread, simple, in black and white—well, more like navy and white—with the band's new photos across the top and the interview at the bottom. "Costumes look good," Teru said, and Rei nodded.

"I see no problem."

"There isn't one," Minori said. "Not with the article." But he flipped to the previous page and held it up. "But there's this."

It was an advertisement for the Crisis Cross CD.

240

"It's just an ad," Seika explained.

Minori frowned. "A full page ad. To get it on this page—"

"They've got a label behind them," Seika went on, as though this wasn't the first time he'd explained this. "Bara had nothing to do with it."

"I know. But they're full color, we're black and white, and—"

"Enough." Rei slammed his hand into the mixing board. "You are behaving like children. The article is fine. We record *this* album in half an hour."

Minori opened his mouth, as if to offer a retort, but—apparently thinking better of it—only nodded, and shut the magazine with a glossy slap.

"We're, uh, starting with 'Midnight Higeki,'" Teru said, pulling a stack of rehearsal schedules from the bag.

"All right," Minori muttered. He stepped down into the studio, but had barely unzipped his guitar case when something on the schedule caught his eye. "Teru?" he asked. "What's this 'Untitled'?"

Teru ran over to check Minori's schedule, then looked at his own to confirm. "We listened to it. You know, 'Kusarikitta kono tokai'?" He half-sang the first line of Saki's song, trying to ignore the fact that his stomach felt like a block of ice, and that he couldn't seem to get enough air to fill his lungs.

"I thought we cut that one?" Seika glanced at Minori, then up to the mixing booth, to Rei.

Minori only frowned. "I thought so too."

—✳—

They broke for lunch at half-past noon, Rei refusing to join the others even though Teru made a point of inviting him. "I have work to do," he said.

"Fine," Teru sighed. "I'll bring you something."

He stopped by a convenience store on the way back to pick up a sandwich and a coffee for Rei. He paid for his purchase, took his bag, and was on the way out the door when Seika stopped him.

"Teru? Can I talk to you for a minute?"

"I guess." Teru followed him outside. Seika shook a pack of cigarettes from his jacket and offered him one. "No thanks," Teru said. "I'm trying to quit."

"Suit yourself." Seika shrugged and lit one for himself. "Nice job this morning."

Teru shook his head. "It wasn't good enough for him."

"Probably not." Seika laughed, but it didn't reach his eyes. "I haven't talked to you in awhile. Is everything okay?"

"It's fine."

"Okay." He put a hand on Teru's shoulder. "Because I know this is hard. It's hard enough even without... everything else."

Teru shrugged the hand away. "Yeah. Thanks for the concern, but I'm fine."

"Okay. But... Teru?"

"Yeah? What's wrong?"

"Have you thought about telling the others?"

"About what?" Teru's voice caught in his throat; he wiped his suddenly sweaty palms on his jeans.

Seika shook his head. "You know what I mean. And I

hope you know that normally, I'd tell you to take your time. It's none of their business who you're sleeping with—"

"I'm not—" *I'm not sleeping with him. Not like that.*

"It doesn't matter. It's a conflict of interest."

"I know."

"Think about it." Seika lowered his voice. "I'm not telling you to come out to the world. But if we're working with Rei, and if you're more than just colleagues... Teru?" He frowned. "Minori needs to know."

Teru lingered at the studio until the others were gone, helping Rei collect the equipment and the sheet music before lugging their oversized bag back to the station. It was six o'clock when they got home; the approach to the apartment was occupied by a group of girls in high school uniforms and slouchy white socks, giggling around a magazine. They looked up at the sight of their unconventional neighbor, then turned away and laughed again.

The key turned in the lock. Boots found their place in the entranceway and robes fell from slumped shoulders. Ice cubes tumbled into glasses and a deep golden tonic spilled over them and into parched throats, dulling the world and the day.

"Today went well."

"It did," Teru agreed and, as well as he could with the sofa and the whisky and his own exhaustion to hinder him, began the routine of helping Rei into the same state of undress as he was—a long sleeved T-shirt and cotton pants that could have doubled as pajamas, rumpled and faded and intimate in a way that feathers and fishnets couldn't rival.

"Rei?"

"Yes?"

"Why did you put Saki's song on the schedule?"

"It has been there since the beginning."

"But the guys never agreed to it."

"The *guys* have no choice."

Teru sighed. "It *is* Minori's band, you know. Maybe we should just explain."

"No."

Teru frowned, and pulled Rei closer, until his breath was warm and humid on Teru's cheek. "If they knew what it meant to you, I—"

"No," Rei whispered again. "I can't talk about him, Teru. I can't share him with anyone but you."

"Okay," Teru said. He should have pushed it further, but Rei's eyelids had begun to droop and his head was heavy on Teru's shoulder. He'd seemed fine all day, but it was only the first day of recording, and it occurred to Teru too late that alcohol and painkillers weren't supposed to be a very good mix.

He slipped an arm around Rei's waist, helping him to his feet and into the bedroom. The wig went into the sink, the mask on the bedside table, and Teru made a point of being otherwise occupied while Rei applied ointment to his scars. They slipped into bed with the lights still on, and Rei fell asleep while Teru lay beside him, tired but not sleepy, and tried to think about what he would say to his friends.

Seika was right. He needed to tell them; they needed to know. But no matter how long he lay there, watching the rise and fall of Rei's chest as he slept, Teru couldn't come up with the words.

"I need a drink," he muttered to himself. Or some fresh air. *Or a smoke.* He wasn't sure if Rei would be able to smell it on his clothes in the morning—wasn't sure, for that matter, how much of a sense of smell Rei had left at all—but he had gotten away with it before and if he was careful, he'd be able to do it again.

He slipped out of bed, skirting the kitchen table on his way to the door and padding barefoot down the hall to the music room. The cigarettes were in his bag; he slipped the half-empty pack into his pocket. Then, almost as an afterthought, he glanced at the cell phone he had left lying on the table.

The light was blinking. Three missed calls. All from the same unfamiliar number, all within the last ten minutes. Teru highlighted the number and hit redial.

"Hello?"

"Hello. I had a call from this number...?"

"Teru?"

"Chizuru? I mean, Ms. Sakata?"

"Chizuru," she corrected him. "Are you with Rei?"

"No. I mean, yes. I mean, I'm here, but he's asleep."

"Already?"

"We had a couple of drinks," Teru stammered, like a kid having to explain to his girlfriend's father why he'd kept her out past curfew. "We were in the studio all day, and..."

"Alcohol and painkillers." She sighed. "And let me guess, no dinner?"

"No," Teru admitted. "How did you get this number?"

"I tried to give you *my* number months ago."

Teru cringed at the memory. "I guess I was busy. I—"

"Look," Chizuru said, "I'm not mad. But there are some things I need to talk to you about. You're there now more than I am, and—"

Teru glanced over his shoulder at the closed, silent door. He lowered his voice. "Now?"

"How about tomorrow?" she said. "If you can get away."

———✳———

Teru met her in a coffee shop in Shibuya. He'd told Rei he was going home to get a few more changes of clothes. That wouldn't give him a lot of time to sit around and chat, but Chizuru knew a place inside the station, on an upper floor of the Tokyu Department Store that could be accessed without taking a step outside.

She was waiting for him with two cups of coffee and a plastic binder. "Thanks for coming," she said. "Was he okay last night?"

"Fine," Teru said.

"Good." Chizuru frowned. "He's not really supposed to drink, you know."

"He's an adult. We had a long day. I—"

"I know you don't have a lot of time. Can I be honest?" She leaned over the table, lowering her voice as though confiding a secret. "Rei is... he needs a lot of help."

"I know that."

Chizuru shook her head. "I don't know if you do. He lies, hides it as well as he can. I'd be surprised if he's honest with his doctors. Sometimes I think he's trying to hurt himself. Refusing treatments, skipping appointments, refusing to take his meds or even a goddamn taxi."

"I could get a driver's license," Teru suggested. He'd been thinking about it anyway. He had never really had the money or the need before, but now that he had both.... "I wouldn't mind."

"He could hire a chauffer," Chizuru said. "He won't. There are other things he could do, though, with that money. It is the twenty-first century, now, isn't it? They could build him a new nose, do some more work on that eyelid. But it wouldn't live up to his impossible standards. And I can't get a word in edgewise about that arm."

"Why?" Teru asked. "What's wrong with it?"

"Nothing you don't already know. He's got no function, no feeling but constant pain. It's a dead weight on his neck and back, though, and his doctors think they can relieve some of the pain if they amputate."

"Amputate?" Teru had never heard that word in any sense that wouldn't be horrifying—something to avoid at all cost, to pity. Not something anyone would want.

"You sound exactly like he did. Here." Chizuru pushed the binder across the table. Teru opened it, flipped through the pages. They were test results, X-rays, copies of old prescriptions. Most of it might as well have been in a foreign language.

"What am I supposed to do with this?" he asked. "I'm not a nurse."

"Neither am I." Chizuru laughed. "I was a beautician. Can you imagine?" She ran her fingers through her mousy, unkempt hair. She wore no makeup; her nails were bitten to the quick. "I haven't styled anything but those damn wigs in years."

Teru closed the file. "Why do you do this, then?"

Chizuru picked up her coffee, swirling it in the mug like a tumbler of brandy. "Rei wasn't the only one who had his world destroyed that night," she said softly. "Aeternum. Stupid name for a band. 'Eternity'? Some eternity they got.

"Rei hated me, you know, and the feeling was pretty much mutual. I was dating *his* bassist. I was going to break up *his* band." She shook her head, and her voice softened as her gaze grew distant. "It was Taka's mother who called me, told me to leave now, don't bother to change.

"We had to get to the hospital," Chizuru went on. "Had to say goodbye. It—" her voice cracked, and Teru felt it like a fracture running through him. "It was too late, though. He was already gone when we got there.

"They all had families, the four who died. They came, they cried, they took them home." She shook her head. "No one came for Rei. Saki was smart—he dropped out of law school to join that band. Did you know that?"

Teru shook his head. He knew nothing about Saki, except that Rei had loved him, and now he was gone.

"He'd taken care of everything: the apartment, the insurance, the money in his account. It was all willed to Rei, the week they moved in together. His parents fought the will—it was their money to begin with, but Saki was an adult and everything was in his name. The other driver's insurance covered the hospital bills. No matter what Rei told you, it wasn't technically his fault."

"It wasn't?" That shouldn't have been a relief. People made mistakes—sometimes even fatal ones—and Teru knew that didn't make them bad people. But if it wasn't Rei's fault, if Rei could somehow believe it... That was hope, at least, of a kind.

"The other car drove over the medium, plowed into the side of their van. They went over the guardrail. There was an explosion, a fire. None of them should have survived. The police, the insurance companies... no one ever blamed him. Except me"—she smiled sadly—"when there was no one else left alive to blame.

"I felt guilty, for blaming him. For surviving myself. For hating him for surviving too. And so when he was awake and coherent enough to talk about it, I started taking his songs to the record labels, selling them to pay for everything insurance didn't cover. When he was finally released, after more than a year, I came back to Tokyo with him. What else could I do? My boyfriend was dead, my job long gone. It was stay or go back to my parents' house, and he wasn't going to last a week on his own."

"Thank you." It wasn't enough, but Teru didn't know what else he could say. "I—"

"Forget it," she said. "That was almost six years ago. I did what I had to, but... I can't anymore. I'll be his assistant, his manager, whatever you want to call it, but I can't keep staying up at night wondering if he's eating or sleeping or lonely or in pain. I need to move on, and I don't know if he ever will. But I think if he does, it'll be with you."

No pressure, right? "What do you want me to do?"

"Take care of him. Make him take care of himself. He

actually listens to you."

"I don't know about that." Teru didn't think Rei really listened to anyone.

"He loves you."

Loves. He shook his head in protest, or maybe denial.

"He cares what you think."

"I guess." And even though he wasn't sure of even that, Teru slipped the binder into his bag.

"He's supposed to go to the pain clinic on Friday," Chizuru added. "See if you can get him to show up. And Teru?"

"Yeah?"

"Try not to lose my number this time."

Chapter 24

They took Friday off, and Teru walked with Rei—who had been surprisingly agreeable about the whole thing—to the Meguro Ekimae Pain Clinic. The waiting room was full of older people—grandmothers hunched over walkers and old men grumbling to themselves as they watched the clock. The air had an antiseptic tang to it, and tinny muzak piped in over the PA system gave the place a sense of timelessness, like you could wait forever and never be called.

Rei disappeared eventually into one of the treatment rooms, but Teru stayed behind, tapping his foot to the song in his head and flipping through back-issue magazines. "Top Ten Post-Retirement Investments." "Better Living After Sixty." There were a few newsmagazines as well, and a handful of battered children's books that seemed out of place in such an astringent setting. Teru hoped their readers were the children and grandchildren of patients, and not patients themselves.

"Was everything okay?" Teru asked when it was over.

"Fine."

That was all either of them had to say.

———※———

Teru decided to tell his friends that Saturday. Minori

had called them out for a dinner meeting, and it would be easy enough for Teru to slip his own news—or confession—into that conversation, rather than dealing with each of his bandmates on their own.

As always, Rei was invited. As usual, he declined, and Teru made no effort to change his mind. "I'll see you later," he said, letting his fingers brush Rei's over the mixing board and wondering if next time, once everyone knew, he would be able to do something more.

He felt good about it until they sat down at the restaurant. The first item on Minori's agenda, apparently, was his deep dislike for Saki's song.

"We've got eight tracks," Minori said, "and two more to lay down next week. I say we make that one. Either that, or re-record something."

Nao and Yasu nodded their agreement. Teru glanced at Seika, but he only looked away.

"Teru, can I get you to talk to Rei?"

"I guess," Teru said. "But are you sure? I kind of like it."

Minori frowned. "I like it too. But it sounds like 80s metal. It doesn't belong on this album, and it doesn't sound like this band. We're supposed to be moving forward, not going back in time. Now, as far as the schedule..." He took out a sheaf of papers and passed them around. The issue of the song, it appeared, had been settled.

"Most of these dates you already know. Neurosis next week, Rock Eden the week after that. We're doing the countdown again this year"—Teru had to stop himself from cringing; he didn't like the idea of leaving Rei alone on New

Year's Eve—"and Vicinity on January fifth is a three-man."

"A three-man?" Yasu sounded surprised. "Are we selling enough tickets for that?"

"I think we will be by then," said Minori. "The album should be ready for release in... early December? Unless we want to deliberately push it back. Crisis Cross comes out on the twenty-third."

"We need to ask the producer," Seika added, giving Teru a sidelong glance.

"I agree." Minori nodded. "Look, Teru, I hate to ask you to be the one to deal with this, but if we're going to work with Rei, he needs to work with us. If he won't, or can't, or whatever... well, I don't see the need to make things more complicated than they already are."

Teru nodded and reached for a glass of water; his throat was suddenly dry. "Okay," he said. "I'll talk to him."

"Just give him my phone number," Minori said. "If he's going to manage us or produce us or—fuck." His cell phone started buzzing on the table, and he picked it up with a frown. "Sorry, guys. I've got to get this."

"What's up with him?" Yasu asked as Minori disappeared into the men's room.

He was only gone for a couple of minutes, but it was long enough to break whatever rhythm the meeting had had. He kept looking at his phone, even after he got back, and seemed to have completely forgotten about the issues he had with Rei.

"So, next week's set list," Minori said, absently handing a set of photocopies around the table, "and recording again on Monday. If no one has any questions"—he glanced again at his phone—"I guess we can call it a day."

Teru could have stayed silent. For a moment, looking at the tired faces of his bandmates around the table, he almost did. But when he thought of Rei, of the way he stepped out of his comfort zone every time they left the house together, the way he believed in Teru and trusted him—with his music, with his face, with Saki—saying nothing at all felt like too much of a lie.

"I, um. I've got something," he said.

All eyes turned to Teru; a hot flush spread across his face. He shrugged, looked down at the table, moved his water glass a centimeter to the left. "It's not a question or anything."

"What's wrong?" Yasu asked.

"Nothing!" Teru said. "I mean, it's nothing bad. It's just... I'm, uh...seeing someone."

Yasu laughed. "I knew it! Congratulations! I—"

"No. It's not Kiyomi. It's..." He took a deep breath. "It's Rei. I'm... seeing Rei. I just thought you should know."

He breathed in. He breathed out. His friends said nothing at all. Teru closed his eyes. An eternity passed. And then a friendly voice broke the silence.

"Congratulations," Seika said. Teru looked up; he was smiling, as if at an inside joke, and Teru couldn't help but crack a half-smile back.

"That's great." Nao spoke up next. "Congratulations."

Yasu's eyes grew wide. "Wow," he said. "That's... does Kiyomi know?"

Teru shook his head. "Tomorrow. Please don't tell her before then."

"Shit," Yasu said. "How *old* is he, anyway?"

Teru would have laughed, if he hadn't wanted to cry. "Not that much older than we are," he said, although that wasn't exactly true.

Minori gave him a thin-lipped smile. "Okay."

"That's it?" Seika scolded.

"Yeah. That's it." He took the check from the table and glanced at the amount. "The band'll cover it. Yeah. Okay."

Teru came home to the sound of his own voice, belting out one of La Rose's ballads from the music room. "What do you think?" Rei asked, as he dragged a couple of tracks into the workspace. "This one? Or this one?"

The two versions weren't exactly the same, but Teru wasn't sure they were different enough for either to be considered better. "I guess I like the first one."

"Ah." Rei nodded and continued with his work, giving no indication as to whether Teru's answer had been correct.

"Do you have a minute?" Teru asked. "We've got some new shows booked. A three-man in January."

Rei stopped the music and swiveled his chair around. "By this time next year you will be the only band on that stage."

"That would be nice." Teru tried, but not as hard as he could have, to keep the tired, sarcastic edge from his voice.

"Is something wrong?"

"Not really." Teru shook his head. "I'm just..." *I'm just fucking exhausted.* "Minori keeps asking me to get you to these meetings. You know the guys don't care about..." He waved his hand in a vague gesture that he hoped encompassed everything.

"I care," Rei said quietly. "You know that."

"But don't you want more of a say on what we do with your songs? And you could help us with things like this." Teru tossed the schedule to the table. "You did this before, right? Your band was pretty big. You must know where we should play, what we should do, how we should promote ourselves."

"You know nothing about that band."

"Rei..." Teru pressed his fingers against his temples, suddenly aware that his head was pounding and not quite sure when it had begun. "Why does this make you so mad? They want you to help. They value your opinion!"

"And I am happy to give it."

"But you'll barely talk to anyone but me! Nobody cares what you look like. You did it, okay? You proved yourself with your music. Wasn't that what you wanted? Fuck..." Teru shook his head. "You don't even know what you want.

"Oh, and by the way," he added as he got to his feet, suddenly spiteful, suddenly wanting to hurt Rei, to make him understand this frustration. "They're not going to play that song, you know. They don't want it on the album."

He was almost to the door when Rei spoke. "Why not?"

"It's old. It's out of date. You know that as well as they do."

"It is an album. Every song does not need to sound the same."

"No," Teru agreed, "but every song needs to sound like it belongs to this band."

"They are ungrateful."

"What do they have to be grateful for? None of them asked for your help, Rei. How would you have felt if a stranger showed up at your rehearsals and started telling you what to sing?"

"I have helped you."

"Yes, you have. And I appreciate it, because I don't care what I sing as long as it's brilliant. But there are five people in that band. Five careers. Are you thinking of any of them? Because if you were, I think you'd want to make the best possible album for *them*, not for you."

"You... agreed with them?"

"No." Teru slammed his hand into the closed door. "No, damn it. I stuck up for you, even though I had no reason to. Even though I know they're right, and the only reason you want that song on the album is because... because your dead lover wrote it, and—"

"Go."

"I'm going!" Teru whirled around, surprised at both the strength in his own voice and the fury in Rei's eyes. "Look, Rei, I get it. I do. If you were dead, and I were the only person who could keep your music alive—"

"I am dead!" Rei roared. He rose, took a staggering step forward, and fell, trembling, against the coffee table. "I am dead," he repeated. "And you are the only one who can keep this music alive."

Teru closed his eyes, forced himself to turn away. He wanted to go to Rei, to make sure he wasn't hurt. But he couldn't. He opened the door and ran to the bedroom, where he collapsed onto the bed, awake but unthinking, in a daze.

He was dimly aware that a lot of time had passed when

he heard the door open and slow, shuffling footsteps enter the room.

"Teru?"

He rolled over, opened his eyes. "Are you all right?"

"I should apologize."

"No." Teru sat up. "I'm sorry. I had a bad day. I shouldn't have taken it out on you."

"You were right." Rei limped to the edge of the bed, wincing as his cane and his wrist took the brunt of his weight. "I have been thinking of myself first." He sat, and Teru inched over to sit beside him.

"What should we do?"

"Forget about it. There will be other albums. Other shows."

Teru nodded. "Are you sure you're all right?"

"I'm more concerned about you."

"I'm fine," Teru said. "It's just... I told them about us."

"And?"

Teru frowned. "Seika had already figured it out. Nao had no reason to care. But Yasu was weirded out, I guess. And I think Minori was mad. This band is his baby. I guess I kind of get it, but..."

"It hurts."

"Yeah." Teru nodded. "It does."

—⋟⋞—

Kiyomi was waiting for him at Shibuya Station, a halfway point between their apartments whether Teru was coming from Nakano, which she believed, or Meguro, which he actually was. She was dressed for a date, her hair pulled back with a simple clip, pierced earrings catching the warm October sunlight as a breeze teased the hem of her skirt. She saw him across the plaza and stood on her toes to wave.

"Long time no see!" She smiled. Teru tried to smile back, but his face felt like molded plastic. Kiyomi held out her hand to take his, but hesitated at the last minute and reached up, pushing a strand of hair out of her face instead.

"Yeah," Teru agreed. "It's been awhile, hasn't it?"

Kiyomi shook her head. "You've been busy. I was surprised to hear from you. In a good way, of course," she added quickly.

"Look, Kiyomi, this isn't a date. There's something I need to talk to you about. Can we sit down somewhere? My treat."

There was a Starbucks on the second floor across the street. Teru bought a coffee for himself and a nonfat iced latte for Kiyomi, and when two seats at the counter facing the window opened up, they took them. Side by side, they watched the people swarm across the infamous pedestrian scramble—orderly lines that only looked like madness, Teru thought, when you were in the middle of it.

"So," Kiyomi asked. "What *was* the purpose of this non-date?"

Teru took a deep breath. He wouldn't be doing her any favors by dragging this out any longer. "Kiyomi, I can't... I can't see you anymore." He couldn't look at her face, couldn't stand to see her reaction.

"Why not?" she whispered.

"I'm seeing someone else."

There was a very long pause. The pedestrian light

259

turned red, and cars surged through the intersection. The voices of the other customers seemed to swell to a roar. Out of the corner of his eye, Teru watched Kiyomi's hand squeeze her plastic cup a little too hard, denting it and causing a bead of perspiration to slide onto her perfect pink fingernail.

"What?"

"I'm seeing someone else." It was easier the second time. "I'm sorry. I never... I never meant to lead you on."

"Someone else," she repeated. "Who? Why? Since when?" Her voice rose with each question until it threatened to break.

"It's Rei."

Kiyomi froze. Her entire body trembled, and then something in her snapped. She slammed her drink down, dislodging the lid and sloshing coffee over the counter and to the floor. Then she stood and walked out with her head held high, leaving Teru to clean up the mess on his own.

He was on his fifth handful of napkins and about his twentieth apology to the couple on the other side of the mess when she returned. "When?" she hissed. "Was it when you were seeing me? Or..." She threw his studded bracelet at him; it missed and landed on the floor. "I carried that *around* with me! How could you let me...? Just... give it back!" she cried, and took his necklace—the one she had given him—in her bare hand. She pulled at the chain and it shattered, falling into the spilt coffee like ruins sliding into the sea.

"Give it back!" she sobbed as she ran again from the Starbucks. "Just give it all back!"

Teru wished with all his heart that he could.

—⋙⋘—

Their next show was at Neurosis, a smaller live house in the suburbs of Saitama. Minori brought the van, and they parked in an hourly lot, changing and doing their makeup in the backseat as they reviewed rough versions of the album tracks on the car's CD player. The venue was tiny; the merch tables were set up in the back of the hall, in front of the window where customers could exchange their drink tickets for something from the bar. It reminded Teru of the places he had played back in Niigata—inconvenient, but there'd been something fun about those good old days, too.

He had left Rei in bed, reclining on a mountain of pillows and painstakingly rewriting lyrics by hand. The pain, he claimed, was always worse during typhoon season, but Teru still worried. He had run to the supermarket for boil-in-the-bag rice porridge and umeboshi. "It is not the flu," Rei had scolded him, but he'd eaten it.

"Are you're sure you'll be okay?" Teru had asked. But neither of them had seriously entertained the idea of his missing the show.

Now Minori was striding across the parking lot with a piece of paper in his hand, calling Teru's name as loudly as he could without drawing the attention of the neighborhood.

"What's that?" Teru asked.

"Guest list. You invite anyone?"

He meant Rei, of course. Teru shook his head. "Not tonight."

"How about Kiyomi?"

"Kiyomi?" Teru hadn't spoken to her since she'd stormed out of the coffee shop a week ago. "I, uh... don't know. Hasn't anyone else talked to her?"

"Put her down," Yasu interjected from the back of the van. "A staff pass doesn't cost us anything, and if she doesn't show we'll sell the stuff ourselves. That's all the reservations?" He pulled a second sheet from beneath the guest list with a frown.

"Thorne's at Vicinity," Nao offered. "Bigger venue, better location, lots of overlap in fans...."

Minori nodded, apparently no more upset than if Nao had commented on the weather. "Maybe," he said. "Let's worry about the show. We rehearse in an hour; our set's at seven forty-five. No personal drama tonight, okay?"

It was at four fifty, with only ten minutes until the doors opened to the public, that Kiyomi strode into the live house with her teeth gritted and her head held high. She didn't look at Teru, refused to make eye contact even when he glanced her way. "Sorry I'm late," she said to Minori. "This is my last night, okay?"

Minori nodded. "Fine. I understand."

The stage at Neurosis was small, and more than once Teru narrowly missed colliding with a guitar head as he worked the crowd as well as he could in such close quarters. But the size of the venue also worked to their advantage; it was harder for the fans of the other bands to sit down and ignore them when, even toward the back of the hall, they were only a few meters from the stage. Until the moment the stage lights went up, Teru's head was heavy with thoughts of Rei, of Kiyomi, of the band, and of the inconvenience his personal life had caused them—but when the opening strains of the first song wailed into the darkness, that grief was channeled into an anguish that sent his voice into heavenly peals of despair.

"Nice set," Minori offered begrudgingly when they sat down to dinner after the show. They hadn't turned a great profit, but the stack of questionnaires in the middle of the table was thick, and there wasn't a negative comment to be found. "You heard Kiyomi quit?" Minori looked around the table, and the others nodded.

"What are we going to do?" Nao asked. "I don't mind doing that stuff myself, but we've got a lot of shows coming up, and..."

"All right." Minori frowned. He pulled out a stack of postcards and a list of names and addresses. "We were planning to send these out anyway. Make a note at the bottom when you write the address. See if we can't recruit someone, at least for now."

Teru picked up the first card on his stack. They were simple but well made, with a photo of the band above their upcoming schedule. Beside next week's show was a note: *Important Announcement!* They were planning to announce the album's release then, but no one would know until the end of the set whether the announcement was good or bad. Breakups, at least in the world of visual kei, were Important Announcements too.

The three-man in January had a note beside it, too. Since there would only be three bands, they'd play a longer set than usual and there would probably be an uchiage with the fans afterwards. "Vicinity," Teru read aloud. "Takadanobaba." A chill ran up his spine. "January fifth."

"Is something wrong?" Seika asked. "That's not a mistake, is it?"

"No," Minori said. "January fifth. We talked about that. I thought everyone was available."

"I'm available." Teru shook his head. "It's fine."

"You're pale," said Seika. "Is everything all right?"

"Of course," Teru said, too quickly. *Of course it's not. That was the night of the accident.* He couldn't leave Rei alone on that of all nights. But there wasn't much of a choice, was there? It wasn't like Rei was suicidal—if he was going to do something drastic on the anniversary, he'd had five opportunities before. And Teru only knew the date because he'd seen it in the stairwell; if Rei had wanted special attention that night, he would have mentioned it himself, wouldn't he? Teru told himself that, but as he filled in the addresses on the postcards, adding "Staff and Roadies Wanted" under the schedule, his thoughts were full of Rei, lying in bed with a storm raging through his broken body. Suddenly, he wanted to go home.

"Done." He pushed the postcards across the table. "Look, I'm kind of tired. Do you mind if I—"

"Let's call it a night." Minori nodded his agreement. "Does anyone want a ride?"

Teru glanced out the window. The trees lining the parking lot were tossing in the wind. It wasn't raining yet, but it almost definitely would be by the time he got back to Rei's.

"Can I get a ride to the station?" he asked. "Just to the closest station to wherever we are now?"

"You sure?" Yasu frowned. "You're going to get soaked."

That was probably true. But Teru didn't like the idea of giving out Rei's address, didn't like the idea of admitting he'd been sleeping there more often than not, and definitely didn't like the idea of answering any questions the guys might have along the way. "Yeah," he said. "I need to do some shopping on the way home."

That wasn't entirely a lie. He bought a can of beer and a plastic umbrella at the supermarket and, lancing with the umbrella against the sideways-falling rain, made his miserable, exhausted way home. His hair was plastered against his forehead and cheeks by the time he reached the apartment, his socks soaked through the soles of his boots.

"Rei?" he called into the darkness. "I'm home."

There was no reply. Teru had wanted to show Rei the postcard, talk to him about the show—but if he'd managed to get to sleep, that was good news as far as the pain. But the bed was empty, and as Teru peeled the rain-soaked plastic bag from the can and took what he thought was a well-deserved drink, he heard the strains of a complicated keyboard solo from the music room.

"Rei?" He opened the door slowly, trying not to interrupt, but as he let it close behind him, Rei balled his hand into a fist and brought it crashing down on the keyboard with an electronic scream. Teru jumped. "I'm sorry. I can go."

Rei flexed his wrist back and forth, then around in a circle. Silently, he bowed his head.

"Rei?" Teru tried again. "Are you okay?"

"I am fine," Rei replied, but his voice was strained.

"Are you sure?"

"It is the weather." Rei looked up. "Your show went well?"

"Yeah." Teru sat on the sofa, took a sip of his beer and then, on second thought, stood up again and offered the can to Rei.

"Thank you," he said, but handed it back after a single sip.

"Is that for the album?" Teru asked.

"Yes."

"Is there anything I can do?"

"No," Rei whispered, rotating his wrist again. "When the storm passes..."

"When the storm passes," Teru echoed. "Right."

Chapter 25

The storm passed. The skies brightened and the weather cooled; the maple and gingko leaves began to shine in shades of red and yellow. Rei grudgingly allowed Teru to wrap his wrist in drugstore bandages and apply medicated patches intended for muscle aches and fatigue. He wouldn't see a doctor. "What is the point?" he asked, when Teru suggested it. "They will only tell me to stop playing, stop typing, stop using the cane. That is not an option," he declared coldly, but he limped around the apartment without it as much as possible, and when he went out it was with the aid of a forearm crutch, carefully concealed under his robes, that he had dug out of the piles of junk in the bedroom.

Teru worried, but there wasn't a lot he could do. Rei was right—he couldn't stop using the computer or the keyboard, not if they wanted to make the December release date. And if it was him, in Rei's place, he wasn't sure he'd want to hear what a doctor had to say either.

The day before the show, Teru quit his job at the CombiMart. It wasn't planned; he'd come in for a four-hour shift and to turn in his availability for the next two weeks. His manager frowned when he handed in the crumpled sheet of paper; half of the dates he had originally marked as available had been crossed out to make room for rehearsals, meetings, and running errands for Rei.

"This all?" he asked.

"Yes, sir." Teru bowed in apology. "I've been really busy with the band."

"Minimum three days a week." The manager pointed to the help wanted sign in the window. "That was the deal. How about next Tuesday?"

Next Tuesday they were scheduled to hand out flyers in Harajuku. "Look," Teru said, "how much notice would you need if I wanted to quit?"

"Given how little we've been able to rely on you these days? Just about any time would be fine. No hard feelings, Ijima. You're a good worker. If that band of yours doesn't work out, you're welcome back anytime."

"Thanks." Teru shrugged out of his uniform. "I'll keep that in mind." He smiled, but his hands shook as he entered his code into the time clock. That was it. He was officially unemployed.

—⋇—

The next day started on a good note. Teru woke to an empty bed, but he found Rei in the music room looking refreshed, as if he'd actually had a good night's sleep. They ran through the evening's set, and when it was over Rei smiled. "You have come so far," he said, "and you will go far still."

"I better." Teru laughed nervously.

"Don't worry about your job. You made the right choice. Our music is all that matters now."

268

They ran through the announcement Rei had written about the album, then showered and dressed. At eleven, Rei asked Teru to lock the door behind him when he left. "I am going ahead. I will see you at rehearsal."

"We can go together," Teru suggested. "If you want."

"No, thank you," Rei replied. "Your friends are good people. But there will be others there. There are still some who remember me... the way I was." He shook his head, as if to clear away the memory. "Chizuru will let me in. I will see you after the show."

"Sure," Teru said. "After the show."

———————

An hour later, he sat at the mirror, plucking his eyebrows as Yasu's reflection looked on. "What are you laughing at?" Teru asked.

"You." Yasu snickered. "Preening like a girl."

"You do it too."

"I know." Yasu dug around in his guitar case. "But it's funnier when you do it." He laid his guitar in his lap and snipped the first of the old strings with a wire cutter. The two pieces flew into the air and hung there, bouncing back and forth. "What are you so happy about, anyway?"

"Happy?" Teru shrugged. "I don't know. Just the album, I guess. And we haven't played here for awhile."

"Yeah?"

"What do you mean, yeah? You know I like this place."

"Yes, I do." Yasu wound the old strings into a loop, twisting one end under the other to make a circle, and slipped the now-useless wires into his case. He shook his head. "This is fucking hard for me, man. It's weird to think of you with him. I mean, as long as you're happy—"

"I am."

"Okay. Good. That's all I meant, I guess."

Yasu didn't look like he was done, though; he didn't break eye contact in the mirror even though his fingers kept on restringing his guitar. Teru never found out what he wanted to ask, though, because an exhausted-looking Minori, with red-rimmed eyes and hair sticking up in directions that even the strangest of bands wouldn't have deliberately gone for, walked into the room with a stranger in tow.

"Hey, guys," he said.

"Um, hey?" Yasu looked up. "What happened to you?"

Minori yawned. "I'm fine. I've got us some new staff, at least for the night."

"Hey." Teru nodded at the man. He was young, probably a couple of years younger than Teru, with short hair and casual, sporty clothes. "Have you, uh, been into visual kei long?"

"He's not," Minori answered. "He's my brother. Keisuke, this is Teru, Yasu."

"Hey," Yasu said. "You play?" He nodded to the half-strung guitar.

"Not lately." Keisuke shook his head. "I'm pretty busy, studying for university entrance exams."

Yasu nodded. "Cool," he said. "Your parents must be proud."

"No teasing." Minori scowled. "Keisuke's going to help carry our stuff and work the merch table until we find someone new."

"Thanks," Teru said. "We appreciate it."

"And you will appreciate it even more," Seika said as he swept into the room, managing to look like a drag queen even in sunglasses and sweats, "when I tell you we have *two* lovely young men on staff for the evening. Sung-Min?"

He was followed by a slim, attractive Korean man in a black T-shirt and tight-fitting jeans. "So, this is the band," he said, in slightly accented Japanese. "It's nice to meet you at last."

Yasu whistled. "So that's why you live in Koreatown."

"Believe it or not," Seika said, "it actually *was* because of the rent. Meeting Sung-Min was a pleasant coincidence."

"I, um, didn't know you were seeing anyone," Teru stammered.

"He means," said Yasu, "that he thought you were a hopeless playboy."

"Sung-Min thinks visual kei is ridiculous." Seika shook his head in mock severity. "And having him around would be terrible publicity. But yes"—he lowered his voice and smiled—"we've been together for almost three years."

Teru wasn't sure how anyone who thought visual kei was ridiculous could be with someone who looked like Seika... but then again, he supposed he did know what it was like to fall for someone you never would have expected to be your ideal. "That's great." He smiled. "Thanks, both of you. It's a big help."

It was; for a band that had never had roadies, having someone to carry their luggage felt like one step closer to stardom. Once upon a time, Teru had been nervous about playing here. Now, as he ascended the stairs and stood onstage, soaking up the excitement of the crowd, it felt like nothing so much as coming home.

"Good evening, Meguro!" he cried, and the crowd—three or four rows of them now—cried wordlessly in return.

They launched immediately into the first song, one of Yasu's hard rock numbers that Teru had struggled so much with. He still couldn't scream like Bara could, but he'd figured out how to half-shout the heavier sections and sing his way through the rest. It didn't sound the same, but Yasu swore he liked it better, and if the sheer volume of the crowd was any indication, the fans more or less agreed.

The song finished on a triumphant note and Seika, without missing a beat, plunged into the intro for the next. Teru whispered into the mic as Rei had instructed him, his voice barely audible over the throbbing bass. "Tonight," he said, "we have a very important announcement to make. But first..." He turned and raised his hand, letting the spotlight rain down on him as he smiled at Nao behind the drums. "'Phoenix.'"

It was one of Rei's more difficult songs, and they didn't play it often, but it was one of the most requested on their questionnaires. Rei had never told him what the song was about, but Teru had always assumed it was for Saki.

"Rise," he pleaded over the pounding drumline. "Rise!" It didn't matter who the lyrics were meant for; Teru sang them up to the balcony, for Rei.

Sweat poured down his face and slicked his palms; he replaced the microphone on its stand and retreated upstage to take a drink of water and blot at his face with a towel. This was necessary, but also calculated. Make the audience wonder. Make them think.

When he took the mic again, the crowd went silent. "We stand at the beginning of a new era," he said. "Is it a beginning, or an end? Only time will tell."

They played two songs back-to-back then, a love song of Minori's and "Yami no hanabira." Then the lights went down, and Teru lowered his head. "An important announcement," he repeated, in the ambiguous voice he had practiced, still giving no hint as to whether the news would be good or bad. "On December twenty-first..."

"What?" someone cried.

"Tell us!"

"La Rose Verboten..."

"We love you!"

"...will release a new album. And from that album..." He raised his face to look directly at the spotlight. "A new song. 'Sacrament.'"

He tore the mic from its stand, relinquishing center stage to Minori and Yasu, who wailed back-to-back on the intro as the lights strobed red. Teru looked out into the audience, took a deep breath, and began.

"Akatsuki no hikari
Karada wo nazoru.
Yuuyami wa terasu
Chi mamire no sekai."
Morning rays of light
Trace your body.
Dusk illuminates
A bloody world.

"Hitori ni nari."

I'm alone.

"Confession at your altar."

Teru understood the English words only as Rei had explained them to him, but they had drilled the pronunciation until he could sing them with almost as much confidence as the Japanese. The guitars and bass swelled, and Teru raised his voice to match.

"Drink my blood unholy,
My Sacrament."

The next verse was faster, with a drumline like blood in Teru's ears. It was fast enough, passionate enough to headbang to, but the audience was still and silent, listening.

"Hakaba no yuuhi
Kokoro wo tsutsumu
Asu nado
Kiyashinai,"

Dusk in the graveyard
Envelops my heart
Tomorrow
Will come no more.

"Hitori ni nari,
Mienai, your altar."

I'm alone, I can't see your altar.

"Dry my blood unholy,
My Sacrament."

The crowd screamed. The lights shone down. Teru fell to his knees and dropped the mic, sending a peal of feedback from the speakers like a sigh.

—⟶⟵—

"That was some show." Seika smiled at him in the mirror. "And a brilliant song."

"Thanks," Teru said, but Seika's smile faded to a thoughtful frown.

"I remember them, you know. Aeternum."

Teru whirled around, his heart pounding. "You do? Why didn't you say so?"

"I didn't know them. Never saw them play, that I can remember. I didn't know Rei was one of them, at first. Everyone said they all died. But I remember when it happened—an entire band wiped out in a single night. It was big news, at least in the scene at the time. Do you think he wrote that song for them?"

"I don't know," Teru admitted. "I'm not sure what he wrote before, and what after."

Seika nodded. "It's sad, either way."

Teru wasn't sure if he meant the song or the accident, but there was only one answer. "Yes," he said. "It is."

"What is?" Yasu stepped into the dressing room with a pen in one hand and a piece of paper in the other. "And before you answer that, can I put you both down for the uchiage?"

"We were just talking about the new song," Teru said. "And I don't know. Rei thinks—"

Yasu groaned. "Come on, just tell him you've got an important meeting or something. I used to lie to my ex all the time!"

"Yeah." Teru grinned. "Isn't that why she broke up with you?"

"No, she broke up with me because she met a guy with a six-pack and a recording contract." Yasu grimaced. "But, point taken. Seika?"

"He can't." It was Minori's brother Keisuke who answered. "None of you can. Didn't my brother tell you? We need to talk to you, after the show."

Seika frowned. "Is something wrong?"

"I think he wants to tell you himself."

"Okay." Seika nodded. "Did anyone tell Nao?"

Yasu shook his head. "I don't think so. He was up at the merch table with me and Sung-Min." He scratched out both names on the list. "I'll go tell him. Where's Minori?"

"I'm here," he said, slipping into the crowded room. "Kei told you?"

"He told us something." Seika frowned. "What's wrong?"

"I'd rather not talk about it here, if that's all right. Bring your boyfriend, if you want." Minori turned to Teru. "Yours too, if you think he'll come."

An hour later, they stood outside the izakaya: the five band members, Keisuke, Sung-Min, and Rei. At a glance, it was Keisuke and Sung-Min who stood out; they were the only ones with short hair and more mainstream taste in clothes. From a distance, Rei was just one of a very unusual crowd—one more colorful head of hair, one more black, unisex wardrobe.

A waiter showed them to a private room in the back, where they were to remove their shoes and place them into lockers.

"This too," Rei whispered, and handed Teru the crutch

he'd been using instead of the cane. Teru raised his eyebrows; a wordless question.

Rei looked away; a wordless answer.

They filed into the room with their arms linked, Rei leaning on Teru and Teru directing as much of the weight onto his elbow and shoulder, away from his wrist, as he could.

"Everything okay?" Minori asked, and Teru nodded.

"Fine."

Rei said nothing. He took a seat against the wall, with Teru on his left—as hidden as he could be in this crowd. The room was Japanese-style, with a hori-kotatsu, an opening under the table allowing customers to adopt a more Western-style position instead of sitting on their feet seiza style on the floor. Even so, Rei had to lean heavily on Teru to get both legs under the table, and Teru didn't want to think too much about having to get out again after a couple of drinks.

"All right," Minori said, when the waiter had left with their order. "I don't want to drag this out. You guys played a hell of a show tonight—and a hell of a song." He nodded at Rei, but the expression on his face was grim. "That was the best turnout we've ever seen."

"'Important Announcement,'" Yasu joked. "Does it every time."

"Yeah. Look, I just wanted to make that clear. What I'm about to say has nothing to do with Bara, or Thorne, or any of our fans. And it has nothing to do with you."

Yasu froze, his cigarette halfway to his mouth. "What has nothing do with us?"

"I'm quitting," Minori said. "The three-man in

January's my last show."

That didn't make sense. "You can't," Teru whispered, disbelieving. "We were doing so well."

"What about the album?" asked Nao.

"We're putting out the album. I'll play the show. I'm not going to walk out on my commitments here, but I've got family commitments"—Minori glanced at Keisuke—"that I've got to take care of as well."

"Why don't we call a hiatus?" Seika suggested, leaning across the table to look Minori and Keisuke in the eye. "We could all use a break, and when things calm down..."

"That sounds all right." Yasu nodded.

For a moment, the air in the room seemed to lighten—but Minori only shook his head.

"Things aren't just going to calm down," he said. "You know I'm my parents' oldest son. I've been supposed to take over my dad's business since before I was conceived... until I decided to go to music school instead. They let me. They supported my dreams. And now we're being run out of business by supermarkets and home centers, and we're going to lose the house and the store if I don't start making some money. It's time for me to get a real job. Start pulling my weight as the heir."

"I'm sorry," said Nao. "I didn't realize."

Minori shook his head. "It's all right. I know I've been a jerk lately. I've known this was coming for a while. But I can't ask my mom to wait tables, or Kei to give up on college. It's time for me to grow up, I guess."

"All right." Yasu nodded slowly. "If you're sure that's what you've got to do."

278

The waiter returned with the beers, and they toasted the night's success with voices that were far from cheery. The show, the crowd, the song itself seemed a million years away.

"What are we going to do?" Teru asked.

Minori tried to smile. "It's up to you. If you want to keep going you can keep my songs, keep the name. Find another guitarist or rescore the songs for Yasu alone. Let's be honest," he said with a bitter laugh, "this hasn't been my band for awhile."

"We can't do that," Seika said. "It is your band. It wouldn't be right."

"Then break up." Minori sighed. "I'm sorry. Kei's going to take his exams in January and there'll be tuition to pay, things to take care of at home. I can't ask my dad to deal with everything alone while I'm off pretending to be a rock star. No offense," he added. "It's been great."

"Yeah," Teru whispered into his beer. "Right."

Beside him, Rei said nothing at all.

—✳—

"You're not even upset," Teru accused him when they got home.

"Why should I be?"

"Everything we've worked for is falling apart, and—"

"I fail to see that."

"And you're just going to sit at the computer and work like nothing happened? Fuck..." Teru sighed. "At least let me wrap your wrist, and take your goddamn medicine."

"I am fine." Rei opened his music program and pulled up one of the guitar tracks, setting it to play at full volume.

"You are not!" Teru cried. "You are not fine, and nothing is fine right now!"

"You're drunk. Go to bed."

"I'm not. And how can you say that? It's your music, isn't it? Your dream?"

Rei sighed. "Minori is a fine guitarist. But there are thousands of talented guitarists in this city."

"You just want to replace him?"

"Do I want to? No. It will take time. It will set us back. But in the end, it won't matter. My music. Your voice. That is all we need. The others... are replaceable."

"So that's what it comes down to? Your music, over everything else?"

"Yes."

Anger rose in Teru's throat. "Would you have replaced Saki?"

Rei turned back to the computer, dragged and dropped another track into the window, and hit play again. "No," he said at last, over the music. "There would have been no need. Saki chose his music over his family, as did I."

"You don't talk much about your family."

"Neither do you," Rei remarked coldly.

"That's true." Teru pulled an ottoman over and sat next to him. "I guess I don't. My mom didn't want me to move to Tokyo, and she hasn't really spoken to me since. My dad runs a propane gas company. Can you think of anything more boring? But it's safe. Recession-proof, right? And I was next in line, just like Minori." He shook his head. "They named me Masato—a correct person. A normal person. That was their dream. I named myself Teru because it was what I wanted. I wanted to shine."

"You will," Rei whispered, and then, "You do."

Teru frowned. "I feel bad. This was Minori's dream. He put this band together, and... I don't know. Maybe we ought to just quit. Move on. Let go."

"Don't say that." Rei spoke through clenched teeth. "Don't *ever* talk about giving up."

"I'm not talking about giving up. I love performing. I love your music. But I can't stand to see what it's doing to you. You don't eat, you don't sleep, you think you deserve to be in pain. You won't fucking stay off your ankle or see a doctor about your wrist. What the hell are we going to do if you fuck up what you've got left?"

"I," Rei said, "am producing an album. Your album, I might add. The album that will make you a star. You want to bandage my wrist so I can't play. You want to drug me so I can't *feel*. How is that any different, Teru? How is that any different from what you say will happen if you don't?"

"I don't... I don't know." Teru pressed a hand to his throbbing temple as he stood. "I don't know anything anymore. You do what you have to do. I'm going to take a walk."

Teru grabbed a hoodie from one of Rei's drawers and pulled it on over his T-shirt. The nights were getting cold, and he hadn't brought over much in the way of winter clothes. He stood on the sidewalk a block from the apartment, smoking. It was closer to dawn than to dusk; the city was dim. Teru's mind was blank, too drunk or too sleepy to think coherently about anything—about the band, about Rei, about where any of them were going from here.

He crushed the cigarette beneath his boot and headed down the hill, past the live house to the 24-hour convenience store. He bought a telephone card and stood outside, staring at the pay phone until he had worked up the courage to pick up the receiver, stick the card in the slot, and dial his parents' house in Niigata.

It rang once; Teru hung up. It was three in the morning, and no one there wanted to talk to him anyway.

—⸼—

Rei was still at the computer when Teru came home. He slipped out of the hoodie, tossed it into the washing machine, and lay down across the sofa. He wanted to fall asleep like that, listening to the music instead of whatever was going on in his head.

"You're back," Rei said, when the track reached its end.

Teru's eyes were closed; he could have pretended to be asleep, but he didn't. "Yeah."

"May I ask you something?"

"Sure."

"Would you give up your music for me?"

"Yes," Teru said, "if it came to that. But first I'd do whatever I could to make sure we could make our music together."

"I see." A pause. "Teru?"

"Yeah?"

"I will rest," Rei said, "when the album is done. For now... please, let me do this."

"Okay," Teru said, burying his face in the cushions. "Fine. That's"—he yawned—"That's a promise."

Chapter 26

It had been two weeks since Teru had been back to his apartment, and the place was starting to smell. There were only two windows, but he opened them both and turned on the bathroom ventilator as well. He hung his futon out to air on the balcony, noticing with a grimace the spots of mold that had started to grow on the bottom. There was another uncomfortable decision to make: Was he ever going to sleep here again, or could the futon be cut up and put out with the garbage?

He dusted, swept, and filled a couple of shopping bags with warmer clothes and sneakers. Satisfied that he had everything he needed or wanted, Teru brought the futon in, closed the windows and left with his clothes and as much trash as he could discreetly stuff into a convenience store garbage can.

At Shinjuku Station, Teru put his bags—minus the garbage—in a locker, and headed out the Southeast Exit to a music store he'd visited a couple of times before. He browsed the sheet music, glanced over the instruments and supplies, but he'd come for the bulletin board at the back, full of flyers from bands looking for musicians, and musicians looking for bands.

SINGER WANTED–Must love The Beatles!

Death Metal Band Seeking Dedicated Guitarist

Wanted: Drummer and Bassist for Luna Sea copy band

"There's a visual band."

Teru jumped at the sound of Yasu's voice behind him. "Don't laugh." He groaned. "You scared me. What are you doing here?"

"Looks like the same thing you are."

Teru looked at the visual band's flyer. "They're looking for a guitarist. You should give them a call."

"No thanks." Yasu snorted. "I did a session with this guy once"—he jabbed a finger at one of the names—"and trust me, once was more than enough."

"So, you're really thinking about it? Finding another band?"

"Yeah, maybe. It'd be nice if you and I could stay together, but the others..."

"You don't think Nao and Seika'll stick around?"

Yasu shrugged. "Nao's a kid. He's in school, lives with his parents. He might stick with it. I hope he does. But I also wouldn't be surprised if he doesn't. And Seika... he'll be doing this until he dies, but I think he'll be just as happy if he never makes it big."

"Really?"

"Just a guess. I'm going to pick up some strings while I'm here. You need anything?"

"No," Teru said. "Not here. I was going to go over to Tokyu Hands though, if you want to tag along?"

They walked around the station through an underpass, past walls of lockers, a Uniqlo, a travel agency. Two young women sat by the window in a Starbucks, their heads bent over a manga. They probably weren't a couple any more than the schoolgirl and the biker chick on the cover, but Teru thought it would be kind of nice if they were.

"So, was Rei pissed off the other night or what?"

"What?" Teru shook his head. "Oh, you mean about Minori? No. He said there were a hundred thousand decent guitarists in Tokyo and we'd find someone new. Like you guys are just replaceable."

"But not you?" Yasu joked.

"I'm already a replacement." Teru frowned. "He'd be singing this stuff himself if he could."

They rounded the corner, and the Takashimaya department store came into view. It was already decorated for Christmas; the tall columns surrounding the entrance were entwined with strings of silver lights, and the canopy overhead sparkled with more of the same. Artificial poinsettias spangled with red and gold glitter caught the light, throwing it back in a million directions around the centerpiece: a magnificent metallic tree that was either beautiful or painfully garish—Teru couldn't quite decide.

"Speaking of Rei," Yasu said with a wink. "You guys have any plans?"

"Plans?"

"For Christmas?"

Teru laughed. "It's November. And no."

"Why not? You're in a relationship, even if it is a really fucking weird one. Isn't that what couples do? Exchange gifts. Have dinner. Get drunk. Get laid."

"I don't even know if Rei knows what day it is today," Teru said, only half joking. "It's hard enough to pry him away from the computer to eat, and you want me to take him to Disneyland or something?"

Yasu shrugged. "Never said Disneyland. And the album'll be out by then."

"Yeah, I guess it will be." Teru shook his head. "But I don't think so."

"Why not?"

They stopped in front of the tree, with its plastic needles and wire branches—well-made, but no one was going to believe it was real. Around them, ads encouraged gift-givers to consider diamonds or perfume, and a rack of travel brochures promised holiday getaways to locations both familiar and exotic.

"Why not?" Yasu asked again. "You ought to at least do a love hotel or something."

"I don't think so." A short, bitter laugh followed the thought. "We tried that once, actually. Didn't go so well."

Yasu looked at him for a long minute, and then shook his head. "No way," he said. "Are you telling me you've never...?"

"I don't want to talk about it."

"Fuck, Teru! You *have* to go, then."

Teru looked at his feet. "I don't even know what to do."

"That's bullshit. Hell, even *I* know what to do, and I'm

286

not the least bit interested in trying it. Look." Yasu's tone was serious. "Let me say this, as the fat kid who wanted to be a rock star, okay? You're dating someone with... body image issues. You *don't* have sex with that person. How the *fuck* does that seem like a good idea?"

Teru said nothing. Yasu was right.

"Do you guys, you know, go on dates, or anything?"

"A couple of times," Teru muttered. "Not recently. He's self-conscious. People stare."

"No fucking kidding!" Yasu laughed and Teru, in spite of himself, joined in. "People are staring at you and me right now. I'm gonna go out on a limb and guess that Rei didn't ask for whatever the hell happened to him. But if you didn't want people staring at you, Teru... you may not have realized this, but there are other colors you could have dyed your hair. So put on a hat and a pair of sunglasses and take your fucking boyfriend to..." He strode across the plaza to the rack of brochures and picked up a handful at random. "Here."

"Hawaii?"

"Why not?"

"I don't have a passport, for one thing. And I don't think I'd have much luck getting Rei on a plane."

"Fine. Then how about this? Kyushu. There are trains that go there, right? Kyoto. Lovely, scenic Niigata."

Teru laughed. "I'll pass on that one."

"Whatever," Yasu said. "But you ought to do something."

"I'll think about it," Teru said, and threw the pamphlets into his bag.

They walked through the first floor of the department

store. Yasu was right—they did draw stares, two men without dates, dressed in studded jeans and leather jackets in a sea of Vuitton and Chanel. *Just passing through*, Teru thought, nodding to the middle-aged saleswoman who followed them with pursed lips and narrowed eyes.

"So, how about you?" Teru asked as they stood in line for the register. "Any big plans for Christmas?"

"No," Yasu said. "Well, yeah... with my mom. Between the countdown show and the three-man, there's no way I'm going to make it home for New Year's. So I promised she could have me till the thirtieth. Your mother asks when you're coming home, by the way. I'm guessing she doesn't know?"

"About Rei? No. And she's not going to."

"Is that a threat?"

"That's an order."

"Yeah? Well, as much as I do love to subvert authority," Yasu said, "don't worry. Telling your mother is one feat you're going to have to perform on your own."

—⭒—

Teru's bags were heavy, but his heart was light as he made his way home. He was glad that Yasu was okay with everything—a little freaked out, maybe, but generally okay. Teru walked into the apartment, humming to himself, and deposited the bags of clothes on the coffee table.

"I'm home," he announced.

Rei nodded, but didn't look up from his work. "That took awhile."

"I ran into Yasu in Shinjuku."

"I see."

"Is everything okay?"

"Yes."

"Okay." An awkward silence hung in the air. "Then I, uh... I guess I'll put this stuff away."

He took the clothes to the bedroom and folded them in the corner, next to the pile that had accumulated over the past few months. Yasu would have laughed, if he'd known that Teru was living here—more or less—without changing his legal address, and without so much as a drawer to his name.

The travel pamphlets he pulled out of his bag with a sigh. It wasn't that it wouldn't be nice to get away. It would probably be good for Rei, too, to go somewhere far from the city's prying eyes, with no shows and no computer and no schedule to keep him from doing what he had promised: resting, just as soon as the album was done. But there was too much to think about. Hawaii went into the garbage, as did Okinawa and Seoul and anything else that would involve a plane. Kyoto would be just as crowded as Tokyo, and Teru had no idea what kind of public transportation system they had.

This is stupid, he told himself, even as he lumped the pillows into a pile and sat on the bed to browse through what was left. "Hot springs?" he muttered. That sounded good in theory; weren't hot springs supposed to help with pain? But that would mean being naked in front of a bunch of strangers, and *that* was never going to happen. Teru was just about to toss that pamphlet aside, too, when a line of text on the cover caught his eye: "Private bath attached to the room."

It wasn't just that hotel either; several of the

Japanese-style inns had suites with attached baths, many of them outdoors on a private balcony. They were expensive, especially during peak season—but for the first time in his life, Teru had money to spare.

"It might work," he whispered to himself. "If they'll let two men check in together, anyway."

He found Seika's number on his phone. It wouldn't hurt to ask, and even if Seika hadn't been to one of those places himself, he knew enough gay men that he'd probably have some kind of answer. But when he called, the phone just rang and rang.

Strange. The club wouldn't be open yet, and if Seika was asleep he should have had his voicemail on. He tried again, with the same result.

Teru had just stuffed the travel pamphlets back into his bag and the phone into his pocket, ready to give up, when it rang.

"Seika?"

"No, it's Minori." He sounded confused. "Didn't my number come up?"

"Sorry," Teru said. "I wasn't looking. What's up?"

"It's..." Minori's voice was strained. "It's nothing bad. I'm not sure if it's good either, but we need to talk. All of us. What's your schedule like this week?"

"I'm pretty much free."

"Okay. Let me ask Nao, and I'll send you guys an email when I come up with something, okay?"

"Sure," Teru said. "Are you sure you're all right?"

"Yeah. I'll talk to you later, okay? Bye."

"Bye," Teru echoed, but the line was already dead. A

minute later, the phone was ringing again.

"I don't have any more answers than you do," Seika said. "Not good news, and not bad? Your guess is as good as mine."

"That wasn't actually what I wanted to talk to you about." Teru lowered his voice, half ashamed to ask his question, but Seika only laughed in response.

"That's ridiculous," he said.

"What is?"

"Weren't you ever on a sports team at school?"

"Uh, no," Teru said. "Were you?"

"Good point. Graduation trip? Indie band on tour? Men share hotel rooms all the time. No one thinks anything of it, and even if they do... it's hardly illegal to have a little fun."

"Thanks," Teru said. He didn't mention that it was the idea of a little fun that was making him consider scrapping the whole idea. Rei had said nothing, done nothing in the way of taking their relationship to the next level since that aborted night in the hotel. Teru didn't want to revisit that night, and he certainly didn't want to remind Rei.

"Sorry, Teru. I've got another call. Is that all you needed to ask?"

"Yeah," Teru said. "It's probably Minori again. I guess I'll see you whenever this big news breaks."

"Have fun," Seika said, and terminated the call.

—※—

They met at a restaurant in Meidai-mae, between Nao's last class and Seika's first shift at the club. Minori's expression was grim, and he looked like he'd aged ten years overnight. "I'm sorry to call you guys out here," he said. "I didn't want to say this on the phone."

"Are you okay?" Teru asked. "Your dad's store?"

"It's fine," Minori said. "I mean, it's not. But my family's no worse off than they were. Sorry." He shook his head. "I didn't mean to make you worry. This would have been good news—great news—at any other time."

Yasu took a drag on his cigarette; Seika sipped his coffee, waiting.

"What is it?" Nao asked. "Another omnibus CD?"

"Better," Minori said. "Or worse." He tossed a business card onto the table.

Junichi Hoshino. Ondera Records.

He laughed through his frown. "We've been scouted."

Chapter 27

Seika picked up the business card. "What are you going to do?"

"I don't know." Minori shook his head. "I want to at least hear what he's got to say."

Yasu nodded; Seika put down the card. Nao said nothing, but glanced around the table at everyone else's reactions. Teru gave him a sympathetic smile; he knew what it was like to be the newest and least experienced member of the band. He also thought he knew what a nineteen-year-old kid with as much talent as Nao had would have to say about being scouted by a record label—and "I don't know" didn't play any part in it.

"What did he say on the phone?" Yasu asked.

"Not a lot. It's not an offer, not yet. I get the impression there's a lot of red tape involved, and even if this Hoshino likes us that's no guarantee we'll get a contract. He just wants to know if we're interested. If we are, he'll get back to us about an initial meeting. And he'd like an advance copy of the album, if that's available." Minori glanced at Teru.

"It's not done yet," Teru said. "Rei is kind of a perfectionist, if you hadn't noticed. But I can probably get a couple of tracks."

Minori nodded. "All right. Get what you can."

"This seems like bad timing," Seika said. "Are you sure we can deal with this right now?"

"No." Minori's voice was soft. "But I don't think we have much of a choice."

"Even if we do go major, that's no guarantee we'll be a success." Nao spoke up with a sigh. "This is all I've ever wanted my entire life. But if you're expecting to make a living with this overnight...."

Minori smiled. "Thanks," he said. "I know that. And you're right—this may not amount to anything. If anyone wants out, I won't stop you. I have no idea if he'll be interested in three or four of us without the rest, but I'm going to talk to him, anyway. If it doesn't work out, there's plenty of time to announce a breakup later."

"Okay." Nao grinned. "Then I'm in."

"Same here," said Yasu.

Seika nodded slowly. "I'm interested," he said. "No promises. But we hear what he has to say. Together?" He looked expectantly at Teru.

"I want Rei there."

Minori frowned. "This is a business arrangement, not an artistic decision."

"He knows people," Teru argued. "He's sold to these corporate types before. He knows more about this business than any of us do."

"Be careful," Seika warned. "The public likes to imagine us doing all kinds of glorious things to each other, but if they found out that either of us really did..."

"I know. Let me at least run this Mr. Hoshino's name

by him, and see if he can tell us anything we don't already know?"

"Okay," Minori said. "And guys? Don't quit your day jobs yet." Teru shifted uncomfortably in his seat, sure that the comment was directed at him.

—※—

Rei, to Teru's disappointment, seemed to agree.

"Don't you even want to talk about it?" Teru threw his coat over the arm of the sofa, but he didn't feel like sitting down. He was restless, pacing the room from one end to the other, full of the need to do something and not sure what that something might be.

"When there is something to talk about, yes." Rei spoke to Teru, but he remained immersed in whatever he was doing on the computer.

"There's plenty to talk about! You've been through this before, right? Can't you tell us what to expect?"

"I was never signed to a major label, Teru."

"But you came so close."

Rei took a deep breath. "Yes. Thank you for reminding me."

"I'm sorry. That was thoughtless."

"It is not your fault."

Teru looked over Rei's shoulder; he was working on something in Photoshop. "Is that for the album?"

"It will be the cover art, eventually."

"The cover art? I thought you hired someone to do that."

"I did," Rei said. "I was unsatisfied with the results."

"You've been doing this all day?" Teru frowned. "You should take a break."

"I'm not tired."

"You look tired. Your eyes are dry, your wrist is stiff, and you probably haven't eaten since last night."

To his surprise, Rei laughed. "You know me too well."

"Do you want to go out?"

"Go out?"

"To celebrate."

Rei swiveled the chair around. "There is nothing to celebrate. You are talented, Teru. Your band is talented as well. But you have yet to play a one-man show, or to tour outside of Tokyo. Your album is unfinished. Your image needs work. The world will hear our music, but not now. You are not ready."

All of that was true.

"Don't you trust me?"

"I do. Of course I do. But... things are different now. Minori was ready to break up the band, and now there's a chance of keeping it together. He needs a job—whether it's this or something else, he needs to support his family. If this Mr. Hoshino thinks we're ready, I—"

"Hoshino?"

"I think that was his name." Teru fished the card out of his wallet and handed it to Rei. "A Mr. Hoshino at Ondera."

Rei's eyes grew wide. "Hoshino," he said. "This is... unexpected."

"Why? Do you know him?"

"I did."

"That's great! If you know him, you can put in a good

word for us, and –"

"Teru," Rei said softly, "Mr. Hoshino must think I'm dead. He's the one who scouted me. Us." He laughed bitterly. "I suppose I should be flattered."

"But you're not going to come."

Rei looked down at his arm, held at an awkward angle by its brace. He looked at the cane, hooked on the edge of his desk—a sign of a good day now that he used the crutch more often than not. He looked at the monitor, at the outline of the mask reflected in the convex screen. "I can't," he said. "Not like this."

"Fine." Teru sighed. "Look, I'm going to get us some dinner. I'm guessing you don't want to go out, right?" He stuffed his wallet back into his pocket. "He thinks you're *dead*, Rei." He paused in the doorway. "And you actually think that this... whatever *this* is, is worse?"

—⋇—

He came back with takeout: two beef bowls in Styrofoam containers and a couple of beers from the convenience store. "Rei?" he called. "I'm home."

The music room was dark; he found Rei in bed with the back raised and a tray on his lap, making illegible notes on a piece of sheet music.

"You came back," he said.

"You're going to starve to death if no one forces you to eat. And drink." He popped the top on one of the beers and set it down on the tray. "I hear it's a hell of a painkiller."

"Thank you." Rei smiled a thin smile. "I should apologize. I..."

"You're tired." Teru pulled the tops off the bowls and took a plastic fork—easier than chopsticks—out of the bag. Grabbing another tray from the kitchen, he sat beside Rei on the bed. "I know that. But I came home today with what should have been great news, and you seem almost *angry* about it. I don't understand. I thought you wanted your music to be heard."

"I do."

"Then why aren't you happy?"

Rei was silent, picking at his food and sipping fitfully at the beer. "I don't know," he said at last. "I don't know."

Teru took a swig from his own can. "That's not very helpful."

"Teru?"

"Yeah?"

"Do you believe in life after death?"

Teru's hand stopped halfway to his mouth. "I don't know. I've never really thought about it."

"I think about it," Rei said, "all the time. If there's nothing, if Saki is truly gone, then this music is all I have left of him. The only way he can live on. But if he's here, somewhere, watching us..." Rei's hand trembled as he returned his beer to the tray. "I hope, sometimes, that he is gone."

"You think he wouldn't want us to be happy?"

"Success is not equivalent to happiness. But I wonder if he would want you to have the success that should have been his."

"It's your success, though," Teru protested. *Our success. Not Saki's.* "No one cared about us before we started playing

298

your songs."

"You will be the one in the spotlight," Rei said softly.

And that, Teru thought, was the problem.

"You wish it was you."

Rei looked away.

"It's all right," Teru said. "Hell, if I was in your place, I...."

"I want to be happy for you."

"Okay," Teru said. "That's a start."

—⸙—

Two weeks later they walked into Ondera's head office, five young men with their multicolored hair pulled back and their clothing as tame as their wardrobes would allow. Nao and Minori had actual suits, and Yasu had managed to dig up a jacket that didn't look too bad with his black jeans. Seika was dressed the way he always was, in clothes that were nice enough, but more visual kei than big business. As for Teru, Rei had taken him shopping for a suit that managed to be both. It had felt more like a costume fitting than a date, but Teru knew it had been intended as an apology.

They were greeted by a man with a shaved head and a lower lip scarred with a dozen long-healed piercings. "I'm Hoshino," he said. "Don't look so surprised. They've got me scouting the visual bands for a reason." His voice was gravelly, like he'd torn it up with too much screaming or too much smoking or—more likely—a combination of both. "Come on back to the meeting room, let me tell you about our company and what kind of a deal we'd be looking at, if the higher-ups like you as well as I do."

Most of what he had to say was old news to Teru. Rei's knowledge of Ondera was almost six years out of date, but Chizuru had dealt with them a few times since then, and between the two of them he had gotten a fairly thorough briefing. "They'll get your name out there," Chizuru had said. "Their marketing department is first-rate, but they haven't signed any visual bands recently. Whether that means they're trying to get out of the genre, or just waiting for the right group to come along...?" She'd looked at Rei for confirmation, but he had only frowned.

"I don't understand," Teru complained to her later. "This is the same deal he was going to take five years ago, and he didn't have a problem with it then. I thought that was what we were working for, but he doesn't seem happy at all."

"Things were different back then," she said. "Saki had money, but it came from his parents. They wouldn't let him spend it on the band. Rei sells the songs he doesn't care about, but the ones he hangs on to... I think they're the only thing left that he feels he can control."

"So you think we shouldn't do it?"

"Me?" Chizuru shook her head. "Ondera's got a good reputation, and they've dealt with visual bands before. Let me see any contract before you sign it. I'm not an expert, but I know a couple of entertainment lawyers. Honestly, though? Visual kei is on the way out, and I don't think you're big enough to be making many demands. He's jealous, Teru. That you're getting what should have been his." She sighed. "And he's worried about losing you, too."

Looking around the table at his bandmates, Teru didn't know that there was anything to be jealous about. He

300

and Nao would probably be all right, no matter what happened—they both had other people who could pay the rent and put food on the table if the royalties weren't cutting it. Yasu, flipping through the company's brochure with a bemused smile, would probably get by as well. There was no reason he couldn't keep pumping gas at night if things took awhile to take off, and if push came to shove he could probably borrow money from his parents. Seika's private life was a mystery; Teru didn't know what his boyfriend did or how lavish a lifestyle they led, but it was unlikely that Ondera would let him keep working at the nightclub if and when they were signed. And there was Minori, following Hoshino's presentation to the letter, making notes in the margins of his pamphlet that spilled over onto the back and into his planner. He needed a job. If there was money to be had as a guitarist, so be it. But if there wasn't, Teru knew, he would be gone, and the band would most likely be gone as well.

"All right, if there are no more questions...?" Hoshino glanced around the table before continuing. "I want to run over some of the legal issues regarding your material. You are not currently signed to any indie label, is that right?"

"Yes," Minori said. "That's correct."

"Good. That makes things a lot easier. Does anyone else hold the copyright to any of your music or lyrics?"

Minori glanced at Teru; Teru shook his head. Rei's instructions regarding the rights to his songs had been perfectly clear. The band—and no one else—was listed as composer and lyricist on both the single and the album.

"Okay." Hoshino made a note in his planner. "I think what we're going to want to do is this: You've already got shows planned for December and January, so any contract we draw up is going to be effective February first, at the earliest. I don't want to change the release of your album. You've hired people to deal with that, and your fans are expecting it next month. Go ahead and put out the first press, and we'll buy up the rights if and when we sign you to put out some new material. We've got an in-house management team who'll set you up with a tour—smaller venues at first, just to get your names and faces known.

"We'll get a stylist in here, see what we can do about your image. Visual kei's not as big as it used to be; we may have to tone down your look a little, see if—"

"Wait a minute," Teru interrupted. "We're a visual band. If we change that—"

"Relax." Hoshino smiled. "We're not out to alienate your current fanbase. Makeup and melodrama sell. We're just trying to get you guys into the twenty-first century, appeal to younger listeners who may not have grown up with the musical influences you did."

"Okay," Minori said. "We appreciate that. Is there anything else we need to do?"

"For now..." Hoshino glanced through their file, shaking his head. "Not really. I'm going to pass this along to my bosses. If they want to make a deal—and just between us, I think they will—it should happen soon. We don't want to wait too long, let people start to lose interest. We'll be in touch. In the next few weeks, I would think."

—>¦<—

"I don't like it," Rei said that night, as they sat on the

sofa with a bottle of whisky and Teru's copy of the company pamphlet.

"It sounded all right to me."

"They're trying to turn you into a boy band."

Teru laughed. "Do you have any idea how ridiculous that sounds? It's a great opportunity and you know it."

"You don't know what you're saying." Rei pulled away, and when Teru tried to take his hand he grabbed his crutch and stood. "I want you to turn it down."

"There's nothing to turn down yet. And Rei?"

"Yes?"

"Sit down."

Rei sat, but his back was straight and his hand rested on the crutch—ready to walk out of the conversation at any time.

"I want to do this for you. Not just for myself, or for the band."

Rei's knuckles whitened; he gritted his teeth. "How is it to my benefit to turn my music over to a corporation with nothing to lose? I gave those songs to you, Teru."

"And I still have them. It's not too late to put your name in the credits, too, if you want. But you never sleep. You hardly eat. You're at the computer all day trying to be composer and producer, manager and publicist, keyboardist and graphic designer and I don't know what else all in one. You're killing yourself, and—"

"Killing myself?"

"Someday, maybe. People die of overwork all the time."

"I thought you understood me, Teru." Rei sounded genuinely sad. "I thought that you, of all people, would understand that this... that our music was the only thing keeping me alive."

"I just..." Teru's shoulders slumped and he let out a sigh. "It doesn't matter anyway, does it? Either we get this deal or we break up."

"That," Rei said, "is not necessarily true. Wait here." He rose again, and disappeared into the hallway. Teru heard a door open and then, a minute later, close.

Rei returned with a paper shopping bag clamped between his teeth. He set the crutch aside, transferred the bag to his hand, and passed it to Teru. "I apologize for the inelegant delivery."

"What is this?" Teru opened the bag. "A CD?"

"Your CD."

"The album? I thought you were still working on it."

"The jacket, the liner notes... those will be completed soon. But the music... Listen to it," Rei urged. "Tell me what you think."

Teru grimaced; he was almost used to singing onstage, but he still hated hearing his voice on a recording. "Do we have to?" he asked.

"Please."

He slid the CD into Rei's computer, and it began to play.

"Turn the volume up."

"Okay," Teru said, but it took him awhile to find the controls, and awhile longer to remember that the mouse was configured for the other hand. "Is that all right?"

"You tell me."

The first song, a seven-minute rock anthem called

304

"Midnight Higeki," or "Midnight Tragedy," was one they hadn't performed yet. For most of the fans, this album would be the first place they'd hear it. "It doesn't even sound like me," Teru said. "It sounds too... professional."

"You don't need a record label to sound like this," Rei said softly.

Teru couldn't argue with that, so he didn't try. He slid across the sofa to rest his head on Rei's shoulder, to slip an arm around his waist and massage the tense muscles in his back. "What was it like?" he asked. "When it happened to you?"

Rei said nothing. Teru held him—listening to the music, listening to him breathe.

"Were you worried?"

"About what?"

"I don't know. About money? About scheduling? About losing creative control?"

Rei shook his head. "I would have done anything for that contract."

"Then I don't understand"—Teru raised his voice to be heard above an angry crescendo—"why you don't want the same for me."

Rei stood, pulling away from Teru's embrace and limping across the room to the computer. "This can wait," he said. With a click of the mouse, the music stopped. "Come with me," Rei said.

He took Teru to the front room, to the bookshelf, and pulled a VHS tape from the shelf.

Aeternum, the label read. *December 21, 1994.*

"Your last show," Teru said.

"Not quite. But this is the last video. The last I have... of him."

"Can I see it?"

"I think you should."

Teru took the tape to the bedroom and put it in the VCR. They lay together on the bed.

"I used to watch this," Rei said, "when I wanted to punish myself."

"Is that what you're doing now?"

Rei closed his eyes. "I don't know. I don't think I'll know until we begin."

Teru pushed Play, and the static was replaced by horizontal lines that scrolled away as the audio kicked in. An invisible crowd chattered in the darkness; from beneath the curtain, a snatch of sultry bassline throbbed.

They were standing on the balcony—or at least, the cameraman had been, and with the bedroom lights dimmed it was easy for Teru to imagine himself there, where Rei had watched him. Someone coughed. The snare drum gave a brassy bark, and the air hummed with the untapped energy of silent amps. The already dark image grew darker, the crowd fading to shapes and blurs. And then light streamed in as the curtain was pulled away to the thunder of the drums and the scream of an electric guitar.

They stood backlit onstage, four shadows of the past until the spotlights colorized them into life. From stage left, a slight man with long purple hair stepped forward and, with a grin that seemed meant for the camera, ran his fingers down the neck of his guitar, milking it for every note of the violent, sensuous opening phrase.

306

Rei tensed, and Teru leaned closer, their bodies touching at every point in a straight, unbroken line. Teru squeezed Rei's hand, and Rei squeezed back—but neither of them took their eyes from the screen.

"Aeternum!" the crowd screamed. "Aeternum!"

The lights went down, the drums became gunfire, and someone—Teru couldn't tell whether it was Saki or the other guitarist—played a heavy, mournful riff that faded only when a fifth figure, clad in a familiar black cloak, climbed out of the stage right door and, with the air of a conqueror, held the microphone, still in its stand, over his head.

"They love you," Teru whispered, as the crowd roared again.

Rei's voice soared over the screams and cheers—higher, maybe, and clearer, but largely unchanged by time. He was an actor, telling a story with his voice and his body, silhouetted against the flashing lights as the song swelled to a climax—young and vibrant and strong.

The first song segued into the second, a rough, heavy number driven as much by the guitars and bass as by the melody. After the second chorus, Rei stepped aside, giving the spotlight to Saki and his guitar. The stage was small, but Saki ran across it, holding his instrument over his head like a prize. The camera zoomed in as his fingers flew faster over the fretboard, titillating the strings to produce a light, playful sound. Teru smiled; he knew that what Saki was doing was difficult, but he made it look like nothing more than a bit of fun.

"He was good," Teru said.

"He was great," Rei amended. "Painfully shy, but once

he stepped onstage..."

"He was brilliant."

In the video, Rei stood behind Saki, hands on his hips as he launched into the final phrase. Saki spun away, a look of mock horror on his face, and Rei leaned in, tracing a path down Saki's body with his tongue—never touching, but eliciting a wail from the audience all the same.

Teru's body ached—with jealousy, with longing, with shame.

"Don't hate him," Rei pleaded. "This isn't his fault."

"You would have gone all the way together."

"Yes. I think we would have."

"I don't want to do this alone."

"Then don't," Rei said, and he pulled Teru close.

Teru spoke into Rei's shoulder. "You still want me to turn it down."

"I want you to stay with me."

"I'd still be with you, Rei. I'd go to work, and then come home. Like any couple. And besides..." He reached up to caress Rei's cheek, then slipped his hand beneath the wig, beneath the mask and lifted them away. "Would it really be so bad to let someone else handle it? The production, the publicity, the scheduling? There'd be more time for us." He sighed, reaching for a tub of ointment. "And we don't have much of a choice."

Rei closed his eyes as well as he could, shivering as Teru rubbed the cool medicine into his twisted skin. "You have," he breathed, as though in the middle of a sexual act, "all the choice in the world. We can start our own label. You can go solo. With your voice and my music, no one will care about the others."

"I care," Teru said simply, massaging Rei's temple, his cheekbone, the nub of his ear. He could hear Yasu's voice, echoing in his head: *How the fuck does that seem like a good idea?* But his hands strayed no further than Rei's back and chest. He screwed the top back on the ointment and lowered the bed. "This is our chance. *Our* chance. The band's. And I think you know already that."

"You should take it." Rei turned away. "I don't want you to. But you should."

"It's not a choice between you and my career. You know that, right?"

Rei said nothing. Teru sat on the edge of the bed, watching the comforter rise and fall with his breath. When he could take it no more he excused himself to the shower to release his pent-up longing as he imagined another world, with no Saki and no accident, in which he was the one being felt up by Rei as the world, and the universe, cheered them on.

Chapter 28

The album arrived on a Monday. It was one of the worst pain days Teru had ever seen; Rei was restless and cranky, uncomfortable even in bed and frustrated that there was so little he could do to help. Teru was left to carry twenty shipping boxes into the music room and to search through the computer by himself, trying to find the spreadsheet that would tell him how many copies went to each store, and then to figure out how to print it.

He brought what he had into the bedroom, and Rei flipped through the stack of paper with an expression that fell somewhere between thoughtful and exasperated.

"There should be two more pages."

"There weren't."

"Is the printer out of paper?"

"I don't know," Teru said. "How do I check that?"

"Open the paper tray," Rei said through gritted teeth, "and check."

In the end, he dragged himself out of bed and into the music room, his taped wrist taking the weight that his leg refused to support.

"You should rest," Teru urged. "I can do this."

"No..." Rei refilled the paper tray in a fraction of the

time Teru had spent looking for it. "I need something to think about. What can I do?"

He sat on the sofa with the spreadsheet and read aloud the names and addresses of the shops and how many copies they had ordered. More than once Teru had to check the address himself, to confirm the kanji characters in the names of unfamiliar places, but it was nice to have Rei there, even if he was doing most of the work alone.

This was what they'd be losing, if the band really did get a record deal. Teru would go to rehearsals, to recording sessions, on tour, and Rei would stay behind—composing, or wallowing in the past. It would mean hiring someone, an assistant if not an actual nurse, to wash the wigs and do the laundry and make sure Rei didn't skip too many doctor's appointments. Without the band, without a project to obsess over, would there be any reason for him to get out of bed?

"What are you thinking about?" Rei asked, as Teru attached the label to a package bound for Osaka. "You seem unhappy."

Teru added the box to the "ready to ship" pile, and opened another empty one. "How many to Rock Amour?"

"Two hundred," Rei said. "You're angry."

Teru frowned. "Where did you get that idea? I'm just thinking. About how this might be the last time we ever do this."

Rei nodded, wincing at some unseen pain. "You're meeting with Ondera again tomorrow."

"Not until two. I can go to the clinic with you in the morning, if you want."

He didn't even know what he was hoping for, as far as

Ondera went. If they were offered a contract, he risked losing this—or at least having it changed. If they weren't, Minori would be out of the band, and the band itself would most likely be gone. As much as Rei talked about having options, Teru didn't feel like there were many good ones. He didn't know how much money Rei had, or how much it would actually cost to start a record label, but even assuming it was possible, Teru didn't see it happening. Rei was too much of a perfectionist to delegate any of the artistic work, and he didn't have the strength to keep up the pace of the past few months for much longer.

When the last box was packed and the label affixed, Teru loaded as many as he could onto a folding cart and took them to the convenience store to ship. It took three trips, and by the time he was done, sweat was pouring down his back on the December afternoon.

"That was the last?" Rei asked.

"Yeah." Teru nodded. "That's all the shops, advance copies to the magazines for review, and one to Ondera." There were six copies left in a neat stack on the coffee table, for Rei, for Teru, and for his bandmates.

"We should celebrate," Rei said, but he was pale and shivering in the cold that Teru had stopped feeling ten boxes ago. "I'm sorry, Teru. I wish this had been a better day."

"It's all right." Teru took off his coat. "We should rest. This week is going to kick both of our asses." He smiled, and was relieved when Rei cracked a half-smile in return. "We'll celebrate on Sunday, okay?"

—⁕—

As he sat in the waiting room at the pain clinic, despite the fact that he had a meeting with a major record label in less than three hours, Sunday was all Teru could think about. It was Christmas Eve, and under the weight of Yasu's urgings and his own longing and guilt, Teru had booked a room in the hot spring resort of Hakone. So far, he had managed not to spoil the surprise, but with as many bad days as Rei had been having lately, he was starting to wonder if he shouldn't break the news early, to ask if he thought he'd be up to it.

He looked better, though, after the appointment, and Teru didn't feel too bad leaving him at the apartment alone. Neither of them said anything about the meeting, but it hung in the air between them. "I'll try not to be too late," Teru said, and began the walk back to the station.

The contract, when it came, was as thick as a magazine with print half the size. Teru flipped through it with one hand, barely hearing what Hoshino was saying as his brain attempted to process the barrage of legal terms. "A lot of this is industry standard," Hoshino explained while two older men—his bosses—looked on. "This is as good a deal as any new band is going to get. But take your time, look it over. Consult with your lawyers—just keep it quiet with the general public until you actually sign."

"When do you need to know?" Minori asked, and the higher-ups exchanged a look.

"How does mid-January sound? Let's say the fifteenth. Think about it over the holidays and let us know. We're confident you won't get a better offer."

Yeah, Teru thought, surprising himself with his bitterness. *You know as well as we do that we're not getting any other offers at all.*

"What happens," Seika asked in a slow and careful voice, "if not all of us agree to sign?"

Hoshino cleared his throat. "This contract, as it is, is for the five of you as a band."

Seika nodded. "And this non-competition clause applies, I assume, to my current job?"

"It's considered performing, yes. I know the pay looks low, but you'll be earning royalties from your music, as well as anything you make on TV and radio performances, appearances at events. We'll do our best to get your name out there, make sure you don't regret making the move."

They met the next day at Minori's apartment. Other than Yasu, who had been a friend long before he was a bandmate, it was the first time Teru had been to one of the other guys' homes. It made the whole thing seem realer, somehow, and more serious; they couldn't let any rumors get out, and if they discussed this in public, there was a chance they would.

Both Rei and Chizuru had agreed to come, and Seika brought Sung-Min as well. With eight people crowded around a kotatsu table intended for two, the apartment seemed even smaller than it already was.

"I talked to my dad," Nao said. "He's not a lawyer or anything, but he used to work in HR. He says it looks all right, as far as labor laws go. But you guys already know I'm in, as long as the rest of you are."

Yasu nodded. "Same here."

"All right." Minori looked at Teru and Seika, but when neither of them spoke he turned his attention to Chizuru.

314

"Teru says you've worked with this label before. What do you think about their offer?"

"I think..." She glanced at Rei, seated in the apartment's only chair. "I think it looks all right."

Rei coughed, and Teru took that as his cue to add, "But we're concerned about creative control."

"That's a typical clause," Chizuru explained. "In the event of a dispute, the management will have the final word when it comes to your musical style, your appearance, and your overall image. In reality, though? The artist does end up making a lot of those decisions, as long as it doesn't go against the business plan."

"But visual kei is on the way out," Seika said, with a glance at Sung-Min. "So many of the old bands are breaking up, or changing their image."

This was true. Superstar Gackt had left Malice Mizer for a pop-star solo career. L'Arc and GLAY refused to be called visual kei anymore, and Luna Sea, second in fame only to fallen giant X Japan, was calling it quits on New Year's Eve. The up-and-comers that were poised to take their place were more like Bara's band than like La Rose.

"We don't even know what they're thinking as far as marketing," Chizuru went on. "I don't think it's worth it to worry about something that's still a what if."

Minori nodded. "What do you think about this, Rei?"

"It doesn't matter what I think," he replied.

"Of course it does. You wrote all our best songs. My parents are fighting with each other every night over whether I get another year to pursue my dreams... but it's not their choice, is it? It's your music. Do you want it in the hands of

Ondera?"

"I want Teru to sing my music," Rei said. "Where he sings it is his choice. Not mine."

Chapter 29

When Teru arrived at the record shop that Friday for the first of three appearances to promote the album, there was already a line wrapped halfway around the block. The promotional poster, another of Rei's Photoshop creations, had been blown up and pasted to a sidewalk sign, nearly eclipsing the much smaller Crisis Cross poster on the door.

"Will you take a look at that?" Yasu said in lieu of hello. "Six months ago we couldn't pay people to come to our shows, and now they're lining up to shake our hands."

At ten, the doors opened and the girls—and a handful of guys—filed into the store, lining up first to buy a copy of the CD and then to get a seat for the in-store event. It was standing room only in the back, and Teru and Yasu exchanged excited, terrified smiles.

The store manager took the floor, thanking everyone for coming and introducing the band. Minori made a statement, and then the floor was opened for questions before the handshake and autograph event.

"Who are your musical influences?"

"What's your favorite song on the album?"

"What brands of clothing do you like?"

Most of the questions were meaningless, and most of

the answers were meaningless as well. "I consider each and every one of you my girlfriend," Seika said when someone asked him if he had one, and the crowd rippled with giggles and sighs.

The only interesting moment came during the afternoon event, when a woman with blonde hair and a spike through her lip stood up and asked, "Can you tell us anything about your schedule from February on?"

"I'm sorry." Minori took the mic with a polite smile. "Beyond what's on our current flyers, our schedule for next year is undecided."

"There are rumors," she went on, "that you're breaking up. And there are others that say you're going major. Are either of these true?"

Minori shook his head. "I'm sorry, but at this point we can't comment on our future plans."

Saturday's only event was in the afternoon. Teru had the morning free, but when he woke to find Rei already dressed and preparing to go out, he decided to head into Ikebukuro early. He showered and changed, packed his bag, and was at Meguro Station a little before eleven.

December 23 was the Emperor's birthday—a public holiday, unlike Christmas and Christmas Eve—and Tokyo's youth were out in force to celebrate. Teru doubted that most of them were thinking about the Emperor's good health, though. They boarded the train with shopping bags and delicately wrapped presents, laughing and chatting under ads for Fujiya cakes and Kentucky Fried Chicken and light

318

displays at every theme park in the Kanto area. Teru wondered if anyone else was as nervous about the weekend as he was, and decided that if they were, they wouldn't seem so damn happy about it.

He was so wrapped up in his worries that he didn't notice the light blinking on his phone until he got off the train at Ikebukuro. *Four missed calls.* He brought up the call history; they were all from Chizuru.

"What's wrong?"

"Teru!" He could hear the relief in her voice. "Where are you?"

"Ikebukuro." He slipped as far out of the crowd as he could, leaning against a vending machine to keep from being jostled. "On my way to the in-store. Why?"

"Shit." Chizuru said something he couldn't quite catch, something intended for whoever was with her. "I forgot about that. I got a call from a hospital in Shinjuku. Rei's in the emergency room there, and—"

"What?" Teru nearly dropped the phone.

"Teru?" Chizuru asked. "Are you there?"

"Yeah." His heart was in knots. "What happened?"

"I'm sorry. I didn't mean to scare you. They're taking X-rays, but it's probably nothing serious. They just need someone to sign him out and help him get home. I'm..." On the other end of the line, a man's voice muttered something, and she replied. "Sorry. I'm not in Tokyo right now. But if you've got your event..."

"It's all right." Teru was already halfway down the stairs, on his way to the opposite platform. "I've got time," he said. "I'll go."

With nothing to go on but the name of the hospital and verbal directions from a couple of railway employees, what should have been a fifteen-minute walk took at least thirty. The reception area was dark and deserted, the shutters over the admission desk closed. "Right," Teru muttered to himself. "It's Saturday. And a holiday."

He followed the signs to the emergency room, where a harried-looking nurse pressed a clipboard into his hand and asked him to take a seat, please.

"Wait," Teru called as she started to walk away. "I'm not sick. I'm... I'm looking for a patient. He was brought in... an hour or two ago, I guess."

"Hold on," she said. "Let me check. They took him up to X-ray. Third floor. Just follow the signs."

The hallways on the third floor were brighter, but even with all the lights on the place had a dingy, depressing look. The lobby might be closed for the day, but up here, where the inpatients waited in their pajamas for the day's barrage of testing and treatments, there were no such things as Saturdays or holidays.

There were two patients outside the X-ray room: a young boy with an obviously broken arm and an old man pushing an IV cart, with a catheter bag sticking out of his pajama leg. Teru tried to focus on the boy; at least he looked like he had started the day with hopes of having some fun. Rei was nowhere to be seen, but the red light above the door indicated that someone was inside, so Teru sat beside the old man and waited.

It was after twelve; he was supposed to be at the record shop at one. He wondered if he should change. He wondered if Rei hadn't already finished and been taken somewhere else, if he shouldn't go back downstairs and ask someone to check the computer again. He wondered how long it would take it to get back to Ikebukuro, and didn't especially like the answer he came up with. When the door to the X-ray room opened and Rei came out, pushed by a nurse in a hospital wheelchair, Teru wasn't sure whether to be relieved or pissed off.

"What the hell happened to you?" he asked.

The nurse frowned. "Are you the family?"

"Um... yeah." Teru pulled his hat down over his forehead, hiding as much of his newly-dyed hair as he could. "Is he okay?"

"Take him down to orthopedics and wait to be called."

As soon as she was out of earshot, Teru pushed the wheelchair to the far side of the hall and repeated his question. "What happened to you? Are you okay?"

"Your event."

"I'll make it," Teru said, annoyance mingling once again with concern. "What the hell did you do to yourself?"

Rei turned away, burying his face as well as he could in his wig. "It was... not on purpose," he said, in a voice that tried too hard to be biting and came out trembling instead. "I fell."

They sat in the hall outside orthopedics until a tinny announcement directed them to Exam Room 1, where the doctor was waiting with a file, a row of X-rays, and a disapproving frown on his face.

"You're the primary caregiver?" he asked.

"The what? No..." Teru fumbled for an answer. "I'm just... a friend."

"Well, your friend was very lucky." The doctor tapped one of the X-rays. "The good news is, nothing's broken. It's a minor sprain. But these plates"—he indicated two white blocks studded with what looked like dozens of screws or nails—"can weaken the bone, making it prone to future injury. He should be wearing a brace, boots or no—"

"You weren't?" Teru glanced at Rei.

"And that cane," the doctor continued, "isn't giving him enough support. I'm worried about arthritis in his wrist and knees; you can see that it's starting to develop in the ankle. Now, it's a holiday, and we're understaffed. I don't see any real reason to keep him here, now, for any further treatment. But I want you to go home, put that ankle on ice, and take these X-rays to your regular doctor as soon as you can make an appointment. Is that clear?"

It was Teru, not Rei, that he looked to for his answer. "I'll make sure he gets some rest," he said.

—⟩⟨⟵

They took a taxi back to Meguro. Rei was silent and pale, his eyes focused on something no one else could see, and he shuddered with visible relief when they pulled up in front of the apartment.

"Wait here," Teru told the driver. "I might be fifteen minutes or so, but I'm going to need you to take me to Ikebukuro."

He helped Rei out of the cab. His ankle was taped and swollen and practically useless; Teru half-carried him as they stumbled to the door.

"Teru," he said. "I'm so sorry."

Don't be, Teru thought, and then, *You should be.* "I've got to get dressed," he said. "Are you going to be okay on your own?"

He helped Rei into bed, elevating his leg and making sure he took a dose of painkillers before hitting the bathroom. It wasn't a problem to change into his costume and do a simple, no-frills version of his makeup, but he didn't have time to do much with his hair. He teased it into something that was more Rei's style—long and straight and falling into his eyes. It wasn't what his fans were used to, but the taxi was waiting. It would have to do.

From the overly polite, falling-over-himself apology to the aloof smile he wore for the autograph session, the entire event was an act. If Teru had stopped a moment to think about where he was or what he was doing, his thoughts would have turned to Rei, to the record deal, to the trip to Hakone that was now almost certainly going to fall through.

He could keep those thoughts at bay as long as the fans were there. It was when they had left that he had problems.

"Where were you?" Minori asked as soon as the doors had closed.

"At the hospital," Teru admitted. "With Rei." He gave the others an abbreviated version of what had happened.

"Is he all right?" Seika asked.

"Yeah, I think so. But I ought to get home. I'll see you guys at rehearsal, okay?"

"Okay," Minori said. But Teru got the feeling that it wasn't okay at all.

———✳———

When he got home, the lights were on, but dimmed as far as they would go. Rei was lying in bed, without his mask or wig, staring at the ceiling in silence.

"How are you doing?" Teru asked, sitting carefully on the edge of the bed.

"Fine." Rei tried, without much luck, to turn away. "I am... so sorry. Your event...."

"It was fine. They thought it was cute."

"I won't let this happen again."

"Okay," Teru said. "Don't." He walked to the kitchen and found the bag of painkillers from the hospital pharmacy. "How many?"

"Three."

Teru took out four. "There's something I wanted to talk to you about," he said, offering the pills and a glass of water to Rei. "Do you need more ice?"

Rei closed his eyes and nodded. "Please," he said, and Teru took the Ziploc bag from his leg, refilling it with ice from the freezer.

"It looks better," he commented hopefully. "Do you mind if I turn on the lights?"

"No."

Teru opened the travel brochure and flipped to the right page. The inn had seemed ideal when he'd chosen it: a private bath and meals served in the room, a late checkout time, about ten minutes from the station. "This was supposed to be a surprise," he said. "It's tomorrow. Too late to cancel. But if you're not feeling up to it, we don't have to go."

Rei looked from the page to Teru and back again. His expression was blank, even the unscarred parts of his face expressionless and immobile.

"We could take the wheelchair," Teru suggested. He had no clue how that would work as far as the train and hotel were concerned, but it was the only thing he could think of to offer. "If you think it's too far to walk."

"No." The reply was immediate. "But I think we should go."

"You do?"

"I do."

"O—okay," Teru stammered. He'd spent the train ride home steeling himself for rejection, and wasn't sure whether to be ecstatic or terrified. "I'll, uh... start packing our things," he said. "Just let me know what you need."

Chapter 30

They took another taxi to Shinjuku. Rei sat with his back stiff, flinching once when another car passed by a little too close for comfort. Teru pretended not to notice; there hadn't been any other options. Their seats on the Romance Car limited express train were reserved and, on Christmas Eve, would have been nearly impossible to change.

The front car was double-decker, with the driver's seat on the upper floor to avoid obstructing the passengers' view. Teru hadn't been able to get seats in the front row, but from where they were seated they still had a good view as the grey Tokyo skyline gave way to a mountainous, evergreen countryside.

Rei sat by the window, lost in thought. His coat was probably the most extravagant thing Teru had ever seen him wear, lined with fur and with long, draping sleeves that were half kimono and half Transylvanian queen. He had probably chosen it for its flashiness, hoping it would draw attention away from his disabilities. Privately, though, Teru thought it had the opposite effect. The right sleeve was conspicuously empty, making him look like the amputee he was fighting Chizuru not to become, and the fitted design made both his crutch and the limp that accompanied it more noticeable than usual.

When they arrived at Hakone-Yumoto Station, there was a line at the taxi pickup point. The people in front of them turned to look, looked again, and when the shock had worn off, returned to the fine art of looking straight ahead. Their taxi driver, on the other hand, took one look at his odd customers in the mirror and gave them a gap-toothed smile.

"You have your ID?" he asked.

"ID?" Teru frowned. He had both of their National Heath Insurance cards in the suitcase, but he had never needed them to take a taxi before.

"Your disability certificate? You get a discount." The cabbie pointed to a sign on the back of his seat.

"I—I don't think..." Teru began, but before he could finish, Rei drew a slim red passbook from his pocket.

"Thanks." The driver hit a button on the meter and the base fare was replaced by a much lower number. "Where to?"

Teru handed him the brochure.

"Nice place," he commented as he pulled out. "Probably full of couples tonight, though. You guys aren't spending Christmas with your girlfriends?"

Teru blushed. "We're, uh... meeting them there."

The entire town seemed like it had slipped a century or two into the past. Across the street from the station, mom-and-pop souvenir shops sold tea and sweets and eggs boiled in the hot springs from beneath wooden, hand-painted signs. Behind them, on the mountainside, white-sided Showa-era hotels stood out among the trees, while the more traditional inns, squat and wooden and quaint, faded into them.

The place Teru had chosen was one of the latter, long and low with a stone approach and a wooden façade that was either very old or made to look like it. Teru slid the wooden door aside with one hand, and held it for Rei to pass through.

They removed their shoes, Rei sitting on a bench to tackle his boots while Teru pulled his off easily. "I'm going to check in," he said. "Take your time, okay?"

Their room was on the first floor, a junior suite with a small, Western-style sitting area in addition to the main Japanese room. "Please let us know if you need any assistance," the clerk said, and handed Teru the key.

Teru turned to Rei. "What do you think?"

"It's lovely," Rei said, in a thick voice that seemed to catch in his throat. "Thank you."

—⁕—

Evening fell early. The sun retreated behind the mountains, casting the last of its rays into the steam rising from the hot springs and painting curls of white and gold over the bare branches and tufts of evergreen that mottled the side of the hill. Below them, in the valley, a river rushed, in sharp contrast to the laconic steam, on its cold and frenzied way.

Teru convinced Rei to dress in the hotel yukata provided for use as pajamas, bathrobe, and room wear during their stay. Whether it was the casual attire, the scenery, or the alcohol that, courtesy of the lobby vending machines, was already flowing through their systems, Teru felt like he had accomplished his biggest goal. He had gotten *away*, and at least to some extent, he had managed to take Rei with him.

Rei declined to take a bath before dinner, admitting that the trip had tired him and reminding Teru that they had all night. Instead, they looked out on their private bath from the Western-style alcove, the only place Rei could really sit comfortably. If Teru had made any mistakes in planning this trip, it was that. A more modern hotel would have had beds and chairs and maybe a desk, but here they were expected to sit on cushions on the floor. Rei propped his leg up on a stack of the cushions, let Teru ice it, and then they just sat by the window and *were*.

Dinner was brought by a woman in a kimono who must have been sixty, but moved with the grace of a twenty-year-old. From her dainty steps to the gracious sweep of her arm, her presentation was as elegant and as essential as the cuisine itself. "A selection of fresh sashimi from our local oceans, hand-selected this morning at market," she explained. "Grade A-5 domestic beef in a soy sauce and onion marinade. Seasonal vegetables, seasoned to perfection by our chef." She explained each dish as she laid it out, and when at last she had concluded with "fresh seasonal fruit from Yamaguchi and Miyazaki prefectures," she looked up at her guests, who had not moved from the alcove, with a polite but questioning gaze.

And then she smiled, her polished façade cracking, laugh lines radiating from her eyes. "Shall I bring you a stool, sir?"

It was Rei, and not Teru, to whom she spoke, and to Teru's surprise it was Rei who answered. "Please," he said. "I would appreciate that."

They ate slowly, Teru adjusting his pace to match Rei's,

as well as to savor the rare and expensive delicacies. He didn't eat food like this very often, and he never drank anything like the hot local sake that flowed down his throat like liquid fire, loosening his tongue as evening became night.

"You know," he said, as the same woman cleared away the dishes, "I've never actually done this before. Taken someone out of town like this."

Too late, he realized that the woman had heard every word and, unless she was far more ignorant than her manner indicated, would also have read between the lines. His face grew hot, but when he glanced at her she smiled and said, as politely as ever, "Please enjoy the rest of your stay."

"I think," Rei said, when the door had closed behind her, "that we should do exactly that." He removed the wig, then the mask, and gave them to Teru, who laid them carefully on the table. "I have never done this before either."

Teru helped him to his feet and, from behind him, untied the obi that held Rei's robe together in the front. It slid from his shoulders, pooling around his feet on the floor. It was an odd sort of nakedness; Rei still wore his underwear, as well as the supporters on his knees and the pressure bandage on his ankle, but he was naked from the waist up and Teru, riding on more than a little drunken courage, kissed him between the shoulder blades where scar tissue met unblemished skin.

"I'm glad we did this," he whispered, and undid his own obi, leaving only the thin shield of two pairs of boxers between them. He wrapped his arms around Rei's waist, tracing the prominent pelvic bones and then, hesitating to ask wordlessly for permission, lowered the boxers as well.

330

Rei stiffened at his touch. "I'm glad we did this too."

The bath and the balcony around it were stone, as hard and cold as the December air that drew lines of goosebumps on their skin. Rei left his crutch and supporters at the door, and made his way to the bath with his arm around Teru's shoulders and Teru's arm around his waist. They entered the water together, letting it warm their bodies as the breeze from the mountains stung their faces and ears. Teru's body grew lighter, softer, until he was sure he would float away, carried on the sulferous steam into a sky so far away that it made the band, the label, and his imminent decision seem... remote, somehow, and unimportant.

He leaned his head on Rei's shoulder; Rei shyed away. With nothing to restrain it, his right arm floated aimlessly in the water, and he was focused on trying to hold it down with his left.

"Stop," Teru said. "I don't mind. Relax." That was the wrong thing to say; Rei sat up straighter, and the expression on his face hardened.

"Relax." Teru slid behind him, wrapping his legs around him on either side and letting his hands trail down Rei's arms. Their fingers locked, Teru's palms against the backs of Rei's hands as he held them both firmly under the water.

The sky was dark, the stars beginning to shine through the bare branches of the trees. Rei leaned into the embrace, his hair rough and ticklish against Teru's chest.

"Rei?"

"Yes?"

"I'm glad you were at the show that night. I'm glad we

met. I'm glad... that all of this happened."

Rei exhaled, his breath melting into the steam. "I am glad too. I shouldn't have loved you. But now, I don't know what else I can do."

"Don't talk like that." Teru held him close. "I'm not going anywhere."

—⋰⋱—

When the heat of the bath had overtaken the chill in the air, and their bodies were red and wrinkled and steaming, they went back inside to find the table pushed against the far wall, and two futons laid out in the middle of the room.

"What you do want to do?" Teru asked. "We can watch TV, or order some more drinks?"

"Teru?" Rei watched his face carefully. "I want you. I want to... be with you."

"Okay," Teru said. He should have been nervous. But his smile could have lit a thousand suns.

They sat in the alcove, naked except for towels, while Teru re-bandaged Rei's ankle. "I'm getting pretty good at this," he joked.

Rei turned away. "I'm sorry."

"Why?"

"You shouldn't have to... to do things like this."

"I don't." Teru shook his head. "Who said I have to? It's no different than the laundry or the dishes. It's no different than you writing my music or mixing my CD. It's just... something I do for you, because I can." Wordlessly, he dug through the suitcase, but Rei brushed him aside.

"No pills tonight," he ordered. "I don't want anything

to dull this."

Teru helped him to the futons, where they lay together, side by side, taking in each other's features in silence. Teru wondered if Rei, too, was remembering that night in Shibuya, when Teru had taken one look at him and fled. He couldn't pinpoint the exact moment when Rei's face had gone from being horrible to bearable and then to... not beautiful. It would never be that, not in any traditional sense. But there were countless kinds of beauty in the world.

"What are you thinking, Teru?"

Teru smiled, and shook his head. "Just how lucky I am. To be here with you."

He propped himself up on one arm, one hip, and leaned over to kiss Rei on the lips. With all of their worries about the band, the future... it had been a long time since they had simply enjoyed the *now*. His hands traced the lines of Rei's neck, exploring the expanse of his chest, his stomach, and beyond.

Rei moaned, arching his back, and Teru let his kisses follow.

"I'm sorry," Rei said. "This face, this body. I..."

"Shhhh." Teru silenced him with another kiss. "It's okay. We'll figure things out as we go."

———※———

Rei slept. Outside, the stars still shone.

Teru lay awake, numb. Every muscle in his body had dissolved to a warm, soft, buoyant jelly. He could float. He could fly. And in the darkness, he could see more clearly than he had in months.

333

Rei's chest rose and fell under the comforter, a peaceful, even rhythm in the night. Teru watched, as nothing at all happened. He could stay here, just like this, until he died.

His mind was made up. If he walked away from the band, he'd be destroying his friends' careers, but abandoning Rei would destroy his life. "I'm here." He mouthed the words, not daring even to whisper them. "Forever. With you."

Then he, too, slept.

Chapter 31

Teru lay on his side, his head snuggled into Rei's shoulder and one arm thrown over his body, breathing a sweet mix of sweat and sex underscored by takeout curry and a faint medicinal tang. The comforter was pulled up to their necks, but beneath it they were naked, their bodies twined against each other for warmth and for pleasure.

"That," Teru whispered, "was amazing."

"So were you."

"Do you..." Teru hesitated, not sure what kind of answer he was hoping for. "Do you want to do more?"

Rei considered this. "Yes," he said. "More than anything. But... this is like the first time for me too. Tonight, I am tired. So are you."

Teru nodded. That was true. The trip back to Tokyo had been uneventful, but it had been long, and he had unpacked most of their things before going out to pick up dinner. He was tired. And beyond satisfied. He only hoped that what he had given in return had been half as good.

"Okay," he said. "We'll take it slow." He closed his eyes. "Rei?"

"Yes?"

"I've been thinking. About the Ondera contract."

"And?"

"I'm going to turn it down. I want to sing your music," Teru explained. "Not whatever the label tells me to. I want to play at the venues you're comfortable going to. And I want to come home to this. Every night, not just every other week or so. I'm going to tell the guys, after the countdown."

"I see," Rei said, his gaze as distant as his tone.

"Is something wrong?"

"Not really," he said. "But Teru?"

"Yeah?"

"Do me a favor. Don't tell them on New Year's Eve. I... want to be with you when you do."

"You do?"

"Let them have their happy holiday. Please."

"...Okay." Teru frowned, unsure why Rei would care if he spoiled anyone else's New Year's Eve. "I guess it doesn't have to be the thirty-first. But we should tell them as soon as we can."

"I agree," Rei said. "We should... get this over with. So everyone can move on."

The countdown started at noon and lasted until half past midnight, with more than thirty bands on the roster and the hall sold to double the maximum capacity. Some bands played more than one, taking an early spot at one live house and a later one at another. Some of the fans flitted from venue to venue too, seeing as many of their favorite groups as possible in one insane day.

La Rose had only one event, but they had snagged a

pretty good time slot. The less popular bands tended to play earlier in the afternoon, and the last two or three slots were reserved for the favorites of the indies record labels. La Rose was scheduled to play at ten fifteen, which wasn't bad for a band that, until six months ago, had had a hard time selling their quota on any given night.

Teru left the apartment at half past eight, wearing most of his costume under his coat. "You sure you're not coming?" he asked, and Rei, as he had expected, said no.

"Have a good show," he said, and kissed him, on the forehead and then on the lips.

Teru shivered. "What was that for?"

"Here." Ignoring the question, Rei reached into his pocket and produced a tiny box.

"Thanks," Teru said. He turned it over in his hand. It was made of thin black cardboard and adorned with a simple gold bow.

"Open it."

Inside was a jewelry box, and inside that.... "It's a pendant."

"Put it on."

Teru fastened the silver chain around his neck, and held the pendant up to the light. It was a red stone with uneven lines running through it—amber, maybe, if amber came in this shade of crimson. "It's like the first sunrise of the year."

"For a new start," agreed Rei. "A new dawn. For your career."

"I love it," Teru said, and turned to leave, but something made him look back. "Is everything okay? You seem..."

"Have a happy new year, Teru."

"You too. I'll see you next year, okay?"

——⁕——

La Rose was ushered out as soon as their set was over, to make room for the night's heaviest hitters backstage. While the rest of the band dragged their equipment back to the van, it fell to Teru to find an izakaya with a table for six still available at eleven-thirty on New Year's Eve.

"To a new year!" Minori toasted, when everyone had arrived. "To new opportunities. Here's to 2001!"

Teru joined the rest of the band as they raised their glasses with a cheer, but he couldn't stop thinking about Rei, and the look on his face when they'd said goodbye. He hadn't seemed upset. More like resigned. But that didn't make sense. He had won. It was the rest of the band that was going to be devastated.

"What's wrong?" Yasu asked, but Teru only shook his head.

"Just tired."

It didn't help when Seika announced, to a chorus of applause, that he had talked it over with Sung-Min and decided that the Ondera deal—non-competition clause and all—was acceptable. Teru felt the eyes of the table on him. This was his cue. He was supposed to speak up next, announce that he was ready to sign the contract as well.

But he held his tongue, and the conversation turned to other things. They rang in the New Year at midnight, accepting free drinks and edamame from the management and toasting 2001 again—and again—with the strangers at the tables around them.

It was after five when the party ended. The world outside was still dark, but the streets were full of revelers with beer on their breath and good cheer in their voices as they called out New Year greetings to Teru and to just about everyone else they saw. Couples with their arms around each other's waists, businessmen holding their drunken bosses up by the shoulders. Underage kids, forgiven as long as they had the money and the holiday spirit to fuel their celebrations. Girls in mini-skirts, apparently warmed by enthusiasm alone. "Happy New Year!" they called to anyone and everyone, gender and age and class distinctions forgotten in the surreal novelty of a yet-untarnished 2001.

Teru echoed the greeting, but every time he did, his unease grew stronger, heavier, colder. Rei had been... strange. The pendant around his neck thumped against his chest, punctuating his heartbeat.

By the time he reached the apartment, his palms were sweating and the fear had worked its way into his throat. The building was dark—which was normal, he told himself sternly, at five in the morning—and hulking like a beast against the washed-out sky.

He wanted to open the door. He wanted to walk away. He wanted to go back in time and tell himself not to leave, not to leave Rei alone. He put his hand on the knob, terrified of something he could not yet bring himself to put into words.

He pulled.
The door didn't budge.

"It's locked," Teru whispered. He dug his keys from his pocket, frozen fingers trembling as he rushed to find the right one. Did it matter? Would one second, one minute make any difference if...? He didn't want to finish that sentence, even to himself.

They key slid halfway into the lock and stopped. Cursing, Teru pulled it out and tried again. He flipped it over, tried forcing it with one shoulder braced against the door. He threw his weight against it, tried turning it even though it was only halfway in. And then he took a good look at the lock.

It was shiny and new, and not even made by the same company as the old one.

"Rei?" His voice was too loud; he would wake up the building. At the moment, Teru didn't care. "Rei! Let me in! Let me in, dammit! Let me..."

He pressed the doorbell. He pounded on the door. He tried calling Rei's cell phone; it rang and rang and eventually went to voice mail. He called Chizuru; more of the same.

He's asleep, Teru told himself. *That's all. There's a good explanation. There's got to be.* He couldn't think of any, though. He kept pounding until a bleary-eyed housewife opened the door to 107 and told him, in a polite tone of voice that didn't match the anger in her eyes, that if his business couldn't wait until a more reasonable hour she was going to call the police.

That wasn't a bad idea, except that Teru didn't legally live here. Rei's neighbors wouldn't be able to vouch for him as anything other than a drunk kid with pink hair and eyeliner banging on the door of an upscale apartment at five... thirty, now, on New Year's Day.

He walked back to the street and called again. It rang

once, twice—and then, to Teru's infinite joy, it stopped. "We're sorry. Your call has been rejected by the party on the other line..." *Your call has been rejected.* Teru's heart soared. Rei had pushed that button. That meant he was alive—right?

Teru walked to the station and sat at the Yoshinoya counter with a beef bowl he hadn't really wanted, hitting the redial button every minute or so. Rei didn't answer, and Chizuru had apparently turned her phone off; he got an "out of service area" recording when he called her. Outside the window, the sun came up. The first sunrise of the new year looked cold and hostile and bleak.

At eight, he pushed the empty bowl across the counter and headed back up the hill. The battery on his phone was almost dead and the charger, along with most of his clothes, was in the apartment. He tried redial one last time, and when that didn't work, he rang the doorbell over and over again until he thought his finger would freeze. Teru slumped to the ground outside the blacked-out window, put his head between his knees, and wondered if he was really going to be sick or if he just wished that he was.

Rei had changed the locks—gotten them changed, but what kind of locksmith worked at midnight on New Year's Eve? And why? Things had been going so well... hadn't they?

Teru held the pendant, warming it with his hand and then holding it up, letting it catch the light of the cruel sunrise. Was there some hidden message there? Something more than a Christmas present delivered a week too late?

A suicide note?

"No," Teru said aloud. Rei had blocked the call. That message meant someone was there, someone had physically pressed the button. But that knowledge didn't stop him from standing up, from pounding on the door again. "Dammit, Rei!" he cursed. "Where are you?" And then, in a softer voice: "Please be in there. Please... be okay."

He held the pendant up again, silently begging it for answers. It spun on the chain, reflecting sunlight onto the door. All Teru could see was the back, the metal setting... and the inscription, which he hadn't noticed before:

SHINE.

Chapter 32

Teru got on the train and went home.

He stopped in Shinjuku on the way, to pick up a cell phone charger at one of the big electronics stores. The New Year's sale was on, and it seemed as if everyone else in the store was buying a computer or a TV or something else with a million accessories that took fifteen minutes to ring up. Teru had no idea how long he'd been standing in line, still half in costume and smelling like a bar, before he was finally able to pay for his purchase and get the hell away from it all.

Nakano wasn't much better, but at least the apartment building was quiet. Everyone who lived there was single; Teru guessed they had gone home for the holidays, or maybe they were sleeping off hangovers. It didn't really matter. They weren't around, and they weren't making noise, and at the moment that was good enough for him.

His mailbox was crammed with flyers and postcards and letters in crumpled, water-damaged envelopes that had been sitting there for a month. Electric. Gas. *Fuck.* The rent came out of his bank account every month, but it had been a long time since Teru had paid any bills.

He scooped up as many of the papers as he could and took them into the dark, dirty apartment. The lights, by virtue of some miracle, worked, and when he plugged his new charger into the socket his cell phone lit up—the first thing all year that had gone according to plan.

The shower was warm—the gas company hadn't given up on him either—but he didn't have much in the way of clothes. He put on an X Japan sweatshirt he'd meant to keep as a souvenir and a pair of snow pants he hadn't worn since leaving Niigata. Then he collapsed onto the moldy futon and, warm and numb and half convinced he was dreaming, fell almost immediately to sleep.

He woke to the sound of his phone.

"Hello?" Teru sat up, almost smacking his head against a rack of CDs that wouldn't have been there if this had been Rei's place. "Hello? Say something!"

"Masato?"

Teru blinked himself back to reality. "Mom?"

Of course. The New Year's Call. The one time a year she deigned to speak to him, and he didn't have the guts to tell her to fuck off.

"Happy New Year," she said. "Is this a bad time?"

Yes. "It's... okay."

"How are you?"

"Fine," he said. "Everything's great. Listen..."

"Yasuhiro was home last week, you know. When are you going to come back home? Your grandmother's eighty years old, and—"

"Soon, Mom. Just as soon as things settle down with the band."

"Oh, are you still doing that?" He could almost hear her frown. "What about your job?"

Teru almost groaned aloud. *My job.* His manager had said he could come back, but.... "We're actually making some money with the band right now," he lied.

"Any girlfriends?" she asked. "I ran into Mr. Uchida at the supermarket the other day, and his daughter..." She launched into a pitch for the marriage of convenience she'd been dreaming about since he had moved away, and it was all Teru could do not to cry.

No, mom. I'm not interested in Mr. Uchida's daughter. I'm not interested in any of your friends' daughters because... because I'm gay. Because I'm only interested in one person, and because he's just walked out of my life for some reason I can't understand, and because I'm hoping he dumped me, because I can't stand to think about the alternative.

"Masato?"

"Hm?" Teru cleared his throat. "That sounds, um... great, Mom."

He got out of bed, pulling the cord to turn on the overhead light. It was dark outside, and the clock on his phone read six p.m. The missed call icon blinked in the corner of the screen, but the calls, when he brought them up, were all from his mother. Teru scrolled down the list until he found Rei's name; their last phone call had been over a week ago. He highlighted the number and hit send.

"The number you have dialed is not in service."

Teru hung up.

He wasn't worried anymore. He was hurt.

It had been six years. Six years since Saki had died, six years since Rei had been injured. And as far as Teru knew, Rei had never once attempted suicide. He had given up on a lot of things—his career, his recovery, his personal happiness—but he had never given up on his music, and on the thought that, somehow, it could keep at least a part of Saki alive. This wasn't a final escape, wasn't a dramatic exit or some elaborate form of revenge. It was a breakup, pure and simple. Rei would go on living, if you could call it that... but he had chosen to do it alone.

Teru tried Chizuru next. It had been over twelve hours; no matter what kind of celebrating she'd been doing last night, she would have noticed his calls by now. If she'd been worried, she would have called back. She hadn't.

She had turned her phone back on, though, and Teru left her a message. "Call me. Please. Just let me know he's all right."

He tossed the phone on top of the futon and walked to the convenience store to pay his bills. When he got back, there was a text waiting for him.

He's fine, Chizuru said. *Don't worry. I'll talk to you soon.*

———※———

Two days later, she came by with his clothes and belongings, folded neatly into four department store shopping bags.

"Come in," Teru offered. "It's a mess, but..."

"I shouldn't." Chizuru bit her lip and frowned. Her clothes were rumpled, and there were dark circles under her eyes. "He asked me to leave your things and go."

"Please," Teru said. "Just tell me what happened. Why would he—?"

"Because he's a fucking idiot." Chizuru's eyes were red,

346

and he wondered if she hadn't been crying as well.

"Is he okay?"

"As okay as he's ever going to be, I guess."

"Then why...?"

"Look," she said. "If you ask me, you're the best thing that's ever happened to him. Saki included. I also think—and trust me, this is saying a lot—that this is the stupidest fucking thing he has ever done. But"—she sighed—"I can't change his mind for him. Honestly, I'm sick of trying. I hope he comes around, but..."

"He changed his phone number."

"I know."

"What am I supposed to do?"

"Wait." She shrugged. "Hope. Don't change yours."

———✳———

It was funny how a person's life—or at least everything in it that mattered—could be crammed into four paper bags. It was funnier still, or maybe just depressing, that all of that stuff couldn't make the apartment feel like home.

Teru re-sorted his clothes into their old drawers, returned his shoes to the shelf by the front door. The room grew smaller, but it didn't grow any more full. At the bottom of the last bag were two black plastic document cases. Teru didn't remember buying them, and he definitely didn't remember taking them to Rei's. He sat down on the futon and opened them one at a time.

In the first, he found the Ondera contract, along with his personal seal and a pen. The message was clear enough. Teru flipped to the last page, where Hoshino and his boss had already affixed their own seals and the corporate one.

"Is this why?" he said aloud as he uncapped the pen and began to write. "Damn it, Rei. We could have done both. We could have made it work." Tears welled in his eyes. "You couldn't even fucking try?"

He wiped his face with the back of one hand and, with the other, set the contract aside. He had to call Minori. Had to tell him he'd decided. Or had the whole damn thing decided for him.

He jerked the second case open, more angry now than anything else. How dare Rei tell him how to live his life? How dare he decide that their—that their *love*, what the hell else could you call it?—mattered less than a contract, an album, a career? There were a million bands in the world with a billion mediocre albums. What he'd had with Rei, though... that had been one of a kind.

Teru wanted to punch something; he wanted to scream. Instead, he steadied his hands and took the papers from the case. It was sheet music—two guitar parts, bass, drums, and keyboards. And at the very bottom, the vocal score, six pages on inkjet paper with a title scrawled across the top in a nearly illegible hand.

Sweet Goodbye.

—⋈—

Not twenty-four hours later, they sat in the meeting room at Ondera Records with five signed contracts and a stack of sheet music between them.

"Thank you," Minori said, "for meeting with us on such short notice."

"Not at all." Mr. Hoshino smiled, and his bosses nodded their agreement. "The earlier we get this settled, the earlier we get to work on your first single and your first tour."

Teru pushed the stack of music across the table. "Here," he said. "That's the single." His bandmates glanced at him in unison—Minori and Seika from his left, Yasu and Nao from his right.

"Do you have a demo?" asked one of the bosses, and Minori shook his head.

"Not yet," he said, fixing Teru with a frown. "And we're open to other suggestions."

"Well, let's run through it in the studio," Hoshino suggested, "and see what we can do. And we'll look into booking a few venues in late March, maybe early April."

"That sounds great." Minori smiled. "One more thing. Would it be all right if we made an announcement at our show tomorrow? Some of our fans are getting anxious."

"No specifics," replied one of the bosses. "But a general announcement would be fine."

—⋇—

"So," Yasu said. "What do you think?" He picked up one of Teru's midriff tops and held it to his much broader chest. "Mind if I borrow this for the encore?"

"You're kidding, right?"

"Only if the answer's no." He pulled up a stool and sat next to Teru at the mirror. Vicinity's dressing room was longer and narrower than Rock Eden's, with about ten years' fewer backstage passes on the walls, but the general feel was the same. "You doing okay?"

"Sure," Teru said. "Why wouldn't I be?"

Yasu passed him a cigarette. "I dunno," he said. "Maybe because your boyfriend wrote you a song called 'Sweet Goodbye?'"

Teru recapped his lipstick and raised the cigarette to his mouth. "Don't worry about me," he said. "I'll be fine."

—⋇—

And he was. In a lot of ways, it was the worst show he had ever done. Every note, every word was stained with memories of Rei, and if he stopped too long to think about it, Teru thought he'd be sick right there, in the middle of the stage with at least a hundred people looking on. But when he shut it out, when he stopped thinking or seeing or feeling and just sang... he sang from his heart, because now he understood.

He understood beauty. He understood pain. He understood life, and how it just got in the way. He knew what it was to love, to lust, to long for something he could never have... and then somehow to have it. To lose it. To hope against hope that he might someday have it again. He sang it all, and the crowd sang back. It came from the same place, whatever they were feeling. Love and loss and longing... when you stripped away everything else, everyone's pain was the same.

"Thank you," he said, as the last note of the last song faded into the spotlight, a ghost of a melody in the night. "Thank you for your support, and thank you... for loving La Rose Verboten as much as I do. There have been"—Teru raised his voice over the screams of the crowd—"rumors, regarding our schedule and our future plans. I want to tell you, to tell you all, that the rumors of our breakup"—someone in the front row wailed—"are not true. As of February, La Rose will be signed with Ondera Records. We will be touring, and putting out new music, and continuing to share this space, and others, with you over the course of this year. Thank you for your support," he said. "Thank you... for all the years to come."

Chapter 33

"Now let's give a warm welcome to our last guests of the night. Celebrating their fourth anniversary with a brand new single, let's hear it for La Rose Verboten!"

The voice came from the other side of the backdrop, swallowed up by the cheers of the studio audience and followed by a second, louder voice from the monitor in Teru's ear.

"Now!"

He pushed the curtain aside and stepped into a forest of flowers: arrangements as tall as he was, towering on either side of the curtain, crowding the dais and spilling down the sides of the stairs to the stage below. There were flowers from the record label, flowers from other bands. Studio musicians and sound engineers, magazines and models and record shops and fans. There were lilies and sunflowers, dahlias and gerberas. But above all else, the display stands overflowed with roses. Red and white and yellow roses, pink and impossible blue.

The lights dimmed, but he could still see the crowd, holding signs with the band's names and faces, waving official tour towels and fans. Behind him, feathers and taffeta rustled. Unplugged guitar strings twanged. The instruments were always faked on TV, replaced with the backing track from the radio edit. Only the vocals were live.

Teru forced his eyes to unfocus; the audience was close, the cameramen were closer, and the lights over the bleachers made their faces uncomfortably clear. His hands were somehow steady as he wrapped them around the mic; if there was one thing nine years on one stage or another had taught him, it was how to keep the shaking on the inside.

Stop it, Teru scolded himself. *You're good at this. It's what you do.* But this wasn't what he had been doing for the past four years. This song, the one that had seemed like such a good idea when the first scrap of a lyric had come to him, when he'd texted it to himself and then passed his phone around the table at a meeting, the one that had seemed only manageably scary when they'd recorded it... it was different now, here. It was one thing to sing someone else's words; it was like ripping his heart out to show the world, to sing these words of his own.

The intro flowed into his monitor, the edge of the melody picked out on a single undistorted guitar. Had he meant it to be this angry, this bitter? Or had Minori done that on his own? Teru held onto the mic with one hand, and wrapped the other around the stand. It didn't really matter now.

> "Suterarenai kyonen no koyomi
> Wasurekaketeita shirabe no kakera
> Futari de sugoshita sugisatta hibi
> Chinmoku no naka de hibiku yo
> Ima de mo."

Last year's calendar, that I can't throw away
Four years ago now, but who was counting?
A fragment of a melody I had almost forgotten
A melody, a lyric, even a chord.
Those days we spent together, that have passed us by
Resound in the silence
Even now.

And then he let the guitars take it, Yasu and Minori draining their silent instruments of every scrap of imagined pain in the world.

—→⁙←—

He'd thought that singing the song would do it, that the final note would somehow melt the ice in his stomach, bring him back to something like the real world. But as they climbed the stairs back to the dais, taking their seats around an oval table surrounded by roses in every imaginable color and size, all he could think about was that it was out there. That someone was going to hear it, and know, and judge.

"Wow," the host said. "That was incredible. So this is the new single, 'Dare mo inai kono yoru,' which will be in stores..."

"Yesterday," Nao said, and a group of girls in the front row raised a handmade poster and cheered. The single wasn't really out yet; the program wouldn't be aired for another month, and their unscripted excitement made Teru crack a nervous smile.

"Just out yesterday. Now, let's talk a little bit about the history of the band."

Teru wiped his sweaty hands on his jacket. The questions were all planned out in advance; they'd had plenty of time to come up with their answers. He knew that no one knew the real history of the band, but still....

"That's right," Minori explained beside him, "it's been four years since our major debut."

"Which, of course, was 'Sweet Goodbye.' Interesting choice for your debut, by the way."

"We weren't even thinking about that." Minori laughed. But of course they had. Ondera had fought them on the title, said it wasn't appropriate for a debut. But Teru had insisted, and....

"You've had quite a few hits since then, of course, but nothing quite on the same scale. Do you feel any pressure at all, any stress about having to live up to that?"

Yes. But Teru knew he couldn't say it. The band was doing all right. They were paying their bills. They'd had their contract renewed twice, and he knew they were holding their own. But it wasn't the same. Teru knew it. And their public—however adoring—knew it too.

"I don't think so." It was Seika who answered, with a wink that made a different section of the audience squeal. "We're proud of that song, and it means a lot to us that it continues to be so loved."

The host nodded. "Absolutely." He glanced behind him, to the promotional poster tacked between the flowers on the wall. "Back to the new single, then. Minori and Teru, you actually wrote this one together?"

"That's right."

"Teru, this was your first time writing lyrics for the

band."

Teru nodded. "Yes."

"So tell us a little about the song. A lot of what you do is on such a grandiose scale, but this one's really personal, isn't it?"

"I don't know about that," Teru said. "I mean, we're always playing characters onstage. I just wanted to write about... about losing someone. About how the worst part of losing someone isn't the moment they're gone, but all the moments after that. All the times they should have been there, and they're not."

There was an "Aww!" from the audience, and the host said. "Well, I think a lot of people can identify with that."

"Yeah," Teru said. That was the end of his scripted speech. "I, uh... hope it might mean something to someone."

"What he means..." Yasu grabbed the mic from the middle of the table and pulled it over to his end with a screech. "What he means is, it's a kick-ass song. So turn off the TV and go buy yourself a copy, okay?"

—————※—————

"Costumes, everyone! Costumes! Wait." Rumiko, the manager, draped the costumes she was already holding over the back of a chair and pressed a jewel-encrusted flip phone to her ear. "Yes? No, we already talked about that. Right. Friday. No, *next* Friday at four. Are you drinking already?"

"Relax." Yasu smiled at her from across the dressing room. "We're off. And I'm taking a cab."

"Fine," Rumiko continued, into the phone. "Thank you. Goodbye." She took a file of business cards from her briefcase and started flipping through it in search of the nearest cab company. "That was the photographer. We've got a photo shoot next week, so please don't spill whatever that is on any of these costumes!

"How many cars do we need?" She counted the raised hands. "Teru?"

"No, thanks," he said. "I'm going to take a drive."

He should have offered to give Yasu a ride. On any other day, he probably would have. But even though he didn't know where he was going, Teru knew he had to to get there alone. He pulled out of the underground garage, blinking in the white light of a cloudy January afternoon. Inside the studio it was Saturday night, but out here it was a Wednesday, and most of the city was cooped up inside, at work or school or whatever it happened to be.

It was barely above freezing, but Teru rolled the windows down just far enough for the cold wind to hit him in the face, drying his hair, still damp from the studio's shower. He turned the stereo off and let his fingers on the steering wheel be his music, tapping and tripping and itching for a cigarette even though he hadn't had one in four years.

The view from Rainbow Bridge was stunning, even in the daylight with the lights turned off. Teru turned a blind eye to Odaiba itself, to the Ferris wheel that ached like a poorly-healed wound. But the other side, the city itself, was a haven. Silver skyscrapers and the sprawling white expanse of the port peeked between the suspension cables, with Tokyo Tower a charm of red amidst the grey. Even though Teru hadn't grown up here, it always felt like coming home, watching the city come into view between the mountains on the way home from a tour—or even now, crossing the bay from the studio which was, technically speaking, also in Tokyo.

He should have veered left at Hamasaki-bashi, taken the route up through Shinjuku that would have taken him home. But he was still on edge, his fingers drumming rapid sixteenth notes while his stomach congealed, trying to convince itself not to be sick at the idea of whatever it was he had just let out into the world. Instead he flew north, around the Imperial Palace and west to Ikebukuro on a whim. There was no reason for him to be in this part of town, but there was no reason to do anything else, either. He could park at the Sunshine City complex and walk around, window shop. Go to the aquarium or the amusement park or hell, even the cat café. Doing something was his goal; it didn't matter what.

The glove compartment, like everything else on the little two-seater, was tiny, but it was big enough to hold an emergency disguise. In the parking lot, Teru slipped on a pair of oversized sunglasses and stuffed as much of his hair under a ski cap as he could. It wouldn't fool a truly obsessive fan, but at least it kind of said *Leave me alone*.

His phone buzzed as he cut the engine, and he almost ignored it. It was probably Yasu. Or Minori. Or someone from the label.

But it wasn't any of them. It was Ryo.

Hey. You still in Odaiba?

Teru groaned silently.

No.

For a second, he considered leaving it at that. Yes, he'd gone out with the guy a few times. Yes, he'd even had fun. But Teru wasn't ready for anything serious, and he got the definite impression that Ryo was.

Sorry, he added. *Long day. Talk to you later, okay?*

As soon as the text had gone through, Teru powered off his phone and shoved it in his pocket, then locked the car and took the elevator to the first floor.

It was the floor below that he'd really wanted, but by the time he'd figured that out, the elevator doors had already closed. Most of the restaurants and coffee shops were downstairs, on what was technically the first basement but also the main floor of the shopping area. It didn't really matter, though. He didn't need to eat. He just needed to walk, to try not to think. He needed to work something out, and wasn't entirely sure what that something was.

The middle section of the floor—and the two above it—was cut away, the opening walled in glass for a clear view of the fountain and the marble-tiled stage below. The stage was sometimes used for concerts, comedy acts, or for Hello Kitty or Kamen Rider to come and shake hands with the kids. On a Wednesday afternoon, though, it was nothing so exciting. Just a piano dealer showing off their wares.

Teru glanced over the rail, watching as a young couple paused at one of the pianos, the girl trying to pick something out with one finger while her boyfriend laughed along. Next to them, a kid struggled through a classical piece with his mother behind him, her face frozen in a frown. "Poor kid," Teru muttered under his breath. His mom had gotten it all wrong.

He turned away from the railing, made a show of looking through some of the bargain bins in front of the stores. Most of the shops on this floor were for women and children, though.

Women and children. That was something to think about. An arranged marriage... or even a charade with a fan. People married people they didn't love every day, and at least it would stop him from being the only member of the band who always spent holidays alone.

Maybe he should take his mom up on her matchmaking offers. Maybe he should turn on his phone and call Ryo. That was the whole point of writing that song, wasn't it? Getting it out of his system. Moving on.

Whatever store he was in front of was playing some Morning Musume song on the PA, and without really meaning to, Teru started slapping the drumline on his pants leg, tapping his foot to the beat. He stayed there until the song ended, browsing through the bins, but when the next track turned out to be Hikaru Utada's "First Love," he cursed under his breath and left the store.

He'd taken two or three steps when he heard it.

A fragment of a melody.

Not "First Love," but it was something he knew.

Something that took him back, for a reason he couldn't name.

Something he'd heard on the radio. On TV. In a bar.

Or somewhere else.

No.

Teru rushed to the rail, needing it to steady himself but unwilling, unable to look at the stage below.

It couldn't be. It didn't make sense. There were only six living people who knew that song. But the melody played on, and it was. Saki's song. The one he had written for...

Rei.

Teru mouthed the lyrics. "Ore no aijin, Ore no hametsu." And a whisper: "Nigeru basho nado nai." His hands were shaking; each breath was ice in his lungs.

The song was right. There was nowhere to run. He couldn't look down, didn't dare to confirm what his brain insisted was true. He was tired. He was hungry. And he'd been thinking of Rei—if not in so many words—all day. There were a hundred reasons it all had to be in his head. But some part of him had to know.

His feet rounded the atrium, took the down escalator two scrolling steps at a time. And the closer he drew, the longer the song went on, the more certain—the more terribly certain—Teru was.

I should stop. I should leave. I should pretend this never happened.

But his feet kept walking—toward the stage, toward the sound.

He came around from the back of the stage, up a carpeted ramp and into a maze of pianos. Upright pianos, digital pianos, and a single magnificent grand. A salesman offered him a pamphlet; Teru waved it aside. He had already found what he was looking for.

"Ore no aijin." The words formed on his lips, half-sung and half-spoken as he zeroed in on the sound.

"Ore no hametsu." This time in a stage voice that rang across the mall.

My lover. My destruction.

The man at the piano froze.

His hair was black, his face in shadows, and he sat in a motorized wheelchair. But it was him. The set of his shoulders, the tilt of his head, his fingers, still and rounded on the keys—Teru would never, *could* never forget those things, not if he'd had a thousand years.

For a moment, Teru thought he wouldn't finish. For a moment, he thought he wouldn't play on. But Rei took a breath. He lowered his hand. And then the song—Saki's song—went on.

"Rei."

Rei shook his head.

"It's me. It's Teru."

"Don't spoil it." The reply was cold.

Around the piano, people had stopped. Kids were pointing; their mothers had gathered to stare. The salesman, armed with his pamphlets and a frown, stood beside them and waited for the coda.

"Do you need any help, sir?" he asked when it was done, and Teru knew what Rei would have to say. All he needed—all he had ever needed—was to be left alone.

Teru took a step backward. He would go. He would get in his car and keep on driving, and—

"Not yet," Rei said. "I want to try one more song."

Teru knew what it was from the very first note. He'd never had perfect pitch, couldn't really have said what note it was. But he knew it with his body, felt it resonate the way it had on stage every night of every tour. This was always the last song—either the last of the main set or the encore, and it had always earned them the biggest cheers. Teru knew it like he knew his own heartbeat, the sound of his shoes on the pavement, or the white noise every night in his ears.

Ondera had hired some guy to play the keyboards, some studio musician Teru had never met before or since. It was their debut single, their best-known work—but he had never been able to sing it for Rei.

He had no mic, and no real audience, but Teru announced it anyway:

"Sweet Goodbye."

It took one line for the shoppers to stop and listen; it took one chorus for them to come. They stood at the foot of the stage, leaned over the upstairs railings, and then, as Rei improvised an approximation of the guitar solo that—in Teru's admittedly uneducated opinion—would have had most two-handed pianists stumped, they began to talk.

"Is that the guy from—"

"Nah, just a cosplayer."

"He sounds like the real thing."

"Look at his hair."

"Who's the other guy?"

"Do you think...? Is it really...?"

"Teru!" A kid with a blonde Mohawk called from one of the shops across the way. "Hey, come here, guys! It's Teru. You know, from La Rose?"

They kept coming: shoppers and store clerks and cleaning ladies with their mouths open and their cell phones drawn. "That's really him!" they cried. "Was this on the schedule?"

The piano salesmen stood there, shaking their heads.

No matter what Teru had said on TV, he wasn't playing a character. He was just himself, singing to Rei. Maybe he always had been. There was too much to say, and he might never have the chance to say it in any other words. So he opened his mouth. He opened his heart. He sang.

"Rei?" Teru said under the applause, in a voice thick with almost-tears. "Look at me. Look at me, Rei. Please."

Rei lowered his head, let his hand fall to the armrest. His body trembled—with breath, with sobs, with laughter? And then, with the quiet whirr of the chair's motor, he turned.

Teru froze. His heart must have stopped; for a minute or two, he was sure he didn't breathe. It hadn't been real, until this moment. Until the moment Rei looked up at him, through a curtain of hair and the eye of a silver mask, knowing Teru—after all this time—better than anyone else in the world.

Rei extended his hand, and Teru took it. Took his weight. Helped him stand.

His body still remembered—remembered everything, even the things his mind had worked so hard to forget: how he was just the right height to rest his head on Rei's shoulder, the way his arm fit so perfectly around Rei's slim—but not as slim as it had been—waist. Teru held him as close as he dared, careful not to jostle his bad arm, careful not to make it look like anything more than the embrace of friends, of colleagues—of bandmates, coming off the stage at their farewell show.

Don't let this be the last show. Don't let this be the end.
"Excuse me?"

It was the kid. The blonde kid from the shop, with his nametag still around his neck, looking up at them with awe in his eyes. "You're really him, aren't you? You're Teru."

Teru nodded. "I guess I am."

"Wow. I mean, I—I love you guys. You're the reason I got into music. Fuck." He stuck his hands in his pockets and pulled out a handful of change. "I don't have anything to ask you to sign."

"Sorry," Teru said. "I don't either. Here." He pulled off his sunglasses and handed them to the kid. They were cheap, a thousand yen at Uniqlo—but he knew they'd be worth a hell of a lot more to a fan.

"Wow. Thanks. Hey, can I ask you something?"

"Sure."

"Can you... I mean, do you think you could do "Yami no hanabira"? I love your indies stuff. It was so epic, right?"

Teru smiled. "Yeah." He glanced at Rei. "What do you think? We have time for one more?"

Rei said nothing, but released Teru's hand and lowered himself back to the chair. He smoothed his cloak, swept his hair into his face, and situated his right arm on his lap. He closed his eyes. He took a deep breath. And he played.

Teru wasn't here, in the bright light of a shopping center on a Wednesday afternoon. He was in another place, another time, midnight in a dark apartment with only two people in the world.

> *Kouya wo oikakusu*
> *Yami no hanabira*
> *Furitsuzuku shikkoku no yuki*

It was like falling into a familiar bed, like curling onto that old sofa with his head on Rei's shoulder and their fingers entwined. They fit together, here as well as anywhere. Like pieces of a puzzle. Like a lock and a key.

Teru's voice grew louder and fuller as he pulled through the key change to the final verse. Four years of vocal training had given him volume and range; four years of silent longing had given him strength.

Itetsuku itami, mune wo sasu
Ai ga...

He held the note until Rei ran out of accompaniment and let his hand fall to his lap. The atrium—all four floors of it—drew a collective breath. And Teru sang, in a perfect pianissimo, the final words:

"...*sakikaeru made.*"

"Do you really believe that?" he whispered. "That love will bloom again?"

Rei closed his eyes. "What's the point of writing anything if it isn't, at least in some sense, true?"

"I hated you," Teru confessed. "For the longest time. What you did was the cruelest thing anyone's ever done to me. But maybe... maybe it was the kindest, too. You gave me my career. I can't ever repay you for that."

Rei spoke to the piano, to his hands in his lap. "I'm sorry. I was a coward. I—"

"Rei?" Teru knelt, then half-stood, unsure of the proper

etiquette but wanting—needing—Rei to look him in the eye. "Listen to me," he said. "We sold out the fucking Budokan."

He almost laughed at the inanity of it, and when Rei looked up, there was a smile in his eyes. "I know," he whispered. "I was there."

It should have been a shock. Maybe, at some level it was. But the tears that stung at Teru's eyes were tears of joy, and gratitude. And under it all boiled a deep well of regret, and bitter grief for all the years that should have been.

"I should have been there for you too," he said. "I should have—"

Teru looked out at the crowd, who still waited, not sure if the impromptu concert was over.

"Look." He took a breath, screwing up all of the courage he'd never really believed that he had. "Do you, uh... want to get some coffee? I've got a car. We could get dinner? Lunch? It doesn't have to be any more than that," he lied. "I just—"

"Teru?"

"Yeah?"

"That... sounds like a good place to start."

Chapter 34

The piano arrived on a Sunday afternoon, carted up the freight elevator and into the studio, into the spot they'd carved between Rei's old keyboard and Teru's new drums, which had gotten the same treatment a few days before.

Rei's new condo was on the top floor of an almost-new building, less than five minutes from Meguro Station. It was bright and clean and fully accessible, with a soundproof studio and a panorama window with a view of Mount Fuji on a clear day.

The hallways were wide and the floor plan open, but at the moment the place was cramped. There were boxes in the halls, in the living room, Teru's plates and glasses piled on the kitchen counter until someone shelved them or threw them away. They had too much of everything now, too much to fill their lives. But it was the piano that made this house their home.

Rei polished it by hand, though the dealer had already done it, shining every square centimeter of the scratched display model the salesman hadn't wanted to let him have.

"We can get you a new one," he'd said. "There are plenty in stock."

But that wasn't the point, and—at some level—the salespeople had known it too.

"One more thing," Rei said. "Wait here." He disappeared into the hall. When he returned, he was holding a photograph, a faded snapshot dressed in a silver frame. He held it out to Teru. "Do you mind?"

It was Saki, in an old publicity shot, caressing the neck of his guitar. About to make love to it. Pouting at the camera, only half-ashamed at being caught in the act.

Teru shook his head. "Of course not." It was Saki—or his song, at least—that had brought them back together, after all. "He's watching over us, right?" he asked, not sure if he believed that in a religious sense but wanting to, all the same.

He placed the photo on top of the piano, where it would be visible from the computer, from the drum kit, from every important point in the room. If they were going to be a family here, Saki would be a part of it. And for the first time, Teru didn't mind.

———※———

It took them two months to make it official. Of course, there were little steps along the way. Teru changed his address, legally this time, at the Meguro ward office and with his credit card companies, his record label, his friends. Their insurance and pensions couldn't go together, since it wasn't a marriage, but other things like their cell phones could. Teru sold his own condo, at a loss that felt like a gain, and used the money to buy half of Rei's. And following Saki's good example, they had their lawyers draw up wills.

Then there was the trip itself. There'd been Rumiko to placate, appointments to reschedule, hotel rooms to book... and the car. Rei had argued against it, but in the end there'd been no choice. Teru took his little red sports car to the dealer and traded it in on a custom minivan with the best sound system money could buy.

It took him another week or two to get used to driving the thing, and he still went the speed limit all the way to Shizuoka, half afraid the wind would blow the van right off the expressway and into the valley below.

Saki slept on the side of a hill, in the shadow of an ancient temple framed by cherry trees that were just starting to bloom. As the tires crunched over the gravel lot, the wind blew a clump of pink buds onto the windshield—ripped from the bough when their colors had just started to show.

The lot was nearly empty on a Thursday afternoon. Teru parked as close to the stairs as he could, but the place had been built centuries ago—no thought had been given to accessibility in its design. He looked over at Rei, in the passenger seat, his hand clenching his robe and his mouth set in a nervous line.

"You going to be okay?" Teru asked.

Rei nodded. "I have been here before."

Teru cut the engine and walked around the van to open the passenger door. He took Rei's hand, wrapped today in a heavy black wrist brace, and helped him ease himself to the ground.

It was Teru's job to carry their things: a backpack slung over one shoulder and a folding chair in the crook of his arm. He wasn't much good at memorials; his father had always paid someone to clean and maintain the family grave. But Teru trusted Rei, that this was what Saki would have wanted. That this would be the best way to say hello—and goodbye.

Every step was a fight, every rise of the crumbling stone steps a triumph. There was no ramp, no handrail—just Teru's hand, and Rei's. The two of them, alone against the world.

The oldest graves were little more than rocks; others had long since had their inscriptions rubbed away. Some had sconces overflowing with half-wilted flowers. Others struggled to raise their blocky heads above the weeds.

Rei stopped in front of a somber grey marker—clean, clear, but unadorned in this springtime between the anniversary of the death and the Obon festival later in the year. The stone dated back to the Meiji era; the first death was in 1906. There were great-grandparents, great-great-grandparents, and maybe an uncle, dead at age 4.

Sakito Koyanagi.

Teru's hand hovered over the newest inscription, not daring to touch it—just tracing it in the air.

Heisei year 7. January 5. Age at time of death: 25.

But that was the old way of measuring age. Unless his birthday was between the first and the fifth, Saki would only have been twenty-three.

Teru unfolded the chair. Rei sat, and together they took the offerings from the bag. Beer. Chocolate. Potato chips. The latest issue of *Guitar Magazine*. A stack of CDs—newer stuff, mostly, that Rei thought Saki would have wanted to hear. Teru put La Rose's single on top of the stack—the song he had written, as much about Rei and Saki as about himself and Rei.

Supermarket flowers went into metal vases; Teru filled a wooden bucket with tap water, and poured it into the vessel in front of the grave.

Is this okay? he wanted to ask. But the silence, even broken as it was by the cry of a bird, by the sigh of a breeze through the pink and white canopy, was sacred. Even the

371

sounds of his breath felt obscene.

They'd brought a whole pack of incense; Teru split the bundle, with trembling hands, in two. He lit Rei's first, touching the lighter to every tip, then waving the incense to extinguish the flame. Rei bent his head and took the incense with his thumb and first fingers; he held an old wooden rosary looped around the rest. He should have clapped his hands, should have held the rosary between them—but Saki, Teru thought, would understand.

He lit his own incense next, and let it fall beside Rei's—the sticks longer, lit later, but smoldering just the same.

Teru didn't have a rosary; the beads his grandmother had given him once upon a time were still in a drawer at his parents' house, unused. He knelt anyway, with his hands together, pressed against one another for strength. He wasn't really Buddhist. He didn't know what he believed. Was Saki here? Was he gone forever? Or was it like that old song—maybe he'd become a thousand winds.

Teru closed his eyes. It was his turn now, to speak to Saki, to ask for... what? His permission. His blessing. His love. He'd rehearsed this a hundred times in his head, but now that he was here, there was nothing. How could any of what he was feeling be expressed in words?

Saki, he began, silently and slowly, letting the name echo in his mind. *Thank you. I'm sorry. I don't know what to say. Rei loves you. Don't forget that. Don't ever think he's really moved on. But he won't be alone, I promise you that. I love him. Can you let me love him, too?*

The sun through the trees was his answer, the wind through his hair an embrace. "Thank you," he whispered. *I don't deserve this. But I sure as hell am going to try.*

Beside him, Rei removed his mask and set it on the altar. His eyes were closed, his head thrown back, and a tear rolled cold and silver down his cheek.

Teru reached over, beneath the robe's long sleeves, and let his hand touch Rei's. The wrist brace was rough against his palm, the rosary smooth and surprisingly warm. "Are you all right?" he whispered. "Is there anything else I can do?"

Rei raised his hand, and Teru's rose with it, the beads clasped between them in the space before the grave. Teru's skin was browner, Rei's fingers longer, but with eyes half closed, half blurred by tears, they might have been the same.

The song of the birds, returned from their southern migration, rose in accompaniment to the swing of the rosary and the dancing of the shadows on the grave. In the distance, a line of cars snaked down the highway. Above them, the cherry blossoms trembled in the wind. But all Teru could see was his hand against Rei's, together for a moment or an eternity—for as long as they had, until the seasons turned.

THE END

Acknowledgements

This book has been a long, long time in the works, and if I am sure of one thing, it is that there is no possible way that I will ever be able to thank everyone who has contributed to its writing and publication. That said, I'm going to give it my best shot, because you guys deserve all of the love.

First, I'd like to thank my family, most of whom have no idea I wrote this, but who put up with my weird hobbies and the fact that I'm always writing *something* at midnight instead of going to bed. To my grandma, thank you for raising me among fishnets and greasepaint. To my grandpa, thank you for introducing me to musicals. I'm not sure either of you would have liked this particular book, but I'm sorry you never had a chance to see me become a published author.

To my mom and dad... if you're actually reading this, WOW. Impressive Googling. Also, stop Googling me and never mention this again. But thank you, for encouraging my love of books and music and not trying to stop me when I ran halfway around the world.

To my kids, for putting up with such a weird and distracted mom, and for my husband, for happily answering my questions about how bands get scouted and how to tune drum heads without ever asking me why I wanted to know such seemingly random things.

To the former denizens of Papen, thank you for

inspiring me to start writing this in the first place and for squeeing for those first early chapters... what was it, 13 years ago? I'm so amazed and honored to *still* have so many of you as friends.

To Becky Albertalli, the very first reader of the finished version and my staunchest supporter over the years... I don't even have the words to say what your friendship and encouragement have meant and continue to mean for me and for this book, through all the good cries and ugly cries and laughs and everything else. Thank you so much for believing in my characters and in me. Platonic soulmates FTW!

To Laura Heffernan, thank you for years of friendship and support and so many virtual shoulders to cry on. Here's to years and years of future cheering for each other's successes!

To J.C. Lillis, thank you so much for the wonderful blurb, for your encouragement as I took the scary, scary leap into self-publishing, and for your own wonderful characters who have always, always been one of my go-to sources of inspiration.

To A.C. Lincoln, thank you for sharing so many of the experiences that inspired this book in the first place, for nostalgia walks around Takadanobaba and for way too many Frappuccinos.

To F.S. Autumn, for all the encouragement and for never letting me give up on my dream. I can't wait to see your name in print, too!

To Cale Dietrich, for being the best almost-time-zone-buddy I could ask for to fill the dark hours of Twitter when the Western Hemisphere is asleep! Thank you for never losing faith in me and in this story... and of course, for the Australian chocolate.

Although they'll probably never read this, I owe a big thanks as well to all of the real musicians mentioned in passing in this book—without your music and your aesthetics, this story and characters never would have come to be. I also have to thank the actual indie bands who put up with my well-intended but probably annoying fannish-ness around the time this book is set, particularly Replicant, Noide, and Grow Jewel. I owe immeasurable gratitude as well to Jim Steinman, who is not a Japanese visual kei musician, but whose music is and will always be a big part of the behind-the-scenes soundtrack to all of my writing and to my life in general, and whose warmth and appreciation for his fans is a constant reminder of the kind of creator I want to be.

Thanks many times to Mia Siegert, for helping me put the final polish on the manuscript before it went to print, and for answering my probably-annoying questions. I wish I had had the emotional energy to take more of your suggestions, and I appreciate every single one.

Thanks to Mayumi, for editing and proofreading the Japanese lyrics, and for suggesting vastly more poetic synonyms than the ones I originally used.

Thanks to MiblArt for the *amazing* cover art that I could never in a million years have imagined.

Thanks to Lily at Gay Book Promotions, Linn at A Novel Take PR, Dahlia Adler at LGBTQReads, and everyone else who helped this book reach its first readers through promotional efforts.

And finally, thanks to all of you, my readers. I hope you've enjoyed spending time with these characters as much as I've enjoyed bringing them to you.

A Note on the Mention of Real People and Places

One of the questions I was most frequently asked by my early readers is, "How much of this is real?"

The short answer is: Any character who performs an action or speaks a line on the page is completely fictitious. All of the venues (except the Nippon Budokan, mentioned in passing in the second-to-last chapter) are fictitious versions of actual places, and the names and specific details have been changed to fit the story. Many of the famous bands mentioned in passing (such as X Japan, Luna Sea, Malice Mizer, and Dir en Grey) are real, although my characters' opinions of their music and appearance represent the characters' fictitious opinions, and not my own.

The deceased musicians memorialized in the graffiti Teru finds in the stairwell are real, although the specific graffiti is not.

Regarding character names, I am aware that several of my characters share stage names with actual people, including musicians. This is fairly common in visual kei and among Japanese stage names in general (for example, Dir en Grey and Luna Sea both have drummers named Shinya), and was, in the case of this book, unintentional. In particular, I apologize for giving my main character the same-in-English name as TERU, the lead singer of GLAY. To be honest, I'm not really a GLAY fan and I didn't make the connection until my Teru had also been Teru for more than five years. For what it's worth, the real TERU spells his name in all English capital letters, and my Teru has always been 輝, a kanji character I wanted to use in one of my children's names but that my husband vetoed. I apologize for any misunderstandings, and stress again that all of my characters are 100% fictitious, and that any similarities (name-related or otherwise) with real people are purely coincidental.

Regarding setting, the general locations in Tokyo and the surrounding areas (such as Meguro, Shinjuku, and Shibuya) are real, but most of the specific shops and restaurants mentioned are fictitious. While a lot of the setting is based in fact, it differs from reality for artistic reasons, for reasons intended to protect the rights of individuals and businesses, and also for the ever-powerful reason of, "It's been almost 20 years, and people forget." So please take everything here with a grain of salt.

Glossary
(in English alphabetical order)

ai ga sakikaeru made (愛が咲き換えるまで): "Until love blooms again"; part of the refrain of "Yami no hanabira"

Botoku no namida (冒涜の涙): "Blasphemous Tears"; one of Minori's songs

demachi (出待ち): To wait outside a venue in the hopes of meeting the artist

ekimae (駅前): Literally "in front of the station." Typically used as part of the name of businesses located near train stations.

izakaya (居酒屋): A Japanese-style pub

kampai (乾杯): "Cheers!"; an expression used when making a toast

live house (ライブハウス): A small performance venue for musicians and other artists; artists typically pay to play, and earn money only if they sell more than their quota of tickets.

omnibus (オムニバス): In the context of music, a

compilation album containing songs by multiple artists

one-man (ワンマン): A concert where only one band or artist performs, occasionally with an opening act. Can also refer, for example, to a train with only one driver on board.

shochu (焼酎): A type of Japanese liquor, usually made from rice, yams, or barley and served on the rocks or with water.

three-man (スリーマン): A concert where three bands or artists perform

uchiage (打ち上げ): A party held after the conclusion of an event, show, or project

Yami no hanabira (闇の花びら): "Petals of Darkness"; one of Rei's songs.

yukata (浴衣): A Japanese-style article of clothing that is similar in design to, but lighter and more casual than, a kimono. Yukata are commonly worn as traditional clothing at summer festivals, and also by hotel guests as both robe and pajamas. They are worn by people of all genders.

About the Author

Estella Mirai lives just outside of Tokyo with her human family and a very spoiled lap cat. When she isn't reading or writing, she works in editing and translation—which means that 99% percent of her day is usually words. In her minimal free time, she enjoys watching musicals, cooking (badly), and slaughtering power ballads at karaoke.

The Stars May Rise and Fall is her first novel.

Connect with the author here:
Twitter: @EstellaMirai
Instagram: @EstellaMirai
Facebook: https://www.facebook.com/EstellaMirai/
Goodreads:
https://www.goodreads.com/author/show/18483732.Estella _Mirai

For rights inquiries and other questions, please email the author at EstellaMiraiBooks@gmail.com.

CPSIA information can be obtained
at www.ICGtesting.com
Printed in the USA
FSHW010834260219
55934FS